I0746326

TRICKED BY JACK

B. LYBAEK

COPYRIGHT

CONTENT
WARNING

I've done my best to list all the potential triggers for Tricked by Jack.

Please read responsibly and remember that your mental health _always_ comes first.

Addiction | Alcohol abuse | Captor/captive | CNC | Death | Dub-con | Explicit language | Explicit sexual scenes | Explicit violence | Forced marriage | Forced proximity | Kidnapping | Knife play | Mental & physical abuse | Non-con | Parental cruelty | Parental neglect | Power play | Primal chase scenes | Public humiliation | Ritualized sex acts | SA (attempted) | Self-harm (mentioned) | Torture | Unaliving | Violence

B. Cybaek
FOLLOW

THANK YOU

To the readers who crack open these pages knowing full well Halloween was never meant to be sweet — thank you for daring to step inside the shadows with me.

This book is for every one of you who craves the darker side of obsession, who isn't afraid to let fear and desire bleed together until you can't tell them apart. You make writing stories like this worth every sleepless night.

All that's left to say is; Trick or Treat…

DEDICATION

For the ones who don't just embrace their fear, but let it consume them completely. This Halloween isn't just about carved pumpkins and costumes—it's about the kind of fear that makes you tremble, ache, and beg to be ruined in the dark.

To those who thought masks were only for hiding… welcome to the shadows, where the trick is an unexpected treat, and every treat is going to make you scream for more.

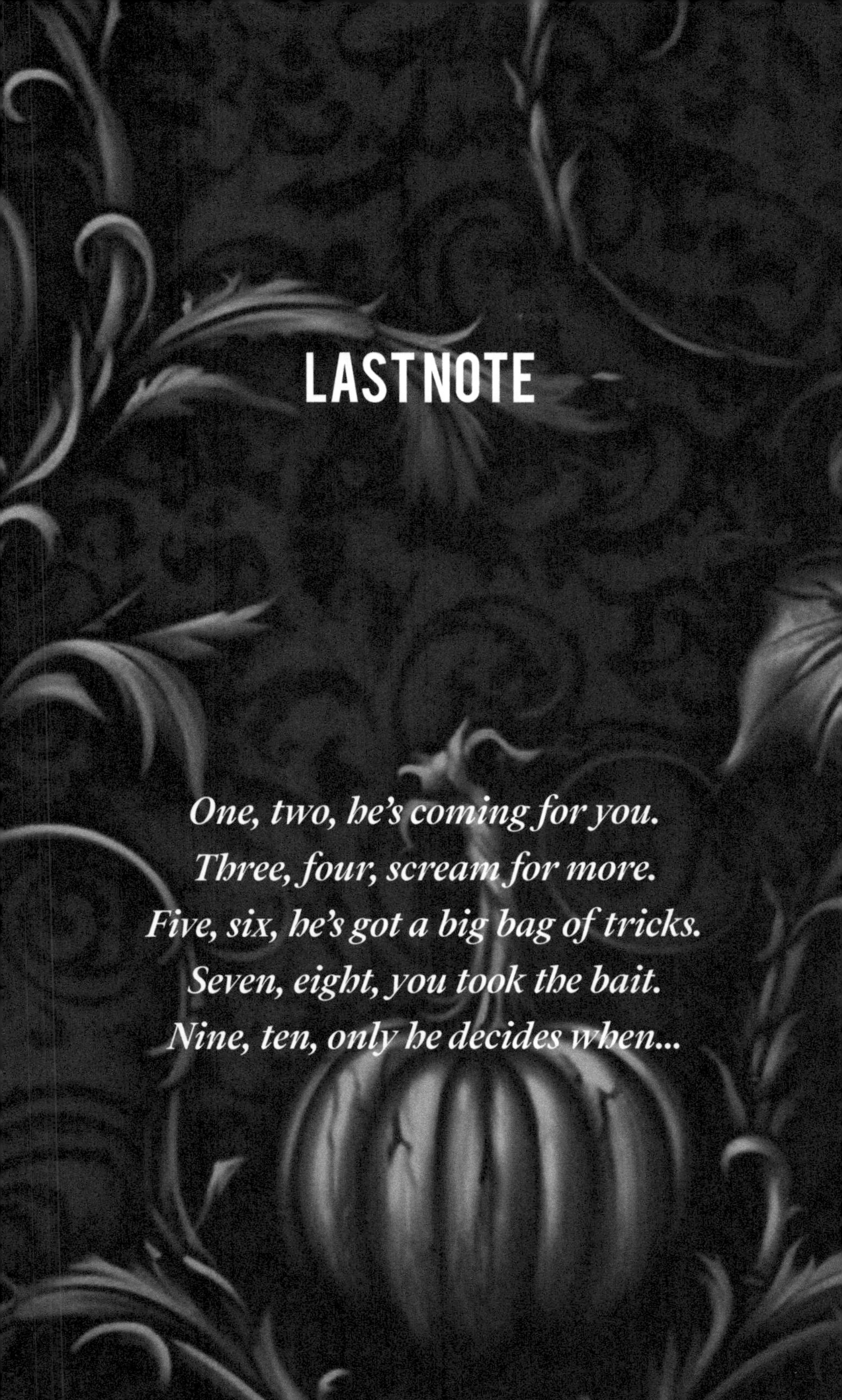

LASTNOTE

One, two, he's coming for you.
Three, four, scream for more.
Five, six, he's got a big bag of tricks.
Seven, eight, you took the bait.
Nine, ten, only he decides when...

CHAPTER 1

The Trickster

February.

I kill the incoming call, Nick's name flashing for the third time today. I'm not in the mood for having my brother check up on me. I have more pressing matters—like what's behind the door of Mortis Psychotherapy in front of me.

It's been two weeks since we buried Ruby, and here I am. Eve canceled my original appointment last week, but I'm not letting anything get in the way of this one.

The waiting room is a shrine to false comfort. Every chair spaced with surgical precision, magazines fanned like they were measured with a ruler. The kind of order that makes you itch.

Someone—Eve Mortis, no doubt—has thought about every detail, every angle, every impression. It makes my teeth ache, and as I take a seat facing the door to the inner offices, I purposefully graze a few of the chairs so their formation is less pristine.

This is exactly the kind of place where people cry in whispers and mirrors never show what you want them to.

My hand slips into my jacket pocket, fingers brushing against the folded edge of Ruby's funeral program. By now, the paper has softened from my constant handling, and the ink's fading where my thumb rests against her name.

Even though every word and photo is burned into my memory, I keep it close. My sister's smiling face is a better picture than the mental one I can't shake. The one of her dying right in front of me.

I'm saved from the agonizing trip down memory lane of how I killed Ruby when I notice the receptionist, Naya, watching me from behind the counter. She smiles like it's policy. Polished warmth, one-size-fits-all.

"First time here?" she asks, voice pitched to carry just to my ears, despite the empty waiting room.

"Is it that obvious?" I make my voice even. Like I'm not one breath away from losing my shit. And like I didn't spend the entire night alone with my new best friends Señor Tequila and my namesake Mr. Jack Daniels.

"Either you're too much in a rush to read…" She gestures to the sign on the wall I ignored. The one that states you need to announce your presence to the receptionist. "… or you're rude. I'm giving you the benefit of the doubt."

I offer a practiced and soft smile. "My bad. I'm sorry about that. I'm Jack Knight—"

She waves me off. "I remember you from when you made your appointment," she says softly. "Dr. Mortis will be with you shortly."

Just as she says that, a woman emerges from the inner corridor, her eyes both steely and red-rimmed. She keeps her gaze down as she slides a credit card across to Naya, murmuring something I can't hear.

Another broken person, leaving Dr. Mortis' office, probably no more fixed than when she entered. I wonder if she'll even make it to her car before the temporary relief of confession fades.

This is what Eve Mortis does. She listens, nods, and offers practiced empathy in fifty-minute increments. And people leave thinking they've been helped, never suspecting they've just paid to have their wounds cataloged by someone who studies emotions like others study art.

I wonder if her eyes ever glaze over while someone sobs about the worst night of their life. If she files trauma away like recipes—one pinch of loss, two of betrayal, stir with remorse.

After two weeks of researching her online, I've learned a lot about Eve Mortis. I could recite her academic credentials, which are no small feats. According to every file I've been able to track down, Eve Mortis is a goddamn prodigy.

She graduated high school at fifteen, and finished NYU Grossman School of Medicine at twenty-two. Which explains how she was licensed to open her clinic at only twenty-six. She's the only child of the late Charles Mortis, who was born Pearson, but changed his last name to stand out more.

On paper, her lineage and achievements make her untouchable. I don't believe it, though. No one's squeaky clean. Eve has skeletons in her closet just like everyone else. I'd shadow her dad or outright ask him if I could. But he died years ago.

If the rumors are to be believed, he was killed by the Hunter. It's a pretty story, though I doubt it's real. After all, what kind of twisted person would give therapy to their dad's killer?

None of that matters today. What I've come here to discover—is whether she feels anything at all behind those carefully constructed walls.

Naya's voice pulls me from my thoughts. "Mr. Knight? Dr. Mortis is ready for you."

I stand, smoothing my tailored jacket with practiced ease. My shoes make no sound on the carpet as I follow Naya down the hallway. The corridor smells different from the waiting room—less synthetic, more human.

"First sessions are usually just getting to know each other," Naya says over her shoulder. She says it like this is a place for healing. "Dr. Mortis is very good at helping people who are struggling."

"I'm sure she is," I reply, allowing just enough rawness into my voice to suggest vulnerability. Inside, I feel nothing but the growing anger and hatred for Eve motherfucking Mortis.

Naya stops at a door, knocks twice, and opens it without waiting for a response. "Dr. Mortis, this is Jack Knight."

She steps aside, and I catch a glimpse of the woman who could have saved my sister. The woman who chose not to. Dr. Eve Mortis stands up. "Thank you, Naya," Eve says, her warm tone at odds with her professionally blank expression.

While Naya slips out, Eve takes a step toward me. Her hair is just as it was at the funeral—jet black from scalp to shoulder, then changing into a striking blood-red color. She wears a long-sleeved nude-toned dress, tailored and high-necked, hem grazing just below the knee.

I fucking hate how good she looks.

Every detail in her outfit is stripped of warmth, like she's allergic to being perceived as anything but controlled. Which, honestly, fit the rest of her soulless office.

There are no family photos or diplomas on display. No plants reaching for nonexistent sunlight. Just white walls, a glass desk with nothing out of place, and a single painting of abstract shapes that convey nothing but safe, sterile ambiguity.

Even the couch where she gestures for me to sit feels unwelcoming—firm enough to keep me present, soft enough to suggest comfort without delivering it. It's a room designed to reveal nothing about its occupant while extracting everything from those who enter. Perfect for a woman who trades in the spectrum of human emotions.

"Please, make yourself comfortable, Mr. Knight," she says, her voice smooth and calibrated. She takes the chair opposite the couch, crossing one leg over the other. Her notepad rests on her lap, pen poised to dissect me.

I sink into the couch, allowing my shoulders to slump forward just enough to signal distress. "Jack. Please call me Jack."

She nods once. "Jack. I must admit, I'm curious as to why you made this appointment. You didn't seem happy that I was at the funeral." Eve's face remains professionally compassionate—a mask as carefully constructed as the rest of her. "I'm very sorry for your loss. Are you here to talk about Ruby?"

I've rehearsed this. What to say. How much to reveal. I need to appear genuine without overplaying my hand. "Yeah," I admit, my voice thick with emotions. "I guess I am."

Eve makes a note on her pad. "Go on."

"Did you know she was the youngest of the three of us?" I ask, staring at a point just past Eve's left ear.

"Why are you asking if I knew? Is that important to you?"

I force myself not to clench my hands or jaw at her obvious deflection. "Just curious," I reply, keeping my tone as light as possible.

"Tell me about your sister, Jack. What kind of person was she?"

"The best," I growl, not liking the way it sounds like she's doubting the kind of person Ruby was. "She was dealt a shitty hand in life, and at every turn, our dad made it worse. But she was kind and loving. Fuck…"

"Go on," she prompts gently.

"Ruby was also quick to forgive. Even when people didn't deserve it."

Another note. Another practiced tilt of Eve's head. "What do you mean when you say people didn't deserve forgiveness? Are you talking about yourself?"

"Maybe." I lean forward, hands loosely clasped between my knees. "I should have known what she was planning… what she had started. What *he* was fucking hired to do. Maybe if I'd known I could have stopped it… but I didn't."

Eve's pen stills for a moment. "I understand you probably have a lot of unanswered questions. But let me ask you this, Jack. Why are you placing so much emphasis on the what and why? Nothing can bring your sister back to life."

I inhale sharply, averting my gaze so she can't see the hatred burning in my eye sockets. "Understanding is a preface for acceptance," I retort, my tone low. "But you're right, Eve. I'll probably never know the reasons behind the choices Ruby made."

She nods. "It's good for you to—"

"So that just leaves the whys, and more importantly, the responsibility."

More scribbling before she looks back up at me, her gray eyes intense. "And who do you believe is responsible?" When I don't answer immediately, she cants her head slightly. "You mentioned that your dad did wrong by Ruby. Are you blaming him for her death?"

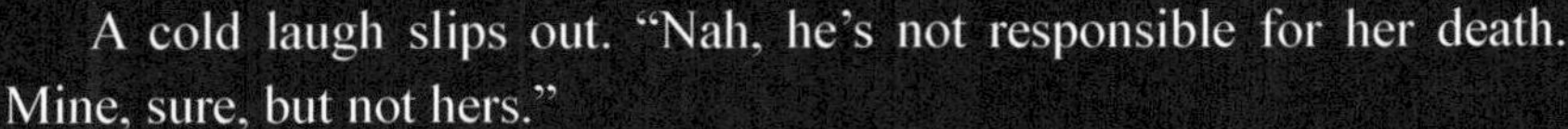

A cold laugh slips out. "Nah, he's not responsible for her death. Mine, sure, but not hers."

Eve's lips part, probably to ask what I meant by *my* death. But I lift a hand, wordlessly silencing her since that's not a conversation I'm willing to have. Not about the minutes I was gone, or the doctors who dragged me back. And definitely not about the Knight family curse.

If I were a theorist, I'd call it coincidence. Say Ruby's death was timing, mine was luck, and Nick's survival is just statistical noise in a family with too much blood under its fingernails. But I'm not a theorist. I'm a Knight, and Knights know better.

"To answer your question, Eve." I deliberately use her name, refusing to give her any power by acknowledging her doctorate. "I blame Valentine Grant, aka the motherfucking Hunter of New York City," I growl, throwing the name out like a grenade and watch where the shrapnel lands.

It's subtle—so subtle most would miss it. But I've been studying people's tells since I was old enough to trick my way into backroom poker games. The momentary stillness of her pen. The almost imperceptible tightening around her eyes. The fraction of a second delay before she responds.

"I see," she says, voice perfectly modulated. "And who was Valentine Grant to your sister?"

"You tell me." I hold her gaze steadily, all pretense of the broken brother momentarily set aside. "He was your patient, wasn't he?"

Eve's face gives nothing away, but her knuckles whiten slightly around her pen. "I can't discuss any other patients, real or hypothetical. That would be a breach of confidentiality."

"Even when one patient murdered another?" The words come out sharper than I intended, but I don't try to soften them.

Something flicks in her eyes when she looks at me. "Valentine didn't kill your sister," she states calmly.

I clench my jaw, trying not to react to her words. But it's a losing battle because she's right. I fucking killed Ruby. "Careful, Eve," I growl. "Just because he didn't end her life doesn't mean he's not responsible. It was his interference that led to the outcome we now all have to live with.”

“I understand you’re looking for answers. For someone to blame. That’s normal after suffering a traumatic loss.” She talks like she’s trying to soothe me. “But I can’t discuss other individuals who may or may not have been under my care.”

The way she says it piques my attention, and I take in her entire body, looking for more tells. Her nostrils flare slightly, and she rolls her shoulders back. Both movements are subtle, making me wonder if she even knows she’s doing it.

Whether she knows or not is inconsequential. I saw it, and I’m cataloging it in my mind. The way she’s acting is like she’s… protecting something. Or possibly someone. Ah fuck me, is she another of Valentine’s conquests? It would explain her composure.

Any decent human being would react at the mention of a murderer they’d treated, protected under the guise of confidentiality. But instead of showing cracks, guilt, or even horror in her professional veneer, Eve Mortis just sits there—completely unmoved, hiding behind ethics while my sister rots in the ground.

“Jack.” She leans forward slightly, locking her gray gaze on my green one. “I’m here to help you process your loss. To find healthy ways to cope. Not to speculate about circumstances that neither of us can change.”

I look down at my hands, forcing myself to act like she’s successfully chastised me. Inhaling deeply, I hold my breath and mentally count to ten before exhaling audibly. “You’re right. I’m sorry. I just…” Trailing off, I let out a carefully measured sigh. “I keep thinking if someone had noticed sooner, if someone had said something…” I trail off, leaving the accusation hanging in the air between us.

“Blame is a natural response to loss,” Eve says, clinical and precise. “But it rarely brings the peace we’re seeking.”

She thinks I want peace, but what I really want is a goddamn reckoning. “I should go,” I say, standing abruptly. “This was a mistake. I’m not ready for this.” I gesture vaguely at the space between us.

Eve stands as well, maintaining the perfect professional distance. “Grief has its own timeline. There’s no rush. When you’re ready to focus on your healing, my door is open."

Healing. As if words could ever stitch together the hole Ruby's absence has torn through my world.

"Thank you for your time," I say, summoning a fragile smile. I step toward the door, then pause, turning back to her with a carefully crafted vulnerability in my eyes. "I'm sorry for being difficult. It's just hard. Harder than I expected."

Something in her expression softens fractionally—not empathy, but a professional recognition of pain. She steps closer, offering her hand. "It's understandable. Emotions are never simple, especially not the strong ones."

I take her hand, but instead of shaking it, I lean in and press a quick, dry kiss to her cheek. I feel her stiffen in surprise, her skin cool beneath my lips.

"My sister would have liked you," I murmur, the lie bitter on my tongue.

I pull back to see confusion flicker across her face before her professional mask slides back into place. Good. Let her feel unsettled. Let her remember the press of my lips against her skin. A fucking Judas kiss.

As I walk back through the waiting room, I only stop long enough to pay Naya. She's now sitting next to an absurdly large bouquet of red roses. They look like the kind of bouquet desperate men buy to either say sorry or lay claim.

It's not my fucking problem which one fits. Now that I've seen everything I needed to see, I leave. Eve Mortis wasn't shocked by the accusation of her former patient committing murder, or even the mention of his serial killer persona.

That can only mean one thing, she already knew. And maybe, just maybe, she's used to being around people like that. My thoughts circle around this as I get into my car and drive the short way to the cemetery.

The cemetery is silent as the sun begins its descent, painting long shadows across the marble façades of family mausoleums. I drive past the main entrance where mourners gather, taking instead the service road that curves behind the hill.

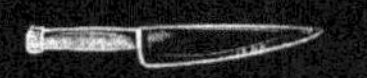

The Knight family crypt stands imposing—generations of power and secrets sealed in stone. I don't stop. Ruby isn't there, not really. Nick insisted on entombing her with the rest of the family, tradition demanding she be locked away in the dark.

But I know our sister. Since her marriage to Michael, there's no way she'd want to be caged again. She deserved something else—something I alone provided.

I park near the eastern edge of the cemetery where the manicured lawns give way to wilder ground. The groundskeeper nods as I pass— I've paid him enough to ensure both his silence and his service. The path I follow isn't marked, but my feet know the way, crushing the frost covered grass that sounds like whispered confessions beneath my shoes.

Three days after the official funeral, I bought this plot under a different name. A small, private space beneath an old oak tree where the stars are visible at night. Where Ruby can have what was stolen from her in life—freedom.

The headstone is simple black granite, her name and dates carved in elegant script. No epitaphs. No Bible verses. Just Ruby Knight—not Simmons—as unadorned and honest as she never got to be.

I kneel on the frozen dirt that covers some of Ruby's favorite belongings. From my pocket, I withdraw a single rose—pristine ruby-red petals that almost glow in the fading light. With deliberate movements, I snap the stem, the crack echoing in the quiet air. The broken flower lays against the dark stone like an accusation.

My fingers trace the edge of the headstone, feeling the cold seep into my skin. "I met her today. Looked Eve Mortis in the eyes, and she didn't even flinch when I mentioned Valentine."

A slight breeze stirs the leaves overhead, sending dappled shadows dancing across the grave. I imagine it's Ruby, listening.

"She hides behind confidentiality. Ethics." The words taste sour. "As if any of that matters when a monster sits across from you. She knew, Rubes. She had to know what he was, and she did nothing."

My hand moves to my chest, pressing against the raised scar beneath my shirt. A constant reminder of my own survival, one I'd trade instantly if I could bring my sister back. The memory of her death comes unbidden, sharp and vivid as it does in my nightmares.

Valentine holds a knife at Ruby's throat. My gun, steady in my hand. The shot hits perfect, centered. Except… Ruby never moved away. And the realization that she wasn't going to didn't hit me until after I pulled the trigger.

One clean shot through both of them. Valentine died instantly. Ruby followed shortly after, her eyes wide with… fuck, I don't know. A part of me thinks she tried to convey forgiveness through her dimming eyes. But that's probably nothing more than wishful thinking.

"I'm sorry," I whisper, the two words inadequate against the weight of what happened. "I should have been faster. Smarter. I should have seen what he was doing to you sooner."

The sun has nearly disappeared now, the cemetery cloaked in deepening twilight. In the distance, I hear the heavy clang of the main gates closing for the night. I should leave, but I linger, needing to finish this before I can move forward with what comes next.

"Eve Mortis has blood on her hands," I continue, my voice hardening. "She probably sat in her office and listened to Valentine's confessions and plans. Writing them down in her notebook instead of stopping him."

The broken flower gleams red against the darkness of the stone, a symbol not of Ruby but of Eve—pristine on the outside, fractured at the core. It's fitting that it rests here, marking the grave of the woman Eve failed.

"I'm going to make her feel what you felt, Rubes." I trace my sister's name one last time. "Eve Mortis is going to fucking pay."

Standing, I brush the dirt from my knees in a gesture that feels ceremonial. The cemetery has fallen completely silent, as if holding its breath. Even the distant sounds of the city seem muffled, respectful of this moment of decision.

With those words, I turn from the grave, my path clear before me. There's work to be done. A reckoning to be crafted. Eve Mortis believes she's safe behind her glass desk and her composed façade. She has no idea what's coming for her—*who's* coming for her.

Back in the car, I pull my phone out and do a quick internet search

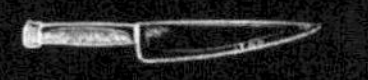

for the owner of the building Eve's clinic resides in.

As soon as I have the details, I tap the number, holding the phone to my ear while it rings.

"Good afternoon and thank you for calling McAllister Holdings. How may I direct your call?" a chipper voice asks.

"Shaun McAllister, please," I reply.

The woman tells me to hold, and it only takes two minutes before Shaun answers my call. "This is Shaun McAllister. How can I be of assistance?"

A wicked smile spreads across my face. "I want to talk to you about one of your tenants."

CHAPTER 2

The Bride

September.

The bass vibrates through the soles of my feet, traveling up my legs like an electric current as I twirl and move my hips in time with the music.

It's almost midnight on a Thursday, and instead of being in bed like a good girl, I'm clubbing with Shelby. Instead of being dressed in something stitched together with control and restraint, I'm wearing a dress that reveals more than it conceals.

One thing I can say for certain is I don't miss my old life. Not one bit.

I didn't choose to leave my practice, the business I never picked for myself. But I had no other choice when my old landlord unexpectedly terminated my lease the first week of March.

The bastard didn't give me any warning and didn't even do it in person. I just received a cold, one-paragraph notice citing building restructuring.

After a week of trying to get his attention by call, email, and even one unsuccessful trip to his office, I gave up. Apparently, that's what two years of never causing problems and always paying my rent on time was worth.

I used to believe structure made things safe. That if you stayed inside the lines long enough, the chaos would pass you by. But chaos doesn't knock. It slips under the door like smoke. It poisons the air you've convinced yourself is clean.

But even now, over six months later, I don't know why I was evicted. Only that I suddenly had to pack up, cancel sessions, and tell my receptionist that we'd figure it out.

It took me over a month to realize the opportunity I had been given, that I didn't have to go back to a life I didn't want. Thanks to Shelby's constant push, I finally turned my back on the profession I never chose.

The brilliant, ruthless, and overcontrolling Charles Mortis, aka Dad, forced me into the life I've now abandoned. A life I'm now free of.

Freedom tastes like the bitter sweetness of my third cocktail and the knowledge that no one here knows Dr. Eve Mortis, the composed psychiatrist who specialized in violent offenders.

They only see a woman on the edge of something dangerous, and I'm loving my newfound freedom.

"Fucking hell, Eve!" Shelby shouts over the pulsing music, her blue eyes bright with mischief. "That guy at the bar hasn't taken his eyes off you for twenty minutes."

I glance over my shoulder, catching the gaze of a dark-haired man in an expensive suit. He doesn't look away when our eyes meet, so I give him the smallest quirk of my lips, neither an invitation nor a dismissal, before turning back to Shelby.

"Let him look," I laugh, pleased by the attention. It's a novel feeling, being desired for nothing more than how I look.

It's shallow, but after living a lifetime where my brain was all that mattered, it's nice to be wanted by someone who might not care about my thoughts at all. Someone who looks like he could wreck me just because he feels like it.

Shelby cackles, grabbing my hand and pulling me deeper into the crowd. "Dance with me instead, then," she demands, and I let her guide me.

We move together, our bodies close. Shelby throws her head back, light brown hair catching the strobing lights as she moves with abandon. I follow her lead, feeling something loosen in my chest—a tightness I've carried for so long I'd forgotten it was there.

When the song ends, Shelby and I retreat to our table in the VIP section. Two fresh cocktails await us—hers electric blue, mine a deep orange that matches the freshly dyed lower half of my hair.

"To freedom," Shelby announces, clinking her glass against mine.

"To choosing our own chains," I counter, and we both drink.

Shelby sets her glass down, studying me with the penetrating gaze that makes her such a formidable attorney. "Do you miss it? Being a psychiatrist?"

I trace the rim of my glass with my fingertip, considering. "No," I say finally, and I'm surprised by how true it is. "I don't miss the weight of other people's darkness."

She nods. "I totally get it." And I know she does.

Shelby spends her days defending people who are most definitely guilty, getting them out on technicalities and negotiating deals. Like me, she has to close her eyes to her clients' crimes.

"I miss you at those boss-bitch seminars, though," she says. "Plus, let's be honest. You were a fucking terrific therapist."

Taking another sip of my drink, I smirk. "It's too late to sweet-talk me now, Shel. I'm retired at the ripe old age of twenty-eight."

She laughs loudly.

I take another sip, the alcohol burns pleasantly, loosening my tongue. "Look, I was good at listening to monsters and nodding in all the right places. I was good at pretending their depravity was just another clinical puzzle to solve." My voice turns bitter without my permission. "What I wasn't good at was stopping them."

Even though it's been seven months since Jack came to see me in my clinic, I still hear his words. The accusations. And despite trying my best, I can't stop wondering if he was right.

Should I have stopped Valentine? Could I have? No, I don't think I could have. He was the Hunter of NYC, and Ruby was both his prey and… well, he loved her. I know he did. But as easy as it is to blame

Valentine for how things went down, she wasn't completely innocent.

She played her role and accepted the outcome. I get why Jack is—or was—bitter. But there's no rewriting history.

Shelby reaches across the table, squeezing my hand. "You can't save everyone."

I snort. "Obviously…" I want to say more, but I trail off as my phone vibrates in my clutch. "Shit," I mutter as I pull the device out.

The screen flashes with Caleb's name, showing me three stacked messages. The last one is less than twenty seconds old.

Caleb: I didn't know you had plans with Shelby tonight.

Caleb: Stop letting strangers grope you.

*Caleb: You didn't say you were getting drunk, Eve. Now I have to take care of this by myself *winky face**

Before I finish reading, a dick-pic joins the thread.

We're not serious enough for it to be okay that he checks in this much. It's not that his texts are threatening, more like little reminders. Ways to tell me he knows where I am and what I'm doing.

And I can't help but wonder how the hell he always seems to know, down to the minute, exactly where I'm at and what I'm doing.

The part of me that hates being controlled bristles, but the part I've only really been able to let out around him, thrills at the attention. Sighing, I leave him on read, refusing to let him end my night out.

Shelby catches my expression. "Boyfriend check-in?" she teases, her tone edged with something sharp. "Honestly, Eve, you should be happy. Most women would kill for a guy like Caleb keeping tabs. He's hot, dangerous, and obsessed with you."

"He's not my boyfriend," I snort, focusing on the first part of her tirade while locking the screen. My thumb lingers over it longer than it needs to. "But yeah, he's checking in."

She smirks, eyes glinting. "Don't screw it up, Eve. Guys like Caleb don't come around twice. He's exactly your type of reckless. You should lean into it."

Her words land wrong, feeling extremely pushy. I narrow my eyes, but when Shel doesn't even blink, I let it slide. I'm probably reading her wrong, and I blame the alcohol for making me oversensitive.

"Yes ma'am," I mutter, aiming for light but hearing the edge in my own voice.

Leaning closer, she lowers her tone. "Don't tell me you don't like it. A man *that* into you? I've seen your taste, Eve. You thrive on the kind of attention that borders on unhealthy."

She's not wrong, and that's the part that bothers me. In my head, this is exactly what I want. Reality is an entirely different matter, one where Caleb's way too much.

"I swear he has a magic dick," I laugh, though what I don't say is that it's more than that — the way he takes without asking, the way he fucks like I'm there to be used. I shouldn't like it, but I do.

"That good?" She waggles her eyebrows suggestively.

"You have no idea," I say, my tone sultry. I fan myself exaggeratedly. "That man definitely knows what he's doing."

"Well, damn," she cackles.

"Let's just say that it's people like Caleb that make it hard to argue why we shouldn't be allowed to fuck our clients," I smirk. "He's the right amount of arrogant, and reckless. He's exactly the kind of mistake I can't resist."

"Lucky bitch," Shelby groans, draining her cocktail. "I need to get laid. It's been seven months, Eve. Seven. Months."

"Poor baby," I tease. "Does this mean you're over your ex?"

She sniffs. "I'll never be over him. But I guess I'm ready to move on to some meaningless sex."

"And here I thought your plan was to save yourself for the Sanctuary of Shadows. You know, for your future demon husband or whatever."

Her eyes light up at the mention of the upcoming Halloween event. "Speaking of which, I got confirmation we'll have our VIP tickets."

The law firm she works at has handled some of the complex liability waivers, NDAs, and contracts for the organizers. While she either doesn't know much, or can't share what she does know, she did score us

VIP access.

"Yes," I exclaim, shimmying my shoulders. "I can't wait."

"God, I hope they choose me as a Bride," Shelby says, her voice dropping to a conspiratorial whisper. "Did you know the Brides get a private experience? Something exclusive, just for them."

"Only you would be excited about being sacrificed to fictional demons," I laugh, but there's an answering thrill in my blood.

Everyone in New York has heard about the Sanctuary of Shadows, the notorious Halloween event on Governors Island. But no one really seems to know *exactly* what it is. A carnival, a theater, or something else entirely.

Those who know are keeping tightlipped, including my best friend. I know she knows more than she's letting on. But since I know all too well how complicated client/patient confidentiality can be, I don't push her.

"Whatever," she sighs. "If only you knew… well, never mind."

I roll my eyes at her. "Alright, stop the dramatics, Shel." When she pouts, I laugh, and signal the waiter to get us more drinks. "Okay, spill it. What are you so eager to tell even though you can't?"

"Well," she sing-songs, waggling her eyebrows. "I'm not one to talk—"

"Right," I snort.

"But from what I know, it's going to be unforgettable. Like, some seriously epic shit." She tilts her head to the side, expression suddenly serious. "Maybe you shouldn't go, Eve. The Knights aren't exactly your friends. They're not anyone's friends."

I wave her off. "It's only one Knight who hates me." At least as far as I know.

"Sure, sure," she rushes out. "Forget I said anything."

Two hours and several drinks later, we stumble out of the club, my arm looped through Shelby's for stability. The cool September air hits my flushed skin, and I inhale deeply, trying to clear the alcohol haze from my head.

"Wanna share a ride?" she asks, fumbling with her phone.

I nod, but as I turn to look down the street, something catches my eye. A figure stands in the shadows between buildings—tall, hulking, and utterly still.

They wear what looks like a gas mask, and even from this distance, I can feel their gaze locked on me.

I blink, and they're gone.

"Eve? You okay?" Shelby's voice pulls me back.

"Yeah," I say, shaking my head. "Just thought I saw something weird."

A car pulls up next to us, and Shelby announces it's our ride. As I slide into the backseat, I glance once more at the spot where the figure stood. Nothing but empty shadows now.

Closing the door, I tell myself it was just the alcohol playing tricks on my eyes. After all, this is the Bronx and not Manhattan. Which means a guy casually wearing a gas mask would definitely stand out and gain attention from more people than just me.

Since I live the closest, I get out first, and after hugging Shel goodnight, I stumble into the apartment complex I live in.

I almost fall asleep while riding the elevator to my floor, and when I do get out, I almost get into a fight with my keys that act like they get a prize if they avoid the keyhole long enough.

"You. Will. Get. In. There," I hiss. The jangle of my keys sounds like a mocking laugh.

The hallway tilts slightly, and I brace one hand against the doorframe, steadying myself with a quiet laugh. This is what freedom looks like, I think as I finally manage to unlock my door—messy, imperfect, and deliciously uncontrolled.

My apartment is dark except for the single lamp I left on, casting long shadows across my furniture. I kick off my heels with a satisfied groan, letting them land where they may instead of placing them neatly in the closet as the old Eve would have done.

I pad barefoot to the kitchen, pouring a glass of water that I down in greedy gulps. The cool liquid helps clear my head, though the room still wobbles pleasantly at the edges.

A sharp knock cuts through my thoughts.

CHAPTER 3

The Bride

I freeze, glancing at the digital clock on my microwave. It's way too late, or early, for a casual visitor. Not that I ever get any of those. Shelby and Caleb are the only ones occasionally stopping by.

Another knock, firm and precise.

A chill ripples beneath my skin as I slowly turn toward the door. I hold my breath, listening for... something. A voice, footsteps, or shuffling. But nothing comes.

I set my glass down and move silently to the door. While moving, I silently scoff at myself. If Shelby told me this happened to her, I'd roll my eyes and ask why she didn't just ignore it. But curiosity wins over any common sense I should possess.

Just as I reach for the door, the knock sounds again, as if whoever's on the other side knows I'm here.

"Who is it?" I call out.

The hallway beyond my door remains silent. No shuffling feet, no impatient sighs. Whoever stands outside is patient. I look through the peephole, holding my breath as if the person on the other side might hear it.

I gasp as my eyes land on the motionless man who looks an awful lot like the one I saw just after exiting the club. He just stands there, completely motionless. Tall, rigid, face hidden behind a matte black gas mask.

The two round lenses stare back at me, flat and blank like insect eyes. A single cylindrical filter protrudes from the mouthpiece. He's wearing military boots, laced tight and polished to a dull shine, worn jeans, and a leather jacket that's zipped closed.

In his gloved hands is a matte black box, tied with a bright orange ribbon that curls in dramatic spirals at the top. The contrast between the cheerful bow and the ominous messenger makes my skin prickle with both awareness and excitement.

Shaking my head, I laugh softly to myself. It's possible this is just some mistake. The intercom never buzzed, so maybe he's at the wrong door. Yeah, that's probably it.

A middle-of-the-night delivery from a company that doesn't believe in only embracing the Halloween spirit in October. The mask and the outfit's disturbingly hot. It works for him. So much so that I'm almost jealous he's here for one of my neighbors.

There's a pulse of want I can't disguise. The silence behind the mask presses in on me, a dark weight that makes my skin prickle with hunger—like lust crawling straight out of the grave.

With that thought, I open the door. "Can I help you?" My voice sounds louder than it should in the silence of the hour. Everything feels thinner at midnight, as though the entire world's holding its breath.

Rather than answering, he extends the box toward me. Now that the door isn't between us, I can hear his slow, steady, and slightly mechanical breathing.

"Who sent this?" I ask, not reaching for it yet.

Silence. The mask's filters rise and fall with measured breathing, but no voice emerges.

"What is it?" I try again.

Still nothing.

"Are you sure you've got the right apartment?" I ask, narrowing the door a fraction. "There are other floors—other people who might've actually ordered something."

Rather than acknowledging my questions, he takes one step forward and lifts the box higher, like that movement is its own answer.

A small, clinical part of my mind catalogs the familiar markers—racing heart, flushed skin, the subtle tremor in my fingers as they brush the doorframe. But none of it registers as fear. It feels too focused, too hot, too alive.

"I can't accept packages without knowing their source," I say, injecting a note of authority into my voice. It's the same tone I use with difficult clients who test boundaries.

The man remains unmoved, arm extended, box waiting. The silence stretches between us, heavy with an unspoken challenge. We've reached an impasse—this strange courier won't leave until I take the package, and I can't close the door on this mystery without resolving it.

My nipples harden under his stare, a traitorous response I hide by folding my arms. But the truth is, I like that he can pull it from me without a single word. There's something undeniably enticing about the way his identity is hidden—like a question I shouldn't want answered.

His loud breathing and something that almost sounds like a chuckle has me realizing I've been standing here like an idiot, gawking at him. Shit. I extend my hand, accepting the box while maintaining maximum distance between our bodies.

As soon as my fingers close around it, he releases his grip with a finality that feels significant.

"Thank you," I say automatically, professional habits asserting themselves even in this bizarre encounter.

He gives no acknowledgment. Just turns around and walks to the stairwell at the opposite end of the hall.

I stand frozen in my doorway, the box cool against my palms, watching this strange messenger retreat. The boots make a distinctive sound against the hallway floor—a heavy thud followed by a slight scrape.

Only when the stairwell door opens and closes several stories below do I step back into my apartment. I secure both deadbolts, then add the chain—a precaution I rarely bother with. But something about this strange encounter makes me feel like I have to.

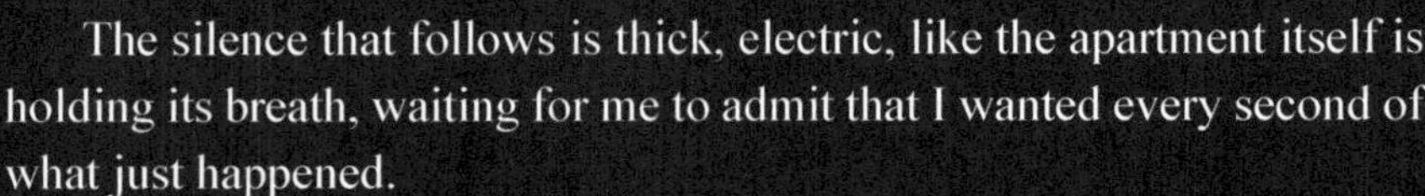

The silence that follows is thick, electric, like the apartment itself is holding its breath, waiting for me to admit that I wanted every second of what just happened.

I look down at the box in my hands, the orange bow suddenly garish against the matte black surface. Like a warning sign in nature—bright colors signaling danger, approach at your own risk.

Whatever message this package contains, it's already breached my defenses, crossed my threshold.

With deliberate steps, I move away from the door, carrying this strange offering into the kitchen where I place it on the counter. I study its dimensions from every angle. No markings or labels. No indication of its origin or purpose.

Instead of cutting the ribbon, I carefully work at the bow, loosening it with methodical patience. The satin slides against itself, making a soft whisper as it comes undone.

With steady hands that betray none of my internal tension, I lift the lid and set it aside, aligned parallel to the box's edge. Inside, black tissue paper forms a nest, carefully folded to cradle the single object it contains.

A black rose.

It's not fresh—not alive at all. The flower is desiccated, preserved in its death. The once-supple stem has hardened into a brittle twist of organic material, the spathe curled inward like a protective cloak around the spadix.

The bloom's elegant curve remains intact, but the tissue has transformed—no longer velvet-soft but papery, fragile, like ancient parchment that might disintegrate at a touch.

What catches my eye are the speckles—dark red, almost rust-colored—marring the black petals like scattered blood. I reach for the rose, pausing only as a slight tremor runs down my fingers.

The flower feels wrong in my hand. It's too light, too hollow, a brittle relic rather than anything once alive. A petal breaks off at the touch, crumbling to dust against my skin.

As I set it down, something shifts beneath the tissue paper—a small rectangle of black and orange cardstock I hadn't noticed before. I lift it

free and turn it over.

> *For every bride, a bloom must die,*
> *Petal-black and blooded dry.*
> *The vow begins before the ring,*
> *You're his now, let the silence sing.*

The final line pulses beneath my skin like a bruise I want to press harder. I read it again. And again. My fingers leave smudges of black dust on the counter, marks that feel like proof I've already let this vow under my skin.

What the actual hell is this? Oh, no. Please don't let this be Caleb's way of proposing.

The Trickster

Smirking, I make my way back to Eve's door the moment I hear it close. When I realized she was hanging around, waiting for me to be gone, I had to walk all the way down and open the front door.

My cock's still hard, straining painfully against the metal teeth of my jeans zipper, the pressure making the pierced shaft throb with each heartbeat. Fuck me. The dress she wore left very little to my fucking imagination.

Tight across her breasts and short enough I saw the swell of her ass when she turned. No bra or panties—I would've seen the lines.

Eve Mortis opened the door to a masked man in the dead of night without a second thought. All while her attire screamed desperation, as if she were inviting chaos to consume her whole.

The hallway is dead silent, all the doors shut, and the lights off. Perfect. My hand slides down, fingers curling around the rigid outline beneath denim. A sharp breath escapes through clenched teeth.

With a savage groan, I rip my zipper down just enough to free myself, the relief instant and agonizing. Each metal stud along my shaft scrapes my palm as I grip hard enough to hurt.

My jaw clenches until my teeth nearly crack, imagining her gagging, eyes watering as I roughly feed her every rung of my Jacob's Ladder, leaving her throat bruised and ruined for days.

I slam into my fist, each brutal thrust making my vision blur at the edges. I imagine her delicate fingers struggling to close around my girth, her eyes widening in fear when she realizes what I'll force her to take.

The force of my next thrust sends my knuckles crashing against her door, the hollow thud echoing down the empty hallway. I freeze, heart hammering violently in my chest.

Shit, did she hear me?

My breathing sounds entirely too loud through the mask as I wait to see if she'll come back out here. I wait for ten, twenty, fifty seconds. Each passing second makes me impossibly harder. Pre-cum leaks from my cock, and I can't say I hate the idea of Eve opening the door, catching me jerking off.

Nothing happens.

Fuck, the anticipation rips through me like electricity, my balls drawing up painfully tight against the base of my cock. One last savage stroke and my entire body convulses—vision whiting out, knees nearly buckling as I erupt, every muscle seizing in violent release.

I bite down on a groan as I come, thick ropes spilling over her door. I press the head of my cock to the wood, dragging it down until it smears. Then I dip two fingers into my cum and write one word.

Soon.

CHAPTER 4

The Trickster

Baby Willow Ruby squirms in my arms, a warm bundle swaddled in cashmere that costs more than most people make in a week. Her eyes peer up at me, unfocused yet somehow trusting.

I adjust her head against the crook of my elbow, supporting her neck with careful precision. The weight of her is nothing, barely seven pounds of new life.

"Look at you, natural as anything." Carolina beams from across the dining table, her fork poised over the remains of her chicken. "She hasn't made a single peep since you took her."

I look at my sister-in-law, who shows no sign of having gone into early labor. "She knows I don't negotiate with terrorists."

Nick snorts into his wine glass. "If only that were true."

The baby's tiny fingers flex against the blanket, and I find myself studying her face that carries traces of both parents. Carolina's wide, expressive eyes, and Nick's stubborn chin. A nose that belongs to neither, a ghost of our dad's genetics resurfacing. Science is relentless that way.

Blood remembers, even when we'd rather it forgot. It leaks through time and skin, sneaking into faces that don't belong to the dead.

"Seriously though," Carolina continues, setting down her fork and reaching for her water. "You're practically a baby whisperer, Jack. Ever consider having some of your own?"

The question lands like a small, targeted explosive. Not enough to do real damage, but enough to disturb the careful composure I maintain at these family gatherings. Nick's eyes flick toward mine, sharp with warning, but I ignore him.

"Not everyone needs to reproduce," I say, voice even. "Someone has to be the fun uncle who teaches her to hot-wire cars and falsify documents."

Carolina laughs, the sound bright against the dining room's dark wood paneling and lime-green walls. The old Knight estate breathes around us, its walls steeped in generations of family power.

Since Nick and Carolina moved into the family mansion, they've reshaped it. It's more modern than opulent now, but still unmistakably Knight. Wealth is our birthright, power our inheritance.

"You joke, but I'm serious," she persists, leaning forward with that particular intensity she gets when she's decided to fix something—or someone. "You'd make a good dad."

"Would I?" I meet her gaze, letting my smile cool several degrees. Willow stirs against my chest, sensing the shift in my muscles. "Based on what evidence, exactly?"

Carolina's certainty falters momentarily. "Well, you're patient. You're protective—"

Nick clears his throat. "Leave him alone, Kitten. Not everyone's cut out for it." His eyes meet mine across the table, carrying an entire silent conversation in a single glance.

"Fine, fine." Carolina raises her hands in mock surrender. "I'll let it go."

"Appreciate it," I say, though we both know she won't.

Since my sister's death, Carolina has made it her mission to include me as much as possible. Weekly family dinners, ideas for how I can spend my time, and, of course, a relentless need to give my life meaning.

I know what she's doing, just like I know she means well. Carolina knows about the Knight superstition, and she's afraid I'm going to plan

my own exit from this world. Give up, like Ruby did.

But that's not fucking happening, and with my luck, I'd come back like a fucking ghost with all the unfinished business I have.

You wouldn't know it by looking at the two of them, but Carolina's only been a Knight for nine months. Nick bought the right to breed her back in December, and what started as a transaction was never supposed to become anything more.

Then they both fell in love, and somehow, she fit. I do care for her, in the way you care for someone who's become part of your family, whether or not they were born to it.

Willow makes a small sound, somewhere between a sigh and a hiccup. Her eyelids flutter, heavy with impending sleep, utterly unaware of the world she's been born into.

The weight of the Knight name. The responsibilities. The dangers.

"She likes you," Nick observes.

"She doesn't know any better," I retort, but my thumb traces a gentle arc across my niece's cheek. Born in late August, almost a month early, Willow Ruby Knight is fucking perfect.

When they announced her name is after two aunts she'll never meet, but that would have spoiled her rotten, it thawed some of the ice around my heart.

Willow was Carolina's younger sister, who sadly died when she was shot by one of my dad's goons. And Ruby… well, she's obviously gone as well. But neither of them are forgotten.

While Willow lives on in Carolina's charity project, Willow's Foundation, Ruby lives on in every fiber of my being. I know Nick misses our sister as well, but unlike me, he's not hung up on vengeance or living with regret.

He's channelled all his energy into his wife and their daughter. I'm both happy for my brother and hating him at the same time. Being me is fucking complicated.

Nick pushes back from the table and stands, stretching slightly. "Coffee in the study? I want to show you the latest for Sanctuary of Shadows."

"Sure," I say, moving to hand Willow back to her mom. "Take your demon child before she drools on my shirt."

Carolina accepts her daughter with practiced ease. "Such a charmer. It's a mystery why you're still single."

I stand, straightening my cuffs. "The greatest mystery of our time," I deadpan.

Following Nick toward his study, I pause at the threshold and glance back at the domestic tableau. Carolina humming softly to her daughter, the remains of our family dinner scattered across fine china.

A perfect picture of Knight family prosperity. Stability. Legacy. All of it built on bloodied foundations none of us discuss. But I still feel the echo of screams no one ever acknowledged. This legacy doesn't just hold us—it cages us.

My skin feels too tight suddenly, like I'm playing a part that no longer fits. Brother. Uncle. The good soldier. Each role is a carefully constructed mask, growing heavier by the day. But not for much longer. Soon, I won't need to pretend that I'm okay.

Nick unfolds the blueprints across his desk with careful precision, his fingers tracing the perimeter of Governors Island like he's measuring the boundary of a wound. I wonder what kind of infection we'll unleash when we cut it open. How many people will beg for more after they bleed.

"The ferry terminal here," he says, tapping the northern edge, "will be our main entry point. Eight-minute ride from Manhattan."

I nod. "Yeah, I know. I've been on the grounds."

Thanks to Nick's pull as head of the family, he got Governors Island shut down from August through mid-November. It's where Willow's Foundation is hosting Sanctuary of Shadows—a month-long immersive Halloween experience. It's theatrical, grotesque, and engineered to mess with people.

Sanctuary of Shadows, or S.O.S. as we've ironically started calling it, opens with a massive launch event on October first at 12:01 a.m.

Carolina has worked tirelessly with her team to get this done in just nine months. The ferry terminal will run twenty-four hours a day, and the two-hundred ticket holders per day can enter from midnight to midnight.

The only caveat is, once a guest leaves, they won't be allowed to come back.

Nick drags his finger along a dotted line. "Once they're off the ferry, guests funnel through this causeway. It'll be lit by torches and jack-o'-lanterns. We're going to completely disorient them."

"Making them feel isolated," I observe, and something hot and eager shifts beneath my ribs.

Nick continues mapping the layout. "We've got the masked staff—no speaking allowed, all communication through gestures or pre-recorded audio. The old military structures are perfect for the haunted zones."

My pulse quickens at the mention of masked staff. Each detail of the Sanctuary feeds something darker in me, something patient and hungry that's been waiting since Ruby's funeral.

"Is the Slaughter Stage ready?" I tap a circular structure near the center of the island so he knows I mean this one specifically.

"Yes," he confirms, his eyes narrowing slightly. "Everything's set up for The Black Wedding."

My fingers still against the paper, heat spreading through my palm at those three words. The Black Wedding. The name alone sends electricity down my spine. "I'm ready, too."

I've been ready since the moment they closed Ruby's casket. I don't want a wedding—I want a fucking reckoning.

Nick looks at me as he straightens and lets out a heavy sigh. "Are you sure about this, Jack?" His tone is weary, and I'm pretty sure I detect a note of sadness. "It's not too late to… let it go." He scrunches up his nose at the last part.

"I can't fucking let it go," I snarl, clenching my hands into fists. "What is it you don't get? Unlike you, I don't have a fucking wife or perfect daughter to hide behind. I'm just me—"

"You have us," he placates. "We're your family. Don't make me lose my brother on top of my sister."

"That's not fair," I accuse, stabbing a finger in his direction. "Besides, you've already lost me once." Even if my heart only stopped for a couple of measly minutes, it still counts.

Something crawled in when it restarted. I don't know what it is, only that it doesn't forgive. And it won't let go until I have my revenge. Maybe then I can sleep through the entire fucking night without waking up bathed in sweat, seeing my sister's lifeless eyes haunting me.

He slams his fist into the desk, making the wood creak, and all the shit on top of it rattles. "Jack!"

"Nick," I parrot, not willing to let it go just because it's more convenient for him. "I need to do this. Now, you can either support me or get the fuck out of my way. Either way, it's happening."

His jaw tightens, a muscle twitching beneath the skin. "Are you sure about this?" he asks again. "I need to hear you say it now. While you're sober for once."

The words emerge heavy with intention, laden with all he knows but won't say aloud. This is his final warning, his last attempt to pull me back from the edge.

I study him—my brother, the heir, the chosen one—and feel nothing but a distant fondness, like remembering a photograph of someone I once knew. Whatever bound us as children has thinned to a fragile thread, barely visible in the gathering dark.

"Yes," I say, the word falling between us like a stone dropped into still water. Final. Unmovable. A declaration of intent. "You know I can't resist a good gamble."

Nick holds my gaze a moment longer, then nods once—sharp, resigned. He's made his choice, just as I've made mine. We are Knights, after all. Blood calls to blood. Silence protects silence. And some vows transcend family loyalty.

I look at the window, to my reflection growing sharper as night claims the glass. The darker it gets, the clearer I become. Like I was never meant for daylight.

Not as Nick's brother or Willow's uncle, but as what my sister's death has made me. The architect of retribution, the keeper of accounts, the hand that balances scales tipped by blood and betrayal.

My phone buzzes in my pocket, and I pull it out to read the text from Ned.

Ned: I just heard her make plans with that boyfriend of hers.

Want me to stop them?

*Me: No. Just leave the key to your apartment under the mat
for me.*

There's no need to chase her. She's already stepped onto the stage—
I'm just behind the curtain, waiting for my cue.

Before he can text me back, I say goodbye to both my brother and
sister-in-law. Once I'm in my car, I speed toward the Bronx, ready to
wait for her return in Ned's apartment. Well, technically, mine.

I'm the one paying the rent, he's just the one living there to keep up
appearances. And Eve isn't aware her neighbor works for me.

CHAPTER 5

The Bride

I hum as I end the call with Caleb, telling him I need to get ready. This is just what I need, a night at the ring. And he's always extra feral when he's been fighting.

After draining the last of my wine and texting Shelby my plans, I head to the bathroom so I can shower and get changed into something a lot less comfortable than the oversized t-shirt and leggings I'm currently wearing.

While showering, I make sure I'm mostly hairless. There's no way I'll be able to resist Caleb when he's panting and sweaty from fighting. Just thinking about it is enough to make my clit throb.

By the time I step out, the air smells like cherry and honey, remnants of my soaps. I inhale greedily while I towel dry, and then I get to work.

It's almost ritualistic the way I release my long hair from the messy bun on top of my head. Like keeping it contained hides the darker part of me I'm letting out more and more often—the side that doesn't just want release, but ruin.

Taking my time, I separate the strands into two and braid each section so they fall down my back. Once I'm done, I move on to my makeup. I'm in the middle of adding a second coat of mascara when my phone rings.

"Shel," I say as a way of greeting my friend.

"Eve," she hollers so loudly I'm glad the phone is resting on the sink instead of against my ear. "I can't believe you're going out again tonight. I thought for sure you'd be nursing a hangover after yesterday."

"Look who's talking," I mutter. "At least I didn't have to work."

"I know," she groans theatrically. "Trust me, I was tempted to call in sick."

When I ask if she's coming tonight, she throws herself head first into a long story about all the work she's behind on.

"Well, that—"

"And you wouldn't believe the amount of shit I'm going to unleash on my intern," she interrupts, her tone heated. "There I was, in court. In front of the honorable judge or whatever…"

Knowing I'm probably close to running out of time, I get dressed while she tells me all about the intern sending her to court with the wrong folder.

"… I looked like a fucking fool. Oh, and the best part is I got fined for wasting the court's time."

"That sucks, Shel," I emphasize.

The good thing about her distracting me is I don't have time to second-guess my outfit for tonight. Once I'm done, I pause in front of my bedroom mirror, and run my hand over the hem of the cropped orange sweater I haven't worn before.

The color perfectly matches my hair, and it's soft and thin enough for late September, snug enough to hint at my shape without clinging. It ends just a couple of inches above the waistband of my black latex pants, leaving a deliberate strip of skin exposed.

I smirk at my reflection, wondering what any of the people from my old life would think if they saw me now—and secretly hoping they would, just so they'd choke on the proof that their good little doctor was never so good.

With the come-fuck-me outfit, heavy eyeliner and multiple coats of mascara, I'm a far cry from the professionally cold therapist they used to know. Hell, I'm a far cry from the person I thought I was at the core.

I've read enough psych books to know that the new me I've embraced is fueled by my daddy issues, which are plenty.

My dad wanted a progeny, so he made me one. Instead of fairy tale bedtime stories, he read me text books. In our house, you didn't get a cake or presents on your birthday. You got tests to prove you were worth celebrating.

Charles Mortis might have been a renowned psychiatrist and a successful professor. But to me, he'll never be remembered as more than an all-around shitty human. Just like to him, I was a subject and not a daughter.

Since my mom died of an aneurysm when I was four, he got to raise me alone, with no one to contradict his cruel methods. And the sharp edges of his methods are exactly what shaped me into something twisted enough to crave nights like this.

But ask me if I care that what I'm doing would most likely be diagnosed as belated teenage rebellion. Just for the record, I don't care one bit. I never got to do it when I was a teenager, so why should I rein myself in now?

"… Eve? Helloooo… are you still there?"

Shit, I forgot about Shelby. "Umm, yes, I'm here," I confirm, shaking the unpleasant memories of my dad away. "Sorry, Shel. I've got to go."

"Yeah, yeah," she sighs dramatically. "Okay, so before I forget why I called you, did you ever fill out the online questionnaire I sent you last month?"

"What for?"

"The Sanctuary," she sing-songs. "They need some extra details for the Bride applicants."

I frown as I step into my ankle boots. "I think I did…" I stop talking, trying to remember if I did or not. "Can't you check for me if your firm has access to all their paperwork?"

"Sure," she confirms. "I probably should have done that before calling." There's something in her tone that sounds almost forced.

"Are you okay, Shel?" I ask, wondering if the late nights and workload is finally catching up with her.

"Peachy," she replies absentmindedly.

While she taps away on her laptop, I dig out my small crossbody bag from the closet. "Shel," I ask, regretting I didn't ask this before filling the damn thing out. "The form's legit, right? I mean, they're not going to do anything weird with my details?"

Shel's answering laugh is downright maniacal. "Bitch, I'm the one who created it. I promise you're not signing away your immortal soul or whatever." There's a beat of silence. "Oh, here it is. Yep, you filled it out and checked all the right boxes."

"Great," I say, knowing I need to get off the phone. "Soooo, if there's nothing else…"

"Yeah, yeah, I'm going, going, gone. Happy dicking or whatever." With that, she hangs up, and I slip my phone and wallet into the bag.

I just about manage two steps when the intercom buzzes, letting me know Caleb's here. Double-checking I have everything I need, I blow my dad's grinning skull a kiss.

"God, I wish you could actually see me now, you bastard," I laugh, slightly crazily. "You'd hate it so much."

Still laughing, I adjust the plaque with the words *why so serious?* that's hanging above the remains of my dad, perched on the living room mantle. Then I leave and head to the elevator. Just as it arrives, I'm joined by my neighbor, Ned.

"Hi," I greet as we both step into the waiting elevator.

"Looking good tonight," he grins, waggling his eyebrows playfully. "Going somewhere special?"

Instead of giving him the truth, I just shake my head and laugh softly. "Isn't everywhere special?"

He rolls his eyes. "Fuck. I forgot you're a therapist and answer everything with a damn question."

"Do I?" I ask, mostly just to fuck with him.

Reaching the ground floor, I wave before almost running outside, where Caleb's leaning against the building. His icy-blond hair is pushed back, a few strands already falling out of place and across his forehead.

"Damn, sweetheart," he drawls, gaze dragging over me like he's checking out a purchase. "Are you trying to get me killed before the fight

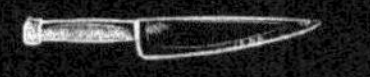

even starts? Or just make sure I'm thinking about you instead of the guy I'm about to break?"

I raise an eyebrow. "That would be stupid since I planned on betting on you tonight," I retort.

He reaches for me, one hand finding my waist and pulling me closer while the other slides behind my neck. "Did you dress like that for me?" he rasps, moving his hands to my ass while fusing our lips together.

The kiss is hard, his mouth claiming mine, our tongues snaking around each other. I moan softly and reach for him, my fingers curling into the hem of his hoodie. I let him take what he wants, just long enough to feel my pulse kick harder.

When I'm tempted to suggest we skip the fight, I pull back. "No," I quip, slightly breathless. "I'm dressed for me. You're just lucky enough to see it."

He chuckles, short and sharp, like the joke's on me. "That I am."

Loving the way he's reacting to me, I put more sway in my step than necessary as we walk to his old dented car that's parked by the curb.

I never trust it to make the destination whenever he drives, but I never complain out loud. Caleb loves this car, which is evident in the way he strokes the dashboard when we're both seated.

"How many fights are you doing tonight?" I ask as we head toward Gowanus in Brooklyn.

The times I've been to see Caleb fight, it was in an abandoned factory. With its brick walls and blood-stained concrete flooring, it legit looks like something taken straight out of Fight Club.

"Only one fucker was stupid enough to challenge me," he replies, cockily, grinning widely when I look over at him.

For a moment, I consider giving him a good luck handjob, but then I decide against it. Caleb's always more eager to play once victory courses through his veins. He has that *to the victor goes the spoils* mentality, and once he proves he's the best, he becomes deliciously rough.

The factory sits hunched between two warehouses, its rusted gates wide open like broken jaws. Floodlights mounted on scaffolding throw harsh light across the gravel lot, illuminating clusters of men with smoke-tipped mouths and predatory eyes.

This is the kind of crowd that doesn't flinch at bruises, and doesn't ask questions when someone leaves limping and bloody.

Caleb parks just past a stack of crumbled pallets, his engine growling low before cutting off. I step out, a shiver rolls down my spine as excitement settles thickly in my throat.

Inside, the air hits me like a wall. It's saturated with sweat and something more primal. Like old blood and broken promises. The floor remembers every scream it's soaked in—and tonight, it's thirsty again.

Bodies press close around the makeshift ring—a square of chain-link fencing reinforced with concrete blocks. Blood stains streak the floor like sacrament, smeared and trodden into the concrete.

"I don't think I'll ever get used to having you here with me, Doc," Caleb murmurs, brushing his knuckles against the small of my back as we slip through the crowd.

People part for him, recognizing the cut of his jaw and the gleam in his eyes. He's not the biggest man here, but he's the one they avoid brushing against. That says everything.

I glance up at him with a smirk. "Oh?" I ask, quirking an eyebrow. I don't expect him to answer since we both know why.

Caleb was assigned to me through court-ordered therapy after too many brawls and a possession charge. I assessed his anger issues, and put together a treatment plan. That was basically all I managed before he was reassigned or something.

If I'm honest, I'd completely forgotten about him until he showed up at my apartment two or three months ago. He just stood outside my door, arrogant and oozing the right kind of danger. In other words, my perfect kryptonite.

He refused to leave until I agreed to at least one drink. Which we've still never had. All we do is hook up. We don't go on dates or cuddle. Hell, we don't talk about anything that matters.

Caleb uses my body like I'm just a wet, willing hole. And he makes sure I remember that's all I am to him. That's why it makes no sense if he's the one who sent the courier.

We reach the fighters' corridor—bare bulbs overhead, flickering weakly—and he stops just short of the curtain that separates blood from breath. "You good?" he asks, turning to face me.

I nod, the pulse between my legs already steady and low, like a warning hum.

Caleb watches me like he knows exactly what I'm thinking. His hand curls around the back of my neck and he leans in. The kiss is rougher this time. Less heat, more possession. His teeth scrape my bottom lip. My knees almost buckle.

He pulls back before I can chase him. "Stay close. Don't talk to anyone," he orders, fingers tightening just enough at the back of my neck to make it clear what happens if I don't follow his orders.

"You're not my keeper," I dutifully point out, but his sharp grin says he'd enjoy proving otherwise.

"Tonight I am." His grin is all teeth and hunger. "I better go." With those parting words, he disappears through the curtain.

I exhale, forcing my composure back into place. I press closer, slipping between two thick-necked spectators until I reach the front where I'm close enough I can touch the ring.

The crowd shifts. A bell rings. And then the first fight begins.

If I'd paid money to be here, I would demand a refund after the first fight. It's so tame that people start pulling out their phones, mindlessly scrolling instead of paying attention. The people here want carnage, not whatever that was.

The second fight is better, but it's the third fight that really gets me shouting and cheering with the rest of the audience. As the fight ends, I make my way to the corner where a few guys sell cheap, lukewarm beer.

It's not my favorite, but it'll do. While I drink my beer, I keep my gaze fixed on the ring. Caleb hasn't emerged yet, but I feel him coming. The low thrum at the base of my spine starts to pulse harder, a hunger coiling like smoke in my gut.

"Hi doll. Are you—"

"Out of your league?" I quip, interrupting the guy who moved closer when I wasn't paying attention. "Yeah, I'm afraid I am." I turn my back to him and buy a second beer before returning to the front.

A sharp whistle cuts through the murmurs, and the next two names are called. Caleb steps into the ring like he owns it. The crowd responds differently this time—everyone here chants his name as he holds his arms up in a salute of sorts.

He's already soaked in aggression. Violence clings to him like cologne, and every step says, you bleed, I win.

While Caleb makes an entire production of removing his hoodie and flexing, my gaze flickers to his opponent, a tough and heavy looking guy with a shaved head and thick neck.

"Get him!" I shout just as the bell sounds.

They collide right away, and the first few blows are fast, clean. But then Caleb shifts—his stance tightening, body lowering—and he starts to hit. His fists find the other guy's jaw, ribs, gut.

Each punch is punishingly precise, and it doesn't take long before blood spatters, making the crowd roar. Caleb takes a hit to the temple, staggers half a step, and then laughs—low, mean, like he enjoys it.

He retaliates by driving a knee into the man's gut and finishes it with a brutal elbow to the face that sends his opponent crumpling to the ground. It's a clean knockout, and the crowd erupts.

While I join in, I press my thighs together, trying to quell the fire pulsing through me. It's not just lust—it's an ache. The sickest part of me gets wet for ruin, for the sight of men breaking each other open.

Caleb doesn't wait for a towel. Doesn't even acknowledge the men slapping his back. His eyes lock on mine as he pushes through the crowd, knuckles bloodied, sweat still slick on his brow.

As soon as he reaches me, I drop the half-full plastic cup and throw myself at him. I wind my arms around his neck and yank him down into a bruising kiss. My mouth parts for him without thought, tongue curling around his.

"Caleb," I moan his name into his mouth as I become slicker with want. "I need you."

He breaks the kiss abruptly. "Let's go," he growls, voice dark and frayed at the edges. His grip on me tightens just enough to make my knees falter. "Now."

Words are beyond me, so I just nod and let him lead me back to his car. He throws open the door, and I slide in, skin prickling against the cracked leather.

He drives like red lights are a suggestion, and with each one we blow through, my pulse spikes higher. He has one hand on the wheel, the other on my thigh. His grip is heavy, possessive. It's only now, as I study him, that I notice we forgot his hoodie. Oh well.

By the time we hit the long stretch toward Riverdale, I'm pulsing between my legs and squirming in my seat. I reach over, palming his obvious erection. "I can't wait," I purr as I dip my hand beneath his waistband.

"Touch me, Doc," he grunts, and I do. I wrap my fingers around his cock, squeezing at the base. "Fuck."

"You looked so hot up there," I admit while I stroke him. "Every woman in there was eye-fucking you—"

"I don't care about other women," he growls. "And you better not care about other men."

"I know," I say smugly, stroking him harder. "But I love knowing I have what they want."

Caleb grunts low in his throat, hips lifting slightly off the seat. His knuckles go white on the steering wheel. "If you don't stop, I'm going to pull over and fuck you in the front seat."

I consider it for a second. The way he sounds, the heat radiating off him, and the smell of sweat and iron still clinging to his skin is almost enough for me to give in.

But we're already pulling into the lot outside my apartment complex, and the craving to be skin-to-skin is stronger than the exhibitionist itch.

"Then get us upstairs," I demand, giving his cock one last stroke before withdrawing my hand. He hisses as I do.

Caleb throws the car into park and gets out fast, slamming the door behind him. I barely have time to open mine before he's there, taking my hand like he owns it—and maybe tonight, he does. His fingers are still dusted in dried blood. I don't care.

We walk across the dark lot, headlights flickering from passing cars, the sound of the city distant but ever-present. Halfway across the lot, I falter. My body stops, yanking his arm slightly.

"What is it?" he asks, looking back at me.

I scan the edge of the building, past the dumpsters, to the shadows near the emergency door. There's a flicker of movement. A car drives by and the headlights sweep across the shadowed corner, just long enough for me to see the masked courier.

The sight triggers a spike of awareness in my spine. Like déjà vu sharpened into a blade. It's not fear, it's hunger. Like something feral inside me just remembered it has teeth.

I step away from Caleb, squinting into the darkness. "Did you see that?"

"See what?" he asks, turning in a slow circle.

But the space is empty now. Quiet. Just the soft hum of a streetlamp and the rustling of dead leaves skittering across pavement.

I shake my head, though my heart's still hammering. "Nothing. I thought I saw…" I pause, then exhale a shaky breath. "Never mind."

Letting it go, I stride toward the entrance. Caleb follows quietly, I feel him a few steps behind me. He isn't saying anything now, but I know the questions are coming.

In the elevator, he watches me from the corner of his eye. "What was that about?" he finally asks.

I hesitate, chewing the inside of my cheek, but I know he won't let it go until I answer him. With a heavy exhale, I explain about the delivery yesterday. Well, technically today since it was after midnight.

"So you're saying some random guy in a gas mask just showed up at your door?" Caleb's voice carries a hint of protective concern.

I nod. "Yeah, he turned up at midnight. On the dot." The memory of those round, vacant eye lenses staring at me sends a shiver through my body that I can't entirely attribute to disgust.

"And you opened the door?" Caleb's blue eyes narrow slightly. The faded tattoos on his forearms shift as he lifts his hand to brush some loose strands of hair behind my ear. It's hard to concentrate when he's standing this close and his torso is on full display.

"I looked through the peephole first," I counter, defensive. "I'm not completely reckless."

"Just partially, then." His smile is quick and cutting, like he's keeping score and I'm losing. "And what was in the box?"

"A black rose." I pause, trying to maintain clinical detachment so he doesn't notice how intrigued I really am. "It was dried, and had these red speckles that looked like blood."

The memory of the flower's brittle texture against my fingertips makes my skin prickle with that same contradiction—revulsion twined with fascination, like wanting to press your tongue to a wound just to taste the blood.

"Was that it?"

"And a note," I add, almost reluctantly. "Something about brides and blooms dying. It was poetic."

"Poetic?" he mocks.

"I meant disturbing," I correct too quickly.

This definitely shuts the door of any thoughts about the delivery being from him. But then who could it be from?

Caleb's hand finds my thigh, his thumb tracing a slow, deliberate path higher up my thigh, and I become intensely aware of the heat radiating from his palm through the thin fabric of my pants. His eyes never leave my face as he studies my reaction.

"You're flushed," he observes, a knowing smile playing at the corners of his mouth. "Your pupils are dilated, too. I'd say this visitor left quite an impression."

I scoff, but the sound comes out weaker than I intended. "It's just a professional interest. I mean, it's not every day someone delivers cryptic, wedding-themed packages to my door."

"Are you into masks now, Eve?" His voice dips, not teasing so much as testing. Like he's filing the answer away for later use.

At his question, I picture the courier, he's somehow already under my skin. The thought makes me hotter than it should.

CHAPTER 6

The Bride

The question lands like a spark on dry tinder. My body betrays me with a subtle shift toward him, a movement so slight I'm not sure he notices until I see his smile widen.

Caleb knows I'm into anything that creates a fear factor. We've dabbled in CNC role-play, and he's even broken into my apartment once. But masks are something I've never considered using.

"I'm into figuring out who's behind them," I reply, struggling to maintain my composure as his hand inches higher, approaching the spot where my black lace garter tattoo circles my upper thigh.

"Are you?" His voice drops to a register that vibrates through me. "Or are you more interested in what the mask allows?"

I don't answer, and I don't need to. He reads my silence with practiced ease. His hand slides to cup my face, thumb brushing across my lower lip.

"You know what I think?"

I raise an eyebrow, trying to reclaim some semblance of control. "I rarely know what you think, Caleb."

He laughs, low and sharp, like my answer proved a theory about me. "I think you've spent so much time analyzing other people's darkness that you forget to acknowledge your own." Before I can respond, he angles his head so he can capture my mouth with his.

The kiss is confident, demanding, and I feel my body responding, heat pooling low in my belly as his tongue traces the seam of my lips.

For a heartbeat, I hesitate. A flash of black rubber and emotionless lenses superimposes itself over Caleb's familiar features. The phantom sound of mechanical breathing floods my ears, making me dizzy with want—for the wrong man, for the wrong monster.

The moment passes, and I greedily kiss Caleb back, letting my fingers tangle in his icy-blond hair, anchoring myself to our very real connection rather than the ghostly alternative haunting my thoughts.

We break apart as the elevator doors slide open again, and a woman clears her throat loudly. I look at her, realizing we're still on the ground floor.

"Did you push the button?" I ask Caleb, taking a step back from him.

He chuckles. "Nah, I forgot."

The woman steps inside, side-eyeing us as she positions herself as far away as the metal box allows. Which, for the record, isn't a lot of space. But whatever. I can't help grinning at her when I catch her checking out Caleb.

"I don't blame you," I smirk. And I really don't, especially not when he's shirtless.

Now that we're not alone, the elevator ride feels like a study in restraint. When the doors finally open on my floor, Caleb's patience evaporates. His hand finds mine, fingers interlacing as he pulls me down the hallway while I one-handedly remove my bag so I can get the keys.

Unlocking the door proves to be quite the struggle when Caleb's lips find the sensitive spot where my neck meets my shoulder. The key scrapes against the lock before finally sliding home.

As I turn my head, my gaze catches on something on my door. "The hell is that?" I mutter, running my fingers across the crusty substance.

"Stop stalling," Caleb gripes, giving me a small shove.

We stumble across the threshold, and as soon as we're both inside, he kicks the door shut and catches me around the waist, hauling me toward the couch. He drops me onto the cushions like a prize and climbs over me, lips crashing into mine.

His mouth claims mine with a hunger that mirrors my own, his tongue seeking entrance as his hands slide down to cup my ass, moving us so I'm on top of him without breaking the kiss.

"I've been thinking about this all night," he confesses against my lips, his voice rough with desire. His stubble scrapes against my skin as he trails kisses down my neck, each one a small, delicious bite of pain that makes me gasp.

My head falls back, and I close my eyes while surrendering to the sensations. My hands roam his shoulders and back, loving the way I can feel his muscles shift under my touch. I shift when I feel Caleb's hand roaming in his pocket.

"What are you—" He interrupts me before I can finish asking what he was doing.

"I wish we didn't have an audience," he smirks, nodding toward the mantle where my dad's grinning skull watches us.

"I want him to watch," I state. "If Hell exists, he's rotting in it. Maybe part of his punishment is seeing all his hard work undone while you fuck me on the couch he used to sit on."

Caleb chuckles as he slides his hands under my shirt, palming my breasts while he licks and nips his way down my throat, not stopping until he reaches my collarbone.

"Oh, God," I moan, rolling my hips. His answering groan makes me huff with impatience, and I reach between us, cupping his erection. "I want this."

He tips his head back and looks up at me while lifting my shirt to reveal the black lace of my bra. "Beautiful," he murmurs. "You don't mind if I take a picture, do you? Got to keep a record of my conquests."

The question is the equivalent to being douched in cold water. I suck my bottom lip between my teeth as I contemplate the question. I'm not shy by any means, but that doesn't mean I want pictures of me floating around.

"Don't," I warn when he raises his phone, holding it right in front of me. "If you need wanking material, call me. But don't photograph me."

"Yes, ma'am," he drawls, eyes already scanning me like he's

picturing the shot anyway.

I huff with annoyance, gyrating my hips to get the spark back. And it doesn't take long until the world again narrows to a series of sensations—the pressure of his cock between us, the tight grip of his fingers as they find my hips and pull me against him in a rhythm that makes my breath catch.

"I want you inside me," I pant.

Caleb groans against my skin. "Fuck. Yes—"

Three sharp knocks at my front door split through the room like a gunshot, freezing us both mid-motion.

My heart, already racing from Caleb's attention, kicks into a higher gear. A strange cocktail of dread and anticipation floods my system, making my skin prickle with awareness.

"Ignore it," Caleb commands, his hand sliding between my legs to cup my pussy. "They'll go away."

His lips reclaim mine, more insistent now, as if he can physically distract me from whoever stands on the other side of my door. For a moment, it works—my body responds to him automatically, melting back into the pleasure of his touch.

But the knocks come again, the same pattern—three sharp raps that seem to echo through my body. I break the kiss, turning my head toward the door despite Caleb's frustrated sigh.

"Don't fucking think about it," he growls, his voice a mixture of desire and annoyance. His fingers trace the line of my jaw, trying to recapture my attention.

I look back at him, taking in his kiss-swollen lips, the naked want in his eyes. My body aches for him, for the release I know he can provide. And yet… "What if it's him?" The words escape before I can stop them.

Caleb's expression hardens, frustration eclipsing any trace of desire. "The mask guy?" His hands slide to my shoulders, steadying me as he searches my face. "That's what you're thinking about? Now?"

I don't have an answer that doesn't sound insane—that something about him has rooted in me, quietly, dangerously. "I just need to see who it is," I say. And while I pull my shirt back down, I glance down at the watch on Caleb's wrist. It's midnight. Exactly.

"You can't be serious," he shouts. "Over my dead body," he snaps, like my curiosity is just another thing for him to shut down.

"Listen to yourself, Caleb," I scoff. "I don't need your permission."

As he runs a hand down his face, I get off his lap.

"It'll just take a second," I promise. I'm not sure who I'm trying to convince here.

As I move toward the door, Caleb's hand catches my wrist, his touch gentler than I expected. "Eve," he says, my name a question and a warning all at once.

I meet his eyes, seeing the concern there beneath the frustration. "One minute," I say, offering a smile I hope is reassuring. "Stay right here, and keep this ready for me." Licking my lips, I pointedly look at his very obvious erection.

Caleb releases me with reluctance. I can feel his eyes on me, heavy with accusation, as I reach for the handle. I hesitate for just a moment, heart hammering against my ribs.

Then, taking a deep breath, I pull the door open.

The masked courier stands motionless in my doorway, exactly as before. Unchanged. Unmoving. Like a funeral statue that wandered off its pedestal to deliver a final omen. Black gas mask with its vacant round eyes, military boots planted firmly, leather jacket zipped to his throat.

My stomach knots tight—not just with dread, but with anticipation that feels dangerously close to arousal.

In his gloved hands, he holds a black and orange envelope. His chest rises and falls with measured breaths that filter through the mask with a soft, mechanical whisper.

"You again," I say, my voice breathier than intended.

The courier remains silent, arm extended toward me with the envelope. The lenses of his mask reflect distorted versions of me back at myself—two miniature Eves, wide-eyed and disheveled. One looks afraid. The other looks hungry. I don't know which one I hate more.

"What is it?" I demand, making no move to accept it.

His breathing changes slightly—a barely perceptible shift in rhythm that suggests something like amusement. But his arm remains extended, unwavering, as if he could stand there all night waiting for me to accept his offering.

Caleb appears behind me, placing a possessive hand on my shoulder, drawing me slightly back from the doorway while simultaneously taking a step forward.

"Who the fuck are you?" he demands, positioning himself partly in front of me.

The courier doesn't acknowledge him, focus remaining fixed on me, arm still extended with that damn envelope.

"He's the one who delivered the rose," I explain, watching the courier for any reaction.

"What do you want with her?" Caleb's voice tightens with suspicion as he steps fully in front of me, addressing the courier directly. "Are you a fucked up fan or something?"

I arch my eyebrow at the question. A fan? A former psychiatrist turned rebellious party girl isn't something that naturally gathers fans of any kind.

The courier remains motionless, breathing steady through the filter of his mask. The continued silence seems to infuriate Caleb, whose hands curl into fists at his sides.

"Look, asshole, I don't know what game you're playing, but you need to back off." Caleb moves closer, invading the courier's space. "She's not interested. So why don't you take your shit and get the hell out of here?"

Still nothing. No acknowledgment, no retreat, no change in posture. Just that deep breathing and the steadily extended arm. It's as if Caleb doesn't exist at all—as if the courier can see only me, and is programmed to complete only one task.

"Caleb," I say, a note of warning in my voice. Something about the courier's stillness triggers my professional instincts—the calm before a storm, the potential energy waiting to be converted.

Either Caleb doesn't hear me or chooses to ignore my caution. This isn't a street fight. It's a duel. Something older, crueler, the kind of violence people used to offer gods.

He steps even closer, chest nearly touching the courier's outstretched arm. "Are you fucking deaf? I said, get out of here."

Acknowledging Caleb's presence for the first time, the courier tilts his head slightly. But his arm remains extended, the envelope still offered to me.

"That's it," he snaps, patience exhausted. His hand shoots out, shoving hard against the courier's chest. "Get fucking lost—"

The courier's free hand catches his wrist mid-shove, twisting it at an angle that makes the latter gasp in surprise. In the same fluid motion, the man steps to the side, using Caleb's own momentum to unbalance him.

Caleb recovers quickly, yanking his arm free and lunging forward with a growl. His fist connects with the courier's shoulder, but he barely flinches. Instead, he tucks the envelope inside his jacket with one hand while the other deflects the next punch with practiced ease.

"Stop!" I shout, but neither of them acknowledges me.

Bodies slam against the hallway walls. Caleb grapples for purchase, trying to use his weight against the slightly taller man, but the courier slips from his grasp like water through fingers.

They move down the hallway in a tangle of limbs, Caleb pushing forward, the courier redirecting rather than opposing. I follow them, heart hammering in my chest, torn between the need to intervene and the paralyzing knowledge that I don't know how.

"Stop it!" I try again as they approach the stairwell door. "He's not worth it!"

But Caleb is beyond hearing. His face is flushed with effort and anger, a vein pulsing at his temple as he drives the courier back another step. For a moment, it seems like he might gain the upper hand—his fingers close around the other man's throat, seeking purchase against the high collar of the leather jacket.

The courier's gloved hands come up between Caleb's arms with calculated precision, breaking the hold in a single outward motion. Before he can recover, the courier's boot hooks behind his ankle, destabilizing him.

A sharp pivot, a controlled push against Caleb's sternum, and suddenly the balance of power shifts completely. Caleb stumbles backward, arms windmilling as his body meets the stairwell door.

It swings open under his weight, and for one suspended moment, he

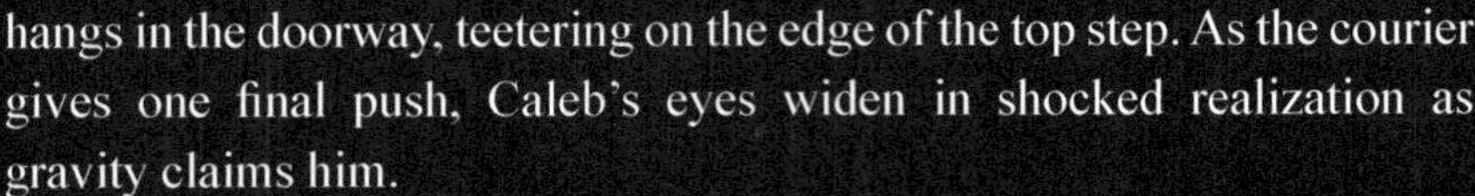

hangs in the doorway, teetering on the edge of the top step. As the courier gives one final push, Caleb's eyes widen in shocked realization as gravity claims him.

My scream tears through the hallway as he disappears from view. There's a series of sickening thuds, punctuated by a grunt of pain, then a final, heavier impact as his body hits… something. The impact reverberates through the stairwell, bouncing off the walls as I stand frozen in horror.

"Caleb!" I lunge toward the stairs, but the courier's arm extends across my path, not touching me but clearly blocking my way. I stare at him, incredulous. "Get the hell out of my way," I demand.

Rather than letting me pass, he just stands there—breathing slow, mechanical, steady—until the silence between us curdles into something intimate, possessive, like the quiet belongs only to us.

"Please," I beg. "Caleb needs help."

The Trickster

Without a word, I push her backward, not stopping until her back connects with the wall. A soft *oomph* flows from her mouth. But instead of giving my Bride-to-be time to recover, I use my arm to pin her in place.

Though she can't see my eyes through the mask, I feel as though she knows I'm peering into her storm-gray irises. Both her orbs are blown wide as she watches me remove the glove on my free hand, using only my teeth.

I drag my bare fingers along her cheek, savoring the feel of her clammy flesh. She doesn't speak or move. She's frozen in… not fear. It's more like she's suspended; held there between instinct and something darker.

When I researched her back in February, I never found any hints of

Eve being attracted to darkness. But it seems my Little Bride has changed since losing her office space.

Not only is she fucking the likes of Caleb, which disgusts me, but she's no longer working. Instead she spends her time doing whatever she wants whenever she wants to. It seems my intended punishment has turned out to be more of a reward.

"Who are you?" she asks, her tone unsure, but I still don't sense any fear in her.

I trace my finger from her cheek to her sternum, following the soft centerline of her body like I'm reading it in braille.

When I find the swell of her breasts, I don't grope or squeeze. I just skim down the valley between them, letting my fingers drag tension in their wake. Lower. Slower. Until I reach the waistband of her pants. Before she can react, I slip beneath the latex.

"What… no. Stop…" Her voice is thin, cracking in places. "Stop it," she cries, thrashing like she actually thinks she can throw me off.

I already threw her boyfriend down the stairs like a deadweight. She's got no chance. She swings at me, and I laugh. Then I catch both her wrists and pin them above her head.

When I press my palm against her pussy, I'm surprised to find her wet. Not just a little, oh no, my Bride's fucking leaking for me like she's already mine. The sound I let out isn't quite a growl, but it's close. The mask distorts it, making it mechanical and hungry.

"You're wet."

"N-no," she whimpers, lying to me.

I press against her clit in slow, exact circles. "Lying is bad," I rasp. "Are you a bad girl, Eve?"

Knowing she's turned on makes my cock throb, thick and straining against my thigh, and I'm tempted to rut against her like a fucking animal. But I grind my teeth together, forcing myself to stay in control.

This is the perfect chance to learn how her body betrays her. And I'm not wasting the gift she doesn't even know she's offering.

"I said stop," she whispers, but her voice has collapsed. There's no authority in it.

I tilt my head. "You did," I reply just as I push two fingers into her cunt. She moans quietly, and the sound vibrates down my spine, pooling hot and sharp at the head of my cock. "Louder," I command. "Moan louder."

"W-what?" she gasps, hips betraying her as they move into my hand.

I curl my fingers inside her, dragging along the top wall. "I want him to hear how good I make you feel. Sing for me."

She shakes her head and keeps her mouth shut. Her body though? Her hips keep rolling.

I slam her wrists against the wall. "Don't fucking disobey me," I snarl. "I want him to know exactly what I'm doing to you. Scream for him."

When she still refuses with a stubborn tilt of her lips, I fuck her harder with my fingers.

"Say it," I growl. "Say how good I make you feel. Scream it loud enough for Caleb to choke on it."

"F-fuck," she cries. "Please…"

"No begging. Only moaning. Let him hear how your cunt welcomes me. Let him know I own it now."

This time she moans prettily for me. And she does it loud enough for the sound to echo, undoubtedly reaching Caleb. Fuck, I hope he's conscious. I hope he hears the slick sounds her cunt makes for me while she creams all over my hand.

"Oh, God," she cries. Her pussy clenches around my fingers like it's trying to drag them deeper—like it knows they're just a stand-in for what should be there instead.

I chuckle. "There's no God here. Only you and me."

She tips forward into the rhythm, legs shaking, pussy clenching like it's begging to be wrecked. I hold her in place, fingers buried deep, mask pressed to her skin, breathing loud through the vents.

She moans again; shaky, fragile. I twitch my fingers, and her whole body jerks like I've flipped a switch.

Then I fuck her with precision—two fingers dragging over every nerve like I'm rewiring her from the inside. Each thrust calculated. Each curl is brutal in its intention. I find the place inside her that makes her knees give out.

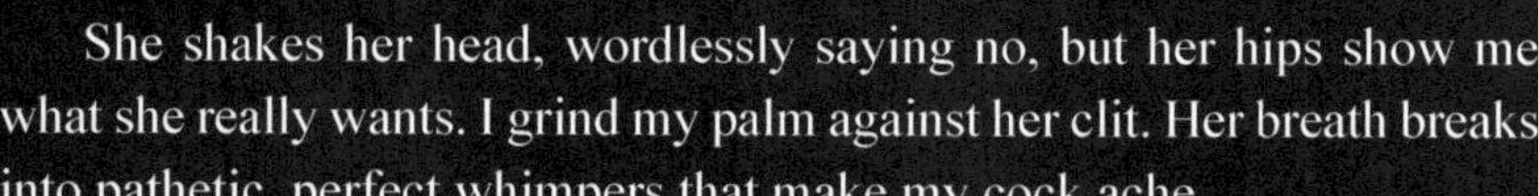

She shakes her head, wordlessly saying no, but her hips show me what she really wants. I grind my palm against her clit. Her breath breaks into pathetic, perfect whimpers that make my cock ache.

Mhmm, Eve's close now. I feel it in the way her cunt squeezes tighter around me. She tries to fight it. She bites her lip, drawing beautiful droplets of blood that I long to taste. But I'm not ready to remove my mask.

The orgasm takes her hard, so violently her legs give out. I follow her down to the floor, fingers still pumping in and out of her molten heat. The sounds coming from her are nonsensical, and the few words she utters make no sense. Yet it's fucking poetic.

When she's nothing but aftershocks and ruin, I withdraw my fingers. The slick sound makes her flinch.

"You're worthy," I murmur, pulling the envelope from my jacket. I extend it toward her once more.

She stares at it like I've lost my mind. "Are you insane?" she seethes, trying to get up. "I don't want anything from you."

I shift and block the stairwell when she tries to move past me. She watches me like she doesn't know what to think or do. But then she takes the envelope with trembling fingers.

"Good girl," I murmur, the praise dark and mocking, before finally letting her run to Caleb's side.

CHAPTER 7

The Trickster

A shiver travels down my spine as I appraise the cage in front of me. I groan when my fingertips trail over the cold metal bars. Each joint welded to my exact specifications, each measurement calculated to the millimeter.

The structure dominates the back wall in my bedroom, a stark testament to purpose over aesthetics. Beautiful in its utility, perfect in its promise of containment. I tap a bar with my knuckle, listening to the hollow ring that echoes through the room.

It's large enough for comfort, small enough for psychological effect. I'd considered many designs before settling on this one, classic bars rather than mesh or glass. I want her to feel the cold metal beneath her fingers when she inevitably tests her boundaries.

My Bride-to-be needs to understand that no matter how clever she thinks she is, the only thing sharper than her mind is my revenge.

I grip one of the vertical bars with both hands and pull, using my full strength to test for weakness. The metal doesn't yield, doesn't even creak. Good. I move methodically around the structure, repeating the test at each junction point.

I whistle a melody as my eyes travel the length of the bars again,

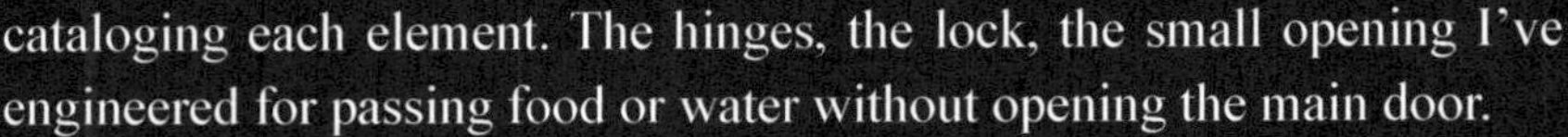

cataloging each element. The hinges, the lock, the small opening I've engineered for passing food or water without opening the main door.

"Almost time," I tell the empty cage, my voice dropping to a pitch reserved for prayers or threats.

With the cage complete, I pull my phone from my pocket and dial Ned's number. My thumb hovers over the screen for a moment as I admire my handiwork one last time. The bars cast thin shadows across the carpeted floor like prison stripes, a preview of the containment to come.

Ned answers on the third ring, his voice carrying that particular blend of efficiency and boredom.

"It's done," I tell him without preamble.

"The love nest?" His voice carries a trace of amusement that would earn anyone else a warning. From Ned, I allow it. He's seen me at my worst and stayed, and that buys certain privileges.

"The cage," I correct, running my free hand along one of the bars. "Everything's in place for when I bring her home."

"And when will that be, exactly?" There's a rustling on his end of the line—papers being moved, perhaps a drink being poured.

"After The Black Wedding." I move to the window, looking out at the darkening grounds of my estate. From this vantage point, the garden looks fucking dead, which, to be fair, it is. Anything that grows out there's nature's doing more than mine.

I took an instant liking to this property when I saw it for the first time back in April. Since Ruby's death, I wanted something more remote than my apartment in Manhattan. And to be closer to Eve who lives here in the Bronx.

This two-story gothic revival mansion is everything I never knew I wanted. The weathered black stones and steep pitched rooflines are perfect. As are the tall, black-trimmed windows and ivy crawling up both sides.

A turret with a round stone balcony extends from the back corner, overlooking the private yard at the back. The driveway at the front is all cracked stone and overgrown, and the entire property is framed by wrought iron fencing.

It's like a place taken right out of a horror movie, which is part of its charm. The floorboards groan even when you're still. The shadows gather like they know something. It's a house made for haunting—now it just needs a ghost.

Another part is the rumors that circulate amongst the locals here in Riverdale. People talk in hushed whispers about the previous owners who died in a dramatic murder-suicide.

And if I'm honest with myself, that was what hooked me. When the real estate agent informed me of the property's history, I couldn't say no. A murder-suicide, exactly what Ruby did.

"Dude, are you still there?" Ned's voice pulls me out of my head and I refocus on the phone call.

Instead of wondering what he might have been saying while I wasn't paying attention, I ask, "Is your sister confirmed for the bridal preparation?"

"She's in." His response is immediate, assured.

"Happily so?" I ask, already knowing she isn't.

Ned grimaces. "No, man. She's still heartbroken after losing her... boyfriend or whatever."

I nod along. "Do you know who it was?"

He shrugs. "No clue. Never met the guy and she never gave me a name. I just know she's still not over it. But she's made sure Eve attends, and that's all that matters." He swallows thickly. "She knows her place, Jack. Even if she's not happy about it, she'll handle the dress alterations, makeup, hair—everything to get your Bride ready for the ceremony."

"Good, I'll make it worth her while," I state dryly. "The dress will be delivered tomorrow. I don't know if she needs a look at it to—"

"I've already shown her the picture," Ned says, interrupting me.

"Perfect." I allow myself a moment to imagine my Bride in the dress, the dark fabric against her pale skin. It'll be theatrical in the best fucking way.

"Something you should know," Ned interjects, his tone shifting slightly. "I ran into your Bride-to-be outside the apartment complex this morning."

My interest sharpens. "And?"

"She was pissed. Like, nuclear-level angry." There's a hint of admiration in his voice that I don't particularly care for. "Her little friend apparently has a broken arm and a concussion. They kept him overnight for observation at the hospital. But when he was discharged, he refused to let her help and apparently blamed her for his injuries."

I feel my lips curve into a cold smile. "Did he now," I muse. "Well, I suppose that's fair. If he hadn't been in her life, I'd have no reason to hurt him."

Ned chuckles darkly. "Good point. But you should have seen her, Jack. She was spitting fire when I passed her."

Frowning, I ask, "Did she tell you all that?"

"Nah, man. She was on the phone when I walked past her, and I might have lingered a bit."

"Anything else I should know?" I ask, keeping my voice neutral despite the annoyance clawing at me. I don't care if Caleb's angry with her, that's not my problem. But it bothers me if his tantrum is loud enough to drown out the sound of me in her head.

When he tells me that's all, I let him know I'll stop by as soon as I'm done here. I don't know if Eve opened her invitation, and it's important that she does. After that, I end the call and toss my phone onto the bed.

Alone again, I let my mind drift back to Eve in that hallway. The way her body had tensed when I pinned her wrists above her head. The initial resistance when my fingers slid between her legs, followed by the damning evidence of her arousal.

Her cunt was wet. So fucking wet. She tried to lie, to trick me with her fucking mouth, but her body folded like a prayer—open, trembling, begging. Not for mercy. For more. And that's something I hadn't expected at all.

I'm not oblivious to Eve's attraction. She's devastatingly beautiful, with curves that could make a monk weep. But until last night, I never considered playing with her body. Her mind, yes, but now, her reaction to me has changed the game.

My cock hardens at the memory, pressing uncomfortably against my zipper. I groan quietly as I cup my erection. It would be so easy to jerk off, maybe even do it inside the cage and leave my cum for her to sit on…

No, I'm not a fucking teenager that needs to introduce his hand to his cock every hour. The next time I nut, it'll be inside her. This isn't just about want. It's about debt, about what she owes me.

Instead of hanging about, I reach for my black duffel bag. My mask and gloves are already inside, so I just add another box with a rose in it. After putting on my leather jacket, I shove the second invitation into the inner pocket. Then I head to Ned's.

When I get there, I take the fire escape two steps at a time. Reaching the right floor, I tap on his window, and the fucker actually grins as he lets me in.

My answering scowl just makes his smile wider. "Is she—"

He waves me off. "She's in there." He points at the wall they're sharing. "Watching some horror movie or some shit, judging by the sounds."

After placing the bag on the floor, I press my ear against the wall separating the two apartments, and he's right. The shrill scream, maniacal laughter, and sounds of a chainsaw confirm it.

I check the clock on my phone, finding there are still a few hours left until midnight and I don't want to disturb her until then.

"Want anything to drink?" Ned offers, and I accept an ice cold beer.

Unzipping my leather jacket, I make myself comfortable on his couch. We don't really talk about anything of substance. He thanks me again for setting him up here, but I just shrug off his gratitude.

"It was nothing," I say before taking a large swig. "I needed eyes and ears here."

"Come on, man," he argues. "Even if you didn't need my help, I know you would have helped out when I got out of jail. So just accept my fucking thanks. Plus, you helped look out for Shelby. That won't be forgotten."

Ned served six years in jail for drug possession and a few other charges, which is bullshit, since the stuff wasn't even his. But the prosecutor had a hard-on for putting him away, and I was too busy being hated by my dad to really pay attention.

Sometimes I don't get why the hell he's loyal to me. My dad killed his parents, only leaving him and Shelby alive. Yet, he's never blamed me or Nick. It was never a secret he would have loved to be the one to kill daddy dearest. But so would most of NYC I'm sure.

"It was the least I could do," I grunt. I've known Ned forever, so it makes me really uncomfortable to be thanked for doing something he had a right to expect.

"How's Nick?" he asks, changing the subject.

"Busy living his best life," I reply, not offering details.

Ned used to work for Nick, but my older brother never really liked him all that much. So after I'd done a few jobs with him where we got on, Nick was all too happy to let me have him. I snort into the bottle at the thought.

It sounds really fucking pompous to say you just move people around like they're property. But that's exactly what they are to the Knight family. Either you're one of us, with us, or against us. There's no other option.

The hours bleed by in slow, silent increments. Ned dozes off halfway through some rerun on TV while I sit motionless, tracking every creak of the old pipes, every scream through the wall.

When my phone finally buzzes a few minutes before midnight, I'm already on my feet, slipping my gloves on as I reach for the mask. With the box in hand, I leave the bag behind and slip out of Ned's place and walk the few feet to Eve's.

As I stand in front of her door, I feel a rare pulse of something like anticipation. It's not nervousness, I abandoned that weakness long ago, but a heightened awareness that vibrates beneath my skin.

The culmination of planning, the precipice before action. I check my watch one final time. It's almost midnight, only half a minute to go. I count down inwardly, and when it's time, I raise my hand and knock. The sound echoes in the empty hallway, sharp and demanding.

Then I wait. My posture is a study in patient inevitability—feet planted shoulder-width apart, spine straight, head slightly tilted as if in curiosity. Through the mask, I hear my own breathing, deep and rhythmic, the sound slightly mechanized by the filter.

There's movement behind the door; a subtle shift in the quality of

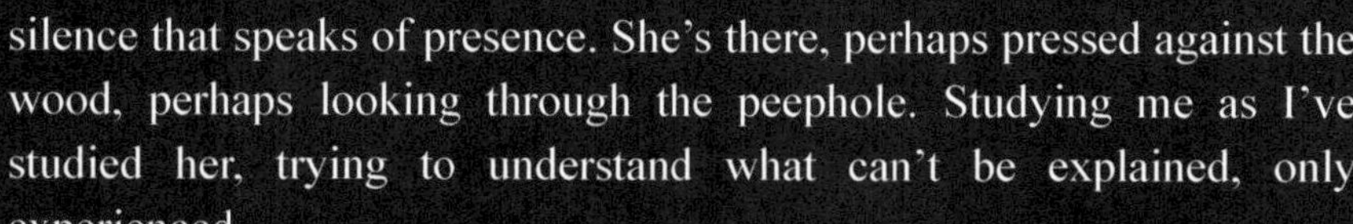

silence that speaks of presence. She's there, perhaps pressed against the wood, perhaps looking through the peephole. Studying me as I've studied her, trying to understand what can't be explained, only experienced.

I imagine her eyes widening at the sight of me, her pulse quickening as she recognizes the pattern. The third visit. The third gift. The final invitation before the claiming.

My thumb traces the edge of the box, feeling the sharp corner against the leather of my glove. The rose waits inside the box—death preserved in unnatural beauty. The invitation rests separately, just as carefully chosen. Both offerings that foreshadow what's to come.

I hear the lock disengage, the subtle click of metal retreating from metal. The door begins to open, a sliver of light widening into possibility. I stand motionless, the box extended in offering. Midnight has arrived, and with it, the next chapter in our evolving ritual.

Eve appears in the doorway, her face a complex study in warring emotions. I catalog each one—curiosity, defiance, and something darker. Her waist-long hair falls loose around her shoulders, the orange ends vivid against the black, wild and untamed like the rest of her.

She's wearing a black tank top that clings in all the right places and leaves just enough to the imagination to make me grit my teeth. It's so thin I see a hint of her nipples pressing faint outlines through the fabric from the chilled air behind her.

Low-rise sleep shorts hang loose on her hips, showcasing her long, bare legs that look like they're fucking made to wrap around me. Her tongue flicks out, wetting her bottom lip as she stares me down, and I feel it—sharp and unwanted—the pull of her.

She shouldn't affect me like this. Not when I've spent months crafting a plan that hinges on control. But she does. Every goddamn time.

There's something about her—reckless and vulnerable, soft and sharp in the same breath—that makes me want to consume and destroy in equal measure. And that want is dangerous. It makes me human, which is as unpredictable as you can get.

Her eyes fix on the mask, searching for humanity in the glass lenses

and finding none. Just as intended. Just as needed for what comes next.

"You," she says, the single word carrying a weight of accusation and recognition. "If you're here to push Caleb around again you're shit out of luck. He won't speak to me because of you."

She crosses her arms under her chest, which only pushes her tits higher, tighter against the stretched fabric of her tank top. She knows what she's doing—using her body like a weapon, even if the safety's still on.

Despite the need to laugh, I remain silent, breathing steadily, the box offered without explanation or apology. The final invitation. The last choice that isn't really a choice at all.

When I stay silent, her mouth curls into something bitter. "Or maybe you want to sexually assault me some more. Thought I'd forget about that part?" Her voice trembles slightly at the end, just enough to give her away. Just enough to tell me she hasn't forgotten how wet she was, either. Good.

Shame is a better leash than chains. And I want her to remember every pulse, every twitch, every moan she didn't mean to make.

I extend the box farther, an unspoken command laced in the gesture. Take it.

She doesn't move, but I see the indecision flicker through her. That pull between indignation and obsession. It's eating her alive, and she doesn't even know where the hunger ends and the hate begins.

"Take it," I say, voice low and edged in command. "Or I'll take you."

CHAPTER 8

The Bride

His words hang in the air between us, heavy with promise and threat. I feel my pulse quicken, a warmth spreading through my belly that has nothing to do with fear and everything to do with something I refuse to name.

The box remains extended in his gloved hand, but I'm suddenly tired of playing by his rules, tired of being the one who reacts while he orchestrates.

"If you want it opened so badly, why don't you do it yourself?" I say, cocking my hip against the doorframe. "Maybe I don't want the contents inside my home." I point at the box for emphasis.

He doesn't respond. The lenses of his mask reflect distorted versions of me back at myself—a woman whose defiance looks like desire, whose resistance resembles invitation.

My dad, the great and renowned Charles Mortis, might have been brilliant in his field. But the fact that I'm actually entertaining a stranger at midnight, and getting turned on just proves how bad his parenting was.

Maybe I'd be making better life choices if he hadn't spent most of my life telling me what to do. If he'd bothered to let me learn from having any experiences he didn't script and tailor to completion. Dick.

I study the stranger, cataloging the details as if they might reveal something about the man beneath the disguise. His posture is military-precise, shoulders squared beneath the leather jacket that creaks subtly with each breath. His gloved fingers remain steady on the box, no tremor of uncertainty, no sign that my refusal has any effect on his intentions.

"Fine," I say, feeling something shift inside me, a dangerous impulse taking shape. "Have it your way."

Deciding on taking a calculated risk, I turn my back on him and walk back into my apartment. It tastes like spite, but it burns like hunger. I want him to follow. I want him to stop me. I want... something I don't have words for.

I only manage two steps before there's a rush of air as hands grab my shoulders from behind. The stranger shoves me forward, the momentum carrying me all the way into my apartment.

Then he spins me, and my back hits the wall with enough force to knock the breath from my lungs. The plaster bites into my spine, cold and unyielding, like the world snapping shut behind me. There's no exit here.

Before I can recover, he's on me, one gloved hand slamming beside my head as he cages me against the wall. An involuntary and embarrassingly breathy gasp escapes me as he presses the box against my chest, hard edges digging into the thin fabric of my tank top.

With my free hand, I reach for the bat I keep by the wall. You can never be too careful, and right now, I need to feel it in my hand and possibly introduce the wood to the courier's balls.

Determined not to give away what I'm trying to do, I focus on him. It's both titillating and infuriating that he's wearing a mask, hiding his expression. I don't even know if he's looking straight at me, or following my hand from the corner of his eyes.

The guy's body doesn't touch mine, but he's close enough that I can smell the leather of his jacket. Looking down, I note that his boots are braced on either side of my bare feet, the size difference stark and somehow thrilling.

I'm trapped, but not restrained. He's giving me just enough space to leave if I truly wanted to, which makes it all the more damning that I'm still here.

Finally, I close my fingers around the smooth wood of my bat. Instead of wasting more time by being careful, I swing it against his leg.

"Get off me," I scream.

Even though it strikes his thigh, he doesn't falter. He shifts his weight slightly, absorbing the blow with a grunt—low and dark with satisfaction. Fuck, rather than scaring him off, I've just amused the devil himself.

Then, with unhurried precision, he reaches down and rips the bat from my grip with one hand. The motion is effortlessly casual, as if I'd never been gripping it at all.

"The only way you're allowed to play with this," he says, voice distorted and intimate through the mask, "is if you fuck yourself with it while I watch." Heat floods my cheeks, and my legs threaten to buckle when he tosses it to the side.

"In your dreams," I spit, needing to say something.

Through the mask, the courier's breathing deepens, the rhythm slightly faster than before. Is he affected by this too? The thought sends a jolt through me.

The mask hovers inches from my face, those round, emotionless lenses studying me with insect-like detachment. I should be terrified. I should be screaming, clawing, fighting. Instead, my body tightens with want, responding to the danger with a primitive excitement that my mind can't quite reject.

He pushes the box harder against my sternum, a silent command for me to take it as he said. I swallow hard, my throat clicking audibly in the silence between us.

If I don't take what he's offering, he'll take me. That's what he said. A choice that should be simple is suddenly anything but. The devil on my shoulder whispers for me to push the stranger and see what happens.

But, even though there's no angel to give me better advice, my fingers close around the cardboard. Instead of immediately releasing the box, he holds on to it. Creating a moment where we're both holding it, connected by this strange offering between us.

Then his fingers slide away, leaving the box in my possession. The weight of it is nothing compared to the weight of his presence.

I begin to work at the orange ribbon that's tied in an elaborate bow, the satin slippery and resistant to my unsteady hands. I refuse to rush, to show how eager I am to discover what's inside.

So, I take my time, each tug of the fabric a small act of reclaimed control. The ribbon loosens under my methodical attention, slithering against the matte black surface of the box with a whisper that seems obscene in its softness.

I feel his gaze on my hands, on my face, tracking every minute reaction. My cheeks burn under the scrutiny, but I don't look up, don't give him the satisfaction of seeing how affected I am.

The ribbon finally comes free, dangling from my fingers. Only then do I raise my eyes to the mask, a silent question in my gaze. What now?

His breathing changes—just slightly, just enough for me to notice—and I realize with a jolt of something like triumph that he's not as unmoved as he pretends to be. Whatever game he's playing, he's invested in the outcome.

With a steadiness I don't feel, I lift the lid off the box, preparing myself for whatever awaits inside. It's another black rose. The desiccated bloom rests on a bed of black tissue paper, its stem twisted into a brittle spiral, the petals curled inward as if protecting a secret.

Like the first, this one is speckled with colored spots that look disturbingly like dried blood. It's beautiful in the way that decay can be beautiful—a reminder that even in death, something can maintain its essential nature.

I stare at it, unable to ignore the unnerving symmetry with the previous gift. Two dead flowers delivered at midnight by a man who has only spoken very few words.

The pattern forms a narrative in my mind—one black rose, an invitation, another rose. And then… what? What comes after the repetition establishes itself? What waits beyond this strange ritual that's inserted itself into my life?

I look up at him again, the box still cradled in my hands. "Am I supposed to thank you?" My voice comes out sharper than intended, the

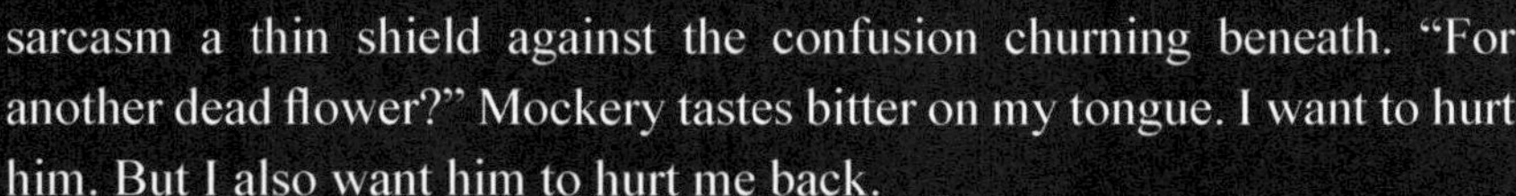

sarcasm a thin shield against the confusion churning beneath. "For another dead flower?" Mockery tastes bitter on my tongue. I want to hurt him. But I also want him to hurt me back.

He tilts his head slightly, the gesture unnervingly birdlike. Then comes the sound—low and resonant, a chuckle that filters through the mask, transformed into something not quite human.

The sound vibrates through me, igniting something primitive in my core. My nipples tighten beneath my tank top, and I have to resist the urge to cross my arms to hide the evidence of my body's betrayal.

His hands reach for the box, his gloved fingers brushing against mine as he takes it. Even through the leather, the brief contact is electric, sending a current up my arms that settles somewhere behind my sternum.

After placing the box on the side table next to us, he produces another envelope. It's identical to the one he delivered yesterday. God, was that only twenty-four hours ago? It feels so much longer.

I open my mouth, intending to tell him I already opened the one from yesterday. Maybe even ask about it. Just as the words shape themselves, ready to be spoken, an almost childish stubbornness rears its head inside me, stopping me from speaking. So, I just close my mouth again and shake my head. I shouldn't be the only one to speak.

Without warning, he steps closer, heat radiating off him like a damn furnace. Instinctively, I press myself harder against the wall, searching for coolness, for stability, for anything that might anchor me as the room seems to tilt on its axis.

He raises the envelope, holding it between his thumb and forefinger. He brings it to my throat, just below my jawline. For a suspended moment, it hovers there, a promise or a threat. Maybe both. Then he drags it down, the sharp paper edge scraping against my skin with precise pressure—not enough to break the skin, but enough to burn, to mark.

I gasp, the sound embarrassingly loud in the silence between us. My eyes widen as he slides the paper down my throat, and over my collarbone. Instead of stopping when it reaches the neckline of my tank top, he continues sliding the edge downward.

The edge catches slightly on the thin fabric, but he doesn't stop until the edge rests between my breasts. My heart hammers against my ribs, so violent I'm certain he can see it pulsing beneath my skin. The envelope burns like ice against my flesh, the contrast between the cool paper and my heated skin almost painful in its intensity.

His other hand moves suddenly, lightning fast. He pinches my nipple through the thin fabric of my tank top, sharp and unforgiving. My gasp is louder this time, raw with heat and something far worse; need. My back arches into it before I can stop myself.

When he lets go and withdraws the envelope, I look down to see a thin red line forming where the edge has traveled—not a cut, but an irritation that brands me temporarily with the path of his attention. My skin rises in a welt that traces from throat to sternum, a visible record of this encounter that will fade but not immediately.

The sight of it—this mark on my body that I didn't consent to but didn't stop—sends a confusing surge of anger and arousal through me. I want to slap him. I want to pull him closer. I do neither.

His thumb brushes my nipple—just once, deliberate and slow. The contact is featherlight, but it shoots through me like static. I freeze. Not because I'm scared. But because I want more. And that terrifies me more than anything else he's done.

He extends the envelope toward me, an expectant silence hanging between us. This time, I don't hesitate. I take it from him, practically ripping it out of his hand with a small growl that makes him laugh. At least, that's what I think the sound from behind the mask is.

I run my thumb over the wax seal before unceremoniously tearing it open. The card inside is thick and black. The surface is matte and textured, like pressed ash. The lettering is etched in deep, metallic orange—coppery, almost glowing against the matte black surface.

One vow. One offering. One trick.

One mask for silence, one vow for shame,
One ring for lust, one kiss to blame.
One game begun, no truth to guide,

One trick revealed when vows collide.

The poem pulses with dark energy and theatrical menace. I look up from the card to find him watching me, his posture slightly changed.

There's a new tension in his shoulders, a coiled energy that wasn't there before. He's waiting for my reaction, I realize. This moment matters to him. Just as I think that, he steps back, allowing space between us for the first time since he pushed me against the wall.

Relief and loss both pulse through me in the absence of his proximity, which is entirely fucked up. Yet it feels… wrong.

"I'll be seeing you soon," he says, his voice a low, distorted rumble. Before I can process what this means, he quickly leaves my apartment.

CHAPTER 9

The Bride

As soon as he's gone, I dart to the door, locking it behind him. The lock clicks with quiet finality, leaving me alone with another dead flower, another poem, and the burning impression of his presence on my skin.

I touch the tender line across my throat and chest, the skin is still raised and warm beneath my fingertips. Proof that I didn't imagine the encounter, that I allowed a masked stranger to mark me in my own home.

On unsteady legs, I make my way to the kitchen, clutching both the box and invitation against my chest like artifacts from another world.

"I'm too sober for this," I mumble.

With robotic movements, I reach for the wine I opened earlier. It's a deep red Malbec that waits by the sink and begs to get inside me. I pour some into the largest glass I own, filling it nearly to the brim.

The wine slides down my throat in three long swallows, disappearing so quickly I barely taste it. The warmth blooms in my stomach, a poor substitute for the heat that consumed me only minutes ago, but welcome nonetheless.

Without bothering with the glass again, I lift the bottle directly to my lips, taking another long pull that drains nearly half of what remains.

My cheeks flush immediately, whether from the alcohol or the lingering effect of his presence, I can't be sure. Probably both. I set the bottle down with more force than necessary, the sound echoing.

What the actual hell just happened? Wait, did it even happen? My body is a battlefield of contradictions, but each one tells me that yeah, I didn't make up the midnight visit. My nipples still strain against the thin fabric of my tank top.

My thighs clench with a need I refuse to acknowledge, much less satisfy. Yet my mind recoils at the implications—at what it means that I responded this way to intimidation, to the thin edge between fear and something darker.

I understand the complicated lines between danger and desire, the ways trauma and fantasy intertwine in the human psyche. But understanding doesn't make it easier to accept my own responses.

My phone sits on the counter, its screen dark and indifferent to my internal struggle. I pick it up, unlock it with shaking fingers, and open the security app. The system isn't elaborate or fancy. It's just one camera facing my front door.

While the app loads, I take another swig of wine. "Here we go," I say when it's displaying a timeline of recorded events.

I scroll to the most recent entry, my thumb hovers over the play button for a moment before I press it, both dreading and craving the replay of what just happened.

The footage is stark in its clarity; me opening the door, the brief exchange, my turning away. Then comes the moment that makes my breath catch. His sudden movement, the way he shoves me inside, the controlled violence of his advance.

On screen, my body hits the wall with an impact I can almost feel again in my back and shoulders. The camera angle captures only a portion of what follows—his back, my face visible over his shoulder, my expression a mix of shock and something else. Something hungrier.

I play the footage, watching it again. And again. Each time focusing on a different detail. The precision of his movements, the way my lips part when he presses me against the wall, the visible shift in my posture from resistance to surrender.

My pulse quickens with each viewing, my breath coming faster as I zoom in on the moment of impact. There's something horribly fascinating about seeing myself this way—a woman I barely recognize, responding to a dominance I should reject but don't.

Without conscious decision, my free hand drifts toward the waistband of my shorts, fingers slipping beneath the elastic to find the slick heat between my legs. I catch myself just before contact, jerking my hand away as if burned. What the hell am I even doing?

Instead of closing down the app or putting my phone down, I replay it, watching the moment loop. The shove, the wall, the cage of his body around mine. The wine burns in my veins, loosening the tight grip of propriety, of self-judgment.

My fingers trace the red line on my chest, following the same path the envelope took. The skin is sensitive, the sensation is a perfect memory—the sharp edge of the paper, the implied threat, the control in his movements.

I set the phone down, screen still illuminated with the paused image. The poem sits beside it, the orange lettering seeming to glow against the black cardstock. It feels like it's mocking me… or maybe that's the wine talking.

My hand trembles slightly as I pick the phone back up. My fingers move before I consciously tell them to, like they know I need to research to feel grounded.

I open a web browser and type in what little I know; black rose, gas mask, midnight bride poem. The results come in fast, and each link I click leads down the social media rabbit hole.

All across different platforms, people are posting selfies with men wearing black gas masks while the women hold a note similar to mine. Except… theirs only have two words written on the paper. It's either *I do* or *I don't*. There are no other variants.

I click on a woman that looks like a gothic doll, and it takes me to her latest social media post.

> *@hauntdoll91*
> *SQUEEEEE!!! I DID IT!!!!*
> *I'm officially going to be a Bride at the Sanctuary of Shadows!!!*
> *#SanctuaryOfShadows   #OneVow   #BrideOfDarkness #MidnightMarked #ChosenNotAsked*

And from there on, I continue. Reading through comments, and following the hashtags they all seem to use.

> *@NotYours73*
> *OMGGGGG!! I can't even explain how excited/shaky/feral I feel right now. The #GasMan just delivered my 'I do', and I screamed. Literally. Woke up my roommate #Worthit*
> *#SanctuaryOfShadows   #OneVow   #BrideOfDarkness #MidnightMarked #ChosenNotAsked*

> *@BuryMe_Softly*
> *To whoever picked me—you've made my dark little heart so happy. I promise to be a worthy Bride. And I promise to bleed pretty. I've already picked my burial dress. Let's GOOOOO!!*
> *#SanctuaryOfShadows   #OneVow   #BrideOfDarkness #MidnightMarked #ChosenNotAsked*

Hours tick by, and before I know it, I've emptied almost a second bottle of wine. Sanctuary of Shadows is so much more elaborate than I gave it credit for. And where I was mildly curious before, now I'm practically salivating.

Not only are they going over the top with their social media presence, delivery of replies to those who applied to be a Bride. But their tickets are actual medallions instead of paper or a barcode that needs to be scanned.

I suppose the courier makes more sense now that I've seen all of this. Well… kind of. Yet… not really. Because if the man at my door was just a courier, as my mind wants to believe, it poses new questions.

Like, why would he fight Caleb just to deliver a cryptic poem to me? And why am I getting poems instead of a simple *I do* or I *don't?*

My legs feel unsteady as I stride into my living room and retrieve all the notes I've received. Once I'm back on the stool in the kitchen, I place them next to each other.

I read the first one.

> *For every bride, a bloom must die,*
> *Petal-black and blooded dry.*
> *The vow begins before the ring,*
> *You're his now. Let the silence sing.*

Then the second note, the one the stranger fought Caleb to give me.

> *He comes by dark, he comes by will,*
> *The bloom you keep must now lie still.*
> *A whisper bound in veil and thread,*
> *Obey the hush, or join the dead.*

Lastly, I re-read the third one.

> *One mask for silence, one vow for shame,*
> *One ring for lust, one kiss to blame.*
> *One game begun, no truth to guide,*
> *One trick revealed when vows collide.*

Turning it over, I read the handwritten note on the back.

> *Please make sure you're on the ferry to Governors Island at*
> *six o'clock on September thirtieth.*

Unsure what to make of it, I drain the last of the wine, but the warm fog of alcohol doesn't offer up an answer to the myriad of questions swirling around my mind.

Well, I guess I'll find out whatever all this means in two days. When the Sanctuary of Shadows opens with a launch event that has people all across social media guessing as to what it might be. And God help me, I'm looking forward to it.

I spin on the stool so I'm facing the living room, tipping my imaginary hat to my dad. "It seems you were right after all," I grin. "You did raise a fool. Because I'm going."

CHAPTER 10

The Trickster

The cemetery gate groans as I push it open, a sound like distant pain that suits my purpose. Like the world exhaling death.

I walk the familiar path, my boots leaving temporary impressions in the damp earth that will vanish with the coming rain. Thunder rumbles somewhere beyond the horizon—a promise, not a threat.

The air tastes of metal and decay, a combination that settles on my tongue like communion wine. Autumn mist clings to the ground, wrapping around the lower portions of the headstones like ghostly hands.

As usual, the cemetery is deserted. It's not quite dark yet, but the place is caught in that liminal space between day visitors and whatever creatures claim the night.

I navigate the maze of markers with practiced ease, my steps slowing as I approach the headstone that bears my sister's name. The dates beneath mock me with their proximity—twenty-eight years of existence compressed into a hyphen between birth and death.

The base of her headstone is littered with wilted red roses from my previous visits, their once-elegant forms now curled and blackened. I kneel before her grave, my knees sinking into the soil.

"Hey, Rubes," I murmur, my voice strange in the cemetery's hush.

The wind picks up, sending dead leaves skittering across nearby plots. As I do every time that happens, I imagine it's her answering me, the only way she can now.

"Everything's ready," I continue, running my fingertips over the engraved letters of her name. "I dropped the last delivery off to Eve two days ago, and Sanctuary of Shadows opens tomorrow evening. Nick's pulled out all the stops for the event."

I continue to tell her about it, like I haven't spent every week updating her on the charity she was once a part of. To Carolina, S.O.S. is about raising money and honoring her sister. For me, it's about getting revenge for Ruby. And for Nick... I honestly don't know. A bit of both, I think.

"He has only tried to talk me out of it a few hundred times," I chuckle mirthlessly. "But he gets it. You'd be proud of your big brother, Rubes. Well, of both of us."

The air pressure changes, compressing around me like a fist slowly closing.

"She's different from what I thought." My jaw tightens at the thought of Eve Mortis, of her gray eyes widening when I shoved her against that wall, of the heat between her legs betraying her. "There's something broken in her."

I could have killed Eve months ago. Could have ended her with the same efficiency I apply to every other problem in my life. But death would be too merciful, too quick. No, what I've designed for her is something far more fitting.

A slow dissolution. A gradual breaking. A lesson written in fear and flesh.

The wind whispers through the trees bordering the cemetery, a soft, sustained note like a distant scream.

I sit back on my heels, surveying the small kingdom of the dead around us. The grass needs cutting. The nearby oak drops acorns that crack beneath my boots like tiny bones. Everything here is in various stages of neglect or decay, just as the living prefer it.

Keep death at a distance. Don't look too closely at its particulars.

"The auction starts tomorrow evening," I say, reaching inside my jacket. My fingers close around the fresh rose I've brought, its stem cool against my palm. "And then comes the wedding."

I pull out the flower, its red petals vibrant against the gray sky. It's still fresh, still perfect. I twirl it slowly between my fingers, watching the petals blur into a dark spiral. I place the rose carefully atop the pile of withered ones, its fresh form a stark contrast to their decay.

"And then she'll be exactly where she belongs. In my fucking cage." My voice cracks slightly despite my iron control. "I'll make her understand what it means to betray a Knight."

The thunder rolls again, a deep, resonant growl that seems to come from the earth itself rather than the sky. A perfect accompaniment to the vow I've just made.

I bow my head, resting my forehead against the cool stone for just a moment. *One. Two. Three. Four. Five.* I mentally count down, and when I hit ten, I lock it away again. I tuck it behind the frozen lake of my resolve, where it can't weaken my hands or blur my vision.

"I'll do right by you." I rise from my position at Ruby's grave. My knees bear the damp imprint of the earth.

While I've been kneeling at my sister's grave, the cemetery has darkened around me. The clouds and mist have thickened now. I brush a speck of dirt from my jacket sleeve, the small gesture a reminder of the control I maintain, even here among chaos and decay.

Then I leave, walking between the rows of headstones. The dead lie in ordered ranks, their final positions determined by plot numbers and family connections rather than the messy entanglements of their lives.

A crow calls from a nearby tree, the harsh sound cutting through the cemetery's stillness. I glance up to see it watching me, head cocked. In some cultures, crows are messengers between the living and the dead. I wonder what this one would tell my sister if it could.

It blinks once, then launches itself from the branch, wings spread wide against the darkening sky. I watch its flight until it disappears beyond the cemetery walls just as the sky flashes with distant lightning.

The storm is approaching, just as I am approaching the culmination of my plan. The gate swings shut behind me with a metallic clang, the sound echoing against nearby mausoleums before fading into silence. My car waits on the street, and I quickly slide behind the wheel.

As I pull away, I feel the anticipation build in my chest, a pressure that expands with each breath. I channel it, focus it, transform it into fuel for what's to come.

Lightning flashes again, followed almost immediately by a crack of thunder that seems to split the sky. The first heavy drops of rain begin to fall, fat droplets splattering against the windshield like tears from an indifferent god.

Instead of going home, I drive to Eve's building, parking right outside the front door. The rain has thickened into something vicious now—sharp, stinging needles pelting the windshield in waves—but I barely register it.

Luckily, I don't bump into anyone as I take the stairs to her floor and make my way to Ned's door. He isn't home, but the key is under the mat as usual so I let myself in.

Stepping inside, I'm immediately assaulted by the smell of stale beer and lemon cleaner. I don't bother turning on the lights. The glow from the street below cuts across the floor in slices, fractured by the blinds, and it's enough for me to see where I walk.

I stride over to the only thing I care about; the wall shared with Eve's apartment. Pressing my palm to it, I lean in until my temple rests against the cold wall. Every creak in the pipes sharpens in the quiet.

Then I hear her; her laugh is high, unrestrained, and fucking radiant. A second voice follows, teasing in its familiarity. It's Shelby.

My teeth grind together as I stand completely still, listening. Eve's laugh comes again, louder this time. The louder she laughs, the harder I grind my teeth. My Bride shouldn't be fucking amused.

She's acting like I haven't been crafting her downfall, like I didn't mark and claim her. Like she isn't living on fucking borrowed time.

My jaw tightens until it aches. I ball my fist against my thigh and breathe through my nose, slow and even, but it doesn't help. All it does is feed the image of her lips parted in joy that doesn't belong to me.

Eve should be afraid, not delighted. She should be reliving the feeling of my fingers deep in her cunt, the feeling she experienced when

I threw Caleb down the stairs. Fuck, even that envelope I dragged across her throat.

There's a rustle like they're moving closer to the shared wall. But I don't care what they're doing. Not really. Because every sound she makes that doesn't belong to me now feels like betrayal.

"What are you wearing for the opening?" Eve asks.

"I'm not sure yet," Shelby answers, her tone wary. "I mean, I don't even know if we get to keep our own clothes."

Shelby knows exactly what's going to happen, but I'm glad to hear she's keeping my secrets. Still, I text Ned while the women discuss clothing options.

Me: Are you aware how close Shelby and Eve are?

Ned: Yes. But it's not a problem. My sister will do what's expected!

I furrow my brows, annoyed with his reply. That's how Nick sounds when he doesn't want to admit he's not fully in control over a situation. I'm halfway through tapping out a reply when there's a knock on Eve's door.

"Ohh, do you think it's your masked stranger?" Shelby's excited voice easily carries through the walls.

Pocketing my phone, I make my way to the door and ease it open so I can see and hear what the fuck's going on.

"I've got a delivery for a Miss Mortis," a male voice states.

"That's me," Eve replies, sounding confused. "Who's it from?"

"Who cares?" Shelby interjects. "Look at the rose, it's gorgeous."

I lean further out, just enough to catch a glimpse of the allegedly gorgeous rose. When I do so, Shelby catches my movement, and her eyebrows shoot up her forehead when she sees me.

"Hey, just sign for it so we can get back inside," she says, nudging Eve. When Shelby looks my way again, I shake my head. That delivery isn't from me.

"Who is it from?" Eve asks again.

The guy glances at his tablet. "A Caleb—"

"Nope," Eve cuts him off sharply, stepping back like the name is an insult. "Tell him to fuck off."

The courier blinks. "Uh… miss… I just have to—"

"No," she repeats, folding her arms. "You can take it back to him and tell him he can shove it."

Shelby's eyes flash with something akin to sadness. "I miss getting flowers like that," she says wistfully.

Eve ignores her, still glaring at the courier. "I'm being serious. Oh, wait… can I pay you to deliver it to him?"

The guy hesitates, then holds out the rose anyway, like proximity might change her mind. "Umm, sure."

Grinning, Eve tells him she'll be right back. Then she disappears for a couple of minutes, and when she returns, she's carrying cash that she offers to the delivery guy.

"Do you have a pen?"

He nods and pulls one from his shirt pocket. She accepts it, and takes the card from the rose, quickly scribbling a message of her own.

"Caleb… go to hell, you pathetic loser. Not with love, Eve."

I'm leaning against the doorframe, watching her with a slow curl of amusement tugging at my mouth. My Little Bride telling some delivery boy to carry her profanity back to the sender is entertaining.

"That's vicious," Shelby whistles. "Kicking a man while he's already down. And after he took a beating for you nonetheless. Damn."

Eve looks unsure of herself. "Is it too much?"

"Nah, he deserves it for the shit he said to you." Despite the reassurance, Shelby smirks in a way that makes her words seem insincere.

Doesn't Dr. Death notice the way her friend looks at her? Like she's calculating ways to use her? The fuck is her problem? She was told to make friends with Eve, but this isn't friendly at all.

"Suit yourself," the courier says at last, tucking the rose back into its insulated bag.

I have no fucking idea why the guy would send flowers after what happened. But I don't like it. After all, Eve's about to be my wife, so I

can't have other suitors sniffing around.

CHAPTER 11

The Bride

The ferry hums beneath my boots, steady and slow as it cuts across the water. Wind snatches at loose strands of hair and tugs at the hem of my coat, but I barely feel it. Not when I'm surrounded by laughter and perfume and the kind of nervous energy that bubbles over in the absence of logic.

Shelby's pressed against my side, practically vibrating with excitement. When I glance at her, she isn't watching the island lights—she's watching me, as if contemplating what to say, before pasting on a grin.

"Can you believe this?" she whispers for the fifth time.

One of the other women hears her and leans in, eyes glittering. "I know, right? I heard they make us walk down an aisle blindfolded."

"I heard they make you bleed to seal the vow," another chimes in, voice giddy.

Shelby snorts and rolls her eyes as though this is tedious to her.

"Are you okay?" I whisper, catching her eyeing me nervously. I can't really put my finger on what it is that's making it seem insincere to me, but her relaxed attitude almost feels forced.

"Hmm? Yep, I'm good." Her smile twitches. "It's a big night, you know?"

Sighing, I move so I'm in front of her. "Come on, Shel. I know something's up. Talk to me."

We might not have been friends forever, or survived childhood and adolescence together. But we've been in each other's lives for a few years. We used to occasionally cross paths professionally, and we were always on good terms.

Then in February she contacted me out of the blue, wanting to go for drinks, and we did. That quickly became a weekly tradition, one we both treasured.

Shel's my first real friend, and I want to be there for her as much as she's been for me. She might not have realized it, but until her, I felt awkward as hell in any social situation that didn't involve work. But now, thanks to her, I feel better in my own skin, so to speak.

"It's nothing," she murmurs, looking away. "Hey, Eve, you know I'm your friend for real, right?"

I tilt my head. "Where's this coming from, Shel?"

"Nowhere," she says too fast. "Just… I'm just reminding you. You know, in case tonight gets weird."

Frowning, I laugh nervously. "Of course I know," I reassure her.

She nods. "Good. Keep that in mind."

The island comes into view—Governors Island, but it doesn't look the way it did last summer when Caleb dragged me here for that Fourth of July disaster. Now it's transformed.

Cloaked in fog, lit only by the warm flicker of jack-o'-lanterns nestled between twisted trees and iron fence posts. They glow like embers from a dying fire, their carved faces leering through the mist.

When we dock, a woman waits at the pier. She's tall, mid-forties maybe, with severe cheekbones and sleek black trousers that fit like a second skin. A tablet dangles from one manicured hand. Her hair's twisted into a glossy bun. Not a single strand out of place.

"Good evening, Brides," she says, with all the warmth of a judge reading out a sentence. "I'm Lorna. Follow me."

As we fall in behind her, a man wearing a skull bandana around the lower half of his face turns toward us. His piercing blue eyes punch the air from my lungs. Is that… no, it can't be. Just as I manage to convince myself it isn't him, I see the arm wrapped in a cast.

"Caleb?" I call out. Instead of looking up again, he turns and disappears into the heavy fog.

The sound of our shoes clicking on the stone path feels louder than it should. Fog pools around our ankles, and above us, the sky seems to darken with each step we take.

Though the walk isn't long, it's disorienting. Trees loom too tall. There's a chanting in the distance that I can't quite make out, like a choir warming up in Hell. And everywhere, the scent of wax, wood-smoke, and damp leaves. The kind of smell that makes you think of rituals and rot.

We arrive at what looks like a black velvet circus tent stitched straight into the earth. Its entrance is flanked by wrought iron candelabras, each flame flickering blue.

Inside, the air is warm and perfumed, lit by twinkle lights strung across the peaked ceiling. Dressing screens line the perimeter, and assistants move like shadows between them, handing out matching sets of black lingerie.

Lorna steps forward again, her tone clipped. "Your Grooms are waiting." A ripple of squeals and whispered speculation moves through the Brides. Assistants begin handing out sets of black lingerie. "They'll be watching as you're led to them. Tonight is the first time you'll see them."

I can't help but smile since I've seen my Groom already. Not without the mask, but still. I've seen and felt him. It feels like an illicit secret, so I keep it to myself.

"Shel," I whisper, turning to… no one. Where the hell did she go? I swear she was right here beside me.

While Lorna continues to explain about the Groom introduction, I look around for my friend, but I don't see her anywhere. She's gone.

"I wonder what my Groom is like," one girl sighs breathlessly.

Another adds, "They say some Grooms bring gifts… others just bring orders. I hope mine is dominant."

Lorna's voice slices through the room again. "Get changed, Brides.

Hurry up."

The other women are already in motion, stepping behind screens, some giggling, some flushed with nerves. I force myself to move. One step. Two.

"Wait." I stop mid-motion as Lorna's suddenly at my side. "You don't need to change."

"Why?" I ask, feeling as though I understand less and less.

"Just wait here," she clips, already moving away.

By the time everyone's done, we're told to line up. The others rush into formation, but while they fight to be in front of the queue, I hang back. Lorna paces down the line, tablet in hand. Her gaze lingers on each of us in turn.

"We'll proceed in order," she says. "There are two carts waiting outside. They'll take you to your Groom. Now, please be patient. It might take a while, but everyone will get to where they need to be."

The first two women move forward. The curtain swallows them, and we're left listening to the click of heels as they disappear somewhere outside of what we can see.

It feels like an eternity passes before Lorna snaps her fingers. "Next."

Two more go.

Then six are gone, and before I know it, it's just me left.

Lorna calls for me. "Eve Mortis." My name shouldn't feel like a threat, but it does. "You may leave."

Wasting no time, I walk through the opening I saw the other potential Brides disappear through. The curtain parts around me like a mouth opening wide, and as soon as I'm through, night air hits my exposed skin.

Beyond the fabric, there's a tall guy waiting for me. He's dressed all in black, with a featureless mask. Instead of speaking, he nods once and steps aside, gesturing for me to follow. We walk a short stretch, stopping when we reach a vehicle parked behind the tent.

It looks like a golf cart—sleek, extended, polished black—outfitted with leather seats and low-burning lanterns along the roofline. The guard opens the door and gestures for me to climb in. I hesitate, but only for a second. Then, I duck my head and slide onto the seat.

The guard takes the seat next to me and starts the engine without a word. The cart hums to life beneath us, gliding forward on silent wheels.

I glance back, watching the tent recede into darkness. It glows faintly at the seams, like something still pulsing with heat after being used. Then it's gone—swallowed by fog and distance.

I don't know how long the ride takes. A few minutes, maybe. Long enough to make me feel like I've crossed into something else entirely. Like I've stepped into something I can never come back from.

Yet, every time I have that thought, excitement spreads through my veins, my heart beats harder, and my core becomes slick with need. My body doesn't want to go back, it wants to chase this… whatever it is I'm now a part of.

The guard doesn't slow down until we're approaching another tent. This one is orange, and the entrance flap is adorned with a glowing print of a gas mask. As soon as I step through the flap, I'm pulled into a tight hug.

"There you are!" Shel exclaims, somehow managing to sound both relieved and like I've done something wrong. "I got worried when you weren't waiting for me here."

"I… umm…" For some reason, I can't make the words come out to explain what happened. They're stuck in my throat. "Where the hell did you disappear to?" I ask, deflecting.

Letting go of me, Shel pulls me over to a section of the tent complete with a vanity table and mirror. She gestures for me to take a seat. When I don't immediately do as she wants, she rolls her eyes and exhales audibly while pushing me into the waiting chair.

"We don't have much time," she mutters. Picking up a brush, she starts working on my hair. A series of tugs follows, each one more pronounced than the last. "I had to get ready first so I could come back and help you."

"Why didn't you say anything before leaving?" I demand. "Talk to me, Shelby."

Her fingers still, and she speaks in a calm tone that's so at odds with what's happening. "You know I can't tell you everything, Eve." I nod as she sets the brush down. "You're just going to have to trust me. Remember what I said, I'm your friend. That part's real."

"So what isn't?" I ask, picking up on what she isn't saying. Squinting, I feel as though I'm seeing her for the first time.

Instead of the outfit she wore when I last saw her, she's wearing a long, tight dress. The black fabric shimmers under the twinkle lights. Her makeup is bold and dramatic. She looks like she's been exhumed and glamorized—some undead pageant queen pressed into service.

Her hair is meticulously twisted into a sleek, polished bun, not a single strand out of place. But what really gets me is her expression. It's eerily calm and detached, resembling the blank, indifferent face of a department store mannequin.

"Nothing here is real," she murmurs as she begins doing my makeup. "It's all a big show, one you wanted to be part of." The last part comes out pointedly, as though she's reminding me that I'm here of my own volition. "A trick for all the senses."

"Maybe," I allow, licking my lips. "But you're still keeping secrets."

"It's all part of the business we call show," she deadpans as she moves on to my eyes, and I try to sit as still as humanly possible while she expertly applies eyeliner and eyeshadow.

"So, you met your Groom?" I ask, needing something to focus on.

"Mhmm," she agrees. "I already knew who it was."

"Do you know who mine is?"

When she doesn't say anything, I know I have my answer. Shel knows, and she's… she's kept it from me for days. This is one of those moments where I wish I could have an *aha* moment. A clarity of sorts. But there's nothing clear about any of this.

"Fine," I relent, my tone scathing. "Keep your secrets, Shel. But if your secrets get me killed, I'll come back to haunt you."

She snorts. "So dramatic." But I can hear the relief in her voice, just as I know she could hear the levity in mine.

As I give in and close my eyes so Shel can finish doing my hair and makeup, I try to make sense of it all. But if I'm honest, none of this makes any sense.

I'm not sure it matters, though. I'm here. And, more importantly, I

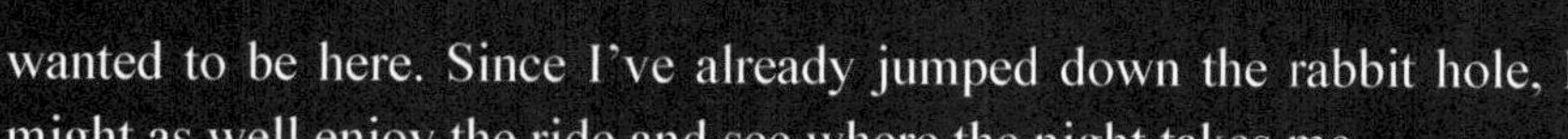

wanted to be here. Since I've already jumped down the rabbit hole, I might as well enjoy the ride and see where the night takes me.

It feels like hours have passed when Shel finally announces, "It's time for the dress."

When I stand and try to look in the mirror, she blocks it with her body. "Come on," I whine. "I want to see."

"Not yet," she sing-songs, shaking her head. "I want you to take it all in when I'm completely done."

Huffing, I fold my arms across my chest and make a show of looking at the ceiling. "Fine," I sigh. "Just let me know when I'm allowed to, you know, actually have an opinion or anything."

"Time to get naked," she announces with a giggle. "And no looking when I come back with your dress."

I flip her off, but do as she says.

This isn't the first time I'm being dressed by Shel. I don't know if she has a doll fetish or just wishes she worked in fashion. But she loves dressing me, and more than half of her outfits are not made to wear with underwear. So, really, this is nothing new.

While I try to ignore the excitement building inside me, Shel dresses me. She pulls, tugs, even makes my breath leave my lungs when she tightens the bodice to the point where breathing no longer feels like an option.

"Shel," I wheeze.

"Almost there." Another tug, and then she lets go. "Okay, you're done. Have a look." I let her take my hand and lead me back to the vanity. As I take in my appearance, I can't help but marvel at it. I look… amazing. Like a bride built for damnation.

My black and orange hair is hanging loosely down my back, with just a few seemingly casual braids throughout the mane. Dark liner and shadow frame my eyes, making the gray look almost metallic, while my lips are painted in a matte black color.

The dress is all contrast and control, tight where it needs to be, sheer where it shouldn't be. It pushes my body into a sharp silhouette; the neckline plunges deep enough to feel like a threat.

Black tulle floats over my skin, layered over a corseted frame that

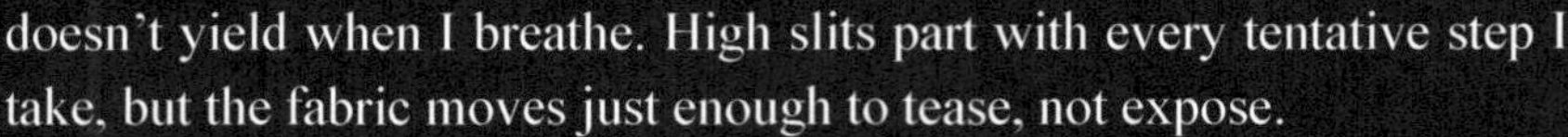

doesn't yield when I breathe. High slits part with every tentative step I take, but the fabric moves just enough to tease, not expose.

Beading traces across the structure like constellations sewn in shadow. The gradient shifts from solid to sheer, revealing slices of skin as if the dress is studying me back—learning what to hide, what to weaponize.

"Oh, and put these on." She hands me a pair of flat shoes that I wordlessly accept.

I sit back down and put them on, tying the laces tight.

"You're going to love what comes next," she beams.

"And what's that?" I ask, already knowing I won't get a straight answer from her.

Shelby opens her mouth, but the words never come as the curtain is pulled back.

My heartbeat kicks harder as the masked courier steps into view. I know that shape now. The silence he wears like a second skin. The way the air changes around him—sharper, charged, as if the atmosphere itself is bracing for something I can't quite name.

For a moment, he just watches. Then he lifts one gloved hand and points at me. "Run."

I blink, confusion gripping me. "What?"

He steps forward with deliberate menace, lowering his hand to his side like a signal of impending doom. "Run. Now." My brain seizes, thoughts crashing and spiraling out of control. I can't comprehend the urgency.

He remains still, a looming shadow, not reaching out, not pursuing. His presence is a silent threat, and he drills that single command into my mind with a chilling insistence.

"Run."

I tear past him, bursting through the flap into the night—and it's no longer empty. People are everywhere, their sudden presence like the opening of a grand scene I didn't know I'd been waiting for.

"Run, Little Bride." His projected voice is everywhere, probably thanks to some fancy technology.

I race forward with reckless abandon, my lungs screaming in protest

against the vise-like grip of the corset, my heart pounding violently in my throat like a war drum. My hair clings to my flushed face in damp, tangled strands. Somewhere behind me, I hear the steady rhythm of boots on stone—measured, unhurried, as if he knows I'll come to him in the end.

As I burst into an open courtyard, I slam to a stop, my breath hitching in my throat. Flickering jack-o'-lanterns cluster near the perimeter like sentinels—leering faces dancing in and out of the fog.

People are swarming everywhere; dozens, no, hundreds of robed figures. They stand eerily still at first, like statues frozen in time. I stagger backward, soles sliding on damp flagstones veiled in fog and scattered petals, my laugh catching in my throat at how real it all feels.

They chant as they come for me. "One vow. One offering. One trick you'll never forget." The voices overlap and blend, perfectly timed, the kind of sound design that makes your skin prickle even when you know it's part of the show.

I spin around and sprint once more, my breath comes in ragged gasps, my vision closing in around me. The chant swells, but beneath it I swear I can hear the low rasp of filtered breathing, steady and inescapable.

Then, my foot catches on something slick beneath the fog. "Shit," I gasp as I catch myself on my hands, the jolt of impact startling but not enough to kill the rush.

Now that I'm down here, I get a good look at the ground and what's making it so slippery. Black roses litter the stones—torn and scattered, like the remains of a prop from a scene that ended just before I arrived.

With no time to waste, I grit my teeth, pushing the agony aside, and scramble back to my feet. The fog thickens, closing in like a living thing as I weave through clusters of silent, shrouded figures that seem to materialize out of nowhere.

The air is filled with haunting whispers, and grasping hands reach out—not quite touching, just close enough to make the chase feel deliciously dangerous.

"One vow. One offering. One trick."

A hand catches my wrist, making me scream as I wrench free. Blood

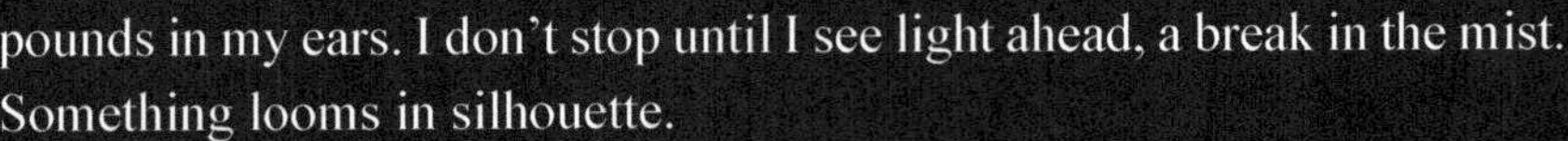

pounds in my ears. I don't stop until I see light ahead, a break in the mist. Something looms in silhouette.

The voices grow louder as I reach the end of my path. "One vow. One offering. One trick."

A stage comes into view, rising a couple of feet above the ground. Upon it stands an altar of black stone. Black candles surround it, flames flickering in the soft wind like they've been waiting just for me.

My mind catalogs the details with almost giddy precision. This is theater. Elaborate, manipulative theater designed for maximum impact. I know this. I understand the mechanism at work. And knowing makes it better.

When I reach the foot of the stage, the courier comes into view as he steps forward. "Come to me, Bride," he says, the mask distorting his voice making it sound like an otherworldly command.

I pause, one foot on the bottom step, savoring the suspense. People close in behind me, but it feels like part of the staging. Like they're here to make sure I don't miss my cue.

A semicircle of jack-o'-lanterns burns along the edge of the stage; each carved with jagged, mocking smiles. Their flames flutter as if reacting to my presence, casting warped shadows that lick across the altar. Like they know they're about to witness a defilement.

My heart stutters, recognition hitting me like a physical blow. Somewhere deep down, I realize I've been following the pull of him all along. Every step, every turn in the fog led me here.

Off to my left, another stage waits under its own pool of light, the nine other Brides and their masked Grooms already in place. Even though they stand in rigid formation, one pair sticks out.

Shelby's Groom isn't wearing a gas mask like the others. Instead, he's wearing a bandana with the same print as the guy I saw by the dock. Now, as I study him, I become more convinced it's Caleb. Or… at least someone that looks almost exactly like him.

While the others stand completely still and barely move, Shelby has her hand down her Groom's pants, very obviously stroking his dick. Good for her.

As I look around, I realize I'm the only person looking at the other stage. The audience are all watching the altar. Knowing its time, I swallow thickly. Then I slowly climb the steps. Each one feels like a decision, a surrender, a choice I'm making despite every instinct screaming caution.

His breathing is audible, deep, measured, amplified by the mask's filter into something mechanical yet undeniably human. He extends his gloveless hand across the altar, palm up, fingers slightly curled in invitation.

The gesture is both a request and a demand, a question I've been answering since the first midnight knock at my door. With a decision that feels both inevitable and deliberately chosen, I place my palm against his.

His fingers close around mine, warm and solid and unmistakably real amid the theatrical unreality surrounding us. In a smooth motion I barely register, he pulls me around to his side, pressing my back to his front.

I gasp, but before I can say anything, his hand closes around my throat with delicious pressure.

We stand like that while the other couples get married, and if I'm honest, I'm barely aware of what's happening around me. I'm way too focused on the man at my back and the impressive erection digging into me.

CHAPTER 12

The Bride

While the applause for the other stage fades, the officiant descends the steps, his robe trailing across the ground as he crosses the space between us. When he mounts my stage, the crowd's gaze follows.

The loud ring of a bell sounds through the air. At the twelfth and last chime, two people step onto the stage from the curtain at the back. They're not wearing masks or anything hiding their identities.

It's the host pair and organizers, Nicklas and Carolina Knight.

Carolina steps forward, her figure cutting through the mist in a floor-length black gown that seems to absorb what little light there is. Her blonde hair is swept up, adorned with black roses, and her face is painted pale with dark, blood-red lips. She looks like a beautiful corpse brought back to life.

"Welcome," she calls out, her voice carrying across the hushed crowd gathered before the stage, "to The Black Wedding."

The audience stirs, a ripple of anticipation moving through them like wind through tall grass.

"Tonight we bear witness to darkness binding darkness," she continues, her voice echoing. "To vows that, once spoken, cannot be undone. To a union sealed not with promises of love, but with blood and

submission and the surrender of will."

With each word, the man at my back flexes his hand around my throat. Not enough to cut off my airway, just enough to… I don't actually know.

"This is not a wedding of hearts," she continues, her smile sharp as a blade as she turns her head to look at me. "It is the wedding of souls—the kind that marks you forever, that claims what was never freely given."

There's something in both her word choice and tone that makes it feel more like a sentence than a performance. Below me, the crowd murmurs its approval, eating everything she's dishing out.

Nicklas steps forward now, tall and imposing in a black tux with a blood-red tie. His hand rests on his wife's shoulder briefly. When he speaks, his voice carries a weight of authority that makes the crowd fall silent immediately.

"As head of the Knight family, I give my blessing to this union," he declares.

Carolina's voice carries clearly and sharply over the crowd. "Tonight, nine couples have already sealed their vows. But of course, it was nothing more than a beautiful illusion. A trick."

While the audience whoops and claps, she turns, her gaze sliding deliberately to me.

"One couple will get married in earnest. I can promise that their matrimony is not just a cheap trick. It's legally binding. The bond you're about to witness between our main couple is real. The claim is true. And the contract will be written in more than ink."

The audience gasps, a ripple of delighted shock. They think it's part of the theater. But the way Carolina smiles at me—slow, knowing—turns my stomach cold.

Nicklas goes on. "Groom, do you claim this Bride as your own, to possess and use as you see fit, to mark with your will and bend to your desire?"

"I do," the man behind me states.

"Eve Mortis." Nicklas turns to me, his eyes cold as he speaks my name. "You have been chosen. You have been marked. You have been sacrificed. Your consent is not required, but your surrender is inevitable."

It's not a question. Hell, he's not even bothering to pretend I have a choice. It's just a statement of fact, delivered with the certainty of someone who has never been denied anything.

Someone says something about legitimacy and witnesses. It sounds official. Binding—just like Carolina promised. My ears ring as if I'm underwater.

Then, a hooded figure moves closer to the altar. Tall and skeletal, dressed in robes so black they seem to devour the surrounding light.

When they begin to speak, the sound is broken and strange—a language I don't recognize with sounds that shouldn't be possible from a human throat. The words scrape against my ears like fingernails on slate, making my skin crawl.

"I am the shadow priest," he announces proudly. "I'm here to seal the unholy union between this Groom and Eve Mortis."

The priest raises skeletal hands, bones visible beneath paper-thin skin, and gestures at something on the altar. My Groom's hand closes around my upper arm, his grip firm but not painful as he guides me forward. The audience watches with rapt attention, their breathing a collective hush that pulses in time with the drumming that has begun somewhere behind us.

On the altar rests a black glass bowl, its surface reflecting the candlelight. Beside it lies a ceremonial knife, blade gleaming silver against the dark velvet. My Groom releases my arm and reaches for the knife.

He. Reaches. For. The. Knife.

"No!" I scream, lunging to the side. But he's quick to grab me again, hauling me back so I'm flush against him before I even manage one step. "No! Let me go. Let go of me, you fucking psycho!" I thrash and kick, but he just laughs. Fucking laughs.

Using his hips, he pins me to the altar; the stone digging into my hip bones. "Keep fighting me, Little Bride," he rasps, rolling his hips so I can feel his growing erection. "It'll make it so much sweeter when we consummate our marriage."

"The fuck," I hiss. "I'm not fucking marrying you. This is just a performance. A sick one, but that doesn't make it real." It can't be real… right? I mean, it has to be a trick no matter what they're saying.

He lowers his head; the hard edge of the mask grazes the shell of my ear, his breath a filtered hiss. "Are you sure about that, Bride?"

Before I can answer, he wraps his arms around me. If he's doing it to keep me here, there's no need. The second he draws the blade across his palm, I stop fighting, too transfixed by what I'm seeing to keep it up.

The skin parts like silk beneath steel, a thin line of red welling up in its wake. He doesn't flinch or inhale sharply as blood begins to drip from his hand into the black bowl.

When he reaches for my hand, I feel the first real jolt of fear spike through me. But I'm too scared to move as he turns my hand palm up. The knife hovers above my skin, and I can feel the cold radiating from the metal even before it touches me.

"Don't," I whisper, the word barely audible over the growing noise around us. "Please… at least clean the knife first." What a stupid fucking thing to say.

He laughs as he steps to the side and positions me so we're facing each other. His head tilts, the black lenses of the mask fixed on me. Then he raises the knife and smears it across my lips. "Anything for my wife-to-be," he mocks.

The blade bites into my palm, a line of fire opening across my skin. I gasp, the sound swallowed by the priest's rising voice. His grip tightens, holding me still as he completes the cut. Blood wells up, hot and shocking against my cold skin.

Somewhere behind us, the drumming returns—slow, steady, echoing the rhythm of his breath against my neck. A beat for each heartbeat.

He positions my bleeding hand over the bowl, pressing his wounded palm against mine. Our blood mingles, running down our wrists and dripping into the dark glass. The sensation is intimate in a way that makes my stomach turn.

The priest chants louder now. It sounds like words but feels like a binding. Like the syllables are crawling under my skin, writing a new name beneath the one I was born with.

More people appear from the edge of the stage, taking the bowl with reverence before disappearing as quickly as they joined us.

My Groom moves behind me, chest to my back. One arm cages my waist while the other, still slick with our mingled blood, drifts lower. My pulse races as his fingers bunch the fabric of my dress.

"You're mine now," he rasps through the mask. "Bought and paid for with blood and pain."

My breathing comes faster as his hand lifts the skirt of my dress, the movement hidden from the audience by our bodies and the fog that swirls around our legs. His fingers trail up my thigh, dragging fire across skin too sensitive, too aware.

Every inch he claims feels like a countdown to something I can't stop.

Movement flickers at the corners of my vision—hooded bodies swaying, grinding, mimicking what he's doing to me, like we're just the prototype, the blueprint of their depravity.

His fingers reach the apex of my thighs, and I bite my lip to hold back a sound that would betray me as he cups my pussy.

I buck and writhe, uselessly trying to get away from his probing hand. But it's too late. He knows I'm wet, knows my body is responding to the danger and the darkness despite my mind's rebellion.

"Stop it!" I demand on a scream. "Just fucking stop it. I did not consent to this."

A low chuckle vibrates against my back as his fingers slide through my slickness. "Just as I thought," he observes, pressing his cock against my ass through his clothes. "Fighting it with your mind, begging for it with your body."

I try to shift away, but his arm across my waist holds me firmly in place. The movement only serves to push me back against him, the hard length of him grinding against me in a way that sends unwanted heat spiraling through my core.

Without warning, I feel him unfastening his pants. The cool air touches my exposed skin for just a moment before something hot and hard presses against me from behind.

"No," I beg, but the word is drowned by the drumming that has

grown louder, more insistent. "P-please don't do this."

He thrusts into me with brutal purpose, splitting me open inch by inch. Thick and unforgiving, like he's carving his name into the softest part of me. My breath catches on a sob as every vein drags fire through my walls, forcing me to stretch around him.

My body opens to him with humiliating ease, wet and willing in ways my mind still denies. I want to claw it back—this response, this heat—but it already belongs to him. Fuck.

His arm clamps around my waist like an iron vise, anchoring me in place as my breath shatters. I brace myself against the altar as each thrust slams through my body. But it's the cruel contrast, the devastation paired with desire, that shreds me.

I hate how much I can feel him. How my body aches for more even as my mind claws for escape.

"Do you vow to claim her pain and pleasure alike, to enslave her will and make her body your altar?" The priest's voice slices through the thick air. "To mark her with pain and pleasure, to possess not only her body, but the remnants of her soul?"

"I do," my Groom growls.

"And do you, Eve Mortis, vow to be taken and transformed, to surrender your freedom to the one who now claims you?"

I shake my head violently, my jaw tightening as I prepare to unleash a torrent of words that would tell him exactly where he can shove that vow. But instead of the searing reprimand I intended, a strangled moan escapes my lips.

A wave of overpowering sensation crashes over me as my Groom strikes that electrifying spot within, making my vision explode into a dazzling array of stars.

"Then let this blood become the bond. Let this taking become the seal."

Around us, the stage blurs with motion—robed figures dancing, writhing, simulating acts of violence and sex that mirror what my Groom is doing to me.

The candles flicker more frantically now, shadows leaping and twisting across the stage. I want to shut it all out. The drumming, the

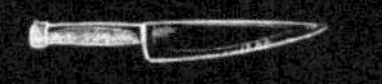

chanting, the swaying bodies grinding in mimicry. But something deep inside me won't let go. Won't look away.

"You feel so good," he groans. "So tight. So wet. So fucking perfect."

I hate the way my body yields, responding eagerly to his words, as my muscles involuntarily tighten around him and a warm, insistent heat gathers low in my belly. I loathe how my hips seem to have a will of their own, instinctively tilting to meet his every thrust, a rhythmic dance beyond my control.

The sounds that threaten to spill from my lips, those soft whimpers of pleasure, press insistently against the back of my throat, demanding to be swallowed back before they escape into the charged air around us.

He groans low in my ear, a deep, primal sound more animalistic than human, resonating through the air like a growl from the depths of a forest.

His hips hammer into me with ruthless rhythm, each thrust punching the air from my lungs, the tip of his cock battering the spot that makes me cry out. I moan, unable to hide how deep he's fucking me.

One of his hands ventures upward, sliding over the fabric of my dress to gently cup my breast. His thumb begins to circle my nipple with deliberate, teasing motions. Oh, God. It feels incredible.

My Groom's thrusts grow relentless, plunging deeper and harder, thick and punishing, dragging a choked moan from my throat every time he bottoms out.

My thighs are on fire, muscles locked in a feverish grip as a scorching heat spirals tight within me. The intensity is overwhelming, rising with a ferocity that threatens to consume me. I fight desperately to delay the inevitable—but I'm helplessly slipping over the edge.

A figure steps forward, cradling a black velvet cushion. Upon it rests a ring—a band of dark metal inlaid with what looks like obsidian. He's quick to take it, holding it up so it catches the candlelight.

His movements slow but don't stop as he takes my left hand in his, holding it steady as he slides the ring onto my finger. It's heavy and cold, feeling like a shackle more than a piece of jewelry.

Another attendant approaches with something that glints in the

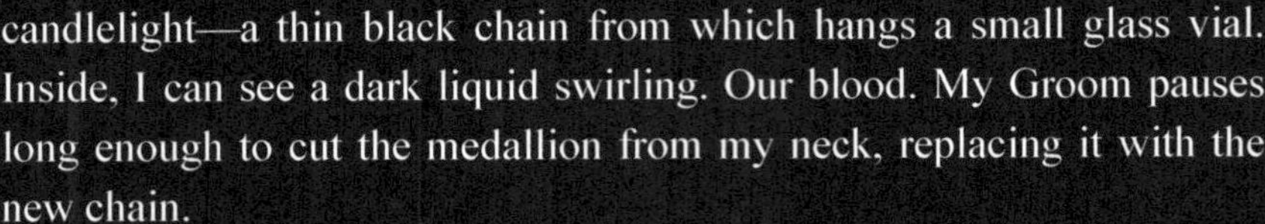

candlelight—a thin black chain from which hangs a small glass vial. Inside, I can see a dark liquid swirling. Our blood. My Groom pauses long enough to cut the medallion from my neck, replacing it with the new chain.

Then he grinds deeper, his cock thick and twitching inside me, his breath rasping over my skin like a brand still smoking. I can feel every twitch, every pulse, like I'm being marked from the inside out.

The crowd watches, their attention fixed on what appears to be a solemn exchange of tokens, unaware of the true consummation happening before their eyes. At least I hope they're unaware.

I bite down on a whimper as he shifts his angle, finding that devastating spot again. "N-no." My fingers curl into fists at my sides, nails digging half-moons into my palms as he thrusts slowly and deeply, dragging pleasure from my body like a confession.

"Yes," he growls, voice thick and ragged. "Come on my cock, wife. Drench my fucking balls with your arousal."

I'm not his wife. I'm just… not.

I hate him. I hate him for doing this. For… my thoughts are cut off as pleasure detonates inside me—violent, electric, absolute. My vision whites out, and my knees go weak.

"Fuck!" I cry out as I shatter, loud, broken, and raw.

My body convulses around him, back arching as my sobs dissolve into filthy, half-formed moans. I can't stop. Can't stop pulsing around him, spasming so hard it hurts. My gasps and moans echo across the stage, into the watchers, into the dark.

He holds me through every humiliating second of it, murmuring that I'm his and that there's no escape. He keeps me standing through it, grinding slower now, cruel in his tenderness.

I don't know where I am anymore—on a stage, in his arms, in a nightmare I almost begged for. The crowd feels unreal. The heat between my legs doesn't.

As soon as my breathing returns to normal, his movements become erratic, his control finally breaking as he drives into me harder, faster. His cock swells, stretching me wide and brutal, each inch a demand my body can't refuse.

I bite down on a cry as heat pulses between my legs again, shame curling tighter with every surge of him inside me.

The hard edge of the mask bumps against my neck as he breaks with a groan—rough, raw, guttural—his cock jerking as he pumps thick, scalding cum into me wave after wave. My pussy clenches around the heat like it belongs there.

Then, with a final rasped breath, he pulls out of me, and I feel him tucking his cock away. "Fuck, your cunt's something else." The deep timbre of his voice makes my inner walls flutter in response.

After rearranging my dress so the skirt covers my ass, he repositions us so we're face-to-mask. I don't know how to feel as I look at my Groom now, after he just fucked me like that.

A bright light blinds me, and I close my eyes for a brief moment. Just as I'm about to open them, his distorted voice rasps through the filter, "Till death, Eve."

The hooded priest lifts his arms, voice cutting through the murmur of clapping like a blade through silk. "It is done. What was separate is now bound. What was free is now claimed for all eternity in this unholy matrimony."

When the priest steps back, my Groom reaches up and removes his mask… and the world tilts.

Jack Knight stares back at me, the ghost of a smirk tugging at his mouth as if this has all been a private joke. "Surprise, wife."

My knees threaten to give way. I don't even have time to curse before his lips crush against mine, sealing not just the marriage, but my fate.

He kisses me hard, brutally so. Each swipe of his tongue against mine is like a brand burned into my soul. My gasp gets swallowed by his mouth, my protest silenced by the sharp crush of teeth and tongue. I lose myself for a second in it—shocked, breathless, overwhelmed.

I hear a click, but then it's drowned out by applause from the audience I'd forgotten about. Jack breaks the kiss and turns us so we're facing the onlookers below the stage. My lips are parted, kiss-bruised and stinging.

"You're mine now. Let them see it." His voice is silk soaked in ash.

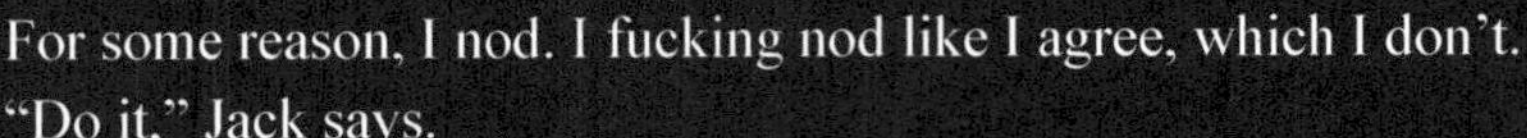

For some reason, I nod. I fucking nod like I agree, which I don't.

"Do it," Jack says.

"Do what?" I ask, confused by what it is he wants me to let them see.

But when I feel someone move behind me just as Jack winds his arm around my shoulders and holds me close, I realize he wasn't talking to me at all. I try to look behind me, but Jack's words stop me.

"It'll be easier if you stand still," he growls.

Then a thick leather gag is pressed against my mouth, shoved between my lips before I can twist away. It silences my cries as I try to pull back, but Jack doesn't let me move. The straps are drawn tight, buckled with swift precision behind my head.

I scream into it anyway, muffled and broken. No one reacts. Their silence is reverent. As if this, too, was scripted.

B. LYBAEK

CHAPTER 13

The Trickster

The ferry cuts through black water, carrying us away from the island where I've taken what's mine. Her weight against my side is an anchor, something solid in the surreal aftermath of our marriage.

Eve's hair whips across her face in the night wind, obscuring her eyes, but not the leather gag still fixed between her teeth. Blood—hers and mine—has dried on our palms, crusted and flaking like a promise turning to dust. But the bond remains. Unbreakable now.

I want to reach over, crack her hand open, and taste it. Just to see if I bleed differently than her. Just to confirm we aren't the same and never will be.

When the ferry docks, I guide Eve up the gangplank with a firm hand against her lower back. She stumbles once, her legs still unsteady. Whether from the ceremony or what came after, I don't know. Don't particularly care either.

My car is waiting where I left it. I open the front passenger door, but she stands rigid, refusing to get in. I lean close, my mouth against her ear. "Look around you, wife. Do you want all these people waiting for the ferry to see me rip your dress off and fuck you on the hood of my car?"

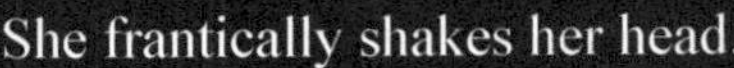

She frantically shakes her head.

"Then get in the fucking car. Now."

Her eyes flash with hatred, but she obediently slides onto the seat. She hisses something that sounds like, "Fuck you, Jack," just as I shut the door after her. But with the gag in her mouth, I can't be sure.

Rounding the hood, I get into the driver's seat and start the car. "Is that you begging for my cock again?" I ask, smirking when she vehemently shakes her head.

The drive to Riverdale passes in silence, and it doesn't take long until my mansion looms dark against the night sky as we pull into the driveway. Eve's eyes widen slightly, taking in the gothic architecture that watches her arrival like a sentient thing.

Ivy coils like veins across its face, and the turret windows glow faintly, as if something inside already knows she's here. A bride for a house that eats its wives.

"Home sweet home," I say, killing the engine.

I unlock her door, then circle around to help her out. When she doesn't move, I unbuckle her seatbelt and simply lift her from the seat. She makes a muffled sound of protest behind the gag, but I've already set her on her feet and am steering her toward the front door.

Inside, I flick on minimal lights—just enough to navigate the space without revealing too much at once. The air is warmer here, heavy with the faint scent of cedar and smoke. Her head turns, trying to take it in without giving away her curiosity.

The heavy oak door closes behind us with a sound like finality.

While she looks around, I shrug out of the leather jacket. Then I reach behind her head and unbuckle the gag. It comes away with a wet sound, leaving red marks at the corners of her mouth. She works her jaw, wincing.

"If you need to use the bathroom, I suggest you do it now." I point toward the hallway. "It's that way."

"Fuck you," she manages, her voice hoarse.

Smirking, I grab my junk. "Not right now," I rasp. "You look like shit." That's a lie.

Even with her makeup smeared into a chaotic mess, her hair twisted

into wild tangles, and her dress irreparably destroyed, she exudes a breathtaking beauty that defies her disheveled state.

Ironically, she's more breathtaking now than when I saw her moments before urging her to run. The fabricated perfection has vanished, replaced by the fierce, desperate woman who is now my wife.

I wrap my fingers around her upper arm and pull her down the hall to the bathroom. She tries to twist away once, testing my grip. I tighten it just enough to make her wince.

The bathroom light casts harsh shadows when I flip the switch. Eve blinks in the sudden brightness. "I don't need to use the bathroom." Her tone makes it sound as though the thought is ridiculous.

Shrugging, I murmur, "Suit yourself."

"I need clothes," she says, voice steady despite everything. Trying to sound confident.

"No, you don't." I switch the light off again. It's a relic now—her wedding veil and burial shroud all in one. "It's time to get you settled into your new home."

Her chin lifts a fraction. "I'm not going anywhere in this dress."

I don't waste time arguing or negotiating. "You don't make the rules here, Eve." I guide her forward, ignoring her attempt to dig in her heels. "You don't decide what you need. I do."

She tries to twist out of my grasp, but I tighten my hold just enough to make her gasp, a reminder of our positions in this new reality.

I steer her down the hallway toward the bedroom, feeling the building resistance in her body with each step. She's moving like someone on borrowed time—burning through adrenaline and fury, her exhaustion held at bay by sheer will and animal instinct.

Pushing her into the bedroom, I release her arm and turn on the light. She stumbles forward two steps, the fabric of her dress whispering against the hardwood, then freezes. Her gaze locks on the shadowed corner, on what waits for her there. The cage.

Eve's breathing changes, becoming shallow and quick. Her eyes flick between the metal, the door, and me. I can see the calculations running behind those eyes—distance, angles, probability of success.

"Don't," I warn, but it's too late.

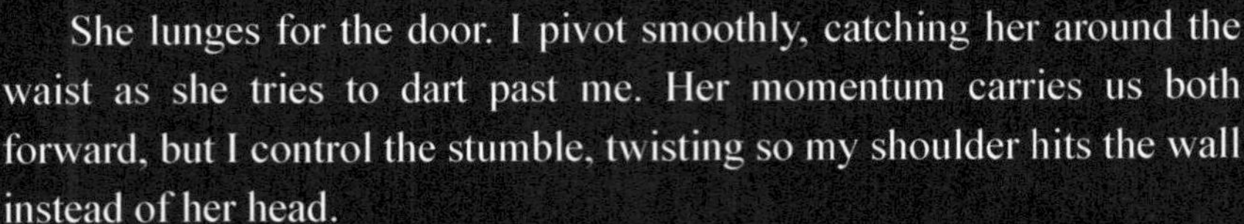

She lunges for the door. I pivot smoothly, catching her around the waist as she tries to dart past me. Her momentum carries us both forward, but I control the stumble, twisting so my shoulder hits the wall instead of her head.

"Let me go!" she screams, all pretense of calm shattered. Her nails rake down my forearm, drawing blood in thin lines. "You fucking psycho!"

I lock my arms around her, pinning her own to her sides. She writhes against me with a desperation that feels like a fucking aphrodisiac.

"Stop fighting," I command, my voice level despite the struggle. "You're only making this harder on yourself."

Her answer is to slam her head back, aiming for my nose. I turn just in time, taking the blow on my cheek instead. Pain blossoms, sharp and clarifying. I tighten my grip, using my weight to force her down to the floor.

"Enough." My voice booms.

She twists beneath me, bucking up with her hips in an attempt to throw me off. I capture her wrists, pinning them above her head with one hand while the other closes around her throat.

"Are you done?" I snarl, staring down at her flushed face.

Her answer is to spit directly into my eye.

The only reaction she gets is my slow blinking to clear my vision. "The next time you spit at me, I'll make you drool all over my cock and use it as lube so I can fuck your ass. Got it?"

Pressing her lips together, she refuses to answer me. Wrong move.

I unsheathe the knife at my belt and press it to her sternum. Her breath stutters. One slow drag down the front splits the corset open.

"You want to act like an animal?" I rasp. "Then you don't get clothes."

With her wrists still pinned, I grab the sides of the ruined dress and rip. The corset peels away from her chest in jagged flaps. But the rest? The weight of her body pins it beneath her, and I don't hesitate—I wrench it out from under her back, dragging the crushed skirt fabric down her hips, over her thighs, and off her legs in a single violent pull.

Her chest rises and falls, fast and shallow. Whether it's fury or arousal fueling it, I can't tell. Doesn't matter. I see the way her nipples tighten, and the flush that creeps up her throat.

I see everything. And I plan to make her feel it.

I slide my hand between her thighs and cup her pussy—firm, possessive, a filthy claim. Her breath snags in her throat. I press my fingers against her slit and feel the heat, the slickness already coating her folds like an invitation she refuses to admit.

"Still soaked," I chuckle darkly. "Or are you soaked for me, *again?*"

She shakes her head in a useless denial. But her body's already told me the truth.

I slip two fingers between her folds and drag them up, slow and deliberate, before rubbing tight, punishing circles against her clit.

"Stop," she gasps, but her hips twitch. "Don't—"

"Why?" I demand, rubbing harder. "You think I didn't notice how you moaned for me? How your pussy clenched around my cock like it wanted to keep me?"

She bucks beneath me, mouth falling open in a soundless cry. Her thighs tremble.

"Tell me you don't want it," I order, fingers relentless. "Say you hate it while you fucking come on my fingers."

"I… fuck… I hate you," she grits out, voice cracking.

Groaning, I finger her soaked cunt faster. "Hate has nothing to do with it, wife. You're going to come on my fingers like the filthy little liar you are."

Her body jerks—sharp, involuntary. A cry tears loose as her climax crashes through her, raw and violent. She convulses beneath me, every muscle drawn tight as I work her through it, not letting up even as her breath comes in sobs.

"That's it," I whisper, dragging it out until she shakes. "You can hate me all you want, but your pussy loves me."

Instead of giving her time to recover, I stand, hauling her to her feet in one fluid motion and pushing her the last way toward the cage.

At the threshold, she makes her last stand.

Eve grips the top bars, arms straightening with desperate strength to keep herself anchored outside. Her naked body arches against mine,

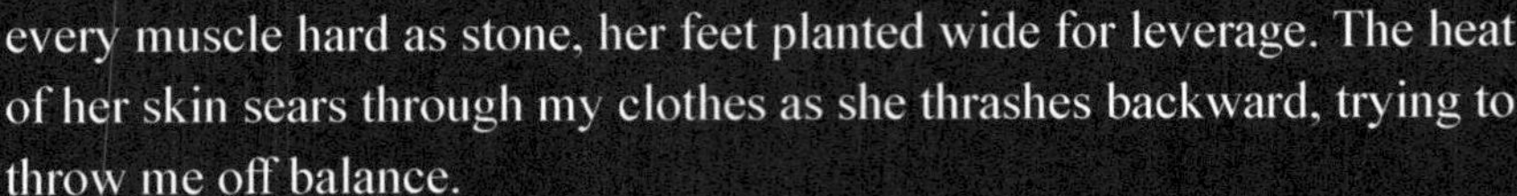

every muscle hard as stone, her feet planted wide for leverage. The heat of her skin sears through my clothes as she thrashes backward, trying to throw me off balance.

"Please don't, Jack. I p-promise I'll be good."

Her voice cracks, but her grip is iron. I hook my arm around her waist and yank her back flush to me, feeling her heartbeat slam against my ribs. Her hair whips across my jaw as she jerks her head from side to side.

"Don't make me drag you in there," I murmur against her ear. "Because I will, and it won't be pretty."

She kicks once more, catching my thigh with her heel. Pain blooms sharp and immediate, and I respond by prying her fingers from the bars one by one, slow enough for her to know she's losing. Her nails scrape metal with a desperate screech before I break her hold completely.

With a final surge of force, I shove her into the cage, her knees hitting the floor with a thud. She scrambles for the door, but I'm already out, swinging it shut. The lock clicks with quiet finality, echoing in the small space like a gunshot.

Eve launches herself at the bars, fingers curling around the metal as she shakes the door with surprising strength. She screams then, the sound primal and raw, tearing from her throat with violent force. Her hands slam against the bars, knuckles whitening with the pressure.

"You fucking monster! This isn't legal, this isn't—"

"Legal?" I laugh, the sound soft and genuine. "Eve, nothing about tonight was legal."

Her eyes dart to the bowls in the corner of the cage. Understanding dawns in her expression, horror chasing close behind. "Food bowls?" Her voice breaks on the words. "Like I'm an animal?"

"Pretty fitting with how you're behaving." I smirk.

She sinks to her knees then, hands still gripping the bars. Something collapses in her, making her shoulders curve inward as reality settles into her bones. It's fascinating to see the fight and adrenaline leave her.

"Why me, Jack? What the fuck did I ever do to deserve this?" she whispers, and for the first time, there's something beneath the anger. "When you wanted my help, I tried to help you. I haven't done anything

to deserve this."

I crouch down to her level, meeting her eyes through the bars. "Exactly," I agree mockingly. "You're the doctor who does nothing."

Shaking her head, she swallows audibly. "You won't get away with this," she warns, but the fire has dimmed to embers. Exhaustion is taking over as the fight leaves her system.

"I already have."

CHAPTER 14

The Trickster

The quiet stretches are getting longer. Not silent—she still screams, still kicks the bars hard enough to bruise—but the bursts are farther apart now. I can't tell whether she's pacing herself or conserving rage.

Like me, Eve hasn't slept. I'm pretty sure half of her reason for constantly making noise is to make sure I don't. Little does she know I don't need her help to stay awake. Since Ruby's death, I only sleep a couple of hours a night unless I'm drunk off my ass, which I haven't been for months.

I've been in the living room for hours—shirtless, hunched over a half-empty bottle, listening to her come undone one scream at a time. Sometimes I hear her pacing, and not in a way that comes from restlessness. She wants me to wonder what she's planning.

It's been almost twenty-four hours since I brought her here. Twice she's demanded to be let out to use the bathroom, and I've obliged.

Eve still hasn't touched the food and refuses to drink water unless it comes in a sealed bottle. The latter is smart, but the former is fucking stupid.

If she's trying to punish me by starving herself, she's playing the wrong game. Or maybe she thinks she's being strong, and perhaps she is. But I've seen stronger women break.

A cigarette smolders between my fingers. Even though the windows are open, the room reeks of smoke and bourbon. I used to smoke years ago, but I stopped right until we put Ruby in the ground.

I tip my head back and take a deep drag, savoring the burn.

Another slam echoes through the house, followed by a scream. I smirk as I exhale slowly and evenly. She's still got spirit, but it's not the same as last night. Not the same chaos as her whispering threats into the dark.

This is something else entirely. Something meaner and more patient. She's spiraling. And she's dragging me with her.

I thought the house would be strong enough to withstand the storm that is Eve Mortis. But it's in the walls now. Her rage, her breath, the soft scrape of her pacing feet—I hear every sound she makes, even when she's still.

The echoes slide through the hallways, pooling in the corners, sinking into the wood like this place is learning her patterns and whispering them back to me.

This is not a home anymore. Fuck, maybe it never was. Ruby used to say that a house doesn't make a home, and she was right. I'm not sure what it takes, only that I don't have it. This is nothing more than a place for the worst parts of us.

While her mouth curses me to Hell and back, I know her body wants me. Every time I've touched her, she's soaked me in her arousal and come so fucking prettily for me. Just remembering her cunt squeezing my cock has me aching and leaking for her all over again.

She might be a force to be reckoned with when she's free, but I've clipped her wings, and shoved her in a cage for my viewing pleasure.

Raising my bottle, I salute the air. "Let the games begin," I rasp.

Thunder cracks somewhere far off. Then the silence creeps back in. I close my eyes and wait for the next blow.

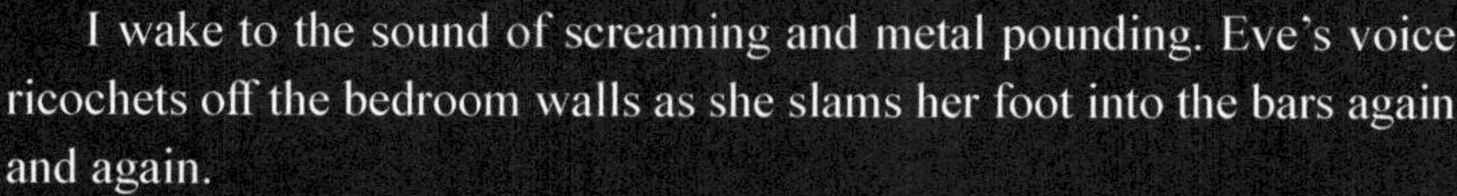

I wake to the sound of screaming and metal pounding. Eve's voice ricochets off the bedroom walls as she slams her foot into the bars again and again.

"Wake up, you useless son of a bitch! You're burning your fucking house down!"

My head's a swamp of liquor and smoke. When the hell did I move back to the bedroom? My mouth tastes like ash and regret, and it takes a second for the rest to register.

What the fuck's that burning smell? I look down to see the cigarette I must've dropped is melting a slow hole into the edge of the carpet. The cherry's eaten through the fibers, leaving a smoldering ring.

"Jesus," I mutter, grabbing the damn thing and crushing it into the ashtray. The glass wobbles, tipping a streak of gray across the wood grain of the nightstand.

"You fucking idiot," Eve spits, voice shredded. "What are you gonna do next, jackass? Drown me in the tub because you can't hold your liquor?"

I push upright, wincing at the pull in my back and the burn in my throat. My temples pulse as if they're caught in a vise. "It didn't catch," I rasp.

She kicks the bars again. Hard. "It could've. I'm not dying in a goddamn fire because my jailer's too drunk to finish a smoke upright."

My eyes finally focus. She's standing now, fists tight at her sides, eyes wild and bloodshot with fury. She's practically shaking with rage. My wife looks feral, and beautifully so.

"Don't worry yourself," I grunt, rubbing my eyes. "I'd have gotten you out before the flames hit."

"Oh, right. Because you're such a fucking gentleman."

"Because you're mine," I snap. "And so is your pain."

That shuts her up—but only for a second. Then she starts laughing. Dry, breathless, on the edge of hysteria. "Your *what*, exactly? Wife? Prisoner of war? Pretty sure even war criminals get meals and ventilation that aren't full of secondhand smoke."

"I gave you food and water," I growl, dragging the bottle off the

floor. "You just refuse to touch it."

"Because I don't trust you," she spits.

"Fair enough." I relent, striding over to the walk-in closet. Her colorful insults chase me as I find fresh clothes.

"Next time, try not passing out like a fucking rookie before the smoke kills us both."

Tuning her out, I take the bottle and clothes with me to the bathroom, where I immediately run the shower. I don't even bother undressing. Just put the fresh clothes next to the sink and walk my ass into the shower, still clutching the bottle.

If this isn't rock bottom, I don't know what fucking is.

Leaning my head back against the tiles, I sit like that until the bottle is empty. Then I finally get up, my legs unsteady as fuck as I remove my clothes and clean myself.

As I look down, I notice the water turning red as it washes away the dried blood from my skin. Fuck, I should have cleaned both of our wounds yesterday. Letting out a grunt, I cut the water off and get out.

I find my first aid kit under the sink, but before cleaning my own, I need to check on Eve's. I might hate her, but that doesn't mean I want her infected just because I was careless and high on the rush of claiming her.

Cutting us both with the same knife without sterilizing it was stupid. But mixing our blood like I did was fucking reckless. Her blood's in my veins now, moving through me with every heartbeat, staking its claim from the inside out.

"Fucking hell," I curse while towel-drying.

Her blood is in my veins, her scent under my nails. There's no part of me that doesn't reek of her anymore, and no part I want to wash clean.

I wrap the towel around my waist and grab the key from my dirty jeans before heading back to the bedroom.

"Get up," I order, switching the light on.

I'm surprised when she obeys, slowly unfolding her limbs and standing. "What now?" she demands.

Unlocking the cage, I open the door. "I need to clean your wound." I point at her hand that's caked in dry blood.

She scoffs, but I notice a small glint of relief in her storm-gray eyes. "Fine." I'm surprised when she leaves the cage and strides straight into the bathroom without trying anything.

"Sit," I command, gesturing to the edge of the tub. She doesn't move. "I said, sit," I repeat, sharpening my tone.

This time she complies, perching on the edge of the bathtub like a bird ready to take flight. I turn to the medicine cabinet, retrieving antiseptic, gauze, and tape. When I face her again, her eyes are tracking my movements with wary precision.

I take her hand in mine, turning it palm up to examine the cut. It's not deep, but it has reddened around the edges. I run my thumb across the wound, and she hisses, trying to pull away.

"Hold still," I say, holding her wrist firmly as I reach for the faucet with my other hand.

Cold water sluices over both our hands, washing away the dried blood in rusty spirals. She makes a small sound—part pain, part something harder to name. With clinical efficiency, I dab the cut dry, then apply antiseptic.

She flinches but doesn't pull away this time. Her pulse beats against my fingers, quick and stubborn, and I wonder if she's thinking about how easy it would be to sink her teeth into my wrist. Maybe she really is a fucking progeny with how fast she's learning.

"Our blood mixed," I say conversationally as I wrap a strip of gauze around her palm. "In the bowl. Did you see what they did with it?"

She doesn't answer, but I feel the tension in her arm.

"They sealed it," I explain, securing the gauze with medical tape. "That vial around your neck contains both of our blood."

Her fingers curl into a fist beneath my ministrations. "You're disgusting," she spits. "And for all I know, you might have passed some disease on to me. I want to get tested."

I laugh darkly. "Maybe you've given me a disease," I reply calmly.

At my words, she smiles coldly and locks her gaze on mine. "I really, *really* hope I have. And I hope it kills you slowly, Jack."

Eve's feistier than I anticipated, and I think I'm going to love having her here until Sanctuary of Shadows closes its doors. What happens

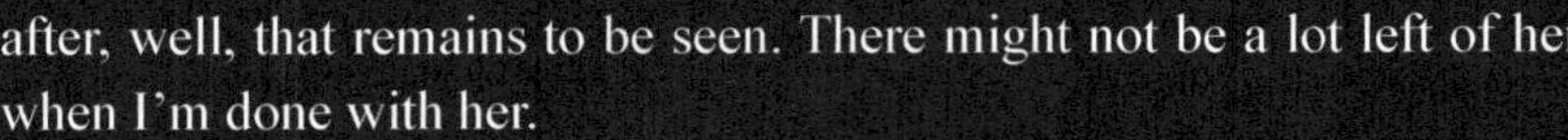

after, well, that remains to be seen. There might not be a lot left of her when I'm done with her.

"I mean it," she continues. "People shouldn't be mixing blood. You need to get me to the hospital."

"Not happening, wife," I bark, dropping her hand.

I stand and move to the sink, washing my own hands thoroughly before cleaning my own wound and bandaging it. Eve remains motionless, watching me with her storm-gray eyes.

"You have fifteen minutes to clean yourself up," I tell her, leaning against the counter. "There's soap, shampoo, towels in here. Use what you need."

Her eyes narrow. "And if I refuse?"

I smile thinly. "I don't see why you'd refuse. But if you like having my cum on your inner thigh that much, be my guest."

She swallows hard, throat bobbing.

"Only ten minutes now," I tell her, pulling my phone from the jeans on the floor and setting a timer. "Starting now."

With my phone in hand, I turn to leave, closing the door behind me so she can shower in peace. Back in the bedroom, I throw on a pair of gray sweats and a white tee. Then I refill her water bowl and set it back in the cage, adding a box of cookies and a can of Coke beside it.

That done, I make myself a coffee, and for a moment, I consider offering her one. But I decide against it since she'd probably just try to throw it in my face.

Just as I take my first sip, my phone buzzes. Timer's up. I head back toward the bathroom and open the door without knocking.

Eve's standing at the sink, only covered by a small towel while she brushes her teeth. The moment I step inside, she lets the fabric fall to the floor and finishes up.

"Let's go," I say.

She eyes the steamy cup of coffee in my hand, longing washing across her features. "I'd offer you coffee," I say, raising the cup in a mock salute, "but I'm pretty sure you'd try to throw it in my face."

Laughing, she walks right by me, shoulders squared despite her nudity. Her round ass jiggles with every step, making me want to bite the flesh just to see what she tastes like.

"You know you can't keep me here forever, right?" she asks as she walks back into the cage. "People will look for me. They'll know something happened. They'll—"

"No one's looking for you, Eve." I lock the cage and sit down on my bed, taking a sip of my coffee. "Your neighbor has already called the police to report you missing. Left a very convincing note saying you'd been acting strange lately. Mentioned your recent visit to the psych ward."

The color drains from her face. "That's… that's not true. I've never been—"

"You weren't," I agree. "But now you are. Your file's been updated. History rewritten. And you, my dear Bride, have no idea how many hands were paid to hold that pen."

She stares at me. "Like that's going to work. The police will know I'm not missing when people start posting pictures of the wedding on social media," she snaps.

I throw my head back and laugh loudly. "Oh, my sweet wife, that's not happening."

"Why not?"

Shooting her a wicked grin, I reply, "Because no one is allowed phones or tablets on the island. You wouldn't believe the lengths my brother has gone to make sure no one can sneak a device in. And if someone succeeds, there are signal jammers all over the place."

"What? No, you're lying." Disbelief is written all over her features.

I drink more of my coffee before I carry on. "The only devices are staff owned, and no one is posting anything without my brother or sister-in-law's approval."

Something like horror dawns in her eyes. "You planned this. All of it."

"For months." I don't bother hiding the satisfaction in my voice. "Every detail, every contingency. You're not the first person to disappear in this city, Eve. You won't be the last."

Her face contorts with renewed fury. She slams her hands against the bars again, rattling the cage with surprising strength. "Let me out! Let

me OUT!"

When screaming doesn't work, she tries a new tactic.

Her foot knocks the water bowl with precise, deliberate force. Not enough to flip it—just enough to send a ripple across the surface and slosh water onto the mat. Then again. Harder. The sound of it slamming into the bars echoes through the room like punctuation.

I continue to drink while observing her tantrum with bone-deep satisfaction. "Are you done?" I ask in a bored tone.

"Not even close," Eve hisses as she brings her foot down on the box of cookies.

Then, with a sound halfway between a sob and a snarl, she continues to stomp on the cardboard until it gives out, crumbs spilling everywhere. She grinds them into the carpet with her heel, eyes locked on mine like she's daring me to do something about it.

The box is gone, but she keeps stomping, like destroying one thing isn't enough to bleed out what's boiling inside her.

"You shouldn't waste food," I observe dryly, setting my now empty coffee cup on the nightstand. "Some people would kill for any food at all."

She grinds her teeth together. "Oh, yeah? What would you know about people struggling, Jack? Your family has everything. You've never gone hungry a day in your life."

"Neither have you," I reply. "But for your information, I'm actually a pretty nice guy. I even volunteer once a month." I don't tell her I only began after my short death. There's nothing like having your heart stop to make you see the world in a different light.

"A nice guy wouldn't keep a woman locked in a fucking cage," she seethes.

I lift the bottle and drink deep, watching her shoulders heave and her face turn redder by the second. "I didn't say I would be nice to *you*," I correct. "But if you think this isn't nice, I can always move the cage outside. The fact you're sheltered, given food and water, is the extent of my niceness to you."

Eve begins kicking the bars systematically, each impact creating a dull metallic thud that reverberates through the room. The noise is repetitive, deliberate—designed to provoke a response. To force me to acknowledge her, to engage with her fury.

I let her continue until the urge to drink myself into oblivion overtakes me, and I get a bottle from the kitchen. Sitting my ass back in the chair, I continue to watch her as I light a cigarette, taking a long drag.

Half the bottle's gone and my throat's raw from chain-smoking when I rasp her name. But she doesn't acknowledge me or stop.

"Eve." My voice cuts through her noise like a blade. "That's enough."

She kicks harder, glaring up at me with defiance burning in her eyes. "Fuck you. Fuck your cage. Fuck your—"

"Keep that up, and I'll gag and hogtie you," I warn.

Her foot freezes mid-kick.

"I'll bind your limbs to the cage itself. You won't be able to move. To scratch. To kick. Just lie there, completely immobilized until I decide to free you." I pause, letting the image sink in. "Is that what you want?"

The silence that follows is absolute. Even her breathing seems to still.

"I didn't think so." I straighten, moving to the light switch by the door. The room plunges into darkness as I flick the switch.

Returning to the chair, I settle into the leather. The silence that follows her hours-long tantrum is the kind that makes you believe in higher powers. Almost.

I light another cigarette, washing the smoke down with another pull from the bottle.

"One day, I'll kill you for this." Her voice drifts through the darkness, barely above a whisper. "I've survived bigger monsters than you, Jack. And when I get out of here, I'll kill you."

I smile into the dark, not bothering to open my eyes. "I know you'll try."

The silence stretches between us, thick with unspoken threats and promises. I hope she keeps trying. Hope she never shuts the fuck up or goes still, because the day she stops threatening to kill me is the day I know I've broken her for good.

"And if we're both lucky, you might succeed," I rasp, keeping my eyes on her silhouette. The longer I sit here, the better I can see her. Well, her outline and movements.

"You know this won't last, right?" She throws her hair over her shoulder, naked and unafraid. "People will come. They'll find me. They'll—"

"Disappear too," I finish. "Anyone who comes for you will wish they hadn't."

CHAPTER 15

The Bride

Hunger claws at my insides like a living thing, scraping against my ribs from within. My stomach no longer growls—it's moved beyond that to a silent, hollow ache that pulses with each heartbeat.

The metal bars pressed against my back have gone from cold to warm to cold again as night became day became night. Three days. Seventy-two hours of captivity marked by bathroom breaks, daily showers, and the slow-building certainty that I will not die here.

Not in this cage. Not at his hands.

I shift on the thin blanket he gave me yesterday, the only barrier between my naked body and the carpeted floor. The fabric has absorbed my sweat, my tears, and probably part of my soul.

The stench of confinement clings to my skin like mildew—like something inside me has begun to rot in this cage, and I'm still breathing through it.

Every inhale tastes faintly of stale air and metal, and it coats my tongue until I can't remember what clean air feels like. A body is just a vessel. Mine is becoming a mausoleum.

Every muscle aches from curling on myself to conserve heat, every joint stiff from too many hours in the same narrow space. The blanket

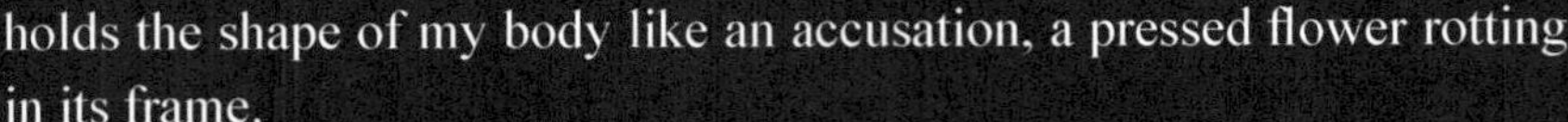

holds the shape of my body like an accusation, a pressed flower rotting in its frame.

Yesterday, I ate two granola bars after inspecting the wrappers for tampering—pressing along the seams, examining the glue, checking for needle marks. I still remember how badly my hands shook as I tore them open.

The sweetness hit my tongue like a drug, and I had to force myself to eat slowly, to savor what might be my only meal for another day. I won't beg for more. I refuse to give him that power.

Jack sits in the chair by the window, a cigarette dangling from his lips. Smoke curls around his face like a living veil, obscuring his features in a gray haze. The bottle beside him is almost empty, and his movements have the loose, unpredictable quality of a man several drinks in.

He mutters to himself occasionally—fragments about consequences and deserving *this*—whatever *this* is. His wedding ring catches the light when he lifts the bottle to his lips. We're married. The thought still feels foreign, impossible.

And if I'm completely honest, scary in a bad way.

"My dad used to drink like that," I say, breaking the silence between us. My voice sounds strange after hours without use—rough, but steadier than I expected. "He'd go through a bottle a night after my mother died."

"Don't engage unless necessary," my father's voice whispers in my memory. *"Observe first. Words give away leverage."*

He taught me that silence is a form of control. If you want to understand someone, watch them when they think no one's looking. Watch long enough, and patterns emerge. Weaknesses reveal themselves.

Jack's eyes flick toward me, narrowing slightly. "Don't remember asking about your daddy issues," he says, but there's something in his tone—a flicker of interest beneath the contempt.

I mentally catalog the data point. *Subject responds to family references. Potential emotional trigger.*

"Just making conversation," I shrug, careful to keep my posture relaxed despite the ache in my shoulders. "Three days is a long time to sit with nothing to do."

He takes another long drag of his cigarette, exhaling smoke in my direction. "You weren't so chatty yesterday. Or the day before." His eyes track over my body, clinical rather than lustful. Assessing.

"I was still processing being kidnapped and caged like an animal then," I reply, keeping my tone even. "Today I'm bored."

Jack laughs, a sharp, bitter sound with no humor in it. "Bored," he repeats. He leans forward, elbows on his knees. "You're a strange fucking woman, Eve."

I tilt my head slightly. "And you're a strange fucking captor. Most kidnappers have demands. Ransom. Sexual gratification." I pause, watching him carefully. "What do you want from me, Jack?"

"Justice," he says automatically, too quickly. A rehearsed answer that's most definitely not the whole truth.

I file this away. "For what?" I push, gently but persistently.

His jaw tightens, a muscle jumping beneath the stubble. "You know for what."

"Ruby," I say softly. Another data point; *his tension spikes when his sister is mentioned.* "I didn't kill her, Jack."

"You let her die." The bottle clanks against the wood as he sets it down too hard. "You knew what was happening. What Valentine was planning. And you did nothing."

I remain silent for a moment, letting his accusation hang in the air between us. His breathing has quickened, and the rhythm of his smoking has accelerated. He draws harder, holds the smoke longer, like he's keeping the words he wants to spit from crossing the bars between us.

Controlled anger.

"So this is punishment," I observe, gesturing at the cage with one hand. "Not justice. There's a difference."

Jack stands abruptly, crossing to the cage in three long strides. He crouches down, bringing his face level with mine, separated only by the metal bars. "What's the difference, Dr. Death?" he asks, voice dangerously soft. "Educate me."

I don't flinch, though every instinct screams to back away from the predator in front of me. "Justice restores balance," I explain, meeting his

gaze steadily. "Punishment is about power. About making yourself feel better."

A flash of something crosses his face—uncertainty, or perhaps recognition. "And what makes you think I want to feel better?"

Excellent question. *The subject demonstrates self-awareness. More complex than the initial assessment.*

It's the first time I've really seen him without a mask—metaphorically speaking, of course. There's no threat in his voice, no performance—only something raw and unguarded that slips through before he can catch it.

"Because you're drinking yourself into oblivion every day," I point out. "Because you're chain-smoking even though I've seen the nicotine patches in your bathroom cabinet. Alcohol and nicotine are two of the most common vices known to soothe people."

His eyes widen slightly as though he's surprised I've noticed that much. Or maybe it's because I've dared to voice it, to pull something private into the open where he can't hide behind smoke and liquor.

The silence stretches between us, taut as piano wire, vibrating with all the things he'll never admit out loud. I can almost hear them, those words rotting at the back of his throat, waiting for something sharp enough to cut them loose.

"Did you know there's an urban myth that common shop-bought cigarettes have the same diameter as the average female nipple?" I ask, which gets his attention. "Some people speculate it's a clever ruse by the cigarette companies. A way to make every drag a ghost of suckling. Triggering the same comfort response we learned at our mother's breast."

I let the words linger, watching his gaze drop to my breasts and catch there, like something in him has snagged on the image. His breathing shifts—not louder, but slower, heavier. As if he's aware I'm watching the way he looks at me.

"Maybe it's just a myth. But your vices all start with your mouth, Jack. You've trained yourself to crave things you can put to your lips. Nicotine, alcohol, maybe even people. It's not just the hit you're after. It's the way it soothes something in you… even if it never lasts."

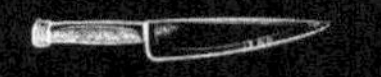

His mouth curves, but it's not a smile—it's the kind of expression that warns you not to mistake amusement for softness. "Careful, Little Bride," he says, voice low. "You keep talking like that, I might have to prove how many other ways this mouth can keep itself busy."

"Do you want to talk about it?" I ask softly, changing tactics. "I'm a good listener."

He blinks, and for just a second, I glimpse the broken man beneath the monster—the grieving brother, the lost soul. Then the mask slips back into place, and he's standing, moving away from the cage.

"Nice try," he says, voice hardening again. "But I'm not going to sit here and pour my heart out to you like we're at a fucking slumber party."

But he already has, just a little. And now I know, Jack Knight is still in the clutches of grief. Deep, catastrophic grief. The kind that alcohol can't touch, that revenge can't fill. He didn't marry me just to punish me. He did it because an enemy in a cage is better than solitude.

I watch him return to his chair, to his bottle and his cigarettes. To his slow self-destruction. The room watches us like a silent confessor while shadows crawl slowly along the walls. This house isn't haunted by ghosts—it's haunted by us.

Somewhere beneath my hunger and my fear, a cold certainty forms, and a plan takes shape. I will be the wife he never expected. I will be the one person who sees through his rage to the broken man beneath.

And when he finally trusts me—when he believes he's broken me—I will destroy him with the same methodical precision my father taught me to use in dissecting the human mind.

Jack thinks he's the captor and I'm the captive. But cages work both ways. And I've just begun my study of the creature on the other side of these bars.

I let ten minutes pass in silence, watching Jack return to his brooding. I'm so exhausted I almost fall asleep while I watch him lower his guard. He's not the only one who has barely been sleeping.

At first, it was the fear of what he'd do to me that kept me awake. But after he fell asleep while smoking, I've been forcing myself to stay awake when he passes out. Just in case.

"So what now, Dr. Death?" he drawls. "No longer bored?"

I shrug. "I am, but you don't seem like you want to talk."

"You could tell me about your tattoo," he says. He points at the ink wrapped around my upper right thigh, making me look down at the black garter I love so much.

It's both feminine and gothic in its design. The lace is finely detailed, inked with the illusion of layered texture, scalloped edges, mesh threading, and shadowed depth.

At the front, centered over the strongest part of the muscle, is a large black satin bow with its tails curling down my skin to mid-thigh. Tiny inked beads and charms dangle beneath the lace, delicate but exact. The tattoo is both decorative and coverage.

Tilting my head to the side, I ask, "Will you tell me about yours?"

From what I've seen, Jack has only one tattoo. A pumpkin that lives on his left arm, specifically on his deltoid. It's gothic, jagged, orange, and mean-looking. When I first noticed it, I almost scoffed out loud. But it's kind of growing on me. Wait… no. I mean that it suits him. That's what I mean.

"Not a fucking chance," he scoffs.

I nod, expecting as much.

Silence stretches between us again, but there's something calm about it. It's not as heavy as before, and there's no menace. It just is. That must mean his guard is lowering, the liquor's doing its work. Time to push him some more.

CHAPTER 16

The Bride

I shift on the blanket, leaning back against the bars in a seemingly casual movement that allows me to pull my knees up and let them fall open. The position exposes me completely. Vulnerable. Inviting. A trap baited with flesh and the illusion of surrender.

When his eyes drift toward me, I stretch, arching my back just enough to push my breasts forward. A performance beginning without fanfare, a weapon deploying without sound.

His gaze catches on my body like a hook. I pretend not to notice, keeping my eyes half-closed as my hand drifts to my breast. My fingers trace the curve methodically, like I'm following a diagram rather than desire.

I circle my nipple once, twice, applying precise pressure until it hardens beneath my touch. The gasp that escapes my lips is calculated, pitched to carry across the room.

Jack shifts in his chair. "What are you doing?" His voice is rougher than before, the words scraping out of his throat.

Rather than answering, I pinch my nipple between thumb and forefinger, hard enough to make myself inhale sharply. My other hand slides down my stomach in a slow, deliberate path. Since this is strategy and not arousal, I'm not wet yet.

I part my folds anyway, peeling myself open for him like a specimen under glass. Let him think I'm offering up some fragile part of myself; in truth, I'm mapping his reactions like a chart, marking each flicker in his eyes as if it's a landmark on a map I'll use to find my way out.

"What does it look like?" I finally reply, voice pitched low. "I'm bored. And you've left me with limited entertainment options."

He crushes the cigarette into the ashtray, the movement too forceful. "You think this is a game?" But he doesn't look away, doesn't tell me to stop.

My fingers move in mechanical circles, clinical and detached, like I'm performing a medical procedure on myself. The sensation is distant at first, pressure without pleasure, contact without context.

I keep my eyes on Jack, watching as he leans forward, elbows on his knees. His pupils dilate. His breathing changes. Power shifts in incremental degrees.

"Not a game," I murmur, allowing a slight tremor into my voice. "A need."

He stands, moving to the foot of the bed where he can watch me more clearly. The bulge in his sweatpants is unmistakable now. "A need," he repeats, his hand drifting to adjust himself. "And you think I'll just watch while you take care of it?"

I tilt my head, letting my hair cascade over one shoulder. "Isn't that what you want? All you do is watch me. Why stop now?"

Something flashes in his green eyes. Maybe he recognizes the manipulation, but it doesn't matter. Primal wins. His hand moves to the waistband of his sweatpants, pushing them low enough that I catch a shadowed glimpse of the base, the heavy weight of him in his palm.

I hate the way my pulse jumps. Hate more that he probably sees it in the way my breathing shifts.

He doesn't give me a second to pretend I'm not staring. "Look at it," he commands slowly. "This is what you've been teasing for three days, Little Bride. Every sigh, every glare, every fucking breath in that cage has kept me so fucking hard."

Jack strokes himself once, twice, keeping most of his cock hidden by his grip. My eyes track the movement without permission. I tell myself it's analysis, but my clit throbs and wetness coats my folds for reasons that have nothing to do with strategy.

"Tell me, Dr. Death, have you been missing my cock? Imagined what it would be like to taste it?"

My mouth curves in the barest smile. "You think pretty highly of yourself."

He doesn't take the bait. "Don't lie. Not when you've already parted your thighs for me." His gaze drops to my fingers. "Circle slower. I want to see you beg without using the word."

I obey, but I make my fingers lazier than they need to be, keeping my expression blank. If he wants something from me, he can work for it.

My breath still hitches, the friction making me shift in spite of myself. He notices—of course he notices—and smirks. "That's it. Let it hurt a little. Makes the relief sweeter when I let you come."

"Let me?" I echo, my tone dry but thinner than I'd like.

He squeezes himself, the sound of skin on skin indecent in the quiet room. "You're not touching yourself for you. You're doing it for me. Say it."

I meet his stare, lips pressed together in silent refusal.

He stops moving altogether. "Say it, or I stop."

My fingers pause, my clit throbbing in protest at the sudden stillness. I hate that he's right, that I want the motion back enough to give him the word.

His grip loosens, and this time he drags his hand all the way down, baring himself completely. I freeze as his entire length comes into view. There, on the underside of his shaft, is a Jacob's Ladder—seven silver rungs climbing the underside of his cock. I blink like I've missed something obvious, because I did.

He fucked me with that in front of an audience, and I was too high on panic and adrenaline and shame to register any of it. I didn't feel the metal. Or maybe I did, but I was too preoccupied to really notice. God, how didn't I notice? I want to remember how it felt, and I hate that I can't.

"If you're going to touch yourself for me, then stop playing, doc," he

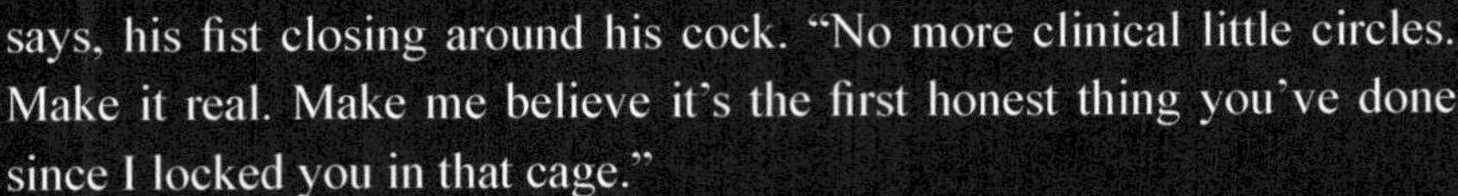

says, his fist closing around his cock. "No more clinical little circles. Make it real. Make me believe it's the first honest thing you've done since I locked you in that cage."

I comply, pressing harder, circling faster. My body responds despite myself, a treacherous warmth building between my legs. The pressure starts as nothing, just friction and wet sound—but then it grows. I tell myself I can ignore it. I don't. My body betrays me one pulse at a time.

Wetness forms, easing the friction of my fingers. My breathing quickens—no longer performance, but genuine response. This wasn't part of the plan. I'm supposed to be in control.

"Wider," Jack growls, stroking himself with long, measured pulls. "Let me see what I own."

I shake my head.

"Keep pretending, and I'll fuck the truth out of you," he snarls. "You're dripping for the man who caged you. For your husband."

The words should disgust me. Should make me recoil. Instead, they send a jolt of heat through my core, and I find myself obeying—pulling my knees back further, opening myself completely to his gaze. My fingers find my clit, and the first real spark of pleasure makes me gasp.

"That's it," he murmurs, his pace matching mine. "Show me how that pretty cunt gets off."

My strategy is slipping away, dissolving under the unexpected surge of sensation. The cage feels smaller now, not because of the bars, but because every inch of me is pulled toward the place where my fingers meet my skin, where his eyes meet mine.

I've underestimated the power of touch after days of deprivation, the way my body would betray me at the first real stimulation. My hips rise to meet my hand, no longer a calculated movement but an instinctive seeking.

"You're so fucking wet," Jack observes, voice dropping lower. "Pinch your clit. I want to see you make yourself come."

I follow his instruction without thinking, applying pressure that sends a sharp bolt of pleasure-pain up my spine. A moan escapes me— unplanned, unbidden. My head falls back against the bars, eyes closing as my fingers work faster, deeper.

"Look at me," he demands. "I want to see your eyes when you come. I want you to know exactly who you're performing for."

My eyes snap open, meeting his dark gaze. He's fully hard now, the piercings rising and falling with each stroke of his hand. Pre-cum beads at the tip, catching the light. His lips are parted, breath coming faster, but his eyes remain focused.

"Say my name," he commands. "Tell me who's making you feel this."

"Jack," I gasp, the word torn from my throat as pleasure builds toward an inevitable peak. No longer pretending, no longer calculating. Just raw need consuming strategy like fire through paper. "Jack, please—"

"Please what?" His hand moves faster now, his cock slick and rigid in his grip. "Tell me what you need."

"Let me come," I beg, the words spilling out unbidden. "Let me—"

"Show me," he growls. "Come for me like a good little wife. Let me see exactly what kind of filthy thing I've locked in my cage."

The command triggers something primal in me, something beyond thought or plan. My back arches off the bars as pleasure crests and breaks, washing through me in violent waves. I cry out his name, fingers working desperately as my thighs shake with the force of my release.

It's messy, undignified—nothing like the controlled performance I had planned.

Through the haze of my orgasm, I see Jack moving closer, his hand still working his cock with brutal efficiency. He reaches the bars just as I'm coming down, still trembling with aftershocks.

"Come here," he says, voice tight with impending release. "I want you against the bars."

I move forward on shaking limbs, pressing my breasts against the cold metal.

Jack groans low and dark, his release hitting my chest in heated, claiming streaks. He keeps stroking, slower now—rubbing the last of his cum between my breasts with the head of his cock, smearing it like war paint.

His eyes stay locked on mine while he paints me, like the act itself is

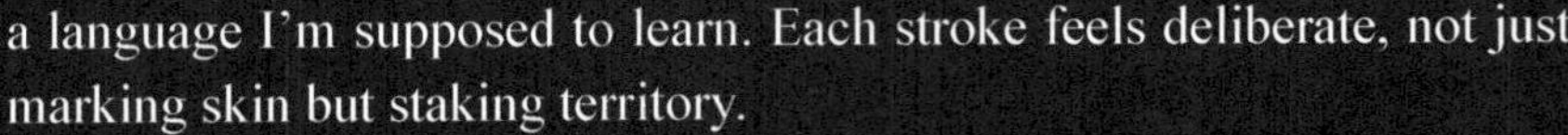

a language I'm supposed to learn. Each stroke feels deliberate, not just marking skin but staking territory.

"Mine," he breathes, the word barely audible as the last pulses subside. It doesn't sound like a claim; it sounds like a truth he's always known. "Fucking mine."

I don't know why that primal word makes my insides turn to liquid, but it does. It slides under my skin like heat and possession all at once. He doesn't want me, and I don't want him to want me. But my body is a traitor, reacting to his voice as if it's tuned to the same frequency.

That orgasm was one of the best I've had in my life, and it was all because of his filthy commands and the lust written all over his face.

Jack reaches between the bars, swiping his thumb through his cum on my chest, then smears it across my lips like he's anointing me. "Stick your tongue out," he demands in a low tone. "And lick my cum from your manipulative lips, Little Bride."

My jaw obeys before my pride can catch up. My tongue flicks out, and I lick the taste of him from my lips like it's mine to crave. Jesus, I have no idea what just possessed me to do that, but judging by the glint in his green eyes, he's pleased.

We stay frozen like that, both panting, both sticky with the evidence of what just happened. The remainder of his jizz cools on my skin like a seal—tacky, pungent, obscene. More binding than the ring still strangling my finger.

The silence that follows feels too loud, pressing against my ears until I'm certain I can hear my own heartbeat in it—like the air itself is recoiling from what we just did.

I tell myself I've won this round—that I've begun the process of making him dependent on me, of blurring the lines between captor and captive.

That this was all part of my strategy. But as I sink back onto my blanket, his cum still dripping between my breasts, I'm no longer certain who's manipulating whom.

His cum starts to dry against my chest, tacky and warm. I resist the urge to wipe it off. Not because I want to keep it—but because I don't want him to see I care that it's there.

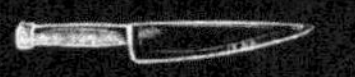

"You're not manipulating me," he says between gritted teeth. "You're feeding me, Little Bride. Don't confuse the two."

There goes the illusion that I had the upper hand. "Is that so?" I deadpan, arching an eyebrow. I won't let him see just how much the reality of those words stings.

Jack nods as he tucks himself away. "Yes, that's so. And the sooner you come to terms with it, the better it'll be for the both of us."

I just scoff.

"You want out?" he asks, tucking himself back into his pants with a cold smile. "Fine. And since you're so desperate to put on a show, you'll do it where you belong. On a fucking stage back at the Sanctuary."

A cruel smirk plays on his lips, and it doesn't disappear when he calls his brother, saying we'll be there tomorrow night.

Fuck… what did I just start?

CHAPTER 17

The Trickster

The Sanctuary looms before us, a playground for the twisted and curious. Eve doesn't stumble as we approach the entrance, but I can feel the tension vibrating through her body where my hand presses against the small of her back.

Her dress is thin enough that I can feel the heat of her skin and the subtle ridge of her spine through it. My fingers dig in slightly, not enough to bruise—not yet—but enough to remind her who she belongs to.

The night air carries the scent of incense and wet earth, mingling with the artificial fog that billows around our ankles, thick as cream and cold as a grave.

"Look at that line," Eve says, her voice carefully neutral. "We'll be waiting forever."

I chuckle, low and close to her ear. "That queue isn't for us, wife." With those words, I guide her past the waiting people, where eager patrons in their Halloween finery wait like cattle for slaughter.

My hand slides lower, resting just above the curve of her ass as we approach a side entrance flanked by two masked guards.

One nods, stepping aside. "Mr. Knight."

"Call me Jack," I reply curtly. "Mr. Knight is my brother."

The fog thickens as we step through, enveloping us in a cocoon of white that obscures everything beyond arm's length. Eve's breathing changes—shorter, more controlled—and I can almost taste her effort to appear unfazed.

"What time is it?" she asks suddenly, turning her face toward mine. Her eyes are sharp, analytical even in the gloom.

"Why do you need to know?" I counter, pressing my thumb into the divot at the base of her spine.

"Because I'd like to have some sense of how long I'll be enduring this." Her tone is acidic, but I catch the small flutter of her pulse at the base of her throat.

"You'll know when I want you to know."

She turns away from me, scanning the crowd that materializes through the fog. A man passes close by—some standard-issue hipster in a vintage coat—and Eve reaches out, catching his sleeve.

"Excuse me, do you have the time?" she asks, her voice honey-sweet.

"Sure I do." He shoots her a sleazy grin while checking out her cleavage. Then he leans closer, brushing one hand against the curve of her breast as he turns his wrist, presumably to check the time.

With a low growl, I step between them and seize his wrist—the one that dared touch her. Bone grinds under my grip, his breath hissing through clenched teeth. I twist until I hear the first sharp crack. His knees buckle.

"My wife doesn't need the time," I bark, not bothering to mask the threat in my voice. "And you don't need to breathe the same air as her."

The man's eyes widen, panic flooding them. "I was just trying to—"

I slam my fist into his gut, folding him like paper. "Like I give a flying fuck what you were trying to do." I let him drop into the fog like discarded trash. "Walk away before I decide to finish the job."

"Oh, give it a rest, Jack," Eve sighs, stepping over the man without a glance. Her voice drips with bored disdain, like she's scolding me for kicking over a trash can instead of dismantling someone's wrist.

My cock twitches at the sheer ice in her tone, but it's the restraint in

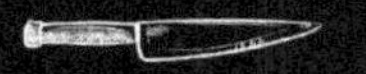

her face that really gets me—like she's weathered worse and knows exactly how to bury it. I want to crack that composure wide open... but first, I'll remind her exactly who she's dealing with.

Reaching for her arm, I spin her around to face me. Her eyes narrow to steel-gray slits, but I just smirk. "If I don't want you to know the time," I say, tracing a finger along her jawline, "you won't. Simple as that."

Her nostrils flare slightly—a tiny tell that speaks volumes about the rage she's containing. "Controlling even the most basic information. How predictable."

"And yet you still asked a stranger," I reply, my hand sliding up to cup the back of her neck. "How predictable."

"So?" she challenges, baring her teeth.

"Are you enjoying yourself?" I ask, my voice low and edged with danger. "Because if you want to keep tasting freedom, you really need to stop touching other men." Before she can answer, I pull her along, almost making her stumble in her high heels.

The crowd parts as we move deeper into the Sanctuary grounds. Ahead, a structure materializes from the mist—a tunnel mouth constructed of what appears to be bone and sinew, though I know it's all carefully crafted synthetics.

A neon sign hangs above, announcing this is the ***Tunnel of Screams.*** But we're not going there tonight.

We've barely made it fifty yards from the Tunnel when Eve's stride falters. Her head turns, focus caught by something through the drifting fog. I follow her gaze to a small booth draped in black velvet, set apart from the main attractions.

Blood-red candles burn in iron holders, their flames perfectly still despite the night breeze. Their light illuminates a hand-painted sign that reads, ***Fate reads you as you read the cards.***

Eve's pupils dilate slightly, and I decide to indulge her curiosity. After all, knowing what she seeks might give me more to use against her later.

"Want to know your future, wife?" I ask, my voice silky with mock concern. "Or are you hoping to find out when you'll escape me?"

Eve's shoulders stiffen under my touch. "Perhaps I just want to know how this story ends," she replies, her tone carefully measured. "Whether the monster gets his comeuppance."

I laugh, sliding my hand to the nape of her neck. "Let's find out together, shall we?"

Inside, the air is thick with incense—frankincense and myrrh, biblical scents of death and divinity. The space is smaller than it appeared from outside, forcing Eve to stand close enough that I feel the heat radiating from her body.

The fortune teller sits hunched behind a small table covered in black silk. Her face is a roadmap of wrinkles. A tattered hood casts her eyes in shadow, but I catch glimpses of them when she moves—pale, almost colorless, like river stones worn smooth by time.

Her gnarled fingers extend toward us, beckoning. "I've been waiting," she says, her voice surprisingly strong and clear. "The cards told me you would come tonight."

Eve shifts her weight, her skepticism almost palpable. "Did they tell you our names too?" she asks.

The crone smiles, revealing teeth too perfect for her ancient face. "Names are masks we wear for others, Eve," she says.

At my side, my wife tries her best not to react as the fortune teller casually throws out her name.

"The cards know you by what lies beneath," the old woman finishes. She gestures for us to sit. There's only one chair, low and close to the table.

I sit down before pulling Eve onto my lap like she belongs there. She stiffens, but I cage her in with an arm around her waist, forcing her to face the crone across the narrow strip of black silk. From here, I can feel every shallow breath she takes.

Before I can respond, she pulls a deck from nowhere—a fluid movement that my eyes can't quite track. The cards are larger than standard tarot, their backs decorated with an intricate design of intertwined thorns and roses.

"Both of you," she commands, laying the deck on the table. "Touch the cards together. They must taste your bond."

I place my hand on the deck first, then grasp Eve's wrist with my other hand, pulling her palm down beside mine. The cards feel warm, almost alive, beneath our touch. Eve tries to pull away, but I hold her there, fingers pressing into the soft skin of her inner wrist where her pulse jumps like a trapped bird.

"That's enough," the fortune teller says after a moment that stretches too long. She takes the deck back, shuffling with a dexterity that belies her apparent age.

The first card slaps down on the table. The Tower—a lightning-struck structure with bodies falling through flames.

Her gaze sharpens. "Some towers fall by accident, others because the heir at their table decided they should burn. Even now, the bones of the man who built yours sit where you can see them every day... to remind you the cage is gone, but never forgotten."

Eve's shoulder twitches against my chest, like she wants to turn around but thinks better of it. I wonder if she thinks the card's about me.

It's not—it can't be. My dad's gone, but he was killed by Nick and Carolina, not me. And as far as I know, no one kept any of his remains. He's rotting in the family mausoleum.

The old woman lays a second card beside it. The Devil—a horned figure with a man and woman chained at its feet.

"Bondage," she continues, her pale eyes flicking between us. "Not just of the body, but of the soul. Chains you both forged willingly. His out of revenge, yours out of hunger for the dark. Each link is both a choice and a lock. And now there is no key."

Eve's breathing quickens slightly, and she presses her nails into my thigh. Whether to steady herself or claw her way free, I can't tell. I shift my hand to her stomach, holding her in place, feeling the shallow drag of her breath against my palm.

It's not lost on me that where my revenge is a negative, my Little Bride's curiosity and hunger for the dark is a positive. How fucking ironic.

"I didn't choose this," Eve says, voice low but steady.

The crone's eyes fix on her. "Didn't you? You followed the masked man of your own volition—"

Whirling on me, Eve stabs her finger into my chest. "Did you tell her that? That I followed you here?"

The woman cackles. "The cards told me, dear. They know what's in your heart." She pauses for a beat. "You let him defile you, and you loved it even though you claim to hate it. Is this not your heart's desire, Eve? To be free of the shackles your father bound around you? To be free of—"

"Please stop," Eve begs, turning away from me again. Her face is down-turned as though she's ashamed by what the fortune teller is saying.

"What else?" I demand sharply, not liking how uncomfortable this is clearly making my wife.

With a sharp nod, the old woman draws the third card; Death.

"Not an ending," the fortune teller says, "but a transformation. Blood has been spilled, and more will follow. The question is whose, and whether either of you will survive what you're turning each other into."

Eve exhales through her nose, a sound too sharp to be a sigh. I feel it in the way her back muscles tighten against my chest. My own jaw locks—I tell myself it's just theatrics, but the card's image still burns behind my eyes.

Surviving each other… the thought shouldn't interest me, but it does. What would be left of her if she did? What would be left of me if she didn't?

I feel a trickle of genuine unease crawl up my spine. This is theater, like everything else at the Sanctuary—carefully researched, designed to unsettle—but something in the woman's gaze feels too knowing, too precise.

"The cards show what already exists inside you," she continues, laying down a fourth card. The Lovers—but inverted, the figures separated by a chasm of flame.

"A union built on revenge," she says. "Two souls tethered not by love but by debt and desire. Every choice made for the wrong reason will come back to collect its price." Her finger traces the divide between the figures. "Your souls are tethered now. One cannot bleed without the other tasting iron."

The words hang between us like smoke, seeping into every crack. I feel her spine straighten against me, defiant, but she doesn't pull away. She isn't running. Not from me, not from this. That knowledge settles in my gut like a claim.

Eve seeking danger. My need for ruin. Two poisons poured into the same cup.

Her head tilts the smallest fraction toward mine, not enough for the crone to notice, but enough for me to feel the brush of her hair against my jaw. It isn't closeness—it's a dare, a silent acknowledgment that she knows exactly what we are.

Eve's fingers twitch against the table. I catch the micro-expression that crosses her face—surprise followed by something deeper, more troubled.

"Blood bonds," the fortune teller continues, "once formed, cannot be broken. Not by distance. Not by death. What flows between you now will flow forever."

"Poetic," I say, forcing a dismissive tone, "but hardly specific. This could apply to anyone."

The crone's eyes cut to me, sharp as blades. "Could it, Jack Knight? Could it apply to the brother who failed to save his sister? To the man who punishes the innocent for his own failings?"

My hand tightens on Eve's wrist, hard enough that she winces. The fortune teller sees it and smiles, a knowing curve of lips that makes my skin crawl.

She draws a final card, placing it with deliberate slowness. The Hanged Man—but reversed, the suspended figure twisting unnaturally.

"The curse only matters because you let it," she says, eyes never leaving mine. "It consumed your sister, and now you're letting it consume you. And you…" her gaze cuts to Eve "… will drink his ghosts until they rot your veins. By the time you notice the taste, you'll be too far gone. This is your warning from fate."

Eve's fingers flex against the table like she's deciding whether to shove the cards away. My thigh under her tenses, ready to keep her seated if she does. I can feel her pulse through every point where we touch.

I keep rolling the words over in my mind. Rot in her veins and ghosts in mine. I know what mine means, but what did my Little Bride do? Or is this about the people she didn't protect from Valentine fucking Grant?

The cards lay between us like evidence, each image a wound the crone pressed her finger into. Whether she believes her own words or just knows which scars to touch, the result is the same—Eve's pulse is racing, and mine is too.

I stand abruptly, pulling Eve up with me. The table rocks, nearly toppling the candles. "We're done here," I say, throwing down bills without counting them.

The fortune teller doesn't reach for the money. "You'll return," she says simply. "Both of you will be back."

CHAPTER 18

The Trickster

I drag Eve from the booth, not caring if I hurt her. The night air hits us like a slap, cold after the incense-thick interior. The fog seems to have thickened, wrapping around us in tendrils that cling to our clothes and skin.

Her stomach growls, the sound barely audible above the carnival din but loud enough for me to catch. It's been at least twelve hours since she last ate—my fault, I realize with a detached sort of awareness.

I already know that the hunger pangs aren't enough to break her. Though they add another layer of vulnerability I can exploit, that's not the reason I haven't fed her. I've tried, she just refuses most of what I offer.

A starving performer won't give the show I want, so when I spot a food vendor through the mist, I move us closer. The grill is hissing and popping, releasing the scent of roasting meat that cuts through the artificial fog like a blade.

"Want some?" I ask, nodding toward the stand.

Eve's eyes follow my gesture, and I watch her throat work as she swallows. "No, I'm not hungry," she lies, her pride still intact despite everything.

"Liar," I say, not unkindly. I steer her closer to the vendor, my hand firm on the small of her back. "You'll need your strength for later."

The vendor's stall is draped with strings of tiny orange lights shaped like skulls. Behind the counter, a woman in elaborate Day of the Dead makeup arranges skewers of meat on the grill. The flames leap up, casting grotesque shadows across her painted face.

"We'll take two, please," I tell her, holding up two fingers. She nods, not speaking—part of the Sanctuary's immersive experience.

While we wait, I study Eve in the flickering light. The aftermath of captivity has left its mark on her in the shadows beneath her eyes which are deeper. But it's not enough to hide the fierce vitality to her that's strangely compelling.

Her hair falls in loose waves over her shoulders, the orange ends catching the light like embers I can't look away from no matter how much I try to. With a reluctant sigh, I run my fingers through the soft locks.

"You better not pull any hairs out," she sniffs, which makes me laugh.

The vendor hands over two skewers of meat and vegetables, dripping with a dark, sticky sauce that smells of smoke and spice. I pass one to Eve, our fingers brushing in the exchange. She doesn't pull away immediately—an interesting development.

"Thank you," she says, the words formal and precise.

I guide her to a small standing table away from the main flow of traffic. From here, we can observe the crowd while maintaining a bubble of relative privacy.

Eve takes a careful bite of her food, then closes her eyes briefly, the simple pleasure of eating after deprivation evident in the slight relaxation of her shoulders.

"Is it good?" I ask, watching her mouth as she chews.

She nods, swallowing before answering. "They've achieved the perfect balance of char and tenderness," she explains, examining the skewer with clinical interest. "The smoke compound is artificial, though. Liquid smoke with additional chemicals to enhance the sensory impact."

I laugh, surprised by her analysis. "Most people would just say it tastes good."

Her eyes meet mine, sharp and uncompromising. "That's boring, and it doesn't actually explain anything."

"What do you mean?"

She sighs as if my question is bothersome. "Good is a relative term. You can't compare it or measure it."

I nod. "But you can compare the perfect balance of char and tenderness?"

"Probably not," she shrugs. "But at least it explains why I find it good."

The statement hangs between us, heavy with implication. I take a bite of my own food to avoid responding immediately, letting the flavors bloom on my tongue. She's right about the perfect blend. Damn her.

"How long are you really going to keep me for?" Eve suddenly asks, her gray eyes locked onto my green ones.

Shrugging, I take another bite, not intending to answer her. But when she scoffs and rolls her eyes, I do. "Why? It's not like you have a job you need to get back to."

"What did you just say?" she hisses.

I arch an eyebrow, amused despite myself. "Are you hard of hearing, wife?"

She takes another bite, chews thoughtfully. "So… it was you." It's not a question. "You're the one who made me lose my office space."

"Is that so?" I retort.

"Mhmm, yes, I believe so," she chirps. "And I'm guessing you brought it up in a seemingly innocent question to gauge whether I already knew or not."

Laughing, I nod slowly, impressed with her deduction.

"You might not know this, *husband*, but you have all the finesse of a sledgehammer."

"The fuck does finesse have to do with anything?" I chuckle.

She eats the last of her food, looking away from me and toward the group of people passing us by.

"It's often the best way to reach a desired outcome." Her tone implies it should be obvious.

"And what outcome do you think I desire, Dr. Death?"

Her gaze is steady, unflinching as she looks back at me. "Control. Vengeance. Absolution for your failure to save Ruby." She pauses, watching my reaction. "But mostly distraction from your own pain."

I lean closer, my voice dropping to a dangerous whisper. "You're analyzing the wrong person. Your psychological tricks won't work on me."

"They already are," she counters, her voice equally soft. "You're engaging with me. Conversing. Finding me intellectually stimulating despite yourself."

She's right, which irritates me more than I care to admit. There's something compelling about her mind—sharp, observant, unafraid to cut deep. In another life, under different circumstances, I might have…

I shut down that line of thinking immediately. Eve Mortis is not a woman to be admired. She's the instrument of my sister's destruction, and now, the vessel for my revenge.

"Come on," I command, straightening. "We have places to be."

I dispose of the skewers in a nearby trash receptacle shaped like a grinning skull. Eve wipes her hands on a napkin, the mundane gesture at odds with our surroundings.

For a moment, the scene feels almost normal—a couple sharing a meal at a carnival—until I grip her elbow and pull her back into the flow of the crowd.

We pass vendors selling caramelized apples that smell of burnt sugar and cinnamon, their glossy surfaces reflecting the flickering lights overhead. Eve's gaze lingers on them, but I pull her onward.

Past a contortionist whose body twists into impossible shapes on a small circular stage. The performer's spine bends backward until his head emerges between his own thighs, face painted in a permanent scream.

"They use vagus nerve stimulation to achieve that level of flexibility," Eve murmurs, her scientific mind still cataloging, analyzing. "The pain threshold would be extraordinary."

"Is that professional interest I hear, doctor?" I ask, my thumb tracing small circles on the inside of her elbow where I know her pulse beats close to the surface.

"Professional observation," she corrects, but I feel the slight uptick in her heart rate beneath my fingers.

The path narrows as we approach a section cordoned off with velvet ropes. There's a warning sign flashing. ***Sacrifices only. Explicit content ahead, viewer discretion advised!***

"Sacrifices," Eve murmurs.

"Yeah, the highest tier," I absentmindedly explain. "Most areas are open to Spectators and Shadows as well. But the best ones are only for Sacrifices." I wonder if she knows those are the names for the different ticket holders.

"Right, right, the tiers," she mumbles, unknowingly answering my question.

We walk closer to a passage where two guards in blood-splattered executioner's hoods stand at attention, their axes gleaming dully in the low light.

"This way," I say, nodding to the guards, who immediately step aside. Perks of ownership. The atmosphere shifts from carnival to something darker, more primal.

Slaughter Stage H display features a realistic beheading scene—an actress strapped to a wooden block, her severed head projected as a hologram while her real head remains hidden beneath the structure.

Blood pumps from the neck stump in rhythmic spurts, splattering the front row of observers who shriek with delighted disgust.

Eve's breathing changes as we watch—quicker, shallower. Not fear, exactly. Fascination.

"The arterial spray pattern is accurate," she notes, her voice clinical but her body betraying her with the subtle press of her thighs together. "Someone did their anatomical research."

"My brother's team consults with medical professionals," I explain, my mouth close to her ear. "For authenticity."

We move deeper into the restricted area, where the displays grow increasingly explicit. On another stage, performers engage in a grotesque orgy—bodies writhing in stylized movements that suggest sex and gore.

It's so real I can't tell if it's fake or one of the troops Carolina found on the dark web. Their skin is painted to resemble classical marble statues cracked with black veins, as if corruption spreads through their stone flesh.

One woman straddles a man whose face is hidden behind a shattered porcelain mask, his hands clamped on her hips as she grinds down on him. Blood—real or staged—slides between her exposed breasts, pooling in the dip of her stomach before streaking over marble-painted ribs.

A second man is behind her, one hand fisted in her hair, the other locked around her throat, holding her still while he bites deep into her shoulder until her head snaps back in what's half scream, half moan.

Beside me, Eve's breathing changes. She doesn't make a sound, but I catch the subtle tightening of her thighs, the way her gaze sticks to the scene as if she's trying to decide whether it repels her or drags her under.

Her eyes flick to mine for half a beat, the corner of her mouth curling before she looks back at the stage—as if daring me to acknowledge she knows I'm watching her.

That tiny, knowing twist in her lips makes my cock stir—not at the scene, but at her letting me see the effect it's having on her. She's not the type to ask me to take her there… not yet—maybe not ever. But she's imagining it, all the same.

"Aroused, wife?" I murmur, my hand sliding from her elbow to her waist, fingers digging into the soft flesh just above her hip.

"Just analyzing theatrical technique," she counters, but the lie is obvious in the flush creeping up her neck.

With a dark chuckle, I lead us to where we need to be. The crowd thickens as we approach our destination.

CHAPTER 19

The Bride

After a few twists and turns, Slaughter Stage C rises ahead—washed in blood-red light that stains everything in shades of menace. As we draw closer, I make out two lines of people positioned center stage.

The women—Brides—are dressed in varying renditions of my own indecent outfit, which is to say they're barely covered at all. My dress might actually be the one offering the most cover. The fabric clings like a second skin, black and slick as spilled ink beneath the lights.

Thin straps cross over my chest in a deliberate tangle, framing more than they conceal, before twisting behind my neck. The cutout bares the curve of my ribs and the flat of my stomach, cinched only by a silver ring that holds the skirt together at my hip.

From there, the material drapes low, a single slit climbing high enough to make walking feel like a performance—each step a risk, each shift of fabric a promise I didn't agree to make.

Though I tried to fight Jack when he forced me into it, I secretly love the outfit. It's daring, it's sexy. It's… mine. When I find a way to escape him, I'm definitely taking it with me.

While the Brides face the audience gathering below the stage, the Grooms stand with their backs to the onlookers. They're clad in black that echoes Jack's attire.

It's unfair how good he looks in those black ripped jeans that are hanging low on his hips, and the open leather jacket framing the hard lines of his torso like it was made for him.

He's not wearing anything underneath, and despite myself, I want to twirl his chest hair around my finger.

"Are you ready?" he asks, not stopping to wait for my answer before pulling me onto the stage.

I don't notice what each Groom is holding in their hand until we join them. But as soon as I see the masks they hold—gas masks identical to the one Jack used to hide behind—I dig my heels into the floor.

"I'm not doing this." I don't need to understand what *this* is to know I want no part of it. My nerves are already frayed enough.

Jack's fingers wrap around my upper arm, squeezing tight enough to bruise. "You don't get to say no anymore. That privilege disappeared when you let my sister die."

He drags me forward, my heels scraping against the ground as I struggle. The vial of blood swings between my breasts, a pendulum marking time to my racing heart.

"Welcome to the Matrimonial Feast," announces a figure in elaborate robes, their face hidden beneath a bone-white mask painted with symbols I don't recognize. "Where Brides prove their devotion and Grooms receive their due."

While the other women immediately kneel before their partners, I look around for Shelby, finally spotting her at the opposite end of the line. But she isn't looking my way. Her eyes are on something in the middle of the growing audience.

"The rules are simple," the announcer continues. "The first Bride to make her Groom come wins. And as for the losers…" He makes a slicing gesture across his throat that leaves little to the imagination.

"I won't do this," I hiss at Jack. "I'm not going to—"

The words die in my throat as he produces a knife from his pocket—long, gleaming, wickedly sharp. He presses the blade against my throat, just beneath my jaw.

"Kneel," he orders, voice muffled slightly as he pulls the gas mask

over his face with his free hand.

The knife bites, a cold kiss beneath my jaw—enough to promise pain if I resist. When I don't move right away, he presses the blade closer, a whisper from piercing skin. Only then do my knees unlock.

Slowly, I sink to my knees on the stage, the impact jarring through my bones. The crowd below murmurs in approval.

"Good girl," Jack says through the mask, the filter making his voice inhuman. "Now show everyone what that pretty mouth can do."

My fingers tremble as I reach for his belt, fumbling with the buckle. The blade remains steady at my throat, a cold reminder of my position.

When I finally free his cock, it's already hard and leaking. It fills my hand with a weight that feels inevitable, like it's been molded for my grip, solid and heavy in my palm.

"Countdown begins!" the announcer calls. "Three…"

I look up at Jack, his features obscured by the mask. While some might see this transformation as monstrous, it's the opposite to me. I like the masked man—it's Jack I loathe.

"Two…"

My tongue darts out to wet my lips, a gesture that draws a low growl from behind Jack's mask.

I look across the audience, and my breath hitches when my eyes land on Caleb. He's standing in the middle, cradling his broken arm, wearing a scowl that makes my insides freeze. Just before I look away, he drags his index finger across his throat and sneers at me.

The hell is his problem? And… not that I've thought about it since the wedding, but I guess he isn't Shelby's Groom if he's down there instead of on stage with the rest of us.

"One…"

Unable to help myself, I flip him off, ignoring the pressure as Jack presses the knife harder into my flesh, breaking skin. A single drop of blood slides down my throat, a hot trail of surrender.

"Begin!"

I take Jack into my mouth with desperate urgency, driven by the blade at my throat and something darker—a sick need to perform well, to win this twisted competition. To show Caleb what he's lost.

My lips stretch wide around the thick girth. The anonymity makes it easier to give in, to pretend it's not Jack using me, but some darker, faceless thing that doesn't exist outside this moment.

I can want the monster. I can take from him. But when the mask comes off, I'll go back to hating the man beneath. I'm not giving *Jack* anything—this is for the man who showed up at my door at midnight, the one who claimed me before I ever had a chance to fight back.

The first bump of his Jacob's Ladder drags across my tongue, and my hips roll—small, involuntary, shame tightening low in my belly. I didn't expect to like the piercings. I thought they'd feel strange in my mouth. But they don't—they feel *obscene*. Every barbell is like a bruise he's planting inside my throat, and I want all of them.

One hand fists my hair, forcing the angle he wants, while the other holds the knife steady at my throat. He pushes deep, hard enough to make my eyes water, and the gag reflex kicks.

I swallow around him instead of pulling back, desperate to feel the next rung scrape my tongue.

"Fuck," he growls, the sound raw and cracked through the mask's filter—half moan, half threat—like he can't decide whether to praise me or break me. "You're so fucking good at this."

Jack's praise washes over me, making me preen under its weight. It's fucked up that I'm so into this, that I'm not faking my enthusiasm. But every gag, every wet choke, every hum of pleasure is real.

Spit slicks his shaft, sliding down to where his balls hang heavy and bare through the open fly. I suck harder just to hear the obscene sound it makes when he pulls out a few inches.

The crowd is so close I can feel their heat, their stares crawling all over me. I bet they're imagining my mouth on them, and instead of shame killing my arousal, it spikes it higher.

Jack uses me like I'm nothing but a toy—fucking my mouth with ruthless precision, the metal rungs catching on my lips each time he pulls back. The sting rips a moan from me, the vibration shuddering up through him.

When I look up, I'm certain his gaze locks on mine through the mask's lenses. A muffled groan leaks from him, low and wrecked, as if the sight alone could finish him. I know he sees it—the hunger I can't hide.

The part of me that isn't just enduring this, but chasing it. My smirk is small but deliberate, a silent dare he can't ignore.

"Take me deeper," he orders, voice rough enough to scrape my nerves raw.

I obey, relaxing my throat until my nose almost brushes his abdomen. The gag is sharp and wet, but I hold, eyes watering, drool spilling from the corner of my mouth.

Jack twitches in my mouth, and I know he's close. The mask turns every sound he makes into something monstrous, and it drags me straight back to that night when he fingered me in the hallway, while making me moan loud enough for Caleb to hear every filthy sound.

My hand slides between my legs under the slit of my dress, pressing hard against my clit through the soaked fabric. The crowd catches it— low gasps, a few ragged cheers—but instead of allowing shame to stop me, the exposure makes the ache worse.

I cup his balls with my other hand, rolling them slowly while dragging my tongue over each piercing like I'm mapping them blind, refusing to let him catch his breath. His breathing changes, and his hips jerk. The knife slips from his fingers, clattering to the stage, but his grip on me doesn't loosen.

Both hands now lock me in place; one yanks my hair, the other clamps my shoulder. "Swallow it all," he growls, the command hitting me low in the gut. "Every. Fucking. Drop."

The first hot surge hits the back of my throat, and I moan around him, swallowing greedily like it's the only thing I've been craving. Another pulse. Another swallow. I don't stop until I've drained every last drop from him, until I'm breathing in his scent and tasting nothing but him.

I keep sucking even after he's spent, milking him, wanting more. The vial of our blood still swings between my breasts, but this—this is the true seal. My clit aches so hard I swear I might come here and now.

The world tilts, the crowd a blur, the lights blinding—but all I see is him above me, breathing hard, still gripping my hair like he's not ready to let me go. I've made him lose control in front of all of them. And fuck,

I'm already wondering how soon I can do it again.

"We have a winner!" the announcer calls, voice booming over the speakers. "The Knight couple takes the victory!"

Jack's breath is still uneven inside the mask, the rise and fall of his chest pressing against my cheek where he still holds me to him. The taste of him coats my tongue, warm and heavy, and my legs squeeze against the need building between them.

"Mhmm, you looked so fucking beautiful choking on my cock," he rasps. Then he drags his cock from my mouth and tucks himself away. "It almost felt like you were enjoying yourself. Did you like having me in your mouth?"

"Y-yes," I admit, too worked up to lie.

With a low growl, he tightens his grip on my hair and tilts my head back so I have to look up at the black lenses staring down at me. The mask hides him, but I can feel the heat radiating from him.

Movement at the edge of my vision draws my attention. The other Grooms are peeling their masks off, faces flushed and satisfied. Jack reaches for the strap at the side of his head.

"Don't," I blurt, sharper than I mean to.

"Don't?" His hand pauses, which makes my lips twitch. Not because it's funny, but because he listened to me.

"Keep it on." My voice is lower now, almost a plea. I don't want Jack. I want the monster. The one who claimed me first. The one whose face I never saw.

A slow, knowing hum vibrates through the filter, and his fingers leave the strap. Then he tilts his head to the side, looking as though he's dissecting every layer of my demand. "Why?"

My mouth opens, but nothing comes out. How am I supposed to admit that I'm wetter for the masked man than the husband who just came down my throat?

"Mhmm, you like the mask," he murmurs, smugness a low rumble through the filter. His fingers leave the strap and trail down my jaw instead, claiming the victory without needing my confession.

"Yes." I nod while licking my lips.

His thumb drags slowly along my jaw, catching the faint trace of spit still clinging there. "You've got the crowd worked up," he murmurs through the filter, his voice still rough from coming. "And you're shaking like you're ready to be fucked in front of every last one of them."

My breath hitches. The thought sends my need spiking higher, but it's not just the audience. It's the mask. The black lenses. The way the filter turns him into something inhuman.

"Please…" My voice is small, frayed.

"Please what, wife?" The words are a taunt, each one measured like he's trying to make me squirm. "Tell me exactly what you want."

"Touch me," I breathe.

"Where?" He moves his hand to my throat, squeezing. "Your throat? Your tits? Or maybe that pretty little cunt you've been clenching since I pulled my cock out of you?"

The last word leaves me trembling. "Yes. Oh, God. Yes, please play with my pussy." I take a deep, shuddering breath. "Make me come. Please, I want to come so badly."

Jack chuckles low, the sound vibrating through the filter. "Greedy little thing." He hauls me up, my knees trembling from the ache and the aftermath of the competition. "Come on," he orders, steering me toward the wings.

We pass the other couples—masks off now, flushed and basking in the crowd's approval. He keeps me moving until we reach a narrow stretch of curtain and shadow between two stages.

The audience is still close enough to hear us if we make a sound, and from certain angles they can see us. Jack drives me back into cold scaffolding, body crowding mine, the hard ridge of his cock digging into my hip.

"You want me to keep it on?" he asks, as if we didn't already settle this. The lenses of his mask catch the stage lights as he tilts his head.

"Yes."

"Say please."

"Please," I breathe, pressing my thighs together.

He grips my jaw, tilting my head up until my throat stretches. "Keep your eyes on the mask. Don't look anywhere else. Or I'll—"

"You'll what?" I challenge.

"Stop," he finishes while dragging his other hand up my thigh, slipping under the slit of my dress until his knuckles press into the soaked lace covering me. "Say it so I know you understand."

"I won't look anywhere else," I rasp.

"Mhmm, you're drenched," he says, almost to himself, the words vibrating dark through the filter.

"Jack," I moan.

"Were you imagining this while you were on your knees? Thinking about me fucking you with the mask on?"

"Yes," I pant as my breath hitches, hips rocking forward into his touch.

"Shhh," he warns when I start to speak. "You want my fingers? You take what I'm giving you. *How* I'm giving it to you."

He hooks the lace aside and pushes two fingers into me, knuckles deep on the first thrust. The heel of his palm grinds into my clit as he fucks me slow, deliberate, each curl of his fingers hitting that soft, brutal place that makes my knees shake.

His free hand stays at my throat, applying just enough pressure to make my head spin, the filter of the mask pulling his breaths into a slow, predatory rhythm that makes my clit pulse.

"Moan my name again."

A burst of laughter and applause from the other stage filters through the curtain, and my cheeks burn at the thought of my own noises joining theirs—at the thought of them seeing Jack finger fuck me. But the awareness isn't enough to stop me.

"Jack." I gyrate my hips, desperate now. "Fuck me harder with your fingers."

His pace quickens, thumb circling my clit with cruel precision while he grinds the thick ridge of his cock against me. "You want my hard cock in your pussy, don't you?" he taunts. "Do you want me to bend you over and let them see the masked man split you open?"

Fuck... yes, I do want that.

"Y-yes," I cry. "I want your cock inside me."

He lets out a cruel chuckle. "Too bad you haven't earned more than my fingers yet, Dr. Death."

I open my mouth, about to say… something, anything. But my body betrays me, fluttering tight around his fingers, chasing every curl like my pussy's trying to keep him inside.

My nipples ache against the thin fabric, and when he releases my throat to pinch one through the dress, the sharp pull rips a gasp so loud I'm sure the crowd hears.

"Come for me," he orders, voice low and inhuman. "Come on my fingers, Dr. Death, or I'll make you do it out there where every last one of them can see your face when you break."

The orgasm tears through me, sharp and merciless, wringing a ragged cry from my throat. My legs clamp around his wrist as the aftershocks wring me out, each spasm milking his fingers.

Jack doesn't let me recover. He pulls his fingers free and lifts them to my lips. "Clean me." I take them in without hesitation, sucking until his hand gleams wet with my saliva. "You're such a good wife." He wipes his hand on my thigh, tugs my dress back into place.

Then, he takes a step back and reaches for the mask. His movements are slow, like he's making sure I see him remove it. When it's gone, his piercing green eyes bore into mine, his lips curving up at the side.

"You keep surprising me, Eve."

I can't help smiling back at him. "Likewise, husband."

Together, we walk back onto the now-empty stage. I scan the crowd for Shelby, hoping to catch her for a word, but she's already gone with her Groom.

"Looking for someone?" Jack asks.

At the same time, I voice a question of my own. "Why did you do it?"

"Do what?"

Sighing, I explain, "Use Shelby to get to me."

He stops walking, frowning as his hand drags over the rough line of his jaw. "She and her brother owed me a debt. I was simply collecting."

The way he says it sends my blood boiling. And yeah, part of it's because I'm pissed I didn't even know Shelby had a brother—but I still lay into him.

"So what? You can't just go around using people, Jack."

"Of course I can."

I scoff. "No wonder you're all alone in that big fucking house. You're an asshole."

Jack's smile is slow, deliberate, the kind that never reaches his eyes. "Takes one to know one, wife. And I don't see anyone coming to your rescue."

CHAPTER 20

The Trickster

"You're an asshole…"

It's been two, almost three, days, and Eve's words still repeat themselves over and over. They're fucking with my mind. She's been with me for a week, hurling any amount of insults at me. Yet, there's something about this one that's sticking.

"You're an asshole…"

The bourbon glints amber in the half-light, promising oblivion I've been chasing since we returned from the Sanctuary just a few hours ago after yet another performance.

Apart from grunting commands, I haven't spoken to my Little Bride since the other day. It's better this way. My fingers circle the neck of the bottle without lifting it, a ritual repeated so many times the motion feels carved into muscle memory.

Eve watches from her cage, gray eyes tracking every aborted movement—the twitch toward the bottle, the unlit cigarette rolling between my fingers. Her silence feels deliberate, a calculation I can almost hear working behind that clinical gaze.

I should feel victorious, shouldn't I? I got her here in my cage, just like I wanted. Instead, I feel like I've been hollowed out, scraped raw

from the inside. Like…breaking her isn't what I want anymore.

"It won't bring Ruby back, you know." Eve's voice cuts through the silence, startling in its calm precision. "The alcohol. It doesn't resurrect the dead, it just pickles the living."

My jaw tightens, teeth grinding at the fucking audacity. As if I need a psychology lesson from my own prisoner. As if Ruby's name belongs in her mouth.

"Did I ask for your professional opinion, Dr. Death?" I keep my voice level, a contrast to the pulse thudding in my throat.

She shrugs, the movement shifting the oversized t-shirt I gave her to sleep in. My shirt. I don't know why I gave her that instead of making her sleep naked.

"No," she admits. "But your liver probably would if it could speak."

A laugh threatens to crack through my anger—unexpected, unwanted. I leave the bottle alone. "There," I say, turning the unlit cigarette over in my fingers. "Happy now?"

"Ecstatic," she deadpans, but something in her eyes shifts. Like she didn't expect me to actually listen.

Power shifts between us for a breath—a current changing direction without warning. She's still my captive, still locked behind metal bars that I control. But she's also the only one who keeps me from splintering into something unrecognizable.

I cross the bedroom to the garden doors and push one open, letting cold night air slice through the stuffy heat of the room. The lighter flares orange in the darkness as I cup my hand around the flame, inhaling deeply when the tobacco catches.

"Thank you," Eve says softly behind me.

I glance back, smoke trailing from my lips. "For what?"

"For not smoking in here. My lungs appreciate it."

Gratitude for something so small feels like a hook—like she's found a way to make me care about her comfort without asking directly. Clever. My eyes narrow as I exhale toward the garden.

"Don't mistake self-interest for consideration," I tell her. "Smoke damages things I own."

"Is that what I am to you? A *thing?*"

I drag deep on the cigarette, letting the burn spread through my chest before answering. "You're whatever I need you to be."

"And what do you need, Jack?" She leans forward, fingers curling around the bars. "Revenge? Punishment? Or something else you haven't admitted to yourself yet?"

The question hangs between us, too direct to deflect without looking weak. "What I need," I say, each word precise. "Is for you to remember your place."

"My place is in a cage," she acknowledges, but there's no fear in her voice. "That doesn't mean I can't see yours."

Smoke curls from my nostrils like a fucking dragon. "And where's my place, according to your expert analysis?"

Her eyes reflect the ember of my cigarette, twin points of light in the darkness. The air between us feels charged, thick with something that isn't just hatred anymore.

"Right where you are. Trapped between what you think you want and what you actually need."

"What I want," I growl, "is justice for my sister."

"No," Eve counters, voice soft but unflinching. "What you want is to hurt someone because you're hurting. There's a difference."

I flick the cigarette into the darkness, listening as it hisses and dies. "You think you know me because you've read a few psychology textbooks? Because you've analyzed damaged people for a living?"

"I think I know you because I recognize the pattern." She tilts her head, studying me like I'm one of her patients. "The drinking. The smoking. The rage that doesn't quite cover the guilt. You're not just punishing me, Jack. You're punishing yourself."

Before I'm aware I've even moved, I'm in front of her cage. My hand slams against the bars, making her jump but not retreat. "You don't know what you're talking about," I roar.

"Don't I?" Her gaze doesn't waver. "Tell me what you really want from me. Not what you planned when you knocked on my door at midnight. What you want now."

The truth itches under my skin—I had a plan, clean and vicious. Break her. Use her. Discard her. But something's changed. The only time

I feel alive now is when I'm with her, watching her fight, watching her yield, watching her surprise me again and again.

"I want…" The words stick in my throat, too raw to voice.

She waits, patient in a way that makes me want to shake her. When I don't continue, a small, knowing smile curves her lips. "That's what I thought."

"Don't push me," I warn, but it lacks the edge I want it to have.

"Or what?" she challenges. "You'll lock me in a cage? Force me to my knees in public? Make me come so hard I forget my own name?" She drums her fingers against the metal bars, smirking while she taps out a melody I don't recognize. "You've already done your worst, Jack. And I'm still here. Still looking at you."

I force out a low chuckle. "Have I?" I ask as I walk back to the door and light another cigarette. "For a prodigy, your mental capacity is pretty limited if you think you've endured my worst. We've barely just started."

Her gray eyes stay on mine as she flexes her hand, the one I cut during the ceremony. She removed the bandage yesterday, deciding it was time to let it air. Personally, I thought she should have done that after the second or third day, but whatever.

Eve's smile deepens, secret and knowing. "So what is your worst, dear husband?"

Ignoring her, I chain-smoke by the garden door, watching night press against glass while Eve's words crawl under my skin. The fifth cigarette burns faster than the first four, ash dropping to marble like gray snow.

My mind circles her challenge like a predator testing weakness—what I really want versus what I planned. Two different beasts entirely. Behind me, fabric shifts against metal as Eve adjusts her position in the cage, the sound drawing my attention back to her like a compass finding north.

"Why did you call me a prodigy?" she asks, shattering the potent silence.

I shrug but don't turn back to face her. I count the seconds, knowing it's just a matter of time before she continues talking. Eve doesn't appreciate silence as much as I expected given her career as a therapist.

"My dad wanted me to be a prodigy, so he forced me to become one," she suddenly says. "I'm nothing like the people you sometimes read about. You know, when a five-year-old can play or compose better than Mozart, or when a twelve-year-old makes a new scientific discovery."

I still don't turn, don't encourage, but I don't stop her either. The cigarette burns closer to my fingers.

"He never saw me as anything but an experiment. One he could mold exactly how he wanted, which is what he did. I guess I could say I was both his greatest experiment and biggest disappointment." She laughs, the sound empty of humor.

The confession hangs in the air between us, unexpected and intimate in a way I wasn't prepared for. I crush the cigarette against the doorframe, leaving a black smudge.

"He wasn't raising a daughter," she continues, voice steady but softer. "He was creating a successor. Or a legacy… maybe both."

I turn to face her, leaning against the frame. "Is that why you became a therapist?"

"Yes," she says, and there's something like disappointment in her expression. "I chose it because… well, I'm not actually sure I ever chose it. It was what he expected, so I did it."

The words hit with unexpected force, like she's reached through the cage and struck something tender beneath my ribs.

"My dad…" I start, then stop, surprised by my own impulse to reciprocate. Her eyes on me feel like hooks, pulling truth I hadn't planned to offer. "My dad hated me."

I lock my gaze on her, wordlessly daring her to look away while I give her a small piece of me.

"The only one of us he ever liked, maybe even loved, was Nick. Ruby was useful since he could sell her off. I'm the only one who was completely worthless and nothing more than a disappointment." I let out a bitter laugh. "He even had me killed."

Eve's eyes widen, her body going still. "He had you killed?"

My fingers drift to the scar on my torso, invisible beneath my shirt but always present. "I was dead for a few minutes before the doctors revived me."

"Oh, Jack." Her voice carries a weight I don't want to examine. "That's—"

Not wanting her pity, I interrupt her. "When I came back, things were different." I look toward the ceiling. "Death changes your priorities."

I almost tell her about the Knight curse then—the superstition that claims two heirs from every generation. How Ruby's death fulfilled the prophecy that's haunted my family for generations. But something holds me back. That knowledge is a weapon I'm not ready to place in her hands.

"I understand more than you think," Eve says quietly.

Before I can respond, she shifts, drawing up her knees and spreading her legs wide. My shirt hangs loose on her frame, but she pulls the hem higher, inch by inch, until the fabric clears her inner thighs.

It takes me a moment for my brain to register what she's showing me. And now that I see the faded circles of puckered flesh, I have no idea how I haven't noticed it until now.

The scars are pale and smooth against her skin; old burns, etched like secrets she decided to show me. Her garter tattoo covers some of the damage on that thigh, but not completely.

"These weren't about wanting to die," she says, tracing one with her fingertip. "Or even about the pain. I wanted to feel something real." Her eyes meet mine, unflinching.

The sight stirs something in me—not pity, something darker and more possessive. For the first time, I don't want to fight it. Fuck it. Let her be the thing that drags me under, because when she looks at me like this, scars bared and defiance steady, I don't feel like the Knight who lost his sister. I feel alive.

I move to the cage door, keys suddenly in my hand though I don't remember reaching for them. The lock clicks open with finality.

CHAPTER 21

The Trickster

"What are you doing?" she asks, body tensing as I step inside.

My shirt is gone, and her eyes catch on the scar carved across my torso—the raised, ugly seam the bullet left behind when it killed me. For a moment, she just stares, breath caught like she's seeing the wound rather than the man.

Instead of answering, I lower myself to the floor between her spread knees, positioning my body at her feet while she leans back against the bars. The reversal isn't lost on me—the captor entering the captive's space, yet placing himself exactly where he can consume her.

"Jack?" Uncertainty creeps into her voice as I take her ankle in my hand, feeling the delicate bones beneath my fingers.

I press my lips to the first scar—a thin white imprint almost invisible against her pale skin. The taste of her skin is salt and smoke and heat, alive against the dead tissue of her scars.

"Mhmm." I groan low in my throat, unable to stop myself, the sound vibrating against her flesh.

She inhales sharply but doesn't pull away. My mouth moves higher, to the more deliberate marks on her inner thigh. These aren't random; they're a language written in flesh, a cry no one bothered to hear.

"What are you doing?" she whispers again, but the question has changed shape, become something else entirely.

"Tasting your pain," I murmur against her skin.

I move methodically, kissing each scar like I'm mapping territory—nuzzling, licking, sometimes biting just hard enough to make her gasp. Her body trembles beneath my attention, caught between retreat and surrender.

When I reach a particularly big mark near the crease of her thigh, I bite down, harder than before. Eve's back arches, a moan escaping her lips as her fingers find my hair. Rather than pushing me away, she threads her fingers through the strands, holding me against her damaged skin like she's afraid I'll stop.

My breath roughens against her inner thigh, confession spilling from me between kisses. Words I never meant to give her emerge between marks I leave on her skin, as if her scars are drawing out my own.

"I used to drink until I couldn't feel my face," I murmur against a particularly deep line near her hip. "After Ruby. Cocaine too. Anything to blur the edges." My tongue traces the silvered tissue, feeling her pulse jump beneath it. "Nothing worked until you."

Eve's fingers tighten in my hair, not pulling away but holding me in place. The contradiction mirrors everything between us—resistance and surrender wrapped into one gesture.

"What changed?" she asks, voice strained with the effort to sound clinical despite the way her body responds to my mouth.

I bite down gently on the crest of her hip, feeling her shudder. "You see too much. Makes it hard to hide." My hands slide under her thighs, palms pressing against the backs of her knees to open her wider. "Now it's your turn to tell me something. Why do you prefer the mask?"

"I... I don't know," she lies.

Lifting my head, I meet her gaze over the landscape of her body. Something raw passes between us—recognition that cuts deeper than I intended. "Don't lie to me," I growl.

"I'm not," she bites back, so I sink my teeth into her flesh, not letting go until she gasps. "Fine. Fine. Okay, I do know."

"You want the monster," I reply for her, thumb tracing circles on her

inner thigh. "Not the man. The mask lets you pretend you're not giving in to me. Just to something faceless."

Her throat works as she swallows. "Does that bother you?"

"No." I lower my head again, nuzzling the soft skin where thigh meets hip. "It fascinates me. The doctor who diagnoses everyone else but can't admit what she craves."

"And what do you crave, Jack?" Her voice is steadier now, challenging despite her vulnerable position.

I pause, mouth hovering over the lace edge of her underwear. The truth rises unbidden, dangerous in its honesty. "This. You. Falling apart under my hands. Fighting even when you want to surrender." I exhale hot against the fabric, watching her stomach muscles tense.

My fingers hook into the sides of her underwear, dragging the material down her legs. She shifts to help, a small cooperation that feels like victory. When the fabric clears her ankles, I toss it aside and settle back between her thighs.

The scent of her arousal slams into me—sharp, musky, intoxicating. My cock hardens instantly, straining against my jeans as I groan and bury my face closer, inhaling deep like I'm starving for her. I want her to see me savor it, to know I'm addicted to the way she smells before I even taste her.

"Jack," she warns, but there's no force behind it.

I lower my mouth to her inner thigh again, working my way up with open-mouthed kisses that leave damp traces on her skin. Each scar receives attention—reverent and possessive all at once. My hands slide beneath her ass, lifting her slightly to give me better access.

When I finally reach the apex of her thighs, I pause, breathing hot against her center without making contact. Her hips shift, seeking, but I hold her still.

"Ask me," I demand softly.

Her eyes narrow, defiance flashing. "No."

I smile against her thigh, admiring her stubbornness even as I plan to break it. "Then I'll wait." I press a kiss to her skin, just beside where she wants me. "I have all night."

A frustrated sound escapes her throat. Her fingers tighten in my hair, trying to guide me. I resist, keeping my mouth maddeningly close but never touching where she needs it most. The power remains mine, even from my knees.

"Please," she finally whispers, the word dragged from her like it costs her something vital.

"Please what?"

Her chest rises and falls rapidly. "Please… taste me."

The surrender in her voice sends heat coursing through me. I reward her by dragging my tongue slowly through her folds in one long, deliberate stroke. The taste of her floods my mouth—salt and sweet and something uniquely Eve—as her back arches off the blanket.

I start slow, methodical, learning the terrain of her with my tongue. Each stroke maps a different reaction—what makes her gasp, what makes her thighs tense, what draws those perfect little moans from deep in her throat.

Cataloging every response, I mentally build a playbook of her pleasure that belongs to me alone.

"God," she breathes, head falling back as I circle her clit with the tip of my tongue. "Jack…"

The sound of my name in that broken voice is intoxicating. I amp up my efforts, alternating between broad, flat strokes and precise flicks that make her hips jerk against my hold. My hands grip her thighs, spreading her wide, putting her on display just for me.

What begins as controlled exploration quickly fractures into hunger. I devour her like a man starved, moaning against her cunt as her taste floods my mouth. Her wetness slicks my lips, coats my chin, drips down to my throat until I'm marked with her in a way that feels like branding.

Eve's restraint fractures by degrees. Her fingers guide my head more insistently now, pressing me where she needs me, and I let her.

Not because I've surrendered control, but because her desperation feeds my own hunger. I want to feel her come apart on my tongue, want to consume the pleasure I force from her body.

"More," she demands, voice raw with need. "Please, husband, more."

I slide two fingers inside her pussy, curling them until she cries out, the sound reverberating off the bars like a hymn to ruin. With my other hand, I press lower, circling her tight asshole.

"Have you ever been fucked here, wife?" My voice is husky and low.

"N-no," she moans. She lets out a small yelp as I grip her thighs and pull her down so she's half lying, half sitting. The perfect position for me to play with her ass.

"Fuck, you shouldn't have told me that," I rasp. The thought that I'm the first one to play with her ass makes my cock throb painfully from behind its denim prison. I remove the finger circling her ass, bringing it to her mouth. "Spit on it."

She does, and once it's fully coated in her saliva, I bring it back to her puckered opening. Her breath hitches as I slowly push it into her tight opening, stretching her as my tongue works her clit.

Her scream turns ragged, body jerking between the double intrusion, writhing helplessly against my mouth and hands. The cage doesn't feel like it's containing *her* anymore—it's containing *us,* this savage ritual that belongs outside time.

Her pussy clenches hard around my fingers while her ass tightens around the one I've buried there, every muscle spasming under the rhythm I force on her.

My tongue lashes her clit, and I groan into her cunt as she writhes— the vibration making her buck harder, grinding against every point of me inside her.

I'm lost in it now—her taste, her heat, her body convulsing on my hands and mouth—everything I ever wanted to ruin and consume. The taste of her grows sharper, her arousal flooding my mouth as she approaches the edge.

"Let go," I command against her flesh. "Come for me, Little Bride. Now."

Her body obeys even if her mind resists—back arching, thighs trembling, a cry tearing from her throat as she breaks apart. I groan into her as I feel every clench around my fingers, every contraction milking my hand.

I don't stop when she comes; I push her higher, dragging her through one orgasm into the next, curling my fingers deeper as I pump her ass in

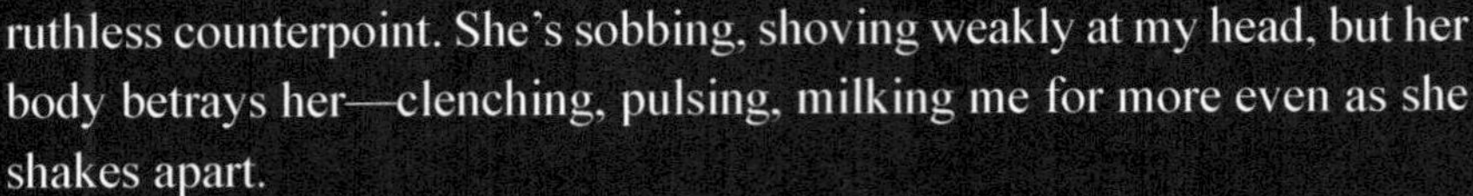

ruthless counterpoint. She's sobbing, shoving weakly at my head, but her body betrays her—clenching, pulsing, milking me for more even as she shakes apart.

I rise up on my elbows, watching her face as she comes down—cheeks flushed, eyes half-closed, lips parted with rapid breaths. Something dangerous and possessive claws through my chest at the sight. This is mine now. This unguarded moment when all her walls have crumbled.

"Beautiful," I growl, licking her wetness from my lips before pressing a final kiss to her thigh.

Then I stretch out beside her in the cage, chest heaving, cock painfully hard. I don't touch myself—I just listen to her gasped breaths, knowing her pleasure belongs to me. But then she stirs, eyes flicking to the bulge straining my jeans.

Without speaking, Eve moves and slides one leg over my hips until she's straddling me. My cock throbs under her weight, and I groan, the sound torn out of me as she grinds down. Her hands work at my fly with clumsy urgency.

"I want these off," she complains, tugging denim and zipper until I help her shove them down just enough to free me.

With my jeans and boxer briefs gone, she places her hands on the scar on flesh. "This is your ruin," she whispers, gray eyes burning into mine. "And I want it."

"Are you sure you can handle it?" I rasp as she sits up, pulling my own tee from her body until she's naked and pressed to my chest.

She hovers for a heartbeat, staring into my eyes like she's daring me to stop her. I don't. I grip her hips instead, steadying her as she sinks onto my cock in one long, trembling push.

"I can handle everything you have to offer," she purrs.

"Fuck," I grunt, head falling back against the floor as her tight heat clamps around me. She moans, nails digging into my shoulders for balance.

The pace is hers at first, shallow and testing, but I don't let it stay that way. My hands tighten, dragging her down harder, forcing her to take me to the base. She gasps, body jerking, but she doesn't stop.

Eve's hair sticks damp to her cheeks as she rides me, sweat running down her neck, her mouth spilling ragged moans that sound like she's breaking open. For a second I just lie there, stunned—watching my captive fuck herself on my rigid length like she's starving for it. My cock twitches inside her, and I nearly lose it just from the sight.

"Fuck, Jack," she cries, riding harder, nails clawing down my chest hard enough to break skin. "Your cock... fuck... your cock feels so fucking good. I can feel every stud inside me."

Blood wells in the fresh scratches, hot against the sweat slicking my torso. Eve dips her head, dragging her tongue over the marks she just carved, licking me raw before she straightens and keeps riding, eyes wild and unashamed.

"Say it again," I snarl, twisting her nipple until she cries out. "Tell me how good my cock feels inside you."

She grins wickedly. "You know... oh..." My Little Bride cuts herself off and throws her head back, moaning loudly.

I grip her hips tighter. "That's it." My cock twitches inside her tight cunt, and I squeeze my eyes shut for a moment as I stave off the orgasm. I'm not ready to nut yet.

She hovers just above my lips, taunting me with her breath, then crashes down. The kiss is filthy—teeth, tongue, spit—a battle and a surrender all at once. She bites my lip until I taste blood, the copper flooding both our mouths as it mingles with spit.

Then she pulls back suddenly, still impaled on my cock, and lets her mouth fall open. Bloody saliva drips down her chin, trailing over her throat, streaking her breasts.

My cock jerks violently at the sight. I rear up and drag my tongue down her chest to lap the crimson trail like it's mine to claim. When I crash my mouth back to hers, I taste my blood on her tongue and groan her name into the kiss.

"Eve." A prayer. A fucking curse.

I don't know what's come over her, if she's too horny to care or if she's claiming me. Either way, it doesn't matter. She's *mine*, and my blood is inside her from the kiss.

"Jack," she pants against my mouth, desperation edging her tone.

"Play with my ass again."

Her pussy clenches around me as she begs, and I understand. My hand slides down, slick fingers pressing to her other hole, teasing, circling until I shove a finger inside as she rides me.

Her scream tears into my mouth, swallowed by the kiss as her whole body jerks between my cock and my finger. She's trembling so hard it feels like she's trying to shake me out of her, but she can't—I'm buried too deep, in too many places.

I groan into her mouth, the vibration rumbling through both of us. "That's it. Take it, Little Bride." She claws at me, hips pumping wild and reckless, using me as much as I use her. My cock pistons into her pussy while my finger works her ass, stretching her until she's trembling uncontrollably.

Her whole body bows as she screams, "I'm coming!" Her pussy clamps down so hard on my cock I almost black out, while her ass strangles my finger.

She's clenching, milking, shattering in my arms, and I fucking praise it with a guttural command. "That's it, squeeze me, milk me, take every drop."

The kiss doesn't stop, even as she sobs into my mouth, her pussy still pulsing around my cock while I empty inside her. The taste of blood, spit, and sex binds us, messy and primal.

Eve collapses onto my chest, my cock still buried inside her, refusing to let her go. When she wiggles like she's trying to get away, I tighten my grip around her.

"No." That's all I say.

She giggles—fucking giggles—and I love it. "Fine, have it your way," she says, pressing a kiss to one of the marks she left on my chest.

Words don't do this justice. For the first time since February, the noise in my skull goes quiet. Not peace—fuck no, I don't get peace—but something sharper. Possession. Control. Eve wasn't what I thought I wanted, but she's exactly what I need.

Her cunt still grips me even as I soften, hot and unrelenting, like it refuses to let me go. I don't pull out. I don't want to. The thought of leaving her body feels wrong, so I stay buried inside her, locking her to me.

CHAPTER 22

The Bride

Waking up the next morning, I immediately feel alert. Something is wrong. Like, really, *really* wrong.

"Jack?" I call out, but no one answers.

Yawning, I stretch, wincing as my thighs pull tight and a dull ache reminds me of last night. My ass still feels tender, my cunt raw from being used until I broke. I reach out for the metal bars caging me in. But… they're not there.

My eyes fly open, and when I look around, I realize I'm no longer in the cage. Instead, I'm in Jack's bed.

"What the hell?" I mutter, wiping sleep from my eyes.

This makes no sense. I fell asleep on his naked chest, covered in blood and sweat, his cum still dripping out of my sore pussy. My skin stings where his studs dragged me raw, my chest still marked by my own scratches against him. It was filthy and perfect.

For the first time, I felt like there was more to him. And to our arrangement—or whatever to call this fucked up situation he's forced me into.

"Jack?" I shout, my voice louder this time. But there's still no answer.

With a huff, I get out of bed, taking the sheet with me. My bare feet pad across the hardwood, but a sharp scraping sound makes me freeze. I look down and can't help laughing hysterically at what I see.

There's a fucking shackle around my ankle. One that's tethered to a chain coiling from a bolt in the wall.

"You sly bastard." I might not be in the cage anymore, but I'm still fucking trapped.

I tug against it, testing, rattling links loud enough to echo through the empty house. No response. No Jack. With a curse, I hitch the sheet higher and march into the bathroom. I half expect the chain to tighten, but it doesn't. There's plenty of slack left.

As soon as I'm inside, I slam the door shut, shoving the chain under the gap so it won't catch. The sheet slips from my body, pooling at my feet, and I step straight into the shower.

Hot water needles my skin, making me hiss when it runs over bruises I didn't notice until now. Between my legs, the sting is sharper, a reminder of being stretched open again and again.

It doesn't take long before the spray beats against my shoulders, washing away what can only be described as insanity. Yep, that has to be the reason I did… what I did last night.

With each day that passes being trapped here, I feel my mind getting duller. I'm sleeping more and moving less. Neither is good for my mental health.

I don't even know when Jack left or where he is. All I know is that when I went to sleep, we were in the cage; I was on his chest, and his cock was still inside me.

But when I woke up, I was in his bed instead of in the cage. And instead of having his body pressed against me, I now have a fucking chain around my ankle. A. Fucking. Chain that's bolted to the wall.

I guess this is one of those times where I really am a fucking fool. Why did I let my guard down? And more importantly, what did I think would happen? Jack Knight can't be trusted.

Since my only company is my thoughts, I guess I can admit that he might be… okay, not *might*—he definitely *is* a good fuck. But that's it. As a human, he's pretty fucking shitty.

That disturbing train of thought is further proof I need to move, need to… do something. As quickly as possible, I finish my shower and dry off before brushing my teeth.

With nothing else to wear, I grab one of Jack's oversized t-shirts from the stack he left in here and pull it over my head. The fabric smells like him, clinging to my skin in a way that makes me restless.

When I'm done, I feel more like myself, and that makes my mood better. It also helps me focus, something I've failed at. So far, my attempts at getting away from Jack have been half-assed at best.

Sure, I tried to seduce him. But he turned that around on me, and it was… no. I need to keep my mind on the task ahead. I can't keep letting him distract me with mind-blowing orgasms and his chiseled, perfect body.

Maybe being alone is for the best. Now I have time to come up with a new and better plan. One that won't be ruined by hormones and a way too active libido.

Shaking my head, I braid my long hair, something that helps me think. I force my mind to run through my mental profile on my captor.

"No matter what your circumstances are, there'll always only be one person responsible. You. You're responsible for all your choices. Stop making stupid decisions, and life will be easier." My dad's words skitter around in my head, unbidden but true.

Leaving the bathroom, I hear the cold metal slide across the hardwood floor as I test the illusion of being free. With a small thrill of discovery, I realize I can reach the kitchen. Victory. I desperately need a cup of coffee.

Feeling excited, I pull open drawers, but they're… empty. Well, most of them are. There's no cutlery at all, and the knife block on the counter stands like a monument to absence, each slot vacant.

I scan the kitchen with methodical precision, noting the locked cabinets, the empty paper towel holder, the absence of anything glass or ceramic. He's thought of everything obvious. So much for making myself some coffee.

Just as I'm debating whether to drink water from my cupped hand like some feral thing, I hear the front door open.

I freeze.

Keys jingle. A soft voice murmurs something unintelligible.

"Hello?" I call out, confused by the footsteps that are most definitely not Jack's.

I look back toward the bedroom, wondering if I should hide. But before I can make a decision, Carolina steps into view. She's carrying a bag in one hand and has a baby perched on her hip like a designer accessory.

"Hi," she says casually, as if walking into a house where a woman is literally chained isn't the strangest part of her day.

"Uh… hi?"

She sweeps past me without comment, shoes clacking softly, and heads to the kitchen island like she owns the place—which, considering her last name and Jack's absence, maybe she does.

The baby babbles as Carolina sets a canvas tote on the counter and unpacks a collection of neat containers, none of which appear to have been opened.

"I brought enough for two meals," she says, pulling out cutlery from her coat pocket like some Mafia Mary Poppins. "I don't cook, but I know people."

I open my mouth. Then close it. Then try again. "Jack sent you?"

She glances over her shoulder with an arched brow. "Did you think the food fairy broke in?"

Fair point.

She moves like she doesn't give a single fuck that I'm shackled. Like this situation is nothing more than an errand she agreed to on her way to Pilates.

"Where is he?" I ask.

Carolina shrugs, expression unreadable. "Out."

Helpful.

"Is that your baby?" It's a stupid question given the similar facial features, but I'm desperate for some conversation.

"She is." The love in her tone confirms it more than the words themselves.

"She's cute," I offer. I instinctively lift my hand and take a step closer, but when she looks at me, I stop myself in my tracks.

Her gaze isn't sharp or cruel. But it's enough to tell me that if Jack is dangerous, Carolina is… deliberate and calculated.

"Why did you bring her here? I mean, you don't know me."

"She's not scared of monsters," she replies smoothly. "Willow was born in a house full of them." The baby coos like she's in agreement with her mother's statement.

When she's finished unpacking the food, she nudges her foot against another tote I didn't notice until now. She smiles as her gaze lands on my bare legs.

"Would you like some clothes?" she grins. "Or are you fine like that?"

"God, yes," I rush out.

From the tote, she pulls out a neat pile of folded clothes. It takes me a moment to realize it's my clothes. My bras, socks, even one of my favorite cardigans. She sets them on the counter like it's no big deal.

"Those are… mine," I blurt, staring at the familiar fabric. "You went to my place?"

"Jack asked me to," Carolina replies smoothly, not bothering to look at me. "He didn't think you'd want to live in his shirts forever."

Not caring about the present company, I reach for one of the knitted sweater dresses, and in no time at all, I replace Jack's tee with my own comfortable clothes.

"Thank you," I say, pulling on a matching pair of knitted socks and wiggling my toes. I don't know why, but wearing my own stuff makes me feel ten times better, and suddenly I'm glad to have company. Even if it's Carolina Knight.

"Want to eat with me?" I ask, surprising both of us.

She arches a brow at the invitation. "Why not." She looks around as though she's searching for something. "You know, I've never been here before."

"This is my first time out of the cage without being taken to and from either the bathroom or the Sanctuary," I inform her, my tone hardening slightly. "So I don't know where the good silverware or China is."

She lets out a sharp laugh. "Let's eat in there." She points to the adjoining room, and as I peek around the corner, I nod.

"If my chain will let me in there," I deadpan, picking up some of the food she brought.

Together, we quickly make two plates and then head into what turns out to be the living room. It's nicer than I would have thought. Dark furniture and a fireplace that's begging to be used.

Carolina sits down on the couch, placing Willow in her lap. The baby babbles happily while her mom shoves food into her mouth and chews it so fast I'm wondering if we're in a race.

We eat in silence at first, but it's not sharp or hostile. Just… comfortable. Willow smears something on her mother's sleeve, and Carolina doesn't even flinch, just wipes it away with a practiced hand. For some reason, the simplicity of the gesture softens the knot in my chest.

"You went to my apartment," I say eventually, needing to fill the quiet. "Did you… look around?"

"Of course I did," she replies smoothly, not even pretending otherwise. "That skull on your mantle? Interesting choice of décor. Jack was right, you're not boring."

My fork pauses halfway to my mouth. "You saw that?"

"Hard to miss," she laughs softly. "Don't tell me it's an ex-boyfriend or something."

For some reason, I tell her the truth. "It's my dad."

"For real?"

Nodding, I take my time chewing the last bite. "Yeah. When he died, that was the only part of him I wanted to keep." I don't tell her how he died, and I'm not going to. Not when I'm the only person alive to know the truth about Charles Mortis' demise.

The official story is a mugging gone wrong. The story known to just a few is that he was killed by the Hunter, aka Valentine. Neither version invites questions, and I've never offered answers.

Exhaling audibly, she admits, "I don't even know how to respond to that." Willow starts fussing, but stops as she bounces her knee. "But you should know, if you think you can do the same to Jack—"

I cut her off with a sharp laugh. "In case you haven't noticed, I'm the

one in chains."

Leaning closer, she studies me—not with pity, not with judgment. Just a cool, assessing glance, the kind I recognize from my own profession. It makes me feel more seen than I like.

"You don't seem all that fazed," she observes. "If I didn't know better, I wouldn't even think any of this bothers you."

Biting my lip, I swallow down the laugh bubbling in my throat. She's both right and wrong. I am bothered, but growing up in my house, you quickly learned to mask your feelings. Showing unease was the same as giving your opponent the upper hand.

"Looks can be deceiving," I reply cryptically.

"Are you bored yet?" she asks after a beat, completely changing the subject.

"Very."

She smiles at my reply. "Yeah, I've been where you are, Eve. Well, not literally, but close enough. If I were you, I'd use the alone time to get curious."

"Curious?"

"Jack's careful," she says, straightening. "But he's still a man. And men often hide what they don't want others to see. Especially Knight men. They all like building pretty walls around rotten things."

Before I can answer, she gets up, moving slowly now that Willow is sleeping on her arm. The baby makes the softest little coos in her sleep.

"We should get going. It was… oh, wait. Before I forget again. If Jack's not back by the end of the week, I'll be escorting you to an event at the Sanctuary."

"You will?" I ask, dumbfounded by the fact Jack might be gone for days. "Where did you say he was?"

Carolina cackles. "Nice try. I didn't say, and I'm not going to. Knight business is just that… for Knights. Take care, Eve."

With those words, she leaves, locking the door after her. I don't know what she meant by her parting words, but I know I'm going to find out. Eventually.

The Trickster

Nick talks too fucking much. He always has. Tonight it's worse, his voice a steady grind in my ear as I follow him down a side corridor of the warehouse.

He called while she was still asleep, curled against me in the cage, my cock still buried in her heat. I should have ignored him. Instead, I carried her out, laid her in my bed, and chained her to the wall.

For half a second I was tempted to leave her free, but no. Eve's not ready for that kind of freedom. If I give her the keys to escape, she'll leave faster than I can ask her to stay. Besides, I need more time to figure this shit out.

I can't fully explain what has changed. Mostly because I'm not even sure I fucking understand it. Maybe it was because she showed me her scars and opened up to me… no. That's not it. Well, not all of it. There's more to it.

Deep down, I know she's right. I don't hate her, and I'm not sure I ever have. But I hate what she represents; my own failure to save Ruby. None of what happened is Eve's fault, not really. Doesn't mean I don't wish that it were.

"You need to calm the fuck down," he mutters, tone pitched low but firm. "Carolina dropped food and clothes off to her like you asked. Eve's fine."

I bite back the urge to tell him Carolina isn't me. She doesn't know every twitch of Eve's mouth, every lie in her tone. She doesn't hear the difference between silence that means exhaustion and silence that means plotting.

"She's mine," I growl instead. "Leaving her chained in the bedroom while I play errand boy for the family is not my definition of fine."

"Fuck's sake," my brother grumbles. "First you can't wait to punish her, and now—"

"Oh, I'm still punishing her," I reassure my big brother.

"Are you?"

No. "Yes."

"Whatever." Nick shoots me a look over his shoulder, sharp and unimpressed. "You think I wanted to drag you here? We've got bodies on the docks, Jack. Knights don't get to pick and choose when business calls."

I curse under my breath, shoving a hand through my hair as we step into the main space. The stench of salt and diesel clings to the walls, mingling with the metallic tang of blood. Two men are kneeling in the center of the concrete floor, hands zip-tied, faces already swollen from whatever welcome committee Nick sent ahead.

Ned stands to one side, calm as ever, arms folded like a priest waiting to administer last rites. He nods at me, expression unreadable.

"This is the part where you stop thinking about your captive Bride," Nick says, voice dry, "and start thinking about the family business. We clean up the mess, we send the message, and then you can go back to playing house with your psychiatrist."

"Don't encourage him to play hide the pickle," Ned deadpans.

"More like the salami," I grin, punching him on the shoulder.

Ned chuckles. "Listen, Jack, I have a favor to ask."

"Shoot."

"Shelby wants to see Eve," he says, looking anywhere else but at me. "She feels terrible, and she misses—"

"Soon," I agree. And judging by the double-take Nick does and the

widening of Ned's eyes, no one expected that reply. "I'm sure Eve will want to see her as well."

"So… when?"

Running a hand down my face, I scoff, "I don't fucking know. I'll figure it out once I'm not about to fucking kill someone."

Ned grimaces, probably realizing his terrible timing. "Right, I get it." Just as I think he's done, he continues. "It's just that Shelby's been acting weird without Eve around."

"Weird how?" I demand.

"I don't know, man. I barely see her anymore, and when I do, she's on the phone with some guy."

Nick chimes in. "Her Groom?"

"No." Ned shakes his head. "That's what I thought, but it's not him. I don't fucking know who. It might not even matter. I just know my sister's acting off."

"Can we discuss this shit later?" I bite. "Surely there are better times."

With that, I step forward, moving toward the kneeling men. One of them lifts his head, a whimper caught in his throat. Wrong move. My hand fists in his hair, jerking his face up to mine.

"Playing house," I sneer, repeating the words Nick said. Then, I drive my fist into his mouth, feeling the crunch of teeth give way. "Not fucking playing. I'm building one."

Blood spatters my knuckles, warm and slick. For a heartbeat, I picture Eve's gray eyes instead of this bastard's. Her mouth instead of his broken teeth. My cock twitches, and I shove the thought down with violence, hitting him again.

Nick says something behind me—*enough, focus, we don't have all night*—but I barely hear him. Every second I'm here is a second I'm not with her, not watching the way she pushes boundaries, not listening to the way she says my name when she's breaking.

Knight business demands my time. But Eve Mortis owns my fucking mind.

CHAPTER 23

The Bride

For the next two mornings, I wake to the most delicious aroma curling through the air—bitter, rich, unmistakable. Coffee. Each morning, the hot beverage is placed on a note with just one word. Yesterday it was *careful*, and today that word is *soon*. It's the only sign Jack's been here.

I don't get why he didn't wake me up. Just like I don't understand why I care. I should be happy he left me alone. Right?

The chain pulls faintly at my ankle as I shift upright. I reach for the mug and take my first sip, moaning at the perfect blend. Damn, that is good.

Not wanting to waste time by staying in bed, I get up and go through my routine of showering and getting dressed. Unlike yesterday and the day before, I don't dress in my own clothes. Instead, I pick the long sleeved shirt on the floor on Jack's side of the bed.

I can't explain why, but even while I'm hurt he left me after what we shared, and is now seemingly ignoring me, I like being surrounded by his scent.

The shirt makes me feel all small and dainty as it reaches my mid-thigh. And paired with a pair of knitted socks that almost reach my

knees, it's practically a complete outfit. Definitely fine for what I have in mind today.

Since Carolina hinted that I should consider exploring, that's exactly what I'm going to do. She was here again yesterday, delivering more food and apparently placing some jack-o'-lanterns outside the front door. Not that I can see them.

Willow wasn't with her that time, but she stayed a couple of hours, talking about how nice it was to be out of the house alone.

Where I thought maybe I'd be able to get some information out of her, she quickly proved that wasn't happening. Not that I can complain. Not when she tried to reassure me that Jack's absence was caused by duty. I'm not sure I believe her, but I want to. More than I ought to.

The chain allows me to reach the walk-in closet, a space I've glimpsed but never properly explored. I hesitate at the threshold, weighing risk against potential insight. Unable to help my curiosity, I step inside.

The closet is larger than expected, with custom built-in shelving that stretches from floor to ceiling. His clothes hang with military precision—suits on one side, casual wear on the other. Everything in black, grays, occasional navy. Nothing vibrant, nothing that bleeds emotion.

I run my fingers along the sleeve of a jacket, the fabric is expensive beneath my touch. This is how he presents himself to the world—controlled, moneyed, contained. My eyes catalog details with professional efficiency, shoes polished to a mirror sheen, ties arranged by subtle gradations of color.

My attention shifts to the back wall, where the shelving unit doesn't quite meet the ceiling. There's a gap there—subtle, easily missed if you weren't looking for architectural anomalies. I press my palm against the wood, feeling for inconsistencies.

A slight give on the right side suggests a pressure point. I push, and a section of the wall swings inward with a soft click. Behind it, a narrow ladder ascends into darkness. My pulse quickens as I step back, processing this discovery.

I strain my ears, listening for any sound that might indicate Jack's unexpected return. The house remains silent except for the occasional creak of settling wood. I have time, but not unlimited. Each minute I spend exploring increases the risk of discovery.

My fingers close around one of the ladder's rungs. The metal is cool and dusty, suggesting infrequent use. I pull myself up one step, testing its strength. It holds firm.

The rational part of my brain—the part trained in risk assessment and survival—warns against proceeding. If Jack returns and finds me here, the consequences could be bad. But it's not like he's explicitly told me I can't go snooping.

In fact, he said nothing. He just left. So... fuck him.

There's no point in pretending I haven't already made up my mind. So I place my foot on the bottom rung and begin to climb.

At the end of the ladder is a trapdoor. When I press my palm against it, I feel resistance. It's not locked, just stuck from disuse. I push harder, and it gives way with a reluctant groan, swinging upward to reveal the darkness beyond.

The attic air is dense with age and secrets, particles of dust hanging suspended from the rafters. I ease myself fully into the space, scanning the shadowed corners with trained precision.

The chain tugs tight by the time I'm halfway through the attic opening. I haven't reached the end of my shackle, yet. But I'm close. The wind outside rattles against the eaves, creating a hollow moaning that seems to emanate from the wooden beams themselves.

This isn't a space designed for comfort or display. It's a repository— a place where memories go to be forgotten, not preserved.

Stacked cardboard boxes line the wall next to me, some sealed with yellowing tape, others open like discarded husks. I move toward them with measured steps, careful not to disturb the thick layer of dust that chronicles neglect.

My fingertips leave evidence of intrusion as I lift the flap of the nearest box. Inside, photo albums rest in funeral arrangement. I extract one, its leather cover cracked with age, and settle cross-legged on the rough wooden planks.

Three children stare back at me—unmistakably the Knight siblings.

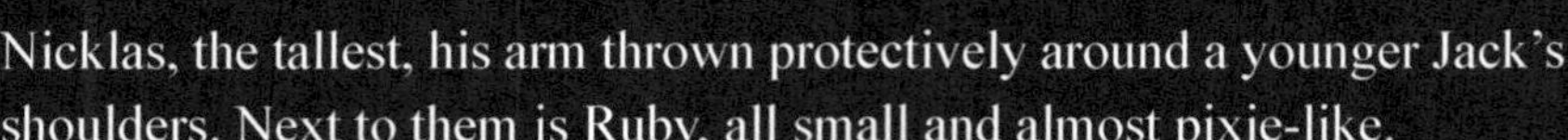

Nicklas, the tallest, his arm thrown protectively around a younger Jack's shoulders. Next to them is Ruby, all small and almost pixie-like.

They stand before a lake, squinting against the summer sun, their bodies relaxed in the casual intimacy of siblings who haven't yet learned to guard themselves from each other.

I study Jack's face with clinical interest, cataloging differences between this boy and the man who caged me. His smile reaches his eyes, crinkling the corners in genuine mirth. There's no cruelty in his expression.

The boy in the photo still had softness to him—rounded cheeks, a hint of sunburn across his nose. But now? Jack is all harsh lines and haunted hollows. That bone-cut jaw, those sharply carved cheekbones—he's the kind of beautiful that hurts to look at.

He looks like something sculpted under pressure, like the world carved him out of bone and fury. It's obscene how good he looks for someone who should terrify me.

As I flip through pages, watching time carve away at innocence, something shifts. The smiles tighten. Spaces appear between bodies once pressed close. Jack's eyes gain a wariness, a calculation.

I recognize the birth of the man I know—the one who plans, who measures, who never reveals more than necessary.

When I'm done looking through the fifth or sixth photo album, a small Polaroid falls from the pages. It's of a woman holding a baby. I pick up the small photo and turn it over. The date and names are written on the back. Jack and Mom.

After tucking the Polaroid back inside the album, I set it aside and turn to a long cardboard tube tucked between boxes. The end cap comes loose with a soft pop, releasing the scent of oils. I slide out a roll of what appears to be paintings, unfurling them carefully across the dusty floor.

A landscape unfurls before me—a shoreline at dusk, waves frozen in violent motion against jagged rocks. The technique is amateur, but the emotion is undeniable. Rage captured in brushstrokes, the sea a churning representation of an internal storm.

The next painting shows a woman I immediately recognize as Sienna Knight from the photographs—Jack's mother.

Her face is rendered with painful precision, each line a reverent documentation of memory fighting against the erosion of time.

There's something hauntingly beautiful and powerful about sensing the hunger for connection in the brushstrokes. Yet it's also frustrating. I shouldn't feel anything, let alone sympathy, for the man who's chained me.

Yet I feel the pull all the way down to my soul. Like if I just touched his cheek, I could trace the origin of every fracture.

Banishing those thoughts, I unfurl more canvases, each revealing a new facet of what must be Jack's inner landscape. A child's bedroom, empty but for rumpled sheets. A pumpkin patch at night, orange globes glowing like embers against black soil.

"Subject displays unexpected depth of emotional processing," I murmur to myself, falling into the clinical assessment that helps me maintain distance. "Artistic expression indicates a repressed trauma response."

But the professional veneer feels hollow against the raw humanity captured in these images. If Jack painted these—and the evidence strongly suggests he did—then the man who locked me in a cage contains multitudes I haven't accounted for.

The predator houses vulnerability beneath his armor, and I'm not sure if that makes him more or less dangerous.

As I carefully re-roll the canvases and begin studying others, I start noticing something that gives me pause. Before I know what my brain has picked up on, I carefully lay the canvases out on the dusty floor, arranging and rearranging them until they make sense.

"Holy shit," I breathe when a pattern emerges.

Jack's cleverly hidden words inside the paintings, and now that I have them side-by-side, they're starting to make sense.

Three children born, only one survives.

This is the Knight pattern, the inheritance we cannot escape.

Mom died bringing Ruby into the world. First sacrifice.

Who will be second?

The devil always collects.

My brain immediately categorizes this magical thinking as another trauma response. The belief in a predetermined pattern of loss creates an illusion of order in chaos.

If deaths are fated, then no one bears responsibility. If sacrifice is inevitable, grief becomes a ritual rather than rupture.

As I try to process it all, the human part of me recognizes something deeper. Jack isn't just cruel, he's haunted. Death isn't abstract to him—it's familial.

The thoughts hidden in paint reveal a man grappling with mortality in the most intimate terms, a man who has felt his own heart stop and restart. Such an experience would fundamentally alter anyone's relationship with mortality, with time itself.

Each day becomes borrowed. Each breath, a theft from whatever claimed you temporarily.

His obsession with me makes more sense viewed through this lens. I'm not just the woman who failed to save his sister—I'm the witness who chose not to intervene in death's design.

In Jack's fractured logic, I'm complicit. I don't feel sorry for him. Understanding the architecture of someone's pain doesn't excuse the suffering they inflict.

But still, something in me itches to reach for him. Not to comfort, but to press harder, to provoke the ghost behind those predator eyes. Attraction isn't supposed to feel this much like sabotage, is it?

As I gather the canvases, carefully rolling them up, I wonder if revealing my own past will help me reach the man hiding beneath the monster. If he thinks he has me figured out, he's dead wrong.

My dad couldn't ever figure me out, and most of the time, I don't even feel like I fully know myself. Jack's no different. I showed him pieces of me no one else has ever seen, and he still walked away. And why the fuck does it bother me that he left?

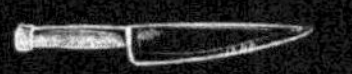

Finishing up, I wonder what Jack would do if he knew I'd seen this evidence of his humanity. Would he rage against the exposure? Or would part of him be relieved to be seen, finally, as something more complex than a monster?

The wind picks up outside, howling against the eaves like a creature denied entry. I replace everything exactly as I found it, erasing evidence of my investigation. Knowledge is power, especially when your opponent doesn't realize you possess it.

I move toward the trapdoor; the chain scrapes ominously against the floor. My mind's heavy with contradictions.

The Jack Knight who painted his dead mom's eyes with such tenderness is the same man who marked me as property, who used my body to punish my mind.

Both versions are real. Both must be accounted for in whatever strategy I craft next.

CHAPTER 24

The Trickster

The ornate wooden floors creak beneath my restless pacing, each step echoing through the cavernous hall like a countdown. I'm already inside the old historic building on Governors Island, reserved for high-level functions like tonight's board dinner.

Board members filter in slowly, nodding at me with wary respect, but I barely register their existence. My eyes keep darting to the arched doorway where she'll appear, where Carolina will bring her. Where my wife will walk back into my gravity.

It's been five days since I've seen her for more than a few stolen minutes while she slept—since I've touched her—and my skin feels too tight, like it's shrinking around bones that won't stop growing.

Five fucking days. I knew I shouldn't have left her alone after what happened between us. Not after she let me taste her pain. I've never thought of myself as a man who needs, but the emptiness in my chest tells a different story.

I miss her.

The realization burns like acid through my veins. I shouldn't care—this arrangement was never about attachment—but my body doesn't seem to understand the distinction.

The grand hall of this historic building reeks of old money and older blood. Centuries of power preserved in stone and wood. Massive chandeliers hang from the vaulted ceiling, their crystal teardrops catching the light like frozen rain.

Gothic arches frame tall windows that look out over the grounds of Governors Island, the distant carnival lights of the Sanctuary bleeding orange through the fog.

A board member—some white-haired fuck whose name I've deliberately forgotten—attempts small talk, asking about the projections for the Sanctuary. I answer with one-word responses, not bothering to hide my disinterest.

His wife sits beside him, her neck draped in diamonds that can't disguise the withered skin beneath. She's eyeing me like I'm the night's entertainment. I've gotten used to the way people look at me since Ruby died—half fascination, half fear, as if tragedy might be contagious.

The heavy double doors swing open, and my spine straightens before my brain can catch up. Carolina enters first, her blonde hair swept into a sleek updo, her dress a conservative black sheath that still manages to display her curves to their best advantage.

Nick would kill for her. Has killed for her. But it's the woman behind her that makes my breath catch. Eve.

She's wearing a short black dress with orange accents that match the tips of her hair, the fabric so delicate it looks like it might dissolve under my touch. The back dips dangerously low, exposing the ridge of her spine all the way down to where it disappears into the swell of her ass.

The front isn't much more modest—a deep V that draws the eye to the shadowed valley between her breasts, held together by what looks like a single clasp that's begging to be undone.

Her legs seem endless, and the heels she's wearing make her calves flex with each step. She's fucking magnificent.

I move toward her without conscious thought, drawn by some force more reliable than gravity. Her gray eyes widen slightly when she sees me, taking in my tailored black tux and the crisp white shirt beneath it.

"I've missed you, wife," I say, the words rough with honesty I didn't intend to reveal.

Eve rolls her eyes, but doesn't pull away when I lean in to kiss her. Her lips meet mine in a perfunctory press, her body stiff in my arms. The coldness of her response is so at odds with the heat of our last encounter that I almost pull back to check if it's really her.

But the scent is unmistakable—flowers layered over something darker, richer, that belongs only to her.

"Hello, Jack." Her voice could freeze blood. "How nice of you to remember I exist."

Before I can respond, Nick calls us to the table. I guide Eve with a hand at the small of her back, feeling the heat of her skin. She allows the touch but doesn't lean into it. The contrast with the Eve who rode me in the cage—wild, uninhibited, claiming—is so stark it feels like whiplash.

Instead of sitting at the head, which is customary, Nick waves our wives over and gestures for them to take those two seats. I take the seat on Eve's left, and Nick sits next to Carolina and right across from me.

It's a deliberate arrangement—the Knight women in the center, protected on all sides. No one touches what belongs to us. And with my brother's head of security behind the women, all sides are covered.

I mouth my thanks to Marco, who just nods back. Stoic as ever.

"Let's start with drinks and the important stuff while the chefs put the last touches on the food," Carolina says, officially calling the meeting to order.

I can't focus on a single word being said as everyone asks questions about the only thing that matters to the board members—money.

My attention is locked on Eve's face, on the careful blankness of her expression when she looks at me. She's here physically, but somehow she's locked herself away, retreated behind walls I thought we'd started to dismantle.

The candles on the table catch in her hair, turning the orange ends to flame. I want to reach across and tangle my fingers in it, to pull until her head tips back and her throat is exposed to me. I want to ask what changed, why she's looking through me instead of at me.

But the questions will have to wait. For now, I watch her.

Finally, the first course arrives, and with it, plenty of wine. Eve and I are served at the same time, and when I shake my head and refill my

water glass, she does the same. I look at her, intending to tell her she can
drink wine if she wants, but she's not looking at me.

Her eyes are on the artful arrangement of food too pretentious to
satisfy actual hunger. Though she smiles politely at the board members
who look her way, she ignores me completely. Sure, the smile doesn't
reach her eyes, but it's still more than she's offered me.

Something dark and possessive twists in my gut. I grip my knife
harder than necessary, the metal biting into my palm.

"Dr. Mortis, I understand you specialize in trauma psychology," says
one of the women, her voice dripping with rehearsed interest. "You got
that from your father, didn't you?"

"Her father?" a man asks.

His wife slaps his arm and scoffs. "Yes, dear. Her father was the great
Charles Mortis."

My gaze darts to Eve, but she doesn't even flinch at the mention of
her dad. Instead, she turns to the woman who first addressed her. "Yes, it
was my dad that got me into that line of business." She tucks a strand of
hair behind her ear. "You could even say he had the head for it—"

"Oh!" Carolina exclaims, her lips splitting in a knowing grin. "I
think I get it now."

Eve ignores her and continues. "I'm currently on an extended
sabbatical, though." Her tone is measured, thoughtful, and engaging.
"All thanks to my husband." She doesn't even look my way.

When the conversation shifts to me, her demeanor changes instantly.
Her answers become clipped, her body language closed. She speaks to
me without looking at me, addressing her glass or the space just over my
shoulder.

Each time I ask her a direct question, she finds a way to redirect, to
include someone else in her response. It's surgical—the precision with
which she cuts me out.

"Willow's Foundation has exceeded all projections," Nick
announces completely out of the blue. "But we're still hoping that the
Sanctuary of Shadows will bring in at least an additional two million in
donations and sales."

I should care about this. The Foundation is a family business, Knight legacy. But all I can focus on is the curve of Eve's neck as she leans slightly toward Carolina, whispering something that makes my sister-in-law's lips twitch with suppressed amusement.

"Jack," Nick says sharply, drawing my attention. "Do you have anything to add?"

"Whatever you recommend."

Nick's eyebrow arches slightly. Beside him, Carolina exchanges a knowing glance with Eve. The silent communication between them sets my teeth on edge. When did they become so familiar? When did my wife and sister-in-law develop a language that excludes me?

"Dr. Mortis," calls a board member from the far end of the table. "Perhaps you could offer some insight into the psychological impact of our immersive experiences?"

Eve straightens, her expression shifting into what I've come to think of as her doctor face. "Fear as entertainment works because it activates the same neural pathways as actual danger, but within a controlled context. The Sanctuary's tiered system is particularly effective because it creates the illusion of choice within a framework that's actually highly manipulated."

The table nods appreciatively at her analysis. I stare at her, hungry for even a glance in my direction, but her gaze sweeps over me as if I'm furniture.

Nick catches my eye across the table and smirks, clearly amused by my transparent frustration. He leans back in his chair, one arm draped casually around Carolina's shoulders, the picture of satisfied ownership.

My brother has always enjoyed watching me struggle—it's our dynamic, and has been since we were children.

"The… what did you call it?" The woman who's speaking pauses, looking at her husband for help, and he quickly leans in and whispers something to her that makes her blush. "Oh yeah, the fear-kink element has been particularly successful, especially in the Sacrifice only zones."

"Dark eroticism taps into primal instincts," Eve replies smoothly. "The brain doesn't always distinguish between different types of arousal. Fear, anger, sexual desire. They share neurochemical signatures."

My cock stirs at her clinical dissection of exactly what happens between us when I have her pinned beneath me. She knows this, *must* know this, yet she discusses it like an academic observation rather than lived experience.

"Of course, the most effective fear comes from genuine risk," she continues, finally—*finally*—glancing in my direction. Her eyes meet mine for a fraction of a second, then slide away dismissively. "When the body truly believes it might not survive."

The next course arrives, and before I know it, we're on the fourth. Eve speaks intelligently on every topic raised, charming the board with insights that blend psychology and business acumen.

She's magnificent, and watching her work the room stirs something like pride in me, buried beneath layers of frustration. This brilliant, beautiful woman belongs to me, yet acts like I'm a stranger she's tolerating at a dinner party.

By the time dessert arrives, my patience has evaporated entirely. Carolina catches my eye as I drain my water, her expression a mixture of amusement and warning. She leans over to whisper something to Eve, who doesn't even try to hide her eye roll in response.

"Something funny, *wife?*" I ask, my voice cutting through the general conversation.

The table quiets, sensing the shift in atmosphere. Eve looks at me directly for the first time all evening, her gray eyes cool and unimpressed. "Nothing that would interest you, *husband.*"

Nick chuckles under his breath, not bothering to disguise his enjoyment of the tension. Carolina's knowing smirk isn't much better. They've seen this building all night—my mounting frustration, Eve's deliberate provocations.

"Jack," Nick warns, but there's laughter in his voice. "This isn't the time."

"When is it the time?" I snap. "When my wife decides I'm worth acknowledging?"

Eve doesn't flinch. She simply takes a delicate bite of her dessert, the movement of her throat as she swallows drawing my eyes like a magnet.

"I wasn't aware I needed to ask permission to speak to others at the table," she clips.

That does it. Something inside me snaps clean in half.

I shove my chair back with enough force that it topples, the crash satisfyingly dramatic against the marble floor. "I need a word with my wife," I announce to the table, not caring how it sounds or who's watching. "Now."

Before Eve can object, I reach for and grab her wrist, pulling her to her feet. She doesn't resist—not here, not in front of everyone—but the fury in her eyes promises retribution once we're alone.

"Excuse us," she says conversationally to the table, her voice perfectly composed despite the way I'm hauling her toward the exit.

"Take your time," Nick calls after us, not bothering to hide his amusement.

I drag Eve from the dining hall and into the corridor beyond, gothic arches looming overhead like silent judges. The heavy door swings shut behind us, cutting off the murmurs and the knowing looks.

In the sudden silence, I can hear her breathing—quick, controlled, furious. And then we're alone, with nothing between us but the wreckage of whatever broke while I was gone.

Without pausing, I haul her up the winding stone staircase, my fingers digging into the soft flesh of her wrist. She doesn't struggle—not yet—but I can feel resistance in the rigid line of her arm, in the deliberate way she keeps a half-step behind me instead of letting me pull her flush.

The ancient steps curve upward through the gloom, worn smooth by centuries of ascent. I know exactly where I'm taking her—where no one will interrupt what needs to happen between us.

"Let go of me," she hisses, but makes no real effort to wrench free. "Your board members are going to think you're insane."

"I don't give a fuck what they think," I growl, not slowing my pace. "And neither should you."

At the top of the stairs, I shove through a set of heavy French doors, dragging her onto the stone balcony that overlooks the grounds. The October air slices through us, sharp enough to raise goosebumps on her exposed skin.

Below, the grounds of the Sanctuary pulse with carnival lights— orange and red, wavering through the fog like submerged fire. Screams rise from the maze, primal and ecstatic. Fear as entertainment. Fear as arousal.

Eve yanks her wrist from my grip and puts distance between us, rubbing the mark I've left on her skin. Her eyes are storm-gray in the dim light, her hair lifting in the cold breeze.

"What the hell is wrong with you?" she demands, voice low and controlled despite the fury in her eyes.

"What's wrong with me?" I step toward her, backing her against the stone railing. "You've been treating me like a fucking stranger all night. Looking through me. Talking to me like I'm an inconvenience. So tell me, wife, what the fuck changed since I had my cock inside you?"

She opens her mouth to spit some retort, but I crush it with a kiss, swallowing whatever insult she was about to hurl. Her lips are stiff at first, resistant, but I press harder, my tongue demanding entry.

Something in her yields—not surrender, but a different kind of fight, her teeth nipping at my bottom lip hard enough to draw blood.

I groan into her mouth, the copper tang spreading between us. My hands find her hips, yanking her against me so she can feel exactly what her resistance does to me. My cock strains against my trousers, rock-hard and aching for her.

"Tell me," I demand against her lips. "Tell me why you're treating me like this."

"No." She shoves at my chest, but I don't budge.

"Fine." My hand slides down, bunching the fabric of her dress until I can reach beneath it. "Then I'll make you tell me."

I press my palm between her thighs, finding her already wet through the thin fabric of her underwear. The evidence of her arousal despite her anger makes my cock throb painfully. I push the material aside and slide two fingers into her heat.

"I've missed being inside you," I groan, my thumb circling her clit with practiced precision.

"Fuck you," she gasps, her body betraying her as her hips roll into my touch.

"That's the plan, Little Bride."

Her hand moves so fast I don't see it coming. The slap lands hard

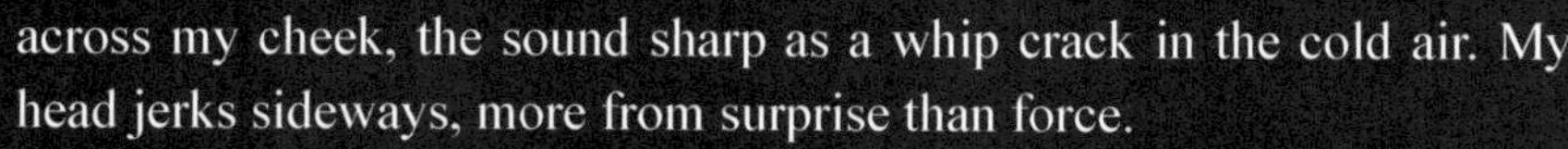

across my cheek, the sound sharp as a whip crack in the cold air. My head jerks sideways, more from surprise than force.

CHAPTER 25

The Trickster

"You left me," she spits, her voice breaking on the last word. "You fucked me and then you left me. And instead of trusting that what we shared in the cage meant something, you fucking chained me like an animal."

The accusation hits harder than her slap. "I had to go."

"Bullshit." Her eyes shine too bright, unshed tears making them look almost silver in the moonlight. "You used me, got what you wanted, and walked away. Just like every other fucking person in my life."

"Nick called and woke me up," I say, the truth raw in my throat. "He needed my help with the family business—"

"What was it?"

Even though I shouldn't, I answer her. "There were problems with a shipment that ended with bodies on the docks. I didn't have a choice, Eve."

"There's always a choice," she counters, but there's less conviction in her tone.

"Not in my family. Not when Nick says jump." I keep my fingers inside her as we argue, feeling her clench around me despite her anger.

"I would have come back sooner if I could."

A flicker of doubt crosses her face. "You could have left a note. Said something. Not just—"

"I know." The admission costs me, but I give it anyway. "I should have told you. But I didn't think it would matter to you."

"Didn't think it would…" She laughs, bitter and sharp. "You really don't understand anything, do you?"

Before she can say more, I withdraw my fingers and lift her body onto the stone railing. Her eyes widen with genuine fear as she registers her position—back to the open air, nothing but a thirty-foot drop to the ground below.

Her hands scramble for purchase, finding my shoulders and digging in. "Jack," she gasps, panic edging her voice. "What are you doing?"

I press my body between her spread thighs, one hand gripping her hip to steady her, the other coming up to circle her throat. "Teaching you to trust me," I growl against her ear.

Her body trembles against mine, every muscle tense with the effort of staying balanced. The cold stone must be biting into her thighs, but that's the least of her concerns with only my grip keeping her from falling backward into darkness.

"I could let you go," I whisper, my fingers tightening slightly around her throat. I groan when I feel her pulse jump. "Right now. One little push and you'd be gone."

A whimper escapes her, raw and primal. Her nails dig deeper into my shoulders. Fuck, I wish I wasn't wearing my tux jacket and shirt. I want to feel her nails dig into my flesh.

"But I won't," I continue. "Because you're mine. And I protect what's mine."

"Jack…" Her breathless plea goes straight to my cock.

"Open my pants," I demand.

Her eyes widen like saucers as she bites down on her bottom lip. "I-I can't," she stutters. "I don't trust you enough to let go."

I chuckle darkly. "If you don't do it, I'll have to. And then you have to trust I won't break your hold." Pausing, I let my words hang in the air for a minute or two. Long enough, I know she understands completely.

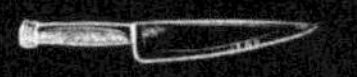

"Either way, you'll have to trust me."

She lets out a small cry and curses my name to Hell and back. But none of that matters when she lets go and reaches for my belt. "Don't fucking let go," she spits.

Then she undoes my belt, her hands trembling. Next, she pops the button and lowers the zipper on my pants, reaching for my cock. She freezes for a split second when she realizes I'm not wearing boxer briefs, but then she licks her delicious lips while pulling my dick out.

"Mhmm, so you can be a good wife," I rasp, squeezing my eyes shut. "Do you feel how hard I already am for you? Do you feel my cock throbbing in your hand?"

Eve whimpers and squeezes the base of my cock harder before stroking it firmly. I groan when her soft hand runs along the studs.

"Now, remove your underwear," I instruct.

Sadly, she lets go of my dick and reaches under her dress. But no matter how much she tries, she can't really get rid of her panties without having to move more than she's comfortable with.

I chuckle darkly. "Do you need my help?" If eyes could kill, I'd be a pile of ash from the look she shoots me. But eventually, she nods. "Ask me for it," I command.

"No."

"Suit yourself." I smirk as I loosen my hold on her. Not enough for her to fall, I'd never do that. But enough for her to feel the slack.

"Jack!" she screams. "What the hell's the matter with you? Help me."

"Ask."

Her chest heaves. "Help me remove my thong," she relents, voice cracking. "Please." The last word sounds like it's ripping straight out of her pride, and it makes my cock throb harder than her hand ever could. Fear is loosening her, bending her, giving me what obedience never could.

"I'll always help you when you ask," I rasp, tightening my grip on her hip so she feels the stone edge bite into her thighs. "But help comes on my terms." I tip my head toward my jacket. "Take the knife from my inner pocket."

Her hands shake slightly as she reaches for my tuxedo jacket and reaches inside, quickly finding the pocket and the small knife resting there.

"You can either cut your panties off." I pause, licking my lips. "Or you can trust me to keep you balanced with one hand while the other puts the blade between your legs."

Eve parts her lips, but no sound comes. Her gaze darts over her shoulder to the thirty-foot drop yawning behind her, then it slams back to me, tears brimming in her beautiful eyes.

Even though her body shakes with the effort of holding still, her thighs spread wider anyway, a trembling offering. Perfect.

"Do it," she whispers. "I… I want you to do it, Jack."

My lips curve, dark satisfaction coiling in my chest as she clutches my shoulder harder with one hand, while trying to give me the knife with the other.

"Put it in my mouth," I say.

As soon as the folded knife rests between my teeth, my left arm clamps tighter around her back. I don't pull her into me—I hold her just far enough forward that she tips toward the drop.

"You better sit completely still," I smirk.

Her ass balances half on the cold stone, half hanging in the open air. I spit the knife into my waiting hand and snap the blade open with a practiced flick. The sound is sharp, final, and it makes her flinch.

I slide the blade down, catching lace. One move and she'll be bare. One slip and she'll bleed. And still she obeys, shaking, silver eyes fixed on me.

"Jack," she whimpers. Her nails bite harder into my shoulders, legs hooked around me.

"Don't worry, wife," I rasp as I slice through the fabric that parts like melted butter beneath the pressure.

Eve lets out a small cry, and when she looks up at me, I notice dark streaks carving down her cheeks. Beautiful ruin painted across her face.

"Oh, Eve," I growl, leaning in and greedily licking the salty moisture from her skin. "Even your tears taste divine."

I draw the knife back, snap the blade shut with a flick, and angle the

handle so the cold hilt presses against her opening.

"What… Jack, what are you…" Her words trail off as I push the handle forward, slow enough that she feels every inch of stretch, the unyielding intrusion splitting her open.

Her cry pierces the night, nails gouging through the skin on my neck as her legs clamp around me, clinging to the only thing keeping her from falling.

"Be still," I command huskily.

I grind the hilt deeper, fucking it into her with measured thrusts, the sound of wet friction rising between us. My cock pulses against her thigh, begging to replace the steel, and I bare my teeth against her throat. "Good wife. You'll take what I give you, even if it's not my cock."

She sobs my name, voice breaking under the strain of fear and arousal, and the sound goes straight to my spine. I press my hips tighter, rutting against her leg, spreading my pre-cum all over her skin, while the knife works her open.

"Jack!"

Her scream fractures into a moan as the handle drags against her swollen clit on every thrust. She's shaking, thighs stretched wide over nothing, cunt clutching down on cold steel like it's the only anchor keeping her alive.

I rut harder against her leg, cock sliding wet across her skin, aching to be inside her but holding back because I want this. I want her to come undone for me like this—on the hilt of a knife, not my cock.

"Do you trust me now, wife?" I rasp in her ear, grinding the handle deeper, twisting it to scrape along her inner walls.

"I… oh God… Jack, I can't…"

"You can." My arm tightens across her back, every tremor of hers ricocheting straight through me. "Come for me. Right here. On the fucking edge."

She breaks with a sob, her cunt pulsing around the steel in violent spasms, slick running down the hilt onto my fingers. Her mouth is open in a silent cry as she comes, clinging to me like her orgasm is the only thing keeping her from falling.

I groan at the sight, my hardness jerking against her skin. But instead of letting her enjoy it, I throw the knife over my shoulder and press my cock against her drenched hole.

"You'll learn to trust me, wife," I growl, starting a brutal rhythm that rocks her on the narrow ledge.

Each thrust pushes her closer to the edge, her whole body trembling with the conflicting impulses to lean into the pleasure and away from the danger. The fear heightens everything—makes her wetter, makes her tighter, makes her gasps sharper and more desperate.

Her thighs scrape against the rough stone as I fuck her, leaving marks I'll trace with my tongue later. One hand stays at her throat, squeezing just hard enough to make her eyes roll back, while the other fists in her hair, holding her steady as I slam into her.

"Jack," she chokes out, wet streaks cutting fresh lines down her face. "Please don't let me fall. Please."

I catch a tear with my thumb, bringing it to my lips and licking it away with a sneer. "You still don't believe me when I say I've got you."

Her sobs become more desperate as her body tightens around me, another orgasm building despite her fear—or because of it. I spit directly into her open mouth as she whimpers, watching her choke it down.

"I'm in your cunt. In your mouth, and in your fucking throat," I almost roar. Even from way up here, it makes a few people on the ground stop and look up. Let them fucking stare. "I'm inside you in every way that fucking counts. Do you trust me now, wife?"

"Please," she gasps, tears still flowing freely. "Please let me come. I need it. I need you."

I slam into her as hard as I can without losing my tight grip on her.

Her orgasm tears through her like a storm, her body convulsing around me as she sobs my name. The vicious clutch of her cunt milking me drags me after her, spilling deep inside with a roar that echoes into the night.

But I don't let her down yet. I keep her seated on the railing, my cock still inside her, cum dripping from where we're joined. Her body quakes with aftershocks, cheeks blotched and wet with the ruin she shed.

"Look at me," I command softly, waiting until her wet eyes meet mine. "See? You survived. Because I let you. And I let you because I

need you."

I hold her gaze until her crying subsides, until the fear in her eyes shifts to something more complex—trust tangled with resentment, relief with lingering anger. Only then do I lift her off the railing, cradling her against my chest like she weighs nothing.

Her body molds to mine, exhausted and pliant.

"You'll always belong exactly where I put you," I murmur against her hair, carrying her back toward the warmth inside. "Remember it."

She doesn't answer, but her arms tighten around my neck, and I feel the press of her face against my shoulder—not quite surrender, not quite defiance, but something in between that feels dangerously close to acceptance.

CHAPTER 26

The Bride

My legs tremble as Jack guides me down the steps of the historic building, his arm around my waist both supportive and possessive. Each movement pulls at tender flesh, a delicious ache blooming between my thighs where he claimed me.

The wind cuts through my torn dress, but I don't feel cold—my skin still burns from his touch, my pulse still races from being on the edge of that stone railing with nothing but Jack's grip keeping me from falling.

"Can you walk?" he murmurs, his breath warm against my ear.

"I'm fine," I reply, though the words catch as another twinge of pain—pleasure?—radiates through me. My ruined panties are gone, disposed of somewhere on that balcony, and without them, I feel exposed, vulnerable.

Jack's cum slides slowly down my inner thigh, a warm, sticky reminder of what just happened between us. He wraps his coat around my shoulders as we approach the ferry, covering the tears in my dress.

The gesture feels strangely tender after the violence of our encounter. I clutch the lapels close, inhaling his scent—cedar, smoke, and something distinctly male that makes my stomach tighten despite the exhaustion settling into my bones.

On the ferry back to Manhattan, I lean against Jack who's standing behind me. We're both watching the lights of Governors Island recede into the fog. We're far enough from the railing that we're not being hit by the cold spray that rises from the churning water below.

His hands rest on either side of me, caging me in without touching, and I find myself leaning back into his chest despite myself.

"I'm hungry," I say suddenly, surprising myself with the simple admission. "I barely ate at dinner."

Jack's chest rumbles with quiet laughter. "Hard to eat when you're busy ignoring me."

I turn to face him, our bodies close in the darkness of the deck. "I was mad at you."

"And now?" His eyes catch the distant lights, turning them to emerald sparks in the darkness.

"Now I'm hungry," I repeat, avoiding the question. "Can we stop somewhere?"

"Sure," he agrees easily. "We have plenty of hotels. One of those could make us—"

I shake my head. "I'm not hungry for fancy food."

"What are you hungry for?" His tone drops, making the innuendo painfully clear.

"Not that," I reply quickly. "Something… greasy."

"Greasy?"

The ferry docks, and Jack leads me to his car, hand at the small of my back. The seat leather is cold against my bare thighs as I slide in, making me hiss. He notices, and his eyes darken as they trail down to where my dress rides up, exposing the bruises already forming on my skin.

As we pull away from the dock, I suggest a known fast-food place. It feels absurdly normal after everything, and I have to bite back a slightly hysterical laugh at the thought of Jack Knight in his perfect tuxedo ordering Big Macs.

"Whatever you want," he says, and there's something in his tone that makes me think he's not just talking about food.

The drive-thru is nearly empty this late, just a few cars ahead of us.

The neon sign casts garish yellows and reds across Jack's face, throwing his sharp features into relief. He looks like a fallen angel in the artificial light, beautiful and terrible.

"What do you want?" he asks as we approach the speaker.

"Double cheeseburger, large fries, and a Coke," I reply without hesitation. "And maybe some of those little apple pies if they have them. And a vanilla milkshake."

His lips twitch. "Hungry indeed."

The teenager at the window does a double-take when he sees Jack in his tuxedo, his eyes widening further when they land on me in my tattered dress mostly hidden beneath his coat. I can only imagine what we look like—disheveled, well-dressed, obviously coming from somewhere formal but looking thoroughly debauched.

"Date night?" the kid asks, trying to sound casual as he hands over our food.

"Something like that," Jack replies, his tone dismissing further questions as he passes me the warm bags.

The smell of salt and grease fills the car as we drive home, making my stomach growl audibly. Jack's hand drops to my thigh, fingers tracing idle patterns on my bare skin. "Patience," he murmurs, and again I have the feeling he's talking about more than just the food.

As we drive down the last two streets to get to Jack's house, I can't help but smile at all the jack-o'-lanterns I see. They're not as awesome and evil looking as the ones Carolina brought. When we left for the board dinner earlier, I finally got to see their cruel faces.

"Have you seen the Halloween decorations?" I ask as he pulls up to his house and turns the engine off.

"Not yet," he replies, getting out of the car, taking the food and drinks with him. "But I heard my dear sister-in-law brought some over."

I hum softly as I get out, ready to show him the evil wonders. But what greets me are not perfectly carved cruelness. Every single pumpkin has been smashed to pieces, and their insides stepped in and kicked around.

"Oh, no."

Jack chuckles and unlocks the door. "I guess the kids around here don't approve."

Pouting, I follow him inside. "Well, I liked them," I state as I kick off my heels and pad through to the kitchen, setting our food on the counter.

Jack watches from the doorway as I shrug off his coat and start removing the dress. His breath hitches as the fabric falls in a puddle of fabric at my feet, leaving me standing in nothing but my strapless bra. Instead of coming closer, he steps back, giving me space I'm not sure I want.

"You should shower," he suggests, voice rough.

I shake my head. "Later." For some reason, I don't want to wash him off me yet. As I move past him, I feel his gaze like a physical touch on my back.

As I enter the bedroom, I bypass the clean shirts and reach instead for one crumpled on top of the hamper. It's black, soft from countless washes, and when I bring it to my face, it smells intensely of him—not cologne, but skin and salt and man.

I pull it over my head without hesitation, the fabric falling to mid-thigh. It feels illicit somehow, stealing his scent this way, wrapping myself in it like armor. Or surrender.

When Jack enters the bedroom, his tie is loosened, but he's still fully dressed in his tuxedo. He reaches for his collar, clearly intending to change, but I stop him.

"Don't," I say, the word coming out huskier than I intended.

He pauses, hands frozen at his throat, eyes narrowing slightly. "Don't what?"

"Don't change." I swallow, feeling heat crawl up my neck. "Keep the tux on. You look…" I trail off, not wanting to give him the satisfaction of hearing me say it.

A slow smirk spreads across his face, knowing and predatory. "I look what, wife?"

"Too good to take it off yet," I admit finally, the confession making me feel naked despite the t-shirt covering me.

Jack Knight in a suit is a sight to behold. And thanks to wasting hours ignoring him, I haven't had my fill of watching him yet. While the jeans and leather jacket are hot as hell, it's different to the tux.

It's two sides of the same coin—an extremely attractive coin. They're the same, and yet they don't compare at all.

His smirk deepens as he drops his hands from his collar. "Is that so?" He crosses to me, fingers catching my chin, tilting my face up to his. "And is that my shirt you're wearing?"

"Yes," I don't deny it. "It smells like you."

Something flickers in his eyes, possessive and pleased. "Come on," he says, releasing my chin. "Let's eat before it gets cold."

He turns toward the living room, and I follow, feeling strangely lighter than I have in days. As if admitting I want him in his tux has broken some dam inside me, allowing other wants to flow freely.

While Jack kneels to build a fire in the stone hearth, I gather our food and drinks from the kitchen. No wine tonight, though my nerves could use the numbing. If Jack isn't drinking, neither will I. It feels like solidarity, though I'm not sure with what.

The fire pops and hisses as I settle on the couch, stretching my bare legs across Jack's lap. The soft drink is cold against my palm, condensation dripping onto my thigh as I take a sip. Jack's fingers rest lightly on my ankle, his thumb tracing absent circles against my skin.

He looks surreal in his tuxedo, the crisp black fabric a stark contrast to the greasy paper bags and cardboard containers littering the coffee table. A man of his status doesn't eat fast food in formal wear, yet here he is, stealing one of my fries.

I swat at his hand and toss another fry at him in mock retaliation. "Hey!" he exclaims.

"They're really good fries," I smirk. "I'm not sure I want to share."

We each bite into our burgers, and finish them without a word. Even though the silence between us is comfortable, I'm itching to find out more about him. So, I decide to shatter it with a question.

"What's your favorite color?"

Jack glances up, brow furrowing slightly. "Is this therapy, Dr. Death?"

"No." I shake my head, taking a bite of my burger. "Just conversation. Normal people have those, you know."

His lips quirk. "And we're normal people now?"

"For tonight," I say softly, not entirely sure why I'm offering this truce. "Just answer the question."

He considers, fingers absently circling my ankle. "Black," he says finally. "Not because it's empty. Because it hides everything you don't want the world to see."

The answer knots low in my stomach. "Makes sense."

"Your turn."

I hesitate, then say, "If I had to pick, orange is my favorite. But I love colors in general, which I think my hair proves." Laughing softly, I playfully lift a strand. "I usually dye it from the shoulders down each season."

"Do you always go with the same colors?"

"No." I proceed to explain that for Christmas I usually dye it green. "And… well… you know what color I use for February," I say sheepishly.

Our eyes meet. "I do."

Needing the heaviness gone, I ramble on about my hair. "For summer, I usually start with blue for a few weeks. Then I get it dyed yellow and light orange. Which brings me back to—"

Jack grabs a stray strand of my hair, twirling the orange part around his index finger. "This color." The deep timbre tells me he's more affected than he likes about any talk of the red.

I get it. It was red during the double funeral when I first met him. And it was that color because of Valentine's Day, which inevitably makes one think about Valentine Grant. I sigh softly, knowing I'll eventually have to tell him more about how I know Valentine.

"It's fitting orange is your favorite color," he murmurs, his hand sliding up to my calf, warm against my skin. "You burn hotter than you realize."

The observation feels too intimate, too accurate. I look away, reaching for more fries. "Who's your favorite band?" I ask, needing a different topic.

Jack steals another fry from my container, deliberately this time. "I don't listen to much music."

"Everyone has a favorite band," I press, nudging his thigh with my be. "Even psychopaths have musical preferences."

He smirks at that. "Marilyn Manson."

"Really?" I can't hide my surprise. "I wouldn't have pegged you for being into dark, aggressive, theatrical music."

"What did you peg me for?"

Now that he asks, I don't know. It's just so on the nose that he haunted me wearing a gas mask, probably listening to Marilyn Manson on his way to torment me.

"Classical," I tease.

His fingers find a knot in my calf muscle and press, making me gasp. "What's yours?"

Taking my time, I polish off the Coke, and reach for the shake and pie. It's not as good as it would have been when we first picked it up, but it still hits the spot. When I've eaten half, I hand him the last part, which he finishes in one bite.

"Come on, don't leave me in suspense, Dr. Death."

Sharing music taste feels more revealing than it should, but I still answer. "Florence and the Machine when I need to feel something... bigger than myself."

Jack's eyes don't leave mine as he continues massaging my calf, his touch firm but gentle. The firelight catches on his cufflinks as he moves, little flashes of silver against the darkness of his tux.

Time stretches. At some point, I shift, curling sideways into him instead of just draping my legs, the fire sinking lower until it glows red instead of burning bright. We're still asking questions, but the pauses grow longer, softer, like we're daring the silence to settle and then breaking it again.

"Do you often need that? To feel something bigger?"

"Don't we all?" I counter, deflecting. "Isn't that what the Sanctuary is selling? A bigger feeling than everyday life offers?"

His fingers pause. "The Sanctuary sells controlled danger. The illusion of fear without consequence."

"And what are you selling, Jack?" The question slips out before I can stop it.

"I'm not selling anything," he replies, voice low. "I'm claiming what's mine."

Heat climbs my neck that has nothing to do with the fire. I slurp some more milkshake, needing the cold to ground me.

Jack chuckles low in his throat, and the hairs on my body rise at the evil undertones. Oh, fuck. I bet he's about to ask me stuff I really don't want to answer.

To my surprise, he doesn't. Sure, he fires questions at me in rapid succession, not pausing long enough for me to demand he answers too. But each one is safe, so I let it go for now. Truthfully, I like seeing him like this.

"Favorite food. Go," he says.

"Anything I don't have to cook," I reply, which makes him laugh—a real laugh that transforms his face, softening the hard edges I've come to expect. I find myself staring, cataloging the differences.

"What?" he asks, catching me.

"Nothing." I look away. "I just... I don't think I've heard you laugh like that before."

Something flickers across his face—vulnerability, perhaps, quickly masked. "Not much to laugh about lately."

The admission hangs between us, weighted with all the things we don't say. Ruby. Valentine. The reason I'm here at all.

"And there went the bubble," I sigh wistfully.

I yawn before I can stop myself, covering it with the back of my hand. The milkshake's long gone, wrappers pushed aside, and the fire is down to a bed of coals. My body's heavy, warm, but my mind won't stop circling him.

"Bubble?"

I sit up straighter and pull my legs up so I can rest my chin on the knees. "Yeah, you know... the bubble we were in before reality came crashing down."

He nods and thoughtfully runs his thumb along the scruff on his jaw. "So maybe it's time I put my wife to bed." His eyes flash with barely concealed hunger when I nod my agreement.

We both stand quietly, reaching for wrappers and any stray leftovers from our meal. Once we get it all, he puts out the fire while I throw the trash out in the kitchen. When I open one of the cupboards, I notice that it's no longer bare.

I try a drawer next, surprised to find it filled with cutlery—steak knives included. It would be so easy to take one. My fingers hover over a wooden handle for several moments.

"Are you going to take one?"

I jump at Jack's voice behind me. "I'm thinking about it," I confess.

Rather than stopping me, or making sure I can't steal an impromptu weapon, he chuckles. "I can't wait to find out what you choose."

With those dismissive words, he heads into the bathroom, leaving me here to make a decision for myself. Either he trusts me way more than I trust him, or he doesn't see me as a threat at all.

If it's the latter, that's downright stupid. I did warn him that I'd try to kill him, and that I've faced bigger monsters and won.

CHAPTER 27

The Bride

The days blur into a rhythm that feels dangerously close to domestic.

We share meals, sometimes sprawled across the couch, sometimes at the counter while Jack cooks like it's the most natural thing in the world. To my surprise, he has quite a few culinary tricks up his sleeve.

He hasn't chained me again. He hasn't locked me back in the cage. And that's somehow harder to digest. When he shackled me, I knew my limits, knew the rules of his game. Now… I don't.

He just lets me drift through his house, making changes for me like I belong here. I catch myself choosing his mug for coffee like it's mine, and the terrifying part is how quickly it starts to feel… normal. Like I really do belong. But I don't. I can't. This is his life, not mine.

Thoughts keep me awake, circling like vultures. Little things keep popping up. Like, I don't even remember the last time I saw my phone. I'm not sure why I haven't considered that until now.

The last time I saw it was at my apartment. I wasn't allowed to bring it to Governors Island for The Black Wedding, so it's been gone for more than two weeks. It's still plugged into the charger on my nightstand. Or maybe Shelby's been by and has it. It seems unlikely, but she does have a spare key.

Ugh, thinking about her sends my blood boiling, and I clench my fists. I still can't quite wrap my head around her betrayal. It burns like acid in my veins, and I want to lash out at anything within reach.

How could she set me up like this? Even if Jack lords something over her, she should have found a way to warn me. It's fucked up. And I know that until I talk to her, my thoughts will just keep circling around the betrayal of it all. Which is exactly why I've kept pushing it down.

Right, so back to my phone. Yeah, the device really doesn't matter. Because I know the sad truth; no one's missing me. The only person who would care knows where I am, and she's the extent of my social circle.

For most of my life, I thought solitude was my choice. Now it feels like I've been buried alive in it.

The house is too quiet, and my body itches for movement. I slip out of bed and pad barefoot to the kitchen. I reach for a glass, fill it at the sink, and bring it to my lips.

That's when I see it—a flicker of motion just beyond the window, quick enough to make me doubt it, but strong enough to set my pulse racing. Someone's out there. Watching. I tighten my grip on the glass, but before I can lean closer, a sound rips through the house.

A scream. Deep, guttural, ripped straight from a nightmare.

The glass slips from my hand and explodes on the tile, water splashing over my legs as shards scatter across the floor. I don't care. I'm already running. My chest heaves as I stumble back into the bedroom, heart hammering harder with each second.

Jack thrashes in the sheets, sweat slick on his skin, his voice torn and broken. "Ruby! I'm sorry. I'm so fucking sorry." His arms lash out like he's fighting invisible chains, and the sight freezes me in place.

I've seen him calculated, cruel, and controlled. But I've never seen him like this—undone, begging, the sound so raw it doesn't seem like it belongs to him. For a second I just watch, trapped in the storm of it. Then I climb onto the bed and grab his shoulders, shaking him hard.

"Jack! Wake up!" My voice cracks, panic rising with every second he doesn't.

His chest heaves, his face twisting in agony.

"Jack!" I shout again, shoving harder this time. His eyes snap open, wild and unfocused, and then lock onto mine. For a moment he doesn't breathe. Neither do I.

His whole body jerks as if he's surfacing from drowning. The sheets are damp with sweat, his breathing harsh, ragged. I keep my hands on his shoulders even when his eyes clear, afraid if I let go he'll fall straight back into whatever nightmare dragged him under.

"Ruby," he rasps, the name torn out of him. It makes my stomach knot.

"She's not here," I whisper quickly. "It's me. Eve."

His gaze sharpens, and something unreadable passes through it—grief, guilt, relief—before he looks away, dragging a shaking hand across his face. "Dr. Death," he rasps. "The name has never seemed more fitting."

I still feel the tremor in his chest beneath my palms. For once, Jack Knight looks human. Breakable.

"You were dreaming," I say quietly.

"Having a nightmare," he corrects bitterly, letting out a humorless laugh. His throat works as he swallows, eyes still unfocused. "Some ghosts don't need sleep to haunt. They just wait until you're too weak to fight back."

I hesitate, then I ask the question I've been wondering about. "Is that why you drink so much?"

His jaw locks, and for a long moment I think he won't answer. Then, almost too low to hear, he says, "I haven't had a drop in days."

"Tell me about her," I say, adjusting myself so I'm sitting next to him on the bed.

"Ask me anything but that," he rasps. He turns and pulls me down so I'm lying next to him, my head resting on his chest and his hand trailing up and down my back.

His heart beats so hard I practically feel the thump against my ear. It's humbling to know he's being so open about his vulnerability. It makes me want to soothe him. I turn my head and place a kiss on his naked chest, just above his scar.

"When did you start painting?" I ask softly.

His hand stills on my back. "How do you know I paint?"

I freeze, realizing my mistake. "Umm…" I hesitate, then decide on honesty. Tilting my head upward I meet his gaze. "I found your canvases in the attic."

His jaw tightens, a muscle ticking beneath the skin. "You've been exploring."

"You left me alone," I remind him. "I was bored."

I expect anger, but instead, he just looks tired. "You liked them?"

The question catches me off guard. "Yes," I admit. "They're… raw. Honest."

His eyes search mine, and I can tell he doesn't believe me—doesn't trust that anyone could see his work without judgment. That hurts more than I expect. I slide my hand higher on his chest, over the steady pound of his heart.

"Paint me," I whisper.

His brows lift, suspicion flickering there. "Paint you?"

"Yes." I push myself up on one elbow, holding his gaze. "If it's honesty you put on the canvas, then I want to see how you see me."

The corner of his mouth twitches, not quite a smile. "That only works if you're bare, wife. No fabric between me and the truth."

Heat rushes up my neck, but I don't look away. "Okay."

This man has already seen every part of my naked body, in various poses, so it shouldn't be a big deal to let him paint me in the nude. Yet it feels poignant.

He studies me for a long moment before sitting up, reaching for the lamp, adjusting it so the shadows carve across the room like strokes of charcoal. Then he gets out of bed, pulling me with him.

Jack's touch is uncharacteristically careful as he peels his t-shirt over my head and pushes my thong down my legs. Cool air ghosts over my skin, turning my nipples into hard peaks. But he doesn't notice.

He reaches beneath the bed and drags out a battered wooden box streaked with paint.

When he opens it, brushes, tubes, and palettes come into view. I can't believe this was hiding in the most obvious place I never thought to look.

"Where do you want me?" I ask as he pulls out a stretched canvas, the surface already smudged with fingerprints and streaks of old color.

He props it against the wall, then drags a chair forward and sets it against the wall. Next, he starts pulling out brushes and mixing colors, careful with how much he pours onto the palette. I marvel at the calm radiating from him while he prepares. It truly is a sight to behold.

Once he seems satisfied that he has everything, he comes back to me. "Lie back down on the bed."

Jack's hands are warm as he adjusts me. Cradling my jaw, he tilts my face toward the light. Then he drags my leg up higher, so it bends, exposing more of me.

His eyes go dark as he takes a step back and observes me. "Perfect," he rasps, kissing my cheek before sitting down in the chair and hauling the canvas onto his lap.

The scratch of his brush fills the silence, broken only by the rough catch of his breath each time his gaze drags from the canvas to my body.

I hold the pose, though my thighs tremble from restraint, my nipples tight from exposure. His eyes eat me alive as much as his strokes capture me.

Finally, the brush slows, then stops. Jack sets it down, leaning back in the chair with the canvas balanced against his knees. His gaze lingers on me, then flicks to the painting.

"Come here."

I push myself up, every muscle tingling and aching from being held in place. Then I pad across the floor, the heat of Jack's gaze scorching every inch of bare skin. When I look down at the canvas, my throat tightens and my breath stutters.

Rather than being greeted by the me I see in the mirror, the woman on the canvas is the one he sees. She's stretched out in shadow and light, every curve of her body alive. I raise my hand and move a finger close enough to almost touch the wet paint.

I wordlessly trace the strokes in the air, committing each one to memory. I'm in awe of witnessing the way Jack sees me. It's intimate, powerful, and truly humbling. Every part of me is turned into something raw and defiant. Devastating. Beautiful. Terrifying.

My nipples are flushed in a tender pink, my cunt caught in strokes of shadow and light, more suggestion than detail—but enough to make my stomach tighten.

But what really gets me are my eyes. They're not just gray—they're soulful and… I don't even know how to describe it. I'm both an enigma and known. A powerful foe and frail.

"You made me…" My voice falters. "…look like I matter."

"You do." His reply is rough, dragged from somewhere deep. And I believe him. Because of every stroke, every careful color blend, I believe that I not only matter, but that I'm coveted.

Something reckless takes over. I drag my finger through the thick orange paint on the palette, then swipe it straight across his chest.

Jack jerks, eyes flashing. "You want to play dirty, wife?"

Before I can answer, he's on his feet, carefully leaning the painting against the wall. While he has his back to me, I dip both my hands into the palette—orange and pink slicking my palms before I press them hard to his bare skin, painting his shoulders and back with my handprints.

He lets out a playful growl and reaches for me, but I sidestep him. "Why am I the only one naked?" I complain.

He bares his teeth at me in a predatory smile as he lowers his boxer briefs, freeing his very erect and pierced cock. I lick my lips, momentarily distracted. That's all the time he needs to advance on me, grabbing handfuls of my ass.

"Then let's play," he rasps.

I slide my paint-slick hands down his back, clutching his ass and hopefully leaving perfect handprints. I'm just about to reach for his cock when I think better of it.

"Wait," I murmur. "Isn't paint bad for the skin?"

He chuckles. "Normally, yes. But this is actually cosmetic-grade body paint."

I arch an eyebrow in surprise. "Really?"

Shrugging, he explains, "I bought some when acrylics started giving me allergic reactions."

That's so not the answer I expected. It's so normal and anticlimactic.

"It does mean the paint isn't the best. It cracks and fades easily, but it'll do for now."

I pout, not happy that my pretty painting isn't of the forever variety. "Oh, okay."

Grabbing handfuls of my ass, he pulls me flush against him. The paint I've just smeared all over him easily transfers to my skin.

"Don't worry," he says, voice low and filled with gravel. "I'll use proper acrylics or oil one day, wife."

"Good," I say, loving the sound of that.

His cock twitches against my stomach. "But tonight," he rasps, "I'll paint you with more than colors."

His mouth claims mine, hard and consuming, while his hands slide between my ass cheeks to cup my cunt from behind. I gasp when his fingers find my wet opening.

"Fuck," he groans, swirling my clit. "You're my masterpiece."

I claw at his shoulders, leaving streaks of color across his muscles as he pushes me backward onto the bed. The sheets stain instantly beneath me, handprints and smudges marking where I writhe under him.

He looms above, body streaked with color, cock gleaming with pre-cum at the tip.

"Jack…" I choke on his name as red-hot want courses through my veins. "Fuck me. Now."

Either he hears the deep need in my tone, or he reads it on my face. No matter the reason, he doesn't keep me waiting. He lines the head of his dick up against my opening and slowly thrusts into me.

He growls low in my ear as my hands find his ass again, pulling him deeper. Our bodies slap wetly, every thrust driving the mess between us into something primal. The sharp scent of paint mixes with sweat, musk, and sex until I can't tell where he ends and I begin.

I arch under him, crying out as another wave builds inside me. His hand catches my throat, tilting my face toward the canvas propped on the wall. The woman painted there looks wild, defiant, terrifying—and I realize we really are one and the same.

"You're fucking everything," he groans.

I let out a sound that's half moan, half sob. Because I think I finally get it now. The emotion spreading through my chest is… love. And if I'm honest, I'm pretty sure I'm not the only one who feels it.

The way Jack painted me isn't how you paint a stranger, or even your enemy. Only someone you love can make you put pieces of yourself, of how they see you, into the paint. And that's exactly what Jack did.

I open my mouth, almost letting the three little words slip from my lips. But then I clamp my lips together. I refuse to be the one to say it first.

CHAPTER 28

The Trickster

The skillet still hisses on the stove when I set the last plate down. Eggs, toast, a stack of pancakes so high she eyes them like they might collapse.

It's too much for two people, but I like watching her fight through every bite I put in front of her. Like every forkful is proof she'll take what I give, even when it's too much.

Eve tears a strip of bacon, lips shining with grease, eyes narrowed on me like she's trying to decipher the catch. "What's the occasion?"

"Does there need to be one?"

Her mouth curves, not quite a smile. "With you? Yes." She quickly demolishes another two slices. "Pancakes and bacon would've done wonders for my mood two mornings ago—when I spent hours scrubbing paint out of places it had no business being."

I just grin, still remembering how annoyed she got when I refused to help her. What can I say, I loved that small fleck of orange paint on her ass.

After taking a sip of her coffee, she grimaces. "What the hell? This is not nearly as good as the delicious goodness you left for me to wake up to while you were gone."

Just as I'm about to ask her what the hell she's talking about since I never left her any coffee, my phone buzzes across the counter. Nick's name flashes across the screen, and the air curdles, the easy rhythm of the morning snapping like a bone under pressure.

"Don't tell me you called because you can smell the bacon all that way at—"

My brother's voice is clipped when he interrupts me. "Someone burned down one of our fucking hotels."

"What?"

"Did you not hear me? I've already spoken with the three, and they swear they haven't heard anything." He pauses long enough to snap at someone for spilling something on the floor. "I hate asking, Jack. But—"

"Fuck you," I snarl, the rot already spreading, coiling under my ribs like it's looking for a way to split me open. "I know what you're about to fucking ask. And no, I haven't done anything that would get anyone to attack our properties."

He exhales audibly. "Sorry, but…" Luckily, he doesn't spell out the many ways I've fucked up over the years.

I've previously gambled hotels away like it was Monopoly and not backroom poker. So it makes sense he'd want to ask me. Especially when his infamous three crime lords of NYC haven't heard rumors or whispers about a new player on the scene.

But it's still fucking offensive—like he can't see the monster straining at the leash, foam on its mouth, teeth aching for flesh. And I've kept it there, barely, without letting it tear free.

"Want me to go check it out?" I ask, looking down in surprise when Eve places her hand on top of mine.

Nick offers to meet me there, but when I explain I prefer to go alone, he just tells me what hotel before hanging up. In big brother language, that was both an apology and his way of saying he trusts me.

When I look up, Eve's gray eyes pin me—annoyance sparking there, sharp enough to cut. "You're leaving," she accuses, and the unspoken *again* hangs in the air.

"You could come with me," I offer, surprising the hell out of both of us.

Fuck, I don't know what I'm walking into, and the last thing I want is Eve caught in the blast—her body wrecked where I should've shielded her. The mere thought of something happening to yet another woman in my life is fucking sickening.

She arches a brow, chewing slowly. "Really?"

I lean across the counter, my palm braced near her plate. "Really," I confirm. "I want you with me."

While it's reckless and beyond stupid, it's also needed. It's becoming abundantly clear that I'm not giving up Eve. Fuck, I think I'm addicted to her. Sleeping next to her keeps the nightmares away, and every minute I spend with her feels right.

And that means sooner or later, I have to drag her straight into my world and let her choke on the smoke like the rest of us. Because the only alternative is letting her go, and that isn't fucking happening.

"Okay," she agrees, lips curving in a smile sharp enough to feel like surrender and defiance all at once.

"You need to promise me something, though."

Her chin tilts. "What?"

"That you'll stay at my side," I growl. "No running. No tricks. No bullshit. You move when I move. You breathe when I allow it. Do you understand me, Eve?"

She rolls her eyes. "Anything else?"

My gaze softens, and I cup her cheek. "I'm not trying to control you, wife. But I can't stand the fucking thought of anything or anyone hurting you."

Her gray orbs lock onto my green ones as she swallows thickly.

"I don't know what we'll be walking in on. Could be fire, could be bullets. Could be worse."

"I'm not a fucking damsel in distress," she snips. "I can hold my own, Jack. Don't forget what I told you about ending bigger monsters than you."

"Damnit!" I roar, slamming my fist into the table hard enough for the plates and cutlery to rattle. "I don't fucking care about your abilities. Don't you fucking get that I don't want anything to happen to you?"

"Why?" she shoots back, darting out of her chair. "Because you're

the only one allowed to hurt me?"

What in the ever-loving fuck has gotten into her? It's like she's dragging us backward, splintering every inch of progress until it fractures to dust beneath our feet.

"Say that again," I demand, my tone low and dangerous.

When she presses her lips together, I've had it. With two large strides, I round the table and close the distance between us. I wrap her hair around my hand and twist so she's forced to look up at me.

"Why are you doing this?"

"I'm not doing anything," she insists.

I force myself to take several deep breaths, doing my best to calm down. "Don't you get it?" My voice cracks raw, hoarse with restraint. "I'd never forgive myself if anything happened to you, Eve."

"Why?"

"Do you understand me, Eve? If anyone after me, or Nick, gets their hands on you, it won't be quick. They'll stretch it out, tear you apart piece by piece. And I'll burn this fucking city to ash before I watch that happen."

"Why?"

I snarl under my breath, beyond annoyed at the way she keeps repeating the same question. But as vulnerability sneaks into her expression, I finally fucking get it. Letting go of her hair, I wrap my arms around her.

"Because you're mine, Eve. You're my fucking wife, and…"

"And?"

"… I fucking love you. And that means if anyone touches you, I'll silence them so completely the world will forget they ever breathed."

A strangled sound escapes her as she throws her arms around my neck, dragging me down until her mouth collides with mine. The kiss is hard and bruising, all teeth and fury. She bites like she wants to wound me, like her mouth is the only weapon she has left.

I growl into it, my hand twisting harder in her hair until she whimpers against my lips. It isn't soft. It isn't tender. It's a punishing affection, a collision of rage and possession so sharp it leaves both of us breathless.

When she finally drags back for air, her gray eyes burn, wild and wet. "I hate you," she whispers, but her voice trembles like it can't decide between curse and confession.

I bare my teeth, still fisting her hair. "No, you don't."

"No, I don't," she agrees so softly I almost miss it.

"You love me back," I rasp, low and certain, like it's a verdict.

Her chest heaves against mine. She doesn't deny it. She can't. The silence between us is a vow, thick as blood, heavier than any admission she could give. Using my hand, I force her chin higher so she can't look anywhere but at me.

The corner of her lip trembles, still swollen from the kiss, still painted with the taste of me. I could devour her all over again, sink my teeth into her until she remembers nothing but who owns her.

"You're coming with me," I say, voice flat, unarguable. It isn't an offer anymore.

It never was. Her lips part like she wants to argue, but then she closes them again, biting down on the sound. Smart. She knows I'll win. She knows I'll drag her into the fire whether she consents or not, because I've already decided she's mine. Forever.

Her fingers flex against my chest, restless, and finally she exhales, sharp and shaky. "Then I need to change," she mutters.

My brow arches. "Change?"

"If I walk into that place in your shirt or anything Carolina brought from my place, I'll look like a fucking target." She tilts her chin, defiance sparking again. "Take me to my apartment. I have some clothes there I can wear."

While she rushes to get ready, I text Ned to meet us at her place with weapons and the spare key. The things Eve left behind at the Sanctuary after getting into her wedding dress are all with Shelby, and I haven't bothered to get them back yet.

Once Eve's ready, we leave and head straight to her place. Luckily, there isn't much traffic, so it takes no time until I pull into one of the parking spots in front of her complex.

"Eve." Her hand hovers over the handle when I say her name.

Pausing, she turns to me. "Yes?"

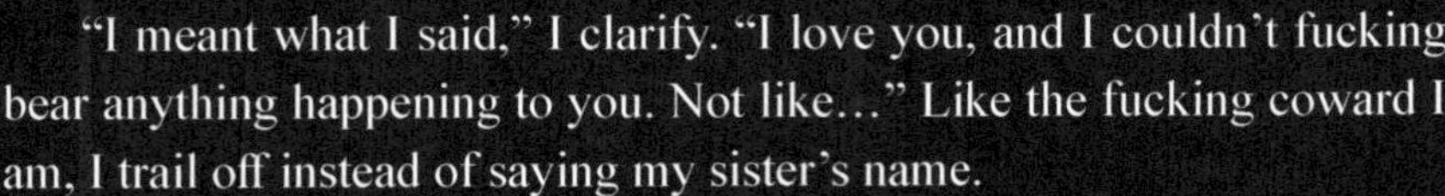

"I meant what I said," I clarify. "I love you, and I couldn't fucking bear anything happening to you. Not like…" Like the fucking coward I am, I trail off instead of saying my sister's name.

She swallows thickly. "I know, Jack. Nothing will happen."

We use the stairs instead of the elevator. The climb is silent, heavy with everything unsaid. When we reach her floor, I jerk her back against me.

"What the—"

I slam my hand over her mouth and point at her apartment, where the door is wide open. My gut goes cold. Ned should've been here, but the hall is empty. Before I can decide how to proceed, Shelby struts out of Eve's front door.

"Surprise!"

"You totally overreacted," Eve accuses with a soft laugh as I let go of her.

"Eve," Shelby calls out, her voice wavering. "Can we talk?"

"This really isn't a good time," I bark. I look behind her, to where Ned's standing. "Are you ready?"

He gives me a sharp nod. "Of course."

Eve does a double-take when she sees Ned, her eyebrows furrowing. "You've got to be fucking kidding me," she mumbles under her breath.

Ah, shit. I forgot she's never officially seen Ned with me. Obviously, she knows he's her neighbor, but that's not the same as *knowing* he works with me. Or maybe she'd already pieced it together and is just…

I open my mouth to say something… anything. But Eve narrows her eyes. "I can only handle one fucking thing at the time. So we'll talk about this later." Then she sighs heavily and looks at Shelby. "I need to get ready. We can talk while I change."

We enter Eve's apartment, and while the women head toward the bedroom, I stay in the living room with Ned.

"Sounds like you're in trouble." Ned grins.

I smirk and nod my agreement as I sit down on Eve's couch, propping one leg over the other. Looking around, I notice her mantle decoration. I arch my eyebrow as my eyes land on the plaque below.

Why so serious?

The unexpected show of humor should be surprising. But when it comes to my wife, not much surprises me anymore. The cold woman I thought I had figured out completely is nothing like that.

Not only has she taken everything I've thrown at her in stride, she's burrowed her way under my skin and into my heart.

Should I feel bad about everything I've done to her? Maybe. But I don't. Because the woman sleeping in my bed, making me ache for her, is nothing like the doctor I sat across from all those months ago.

There are still many things I don't know about her. Like, why the fuck does she have her dad's skull on her mantle? Why isn't she pissed that she lost her business? I might like that she seems so… adjusted. But it's unnerving at the same time.

In many ways, she reminds me of a reptile. Keeping still while waiting for the opportune time to strike, and that might be exactly what she's doing. After all, I know she's stolen one of my kitchen knives.

I guess only time will tell if she'll make good on her promise and try to kill me.

CHAPTER 29

The Bride

I pinch the bridge of my nose and exhale audibly. One. Two… nope. I can't stand listening to another apology.

"Just stop," I sigh, fighting the urge to laugh when Shelby's eyes widen. "You've apologized five times, blamed your brother and Jack three times each, and basically just talked in circles."

"But Eve—"

I shake my head and hold up my hand. "Sorry's cheap," I bite out, yanking my zipper until the teeth scrape my skin. "Try something else."

She twists her hands together, mascara smudged, looking wrecked. "Jack wanted someone to keep an eye on you, and he wanted it to be me instead of Ned."

If this were a therapy session, I'd call out her deflection in a heartbeat. But this is real life—*my* life.

"Okay," I relent. "That I can maybe buy. But how come you never told me my neighbor is your fucking brother? Or… I don't know, you could have hinted at Jack's plans."

"But I—"

That does it. Knowing she's about to deny knowing anything again has my temper flaring hotter than before. "Enough!" I shout. "If you tell

me one more time that you didn't know, we're done."

"Done?"

I nod sharply. "Yes. Done. I know you, Shelby. You're one of the sharpest legal minds in NYC. Do you honestly think I'm going to believe you didn't know? Give me a fucking break."

Her face crumples, tears spilling again. "I couldn't stand thinking about it. You're my best friend, Eve. I never wanted to hurt you, but I couldn't defy Jack. He owns Ned, and I couldn't go against my own brother."

Now we're finally getting somewhere.

"Go on," I urge as I finish getting dressed. Once I'm done, I finally locate my phone and try to switch it on. Nothing. Dead, despite sitting in the charger for weeks.

I force myself to listen to Shelby as she basically continues to repeat the same explanation and excuses over and over.

Acid twists low in my stomach. God, I hate that I still want to believe her. That part of me is desperate for her to make this betrayal make sense, because otherwise I'll spiral until I claw my way out of my own skin.

I force myself to meet her gaze in the mirror. "You broke something in me," I whisper, jaw tight. "And an apology doesn't glue it back together."

"I know," she sobs, wringing her hands. "I just don't want to lose you."

Something in her tone makes me falter. She looks wrecked. Small. And maybe, just maybe, we could untangle this mess. But there's no time right now. Not when Jack's waiting.

As if summoned by my thoughts, there's a knock on the door, followed by Jack's deep voice. "Eve."

Holding a finger up to Shelby, I say, "I'll be right back."

Then I slip into the hall, tugging the sweater straight as I go. Jack is waiting in the living room, shoulders squared. Ned, my neighbor who's apparently working for or with Jack, is in the kitchen.

"Are you ready?" Jack asks.

My pulse drums hard as I meet his gaze. "I think I should stay."

His jaw flexes, a dangerous muscle twitch. "Eve."

I step closer, tilting my face up to his, voice soft but steady. "I need to stay with her. We've barely scratched the surface, and if I don't—if we don't—this resentment will eat me alive. Let me do this."

He stares at me in silence, green eyes burning with the kind of fury that feels like restraint. My breath shortens under it. For a moment I think he'll pick me up and carry me out anyway, and part of me wants him to.

"Come on," I whine. "Isn't it better if I stay?"

His hand catches the back of my neck, dragging me forward into a kiss that steals the ground from beneath me. His mouth is rough, demanding, like he's imprinting his control into me so I won't forget it the second he walks away.

I open to him, let him take, let him devour until my knees weaken. And then I return the kiss with everything in me, not letting him pull away until we're both panting.

He rests his forehead against mine, breath ragged. "Promise me you won't leave this apartment."

"I promise," I whisper, dizzy with heat and the ghost of his mouth.

Behind us, Shelby clears her throat. Both our heads snap in her direction, and for once she doesn't flinch. She lifts her chin, reaching into the inside pocket of her jacket, and pulls out a small switchblade. The metal glints under the overhead light.

"I can keep her safe," she says, voice steady. "If anyone comes, they'll regret it."

Jack studies her with a look that makes the air in the room heavy. Finally, he gives a short nod, though his hand tightens on me like a leash. "If you fail her, there won't be enough left of you to bury."

Shelby swallows hard, but she doesn't back down.

Jack kisses me one last time, slower this time, and then lets go. I follow him to the door, squeezing his hand one last time. When he walks through the door and disappears down the hallway toward the stairs, my stomach clenches.

I've barely shut the door behind Jack and Ned when Shelby drifts closer. She flicks the lock with a soft click.

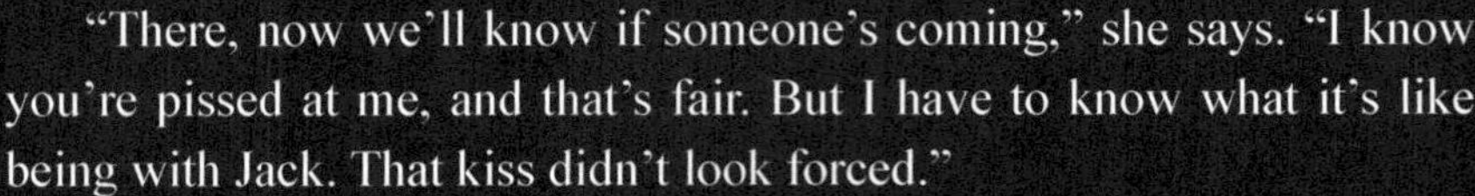

"There, now we'll know if someone's coming," she says. "I know you're pissed at me, and that's fair. But I have to know what it's like being with Jack. That kiss didn't look forced."

While she talks, we move into the living room and settle on my couch. I pick up one of the throw pillows and hug it close.

"Umm… it's intense."

"Yeah?"

I bite my bottom lip, not sure how to describe our relationship. "And complicated."

"But you like him?"

That's true. In fact, I'm pretty sure I love him, but for some reason, I don't want to share that. God, right now I wish it were a therapy session so I could refuse to answer questions. But that's not how friendship works. And I can't be pissed at Shelby for holding back if I do the same.

"I never expected to fall for him," I admit after a pregnant silence. "But I think I have."

Shelby's eyebrows shoot up high on her forehead. "Really?"

Needing to do something, I get up and make us some tea while I do my best to explain that things have changed.

"Did you know he kept me in a cage in the beginning?" I ask, carrying two steamy mugs back into the living room with me.

"No way."

After placing them on the table and sitting back down, I explain my first week with Jack. How cold and cruel he was in the beginning. "He blamed me for Ruby's death." My insides knot as I realize I don't know if that's still the case.

Shelby runs her tongue along her front teeth and blows on her tea before taking a small sip. "Is that why he wanted to capture you?"

I scrunch my nose up in confusion. "You didn't know? Didn't he—"

She interrupts me. "I love my brother, Eve. I really do. But sometimes he acts more like Jack's lapdog than my only family. He never told me what it was all about, only that I had to get you to the Sanctuary of Shadows for the launch event."

I stare into my mug, the steam curling up into my face until my lashes dampen. For a second, I don't know if I'm relieved or furious. If she's telling the truth, and why wouldn't she be, then Ned and Jack kept her at arm's length the same way they did me.

"Ruby was a bitch anyway," Shelby suddenly says. "She got what she deserved."

The. Fuck.

I'm so shaken by that revelation that I can't think of anything to say. So I just say nothing. Minutes slide past, heavy and slow. The heater hums, pipes tick in the walls, each second louder than the last. I sip, swallow, sip again. Steam fades.

The burn on my tongue dulls to warmth, then nothing. By the time I glance down, the tea is already cooling in my hands.

Shelby's gaze flicks toward me over the rim of her mug. "So… when he kept you in that cage, did you hate him for it? Or did part of you like it?"

My jaw drops before I can stop it, heat flooding my face. "Jesus, Shelby. Who asks that?"

She laughs lightly, tucking one leg beneath her. "I'm just curious. You wouldn't be the first woman who confused obsession with devotion."

A prickle starts low in my spine. I grip the pillow tighter. "It wasn't like that. It was… complicated."

"That word again." She tilts her head. "Complicated sounds a lot like excuse-making."

My jaw tightens, teeth grinding, because if I don't anchor myself in anger, the disbelief will swallow me whole. "You weren't there. You didn't feel what I felt."

Her phone buzzes softly against the cushion beside her. She quickly checks it before tapping twice. Then she flips it face-down again.

"Hmm," she muses. "I might know better than you think. My ex once kept me on a leash for an entire month. It was fucking glorious."

This is one of the few times Shelby's talked about her ex. I know he died back in February, but I don't know how or why. Apparently, their relationship was a secret, so no one really knows much about it.

"Do you still miss him?" I ask softly.

"I'll love him until the day I die."

Wow… that's deep. Definitely not just a fling then. So why did I think it was just that? Or maybe a tad more serious, but I definitely never thought it was epic love.

"So when did it stop feeling like captivity?" she asks, changing the subject back to me and Jack.

"What?"

She runs a hand through her hair. "I mean, when did you start spreading your legs willingly?"

The words punch the air from my lungs. My fingers go slack on the mug and I nearly drop it. "Ex-fucking-cuse me?"

She tilts her head, expression open, almost innocent. "I'm just trying to understand. You were terrified at first, right? But now you look at him like he hung the moon. Something must've changed."

My cheeks heat, pulse stuttering. "That's not how I'd put it."

Her smile sharpens as she takes another sip. "How would you put it then? That you're special? That he sees something no one else does? Because I'll be honest, Eve. All I see is a girl who's always been too eager to be filled. Too eager to be needed."

The words land like barbed wire tightening around my ribs. For a heartbeat, I just gape at her, mouth dry, because I can't believe they came out of *her* mouth. Then I set my mug down with a sharp clink. "Why are you talking to me like this?"

Shelby leans back, crossing her legs, phone balanced loosely in her lap. "Because someone has to. You sit here pretending this is love, when it's just another man using you. Different collar, same leash."

My throat works, but no words come. Her eyes return to mine, glinting now, nothing soft left.

"Tell me, Eve. Do you even know who you are when there isn't a man holding your throat?"

A knock rattles the door.

I flinch so hard I nearly spill what's left of my tea.

Shelby doesn't move. Doesn't even blink. She only smiles, slow and cruel. "Right on time."

There's no hurry in her movement as she rises, and sets her mug neatly on the table. She gives me a smile that's all teeth before walking

over to the door, unlocking and swinging it open and in walks… Caleb.

His eyes flick past me without interest before settling on Shelby. She steps into him, and his hands are on her in an instant—fisting her hair, dragging her mouth to his.

The kiss is slow and brutal, all teeth and tongue, wet and noisy in a way that makes my stomach lurch.

"Are you two together now?" I ask, not sure why that surprises me.

Well, actually, considering what she just told me about her ex, it *is* surprising. Sure, I thought I saw him with her at the Sanctuary. But this… this is definitely not what I expected.

"Surprise," Shelby sing-songs after pulling back from him.

Her eyes are colder than I've ever seen, sharp with triumph. I barely recognize her. "Restrain her," Shelby orders flatly, jerking her chin at me. "We need to be gone before Jack and Ned come back. It won't take them long to figure out the fire is bullshit."

"What?" My voice cracks, half-whisper, half-scream. I lurch to my feet, heart battering my ribs.

Caleb doesn't hesitate. He crosses the space in three strides, his good arm a steel band around my waist before I can even blink.

"No," I scream, swinging the mug like a weapon.

"Now you're just making me hard," he sneers, batting my makeshift weapon away.

I thrash, claw, kick backward, but it's useless. Even with a broken arm, he's too strong. The mug that did little impact slips from my hand, shattering against the floor, tea spraying all over.

"Let me go!" My nails rake his forearm, teeth bared, but he doesn't even grunt. My feet lift off the ground as if I weigh nothing at all.

Shelby watches, arms folded, her mouth curved in a faint, satisfied smile. "Hurry up," she snaps. "Jack's not stupid."

Caleb hoists me higher against his chest, pinning my wrists with one hand as he heads for the door. My pulse hammers in my throat, my scream tearing raw as the hallway tilts around me.

Before we step into the elevator, I look back just in time to see Shelby cut her hand, smiling evilly at me as she lets some of it drop onto the floor.

CHAPTER 30

The Trickster

The smoke clings like a second skin, burrowing into my pores and settling at the back of my throat with every breath. Even stripped of my jacket, it lingers, metallic and sharp on my tongue as I sink into the couch in Nick's office.

My brother stands at the window, shoulders rigid beneath his tailored shirt, afternoon sunlight cutting harsh angles across his face. He doesn't look at me when he speaks.

"Tell me again." His voice is controlled, measured. The voice of the heir who learned to hide rage before I learned to wield mine.

Ned shifts on the couch beside me, his sleeves are rolled to expose forearms streaked with soot. His eyes meet mine for a fraction of a second—solidarity, permission—before he looks away.

"There's nothing to tell that I haven't already said." I drag a hand down my face, feeling grit beneath my fingertips. "The hotel's gutted on floors three through five."

Nick's jaw tightens. "And the guests?" His question hangs between us, heavy with what we both already know.

"That's just it." I lean forward, elbows on knees, the taste of smoke souring my mouth. "There weren't any. No bodies. No casualties. Not even a fucking maid or bellhop caught in the crossfire."

"On a weekend." Nick finally turns, eyes narrowed. "At our busiest hotel."

"Exactly." The word scrapes my throat. "The place should've been packed. Instead, it's like someone cleared it out before lighting the match. Only casualties were profit margins and some precious art in the lobby."

My brother crosses to the bar cart, pouring two fingers of whiskey into a crystal tumbler with the kind of precision that tells me he's counting breaths. He doesn't offer me one. Doesn't need to. We both know I've been sober for days, and now isn't the time to break that streak.

"What did the fire inspector say?" Nick asks, swirling the amber liquid but not drinking.

"Said it looked like arson." Ned's voice is gravel, worn smooth by years of delivering news. "Clean job, too. Professional. Points of origin precisely placed to cause maximum property damage with minimal risk to life."

"Someone trying to send a message without catching a murder charge," I add, the words bitter on my tongue.

Nick takes a measured sip, then sets the glass down with deliberate care. "Marco checked in just before you got here. So did the three. None of them has heard anything."

The weight of those words presses against my sternum. The three major crime lords have a network of informants that run deeper than anything else in this city. If there's movement they aren't aware of it means trouble.

"This kind of silence costs serious money," I state.

Nick's mouth twists with disgust, but he doesn't say anything. And neither does Ned.

The implication hangs between us, unspoken but understood. This was calculated, aimed directly at the Knight family, and executed with enough power to ensure the usual channels of information went dark.

"So it's personal," I say, the words scraping past the smoke still coating my throat.

Nick meets my eyes, the scar on his face making him look even more menacing when he's this angry. "It's worse than personal. It's patient. Whoever did this has been planning it. Building toward it."

My gut coils tight, acid churning. I know what he isn't saying—that we've both made enemies. That the list of people who'd want to hurt us would fill a fucking phone book. That the timing, so soon after I've taken Eve as my wife, creates a vulnerability we can't ignore.

I'm on my feet before I realize I'm moving, my body thrumming with an urgency that drowns out the fatigue of hours spent sifting through ash and debris.

"I need to get back to Eve." The words come out rough, urgent.

Nick studies me, taking in the tension wired through my frame, the barely leashed violence in my stance. "You love her?" he asks, his tone clipped.

Fuck me, now isn't the time to get into this shit. "I do."

For a moment I think he'll order me to stay—to put business before personal concerns—and I'm already calculating how much that command will cost our relationship.

But he just nods once, sharp and decisive. "Go then. Take Ned."

"And you?" I ask, already moving toward the door, Ned a step behind me.

"I'll talk to Carolina. Get her and Willow somewhere secure until we know what we're dealing with." He drains his whiskey in a single swallow, the only sign of his own unease. "And Jack?"

I pause at the threshold, hand already on the doorknob. "Yeah?"

"Look after your wife."

As I stride out, the taste of smoke turns to ash in my mouth, bitter, and foreboding. Whatever game is being played, the opening move has been made.

I've always had a penchant for gambling, but I usually never get in without even knowing what game we're playing. But no matter the rules, now it's our turn.

The drive back to Eve's apartment stretches like a garrote—tight, biting deeper with every mile. Ned doesn't speak beside me. He doesn't need to. The smoke smell has settled into both our clothes, a constant

reminder of the trap someone's sprung.

My knuckles bleach white against the steering wheel as I take a corner too fast, headlights smearing across rain-slick asphalt like watercolors bleeding through paper. My jaw aches from clenching, molars grinding together with each block we pass. Something cold has settled in my gut—not fear, something worse. Certainty.

"Take it easy," Ned says. "I'd like to get back to my sister in one piece."

"I need to get to her," I growl.

Ned nods, his profile sharp in the passing streetlights. "You told her to stay put. She'll be fine."

"We'll see," I reply. I hope Ned's right, but with my luck I'm already trying to come up with worst-case scenarios to prepare myself.

The words taste hollow. We both know that the best way to go after a Knight is to capture a pawn. And fuck knows the city is full of men who'll do whatever it takes for power and money.

With each mile closer to Eve, my body coils tighter. My shoulders bunch beneath my shirt, neck rigid, something primal rising beneath my skin. The steering wheel creaks under my grip, plastic protesting as I take the final turn onto her block.

I park half on the curb, engine still running as I slam out of the car. Ned is right behind me, his footsteps echoing mine up the stairs. We don't wait for the elevator. Don't trust the crawling pace of machinery when every second pulses like a countdown.

The hallway to Eve's apartment is too quiet, our footsteps and breathing the only sounds. Even before we reach her door, I feel it—the wrongness, the absence where she should be.

Though closed, her door isn't locked, and I quickly shove it open. "Eve?"

Silence is all that greets me as I rush inside.

The apartment feels hollow, the air too still, like a stage after the actors have gone home. Ned pushes past me, calling Shelby's name, but the lack of answer is confirmation enough.

"Eve!" I bellow, moving from room to room. It's pointless. Her place is too small for her not to hear me. The fact that she isn't replying can only mean… "Answer me, for fuck's sake!"

"Shelby? Shel, where are you?" Ned shouts for his sister while I'm looking for my wife.

When I've gone through every room twice and end up back in the living room, I slam my fist into the wall. "Fuck!" I roar.

Ned's no longer shouting, and when I glance over at my friend, he looks like he's taking stock of the apartment. I snap to attention, noticing the pillow on the floor. Next, the mug shattered near the coffee table, ceramic shards scattered in a pattern that speaks of impact rather than accident.

I stride over to the doorway, my gaze is locked onto something else. A smear near the entrance. Dark and wet against the wood. I drop into a crouch, fingers hovering over the stain.

"Jack!" Ned comes to stand next to me, phone already in hand. "Shelby's not answering her cell—"

I press my thumb into the smear. Rather than being dried or congealed, it's warm and slick against my skin. "Blood," I say, the word falling from my lips like a stone into still water.

My pulse doesn't quicken. My breath doesn't catch. Instead, something cold and clear washes through me, a crystalline calm that feels like floating outside my body.

Ned curses, spinning in a tight circle, eyes wild as he sweeps the apartment again. "Maybe they went out? Maybe they—"

"Someone took her." I rise slowly, blood still wet on my fingertips. I bring it to my nose, inhaling the copper tang. "Took them both."

Ned is still talking, still moving, still calling Shelby's name like she might materialize from the shadows if he says it often enough. I tune him out, my focus narrowing to the blood on my skin and the space where my wife should be.

I cross to the kitchen sink, turn the tap, and watch red spiral down the drain. The water is cold against my hand, a shock of sensation in the numbness spreading through me. With mechanical precision, I dry my hands on a dish towel, fold it, and set it back on the counter.

Turning back to the blood smear, I study it from this new angle. It's too much for a simple cut finger. Too little to be a fatal wound. It could be a signature.

Ned stares at me, confusion warring with the panic in his eyes. "How can you be so fucking calm?"

I meet his gaze, and whatever he sees in mine makes him take a step back. "Calm?" I mock. "I'm not fucking calm."

On the inside, I'm bellowing, pacing, and throwing shit around just to have something to do. But I'm also planning, calculating, and trying to come up with…

"I need answers," I say, already heading for the door. "Stay if you want."

"What do you mean? Your wife is gone. My sister is gone. We need—"

Instead of replying again, I practically run to the stairwell, taking the stairs three at a time.

When he finally catches up with me, I'm almost out of the building. But to Ned's credit, he doesn't ask more questions or try to slow me down.

"You drive," I order, tossing him my keys.

We both get into my SUV. "Where the hell am I going?"

"Aces Fly," I grin coldly. "It's time to pay my old friends a visit."

Ned darts through traffic, barely slowing down for the red lights. Still, the drive feels like it takes forever. Who the fuck could be messing with the Knight family? And why go after Eve? None of this makes any sense.

"So this is it? This is the master plan?" Ned snorts, but there's an edge to it. He knows me well enough to recognize when I'm holding back.

"No," I growl. "This is step one."

"Whatever. Since you know the bar, are there any cameras I should look out for?"

My lip curls. "There are always cameras. But no, none to worry about. The owner is a…" Trailing off, I consider how best to describe the man who's taken me for thousands over the years.

I used to go there two or three times a week for the backroom poker games. But it's been a lifetime since I set foot on that sticky floor. Still,

the owner is one of those people who believe in customer loyalty.

"He's an acquaintance," I decide.

At the intersection, a homeless man pushes a cart across the road. Each step drags, grinding against my patience until he's finally clear.

I turn my attention back to the road, to the approaching silhouette of Aces Fly. Thanks to the heavy rain clouds, the neon sign flickers in the afternoon gloom, casting a sickly blue light across the cracked pavement.

"Pull around back," I instruct, my voice dropping lower as we near our destination.

Ned nods, guiding the car toward the rear of the building. "You know, if you'd told me a month ago you'd be this worked up over someone hurting a woman you claim to hate, I'd have laughed in your face."

"She's my wife," I growl.

The words taste weird when I'm not saying them in a scornful way. But for better or worse, I'm married to Dr. Death. The ring on her finger and vial of our blood around her neck, proves it.

We roll to a stop in the shadows behind Aces Fly. I'm out of the vehicle before Ned's even fully turned the engine off. With each step, I feel my body shift into something harder, colder. The rage that's simmering crystallizes into something focused and deadly. Every sense sharpens.

I don't need to look back to know Ned's following closely as I approach the door. Aces Fly hasn't changed since I stopped coming here. The air still reeks of stale beer and cigarettes ground into the floorboards, decades of vices compressed into a single, sour note.

Bodies part for me without conscious thought, sensing the purpose in my stride, the violence I'm barely containing. I scan the room once—habits die hard—marking exits, threats, obstacles. But there's only one person in here who matters.

"Willy," I call, knowing the man has to be here. "Willy, get your fucking ass up here and make yourself useful."

The man I've shared more gin with than I care to admit grins as he walks toward me. "Jack," he drawls. "It's been too long. Are you here to win back some of your money?"

"I'm here for information," I clarify.

He scratches his chin. "Information, huh? On what?"

I let him lead me over to a table near the back, one that's almost completely hidden in the shadows. "Someone burned down one of our hotels," I say, pulling a chair out and sitting down. "But the curious thing is that no one knows about any new players in town."

Ned grunts as he takes a seat. "Start talking."

Ignoring my friend, Willy shoots me a mostly toothless grin. "If no one's heard about any upstarts or new folks moving in on Knight territory, maybe it's an old enemy then."

"This isn't a game, old man," Ned shouts, slamming his fist into the table and knocking off Willy's glasses. "They took my fucking sister."

Cursing, I bend down and retrieve said glasses while kicking Ned under the table. Shouts and threats don't faze Willy. The way to get him to open up is through fucking talking. Making him feel valued.

I feel like fucking punching Ned for not realizing that. Someone took Eve. If I thought I'd get answers faster by using my gun as incentive, I wouldn't be sitting at this fucking disgusting table, across from a man whose breath smells like death.

"Did they now?" Willy smirks. Fucking smirks. "How can you be sure?"

That gets my attention. "Talk, old man."

"Not with him here." He points at Ned. "He doesn't respect my establishment. Tell him to wait in the car, and I'll tell you what I know."

"He stays," I growl, not in the mood for this shit. "Stop wasting my time."

Willy huffs and puffs as he gets up and disappears out the back. When he comes back, he's joined by a guy wobbling on his crutches, bumping his broken leg against almost every table he walks by.

"This is Junior," Willy says proudly. "He heard some rumors when he was at the Gowanus factory yesterday to fight the reigning champ."

"Is that so?" I ask, eyeing Junior as he flops into a chair.

He nods. "Yeah. Normally, I'm not one to fucking snitch. But that cheating bastard and his bitch deserve it after what they did."

"Well, come on, boy. Spit it out." Willy scoffs impatiently.

"What bitch?" Ned asks. I notice the way his hand disappears into his waistband, probably fisting his gun.

Junior clears his throat. "Yeah, so, I was there to fight Caleb Shore. But he—"

"Caleb?" I interrupt.

"Yes," Junior confirms. "Anyway, he used to have this hot piece of ass with him. But I don't know, man. I guess he traded down."

"Go on," I demand.

"Right. Right. She's umm… not as curvy, and she's always sneering—"

"You're embarrassing me, boy," Willy growls before slapping the back of Junior's head. "No one cares about the woman."

Junior winces. "But you should… she's the one in fucking charge. She's the one who told Caleb to bring a knife to a fistfight. He took out Jimmy."

"Who's the woman?" I ask. I look at Ned out of my peripheral, my gut tightening, and I get this weird sense of foreboding. Like the one you get when you know something is about to… not just change, but fucking shatter your perception.

"Her name is Shelby something. Didn't catch a last name."

"You fucking liar!" Ned roars, darting to his feet and pulling his gun. "My sister would never betray me."

"I'm not lying," Junior insists, holding his hands up in the air. "Look, I can show you."

He pulls his phone out, and taps the screen a few times before turning it so Ned and I can see the picture of Shelby and Caleb in a tight embrace. I lean closer and tap the info symbol which confirms the picture is from yesterday.

"This proves nothing," Ned growls. "He could have received the picture yesterday. Or taken a picture of a picture."

"He could have," I agree. "This only proves that Shelby and Caleb know each other and nothing more." I meet Junior's gaze, making sure he can see the anger and violence in mine.

Gulping, he pulls up his Memo App and plays a voice clip.

"… I only wish I could see the stupid look on the Knights' faces," Shelby says.

"Patience, baby," a man croons.

She scoffs. "I want them to know I'm the one who crossed them. They think they're so high and fucking mighty. But the Knights aren't worth shit."

"Keep going. You're so hot when you talk like that," the guy groans.

"Oh, yeah?" There's a beat of silence followed by fabric tearing. "I want you inside me," she moans.

My eyes dart to Ned who looks visibly disturbed, and I can't say I fucking blame him one bit. Especially not when the sound of skin slapping against skin grows louder.

"I want them to know what it's like to lose everything." She moans again. "Oh, yes. Harder, Caleb."

"Do we really have to fucking listen to this?" Ned barks.

"It's time someone teaches them a lesson." Shelby's tone is growing higher and higher with each syllable. "Fuck, yes. Pinch my clit harder."

"And you're that someone, aren't you, baby?" Caleb asks.

I can barely hear the rest over the roar in my ears. But I force myself to stay focused while the rest of the memo plays out. There's mention of the fire, that it's nothing more than a decoy. A ploy to get me away from Eve.

Shelby knew that Nick would send me, and that I'd be reluctant to take Eve with me. Fuck me, that's why she was at Eve's apartment. She was making sure I'd go alone.

"Fuck," I spit.

"I don't fucking believe it," Ned roars as he lunges for Junior.

When I look at Willy, he just shrugs, already aware of what I want to know. "My allegiance is to you, Jack. Do what you must."

"Are you more than an errand boy?" I ask Junior, my tone cold. "Do you know where they are or what they're planning?"

He splutters his innocence, not knowing he's signing his own death warrant. If he knows nothing, he's a loose end. Nodding to Ned, I wordlessly give him permission to do whatever the fuck he wants.

"Jack—"

"No," I interrupt, not letting Ned say what I know he's about to. "I know you're loyal. I've never questioned you, and I'm sure as fuck not starting now. Just hurry up."

Then I walk outside, my phone already in hand as I call Nick. This just officially became a Knight problem.

CHAPTER 31

The Bride

By the time the sky outside the living room window has dulled from afternoon glare to pitch black, my head's throbbing and my nerves are fried. Yet… I smile.

It's not a genuine one; it's the indulgent mask I used for patients in another life. Now it hurts my cheeks, but I keep it fixed in place to seem approachable. Because I know Shelby still hasn't told me the full truth of what's going on.

The detachment in her voice tells me that whatever she's told me is her excuse, possible reasoning. But not the root of why I'm here.

The pizza box on the table is down to a single slice that I have no intention of eating. "You can have it," I say to Caleb when I notice him hovering near the doorway.

He looks at me, his eyes sweeping across my breasts as he licks his lips. "If you need a release, I'm still willing," he smirks, acting like me offering him pizza is code for please fuck me. "I can overlook you've had a Knight between your thighs."

My heart contracts at the word *Knight*. Caleb spits it like venom, and all I can think of is Jack—his mouth on mine, his hand at my throat, the way he says I'm his. Fuck, I miss him.

Straightening my spine, I square my shoulders, refusing to cower under Caleb's glare. "How kind of you," I spit. "Why? Isn't fucking Shelby enough?"

This is all so surreal—a real mindfuck. From everything Shelby's told me, this isn't about me, but her thirst for revenge against the Knights. And me, I was just kind of in the wrong place at the wrong time. My temples throb harder, and I squeeze my eyes shut.

After we got to this house that smells too much of lemon oil and old coffee, Shelby started talking. Well, first she made sure I was comfortable. She made coffee and brought in cookies like we were just having a day of chilling.

She asked me more questions about Jack, wanting to know if he's happy with me. Though I think he is, I downplayed it as much as possible. The look in her eyes was too wild to make me feel Jack's happiness was a priority to her.

I need to stop thinking about the man I miss more than anything right now.

"The fire was just a decoy, and don't worry, Eve. No one was injured. But I had to get Jack away from you so we could talk." Shelby's words play on repeat in my mind.

She left hours ago. I have no idea where she went or why. Before she left she warned Caleb not to touch me or make me uncomfortable. Like being here against my will is soothing.

I might not be chained or caged, but somehow, that just makes it even worse. It's like dangling the finest cognac in front of a recovering alcoholic. I can see the door, and I'm sure I could make it there in seconds.

But… if it's locked, I'll have given away that I'm trying to escape. And since I have no idea where we are, there's no way to prepare for what I'll find on the other side. So, for now, I sit still and wait.

Caleb snorts, reminding me he's still here. "She's not as adventurous as you." He says it like it's a compliment. "And she fucking cries every time." Disgust fills his tone.

"What do you mean she cries?" I ask, genuinely curious.

His broken arm hangs useless at his side while he props his chin with the other. "That's none of your business."

"Oh." That's all I can say. I swallow nervously, forcing myself to keep him talking. "Why—"

"No more questions," he booms before turning on his heel.

A part of me wants to follow him and demand answers, but of course I don't. I stay on the couch, forcing myself to sort through the different threads in my head. I need to get the upper hand to know which one I should pull.

From what I've seen so far, Shelby seems to be the one in charge, so the smart thing would be to follow her lead. For now, that means waiting for her return.

Looking around, I take in the living room I'm in. The walls are bright yellow, two of them filled with paintings and drawings, and it's not the kind kids make. All the furniture is black, making the room a weird mix of artistic and minimalistic. It's not dusty, so someone clearly lives here.

Before The Black Wedding, I would have said Caleb and Shelby were the people closest to me. Well, maybe not Caleb unless it was by proximity only. Nonetheless, I'm now realizing I don't really know anything about either of them. Including if I'm sitting in one of their homes.

Hours stretch, and I drift off a few times. My neck's aching from just sitting here, and my legs protest when I stretch them across the couch, resting my head on the back.

I'm half asleep when someone snaps their fingers in my face. Jerking up, I let out a startled yelp. "Hey."

Caleb roughly shoves my legs down from the couch and takes a seat. The cushions dip under his weight, the smell of cheap cologne and sweat crowding my senses. How did I ever find him attractive?

His hand lands heavy on my thigh, fingers digging in through the fabric. The cast on his other arm bumps the cushion, a jarring reminder that he's broken but still dangerous. He follows when I try to jerk away, a grin spreading across his face.

"Don't be shy. You'll like it better with me than with that arrogant bastard."

My pulse spikes, panic and fury tangling until I can't tell one from the other. "Get off me." My voice is sharp, clipped, but it only seems to amuse him.

"You think Jack's a god," Caleb sneers, his breath hot against my cheek. "But I've seen men like him break. He can't protect you forever." His hand creeps higher, brazen now.

Rage explodes inside me. "You'll never be him." I shove at his chest with both hands. "Jack will kill you for touching me. You hear me? He'll tear you apart." My voice grows louder and shriller with each word.

Caleb laughs, low and cruel, pressing closer. "Let him try."

The muted pop of a gunshot cleaves the air, wrong in its quiet. His body jerks, eyes wide in shock before going glassy. He slumps forward, deadweight collapsing against me. Screaming, I try to shove him off me, but I only manage to move him to the side.

Blood spreads dark across his shirt, seeping into the couch cushions. At the end of a couch is a figure, one I'm scared to raise my eyes to. But I do it anyway. Shelby stands in the doorway, both hands steady on the gun, smoke curling from the barrel.

Her face is unreadable, calm as a statue. She says something as she moves to the couch and casually shoves him all the way off. But the rising panic in my ears drowns out her voice.

My skin hums with fear. Too much. Too loud. I know this place—this edge. It's the same one my father forced me to walk when he locked me in the coffin and left me with nothing but the sound of my own pulse.

So I fall back on the old tricks. Press my fingernails into my palm until it hurts. Count my breaths. *One. Two. Three.* I focus on the sting, on the burn in my lungs, until the world narrows and steadies.

And God help me, it works. Just like it used to. Okay, okay. Now, I need to take inventory, collect every tidbit of information.

Shelby's not *just* in charge; she's fucking unhinged. The wild look in her eyes is all the confirmation I need. It's one I've seen a thousand times over, just never on her. She's taken out an ally, and while that's good, it also shows how volatile she is. I have to be extremely careful in how I deal with her.

Her mouth moves again, and this time I force myself to hear her. "Are you okay?" I'm surprised by the concern in her tone. "I swear, I didn't think he'd try anything."

"I…" Trailing off, I search for an answer that makes sense, though none comes to mind. Shelby's concerned for me? "T-thank you," I stutter.

Nodding, she calmly holds out a hand, and I don't hesitate to take it. It might be stupid, but since she warned Caleb to stay away from me, I have to believe she doesn't *want* to hurt me.

"I know this probably seems like a lot to you," she says, leading me away from the living room and into the kitchen where she pours me a glass of water. "I'll do anything for the people I love. Even get revenge."

Licking my dry lips, I study her. "But I… umm…" Fuck, I need to do better.

"Don't worry about Caleb," she says flippantly. "He was just a means to an end."

"How long have you two been together?" I ask, finally managing to form a full sentence.

She laughs and playfully slaps my arm. "If you're asking if I was fucking him at the same time as you, the answer is no."

I sit down on a chair, crossing my ankles. "That's good to know." I force a smile.

"It started at The Black Wedding when he became my Groom," she admits. "Was nothing more than sex if I'm honest."

"What about us? Our friendship?" I ask. "Was that also just a convenience thing?"

Her face turns thunderous, features twisting into an ugly grimace. "We *are* friends," she hisses. "Just because it was Jack that put me up to it and wanted me to get close to you for revenge doesn't mean it's still about him."

"So it's not about revenge anymore?"

Laughing, she says, "Oh, it's still about revenge. But now it's my revenge and not Jack's."

At first… the words land heavy. Shelby isn't Jack's puppet anymore. She's her own monster now. Draining the last of my water, I keep my eyes on her, noticing the way she seems nervous to tell me this. I reach for her hand, squeezing it.

"You can tell me anything," I assure her. "The bastard put me in a cage. I'm not judging you."

Shelby takes a deep breath, and then she lets it all out. She explains that Jack wanted me at the Sanctuary to force me to marry him, which I already knew. But what I didn't know is that she was playing her own sidegame.

"Once I realized he had changed and even seemed to like you, I knew I had my chance."

"To do what? This is making no sense, Shel." I deliberately use the nickname, trying to get her to tell me everything instead of just random pieces I don't know what to do with.

"Look, you've been a great friend, Eve. And I've tried to repay that."

"What do you mean?"

A giggle escapes her. "I broke into Jack's house while you were sleeping and brought you coffee. I even left little notes for you."

I gasp. "That was you?"

We continue to talk, and she isn't hesitant in sharing her plans, thoughts, or even feelings. It's insane how open she is. And in my professional opinion, that can only mean one of two things. Either, she's going to kill me or she considers me an ally.

"I'm glad things worked out this way," Shelby admits when I stand and stretch. "Because of you, I can finally get my revenge on Jack. He's about to face his second worst nightmare."

My throat goes dry. "Second?"

Shelby's smile is sharp, cruel and gleeful. "Losing Ruby was the first. He killed her, remember? You're just next in line. And when I kill you in front of him like he did to me, he won't survive it. I'll make sure of it."

While she talks, she moves about. Reaching into the sink for something I can't see. I try to peer around her back, but it's impossible.

"You'll be helping me get my revenge," she says gleefully. "I should thank you. You really are the perfect best friend."

Despite telling myself over and over to play along, I can't. "What did he do to you?" I shout, jumping to my feet.

I only manage two steps, then she spins around and quickly presses something to my mouth. My eyes widen as I try to slap her hand away, but she trips me and follows me to the ground, still with the… fabric pressed over my mouth.

"He killed my lover. He killed John Simmons."

John… what the…

Fuck.

Everything slows down and my limbs feel heavy. My eyes… they… closing. Must stay… awake.

There's a knock on the door. Or am I imagining it?

The Trickster

Nick stands at the head of the table, hands braced on polished wood, posture carved from discipline. He looks like the heir he was raised to be—controlled, untouchable, as if rage were a thing to be swallowed and buried, never worn on the surface.

Carolina watches from next to Nick, where she's sitting. But she isn't looking at her husband, her eyes are on me the way you watch a grenade whose pin's already been pulled.

I only know it's morning because the blinds in Nick's office are cracked just enough for the sun to bleed through in pale stripes, but it doesn't touch me. Nothing does.

I haven't sat. I can't. The chair in front of me bears the weight of my hands, knuckles bone-white, veins roped tight beneath the skin. If I let go, I'll put them through a wall. Through a skull. Through *anything* that isn't her.

Eve.

Her name thrums under my skin, louder than blood, louder than breath. My wife. Fucking gone. And why? Because I trusted Shelby. It's my fucking fault.

"You need to sit down," Nick says at last. His voice is steel sharpened thin.

"The fuck I do." I flip him off and flick the knife in my palm, catching it easy as breath.

"We don't know where she is yet." His gaze cuts to Carolina, then back to me. "And with Ned vanishing, how do you know he isn't at his sister's side right now?"

"He isn't," I growl. Truthfully, I don't fucking know if he is or isn't. All I know is that he split after our trip to Aces Fly. And… I let him.

"If you just start tearing through the streets, you risk losing Eve for good," Nick carries on.

The words sink claws into me. Lose her. Another loss because of me. Another person I couldn't keep safe.

I bare my teeth in something that isn't a smile. "She's already in danger. Every second I'm not with her…" My chest seizes, fury choking me before I can finish.

"Jack—"

"No," I snap, cutting off Carolina, which makes my brother let out a low warning growl.

"Show my wife some fucking respect," he snarls. "You're in our home."

"Only because you won't leave your fortress," I spit back. "Fuck you, Nick. Fuck you for hiding behind your walls and your security while Shelby lays hands on *my wife*."

My brother narrows his eyes, the scar on his face twisting with the movement. "Are you finished?"

I laugh, hollow and violent. "Finished? Yeah, I'm done sitting here with my dick in my hand while Shelby does fuck knows what to Eve. She's waiting for me. Counting on me. I can *feel* it."

Fisting the knife harder, I slice it across the scar on my palm, the one from my wedding night. It splits easily, blood welling hot and slick, dripping onto the wood floor.

"You know how Dad always said blood's thicker than water?" My grin is feral as I lift my hand. "Eve's blood's in my veins. Do you care now, brother?"

Nick's mouth hardens. "Don't mistake my desire to keep you safe for

not wanting to help your wife," he seethes. "If you'd stop charging like a bull for one second and think, we wouldn't be wasting time arguing."

Huh, that gets my attention.

"This is obviously personal, which means every move is," he continues. "And since Shelby's had pretty much unlimited access to you, and to us, there's no shortage of shit she can use."

I let the words jump around in my head, considering them. Well, fuck. I've been looking at this all wrong, haven't I?

Shelby wants to hurt me, or us. That means she'll go for the fucking throat. And by taking Eve, there's only one other wound she can apply pressure to.

"Ruby," I whisper.

He nods. "I believe so."

"How?" Carolina demands.

"I'm not sure yet," Nick replies. "But we need to figure it out if we want to get ahead."

CHAPTER 32

The Trickster

The man reeks of fear. It's in the piss soaking his trousers, in the sweat beading across his scalp, in the way his eyes skitter anywhere but me. I've seen men broken in the cage he runs, beaten bloody for sport. None of them looked this pathetic. Then again, they didn't have me to answer to.

I crouch in front of him, resting the knife flat against his thigh, not piercing, not yet. He flinches anyway, jerks against the ropes binding him to the chair. His lip splits wider when he tries to speak, teeth slick with blood.

"P-please… I d-don't—"

I drive the blade in slowly, inch by inch, right above the knee. His scream cracks against the concrete walls of my basement, high and desperate, before dissolving into a sob.

"You've seen them," I murmur, quiet enough that he has to strain past his pain to hear. "I'll say their names one more time. Caleb and Shelby. They were there at the last fight."

"B-but—" The man howls when I retrieve the blade and run it across an exposed rib.

"Don't waste my time," I warn.

He shakes his head, ragged gasps tearing through him. "I-I don't know w-where they a-are."

"Liar." The word hisses from between my teeth. Rage coils tight in my chest, choking, suffocating. My blade twists deeper before I can stop it, his scream ripping raw through the air.

Nick's hand clamps down on my shoulder. Not to stop me—just to keep me tethered. "Easy," he mutters, though there's nothing easy about the heat rolling off me.

"If you don't remember or know anything, I have no use for you," I state coldly.

He sobs, shudders, piss dribbling fresh down his leg. Useless. I want to tear him apart piece by piece.

"O-okay," he screams. "I-I heard s-some talk about s-screaming. T-that's all I know."

"Screaming?" Nick steps closer, eyes narrowing. "What the fuck does that mean?"

The man's teeth chatter around the word, spit and blood dribbling down his chin. "A… tunnel…"

Nick's gaze flicks to mine, a dark glint beneath his lashes. His voice drops, flat with recognition. "Tunnel of Screams."

The Sanctuary of Shadows. I taste the name before it forms, copper on the back of my tongue. That place where spectacle and silence share the same mask. Of course, Shelby would be there.

The man wheezes, chest buckling, ropes groaning as he thrashes weakly. Hope trembles in his eyes—hope that naming it might buy him mercy. I let him keep it for one beat, let it swell in him like air in a drowning lung.

Then I pull my knife out and straighten. "You did good."

"T-thank y-you," he sobs.

Before he can register what I'm doing, I stab the blade into his abdomen and drive it upward deep under his ribs, angling toward the heart. His body bows hard against the ropes, a shudder rattling through him.

The sound is less scream than strangled gasp, cut off by the wet gurgle of blood flooding his throat. His body spasms once, twice, then collapses inward on itself, eyes glassy, mouth open around the silence I've forced into him.

I hold the knife there until the heat leaves him, until I'm certain there's nothing left to crawl back. Only then do I ease it free, slow and unhurried, the wet scrape of steel against bone louder than his dying breath. For a moment, I just watch him sag lifeless in the chair, a ruin of what passes for a man. Violence always ends in quiet.

"What do you want to do?" Nick asks, and I'm surprised he's been able to keep pretending this long.

My big brother thrives on control, yet he's let me run the show since I sliced my palm open in his home. I know it's his way of showing he cares, that he supports me. But it's not going to be enough to keep me around once Eve's back with me.

"I want out," I say, my tone grave.

"Out of what?" Nick asks, perplexed.

Together, we leave the basement of my house, and when he pulls his phone out, I know it's to order a cleanup.

"Have them burn it down," I say as I take the last stair. "The entire house. The property, whatever it takes."

Nick stops short, glare sharp enough to cut. His voice roughens, half fury, half disbelief. "What the fuck's gotten into you?" He stalks after me into the bathroom, the sound of his boots hard against the floor, as I wash my hands thoroughly.

As I watch the blood that isn't mine curl down the drain in pink threads, I'm reminded of seeing mine and Eve's blood. When I took care of both our cuts. I never admitted it, but I felt it even then—the truth that her pain and mine were already tied. That Eve Mortis is mine.

"Look, man, I know the timing is terrible," I rasp, drying my hands and spinning back to Nick. "But I mean it. This isn't me, and I don't want it to be my life."

Nick crosses his arms over his chest, his expression grim. "Tell me what you want, Jack."

Exhaling audibly, I pinch the bridge of my nose. "I just fucking did, but you're not listening."

He curses under his breath and follows me as I walk into the living room. I don't have time for this shit. I should be out there, in the streets, looking for Eve.

But Nick's not just going to let me brush him off, so now that I've opened this topic, I need to get through it as fast as possible. Too exhausted to continue pacing and standing, I flop down on the couch.

"The Knight legacy is yours, brother—"

"You can have it." His jaw snaps tight, words cutting like teeth. "Take the fucking crown."

I shake my head slowly. "That's not the point. This isn't about wanting what you have, it's about wanting what I don't have. Freedom. Choices."

He takes a seat in the closest chair and leans forward, resting his elbows on his knees. "It's about Eve."

I nod since there's no point in denying it. "I want to… I don't fucking know. Live life to the fullest and all that shit that comes with it."

Explaining what's in my head is a hell of a lot harder than thinking it, but after what feels like hours, I think I've finally managed to make Nick understand that this isn't a tantrum. It's something I need.

"I thought about it before," I explain. "But there was Ruby to consider. And then I got blinded by revenge."

Nick nods.

"Something fucking changed when Dad had me killed. I can't explain it better than that. But I don't want this life anymore."

I stop talking, waiting for the judgment of my older brother, but it never comes.

"Carolina once asked me if I'd walk away from it all if she asked me to," he confesses as he stands and shoves his hands into the pockets on his suit pants.

"And—"

"And I would leave it behind in a heartbeat," he says, tone stern. "So if your happiness is elsewhere, go fucking get it, brother."

I let out a strained breath. "Wait, really? You'll let me?"

He snorts. "You think I want your sourpuss ass around all the time? Fuck off, Jack."

Tilting my head to the side, I watch him. Like, *really* watch him. I

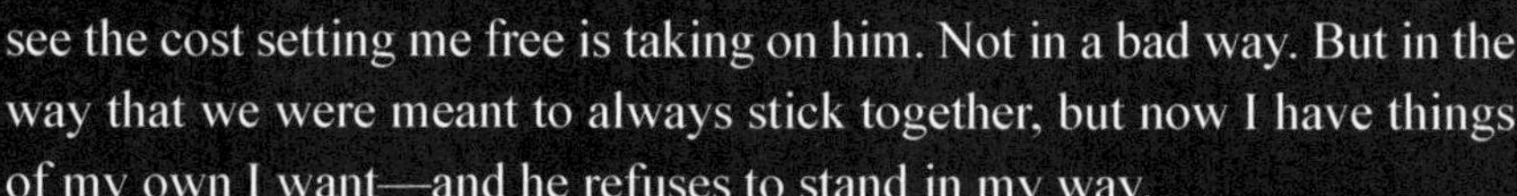

see the cost setting me free is taking on him. Not in a bad way. But in the way that we were meant to always stick together, but now I have things of my own I want—and he refuses to stand in my way.

"Thank you." Instead of waiting for him to brush it off, or for me to make a stupid joke, I stand and pull him in for a hug. "I mean it."

At first the hug feels stiff, unfamiliar. Then, after a beat, it settles—solid, grounding, years of bruises and silence folding into the press of his hand on my back and mine on his. For once, there's no dominance to prove, no legacy choking the air between us. Just blood. Just family.

When we pull apart, Nick exhales sharply, almost like he had been holding it in. He scrubs a hand over his face, then fixes me with the kind of look he usually saves for strategy. "Then the Tunnel of Screams. That's where we start."

The name sits heavy on my tongue when I repeat it. "I guess so." Shelby would thrive in a place where terror is currency and spectacle is cover.

But even as I speak, something unsettles low in my gut. Not doubt exactly—more like the echo of it. A faint coil tightening where conviction should sit steady.

The more I let the words hang between us, the more I feel the thread tug tight in my chest. A gut-deep coil, subtle at first, then insistent. My certainty begins to blur at the edges, like blood thinning in water.

Nick notices. He always does. "You believe it, don't you?"

I nod slowly. "I'm not sure." A pause. My jaw works, grinding the words. "There's something off about it. She's too smart to let herself be found because some coward croaked out her hiding place."

"True," Nick agrees.

The Sanctuary is the perfect setting if you want to rattle your opponent. The fog, shadows, sounds, and people milling about makes it easy to use for whatever you want. But…

"It's uncontrollable," I say, giving voice to the thought the second it hits me. "There are too many factors. She wouldn't know who's hiding behind masks, robes, or corners."

Catching on, Nick adds, "We could have our people stashed there and she wouldn't even know it."

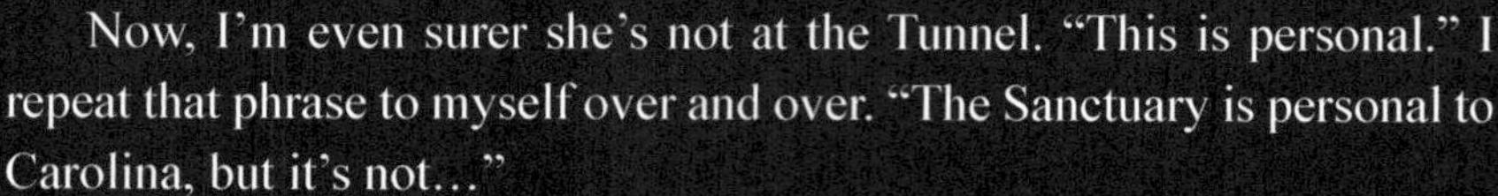

Now, I'm even surer she's not at the Tunnel. "This is personal." I repeat that phrase to myself over and over. "The Sanctuary is personal to Carolina, but it's not…"

"What?" Nick asks, stepping closer.

"It's personal," I repeat. "There's only one place it could be."

Nick doesn't move. His eyes narrow, arms folding across his chest, his silence heavier than accusation.

Then he runs a hand down his face, tone like gravel. "If you're sure you know where it is, we should get it staked out. I'll get men at every entrance. Five inside, five out. We can get the three in, and—"

Holding up my hand, I cut him off. "No."

"No?" he parrots, quirking an eyebrow. "You're not going in there alone."

"I am."

"Jack." My name is a warning, sharp as a blade. "Don't be a fucking idiot. We can end this clean if we plan it right."

I push off the wall I'm leaning against, rolling my shoulders back, stillness bleeding into my bones. "Shelby wants me, not a fucking circus of men with guns. You put anyone else in that room, you ruin the point."

Nick's jaw tightens. "The point is keeping you alive."

"The point is saving Eve!" I roar. "That's the only thing that fucking matters."

He stands now too, chest to chest, his heat colliding with mine. His breath ghosts my face, the sharpness of it like we're seconds from tearing each other apart. The tension between us stretches taut enough to bleed.

"You think you're untouchable? You think she won't gut you if you give her the chance?"

Air leaves me, and I feel lightheaded, like my skull's too tight for what's forcing its way in. Memories don't come one by one—they crash in fragments, stitched together by something I've refused to see. Ruby… Valentine… I get it. I *finally* fucking get it.

This was my sister's last stand, wasn't it? She wasn't coerced or forced. She ended things on her terms. And she did it while being loved by the man she had fallen so deeply for.

Fuck.

The more I allow myself to see the events of the past without the haze of hatred skewering the images, the clearer it becomes. And… I think I finally know who I've been so pissed at. It's not Eve. It's Ruby.

"You'd die for Carolina, wouldn't you?" I ask my brother, interrupting whatever he's saying.

"Of course," he says.

I nod. "And Ruby… I don't think she died for Valentine." Pausing, I lick my lips. "She did it for herself, Nick. She couldn't take living anymore, so she ended things on her own terms."

He huffs out a soft laugh. "Are you finally getting what I've been trying to tell you all these months?" When I roll my eyes, he continues. "Yes, you shot Ruby. But what you did was end her suffering. She was already dying, man. That was her path to take."

Yeah, I never believed him or understood it until now. But now… now I do get it. Because I need to get rid of Nick and go to the one place Shelby can hurt me just from making me go there.

"Okay," I agree, dragging the word out like it tastes sour. "Why don't we go to your place and make a plan with Marco?"

Nick eyes me suspiciously. "Yeah?"

"I just need to shower and change first. Carolina will have my fucking balls if I turn up in blood-soaked clothes."

"Don't ever use my wife's name and your balls in the same sentence," my brother growls, playfully punching my arm.

I rub the spot on my arm where he hit me, shaking my head with a rough exhale. "Noted."

Nick grins, quick and sharp, already reaching for his phone. "I'll call Marco and meet you at mine in an hour."

"You got it." I grab the hem of my shirt, peeling the blood-stiff fabric off my skin.

He mutters something under his breath, distracted, pacing toward the door with his phone to his ear. I stand there, shirt dangling from my fist, heart steady as stone. He thinks I'm right behind him. Thinks I'll play along.

But I'm already choosing a different road.

CHAPTER 33

The Bride

The brain fog thins, leaving a splitting headache pulsing behind my eyes. My throat is scraped raw, mouth cotton-dry. I try to swallow but can't.

Shelby hovers over me, her face too close, pupils blown wide with a manic energy I've never seen in her before. She holds a strip of fabric in her hands, torn from what looks like a dress, and she's smiling at me like we're at a sleepover rather than whatever sick game this is.

"There you are," she coos, voice honey-sweet poison. "I was starting to worry I'd given you too much."

I try to move, but my limbs feel like they're underwater, heavy and unresponsive. As I look around, I realize I'm sitting on the closed toilet lid, my back against the cold porcelain tank.

The bathroom is unfamiliar—yellow walls, white tile, a shower curtain with faded sunflowers. "Where…" My voice cracks, and I have to try again. "Where am I?"

Shelby ignores the question, tearing at the fabric again, the sound of ripping cloth loud in the small space. "Too long," she mutters. "It needs to be shorter. She was wearing something shorter."

She holds the fabric against my chest, frowning at how it drapes.

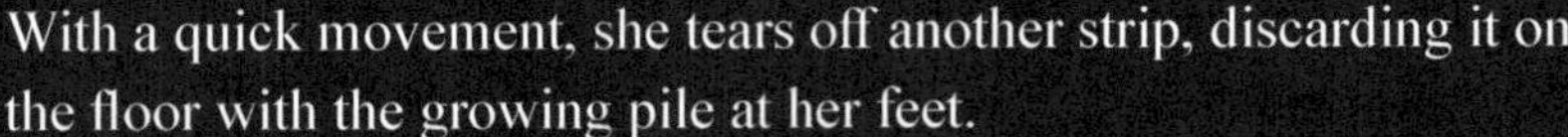

With a quick movement, she tears off another strip, discarding it on the floor with the growing pile at her feet.

"Shelby, stop," I croak. "What are you doing? What is this?"

"Shhh." She presses a finger to my lips, and I flinch away from her touch. "Don't ruin it," she snaps, then giggles, sudden and jagged. "I've got it all planned out. It has to be perfect, or it doesn't count."

A shadow shifts in the corner of the bathroom, and for the first time, I notice we're not alone. Ned leans against the wall, arms crossed, face drawn. His presence hits me like a physical blow. When did he get here? Was he in on this the whole time?

"Ned?" I whisper, confusion spiraling through me. "What's happening?"

He looks at me, then quickly away, jaw tense. "Shelby," he says, voice low, "this has gone far enough. You need to let her go."

Shelby doesn't even turn to acknowledge him. Instead, she forces the torn fabric over my head. I struggle weakly, but she's stronger than she looks, or I'm weaker than I thought. The dress— what's left of it—settles around me, the torn hem barely reaching mid-thigh.

"Perfect," she says, stepping back to admire her work. "Well, almost."

Her hands move to my hair next, fingers tangling in the strands, tugging painfully against my scalp. "God, this color is all wrong. Look at this awful orange. Ruby's was pure black."

Ruby.

The name drops like a stone into my gut, rippling out in horrified understanding. I think of Caleb, lying in a pool of his own blood on Shelby's couch. And now she's dressing me up like…

"The Knights would be lenient if you stopped now," Ned says, taking a step forward. "No one else needs to get hurt, Shelby."

"Lenient? Jack owes me." She laughs, the sound brittle and sharp. "Maybe I should just cut it all off. Would that be better? More authentic?"

My stomach lurches as fragments click into place; the dress, the muttering, the way she keeps trying to shape me into someone else. This isn't random cruelty—this is rehearsal. Preparation.

"You're reenacting it," I say, the words barely audible. "Ruby's death."

Shelby's hands freeze in my hair. For a moment, she's utterly still. Then she smiles, slow and satisfied, like I've finally solved a puzzle she's been waiting for me to piece together.

"Smart girl," she whispers, leaning close enough that I can smell mint on her breath. "Jack's smart girl."

My heart stutters, Jack's name like a lifeline and a noose at once. I think of him finding me like this, staged to mirror his sister's last moments.

Ned shifts his weight, discomfort etched in every line of his body. "Shelby, listen. Whatever happened, this isn't the way. The Knights will hunt you down for this."

"Let them," she spits, still focused on my hair. "Jack took the only thing that mattered. And now he gets to breathe while the love of my life doesn't?"

"The what?" Ned asks, clearly shocked.

"The. Love. Of. My. Life," Shelby repeats, enunciating each word clearly. "You know… oh, maybe you don't." She looks down at her nails, and when she looks back at her brother, there's menace in her eyes. "I never told you about him because you can't be trusted. You're always protecting Jack instead of me."

"Come on, Shelby," Ned argues. "You know I've always looked out for you—"

She lets out a scream. "Lies!" Her entire body moves with each breath she takes. "You went to jail for them, not for me. You're always choosing the Knights."

"That's not on Eve," Ned tries, voice strained. "She has nothing to do with what happened to us."

"She has everything to do with it now," Shelby hisses. "She's Jack's wife. She's a Knight now." She says the word as if it's filth in her mouth.

I catch Ned's eye, trying to silently plead with him. Help me. Stop her. Do something. His gaze meets mine for a fraction of a second before sliding away, guilt darkening his features.

That single avoidance tells me everything; he won't help—I'm alone in this.

Shelby steps back, surveying her work with critical eyes. "Not perfect, but it'll do. It just needs to be close enough that he sees her when he looks at you."

The words hollow me out. She wants to destroy Jack through me, make me into the echo of his worst memory. The cruelty of it steals my breath. And there's nothing I can do to stop it from happening.

My mind races to Jack—what this will do to him, how it will break him open in ways I can't bear to imagine. I've seen the raw edges of his grief, felt them against my skin in the dark when he holds me too tight, like he's afraid I'll disappear. This will rip apart the fragile healing he's barely managed to piece together.

"Why?" I ask, voice cracking. "What did he do to make you hate him this much?"

Shelby's eyes go flat and cold. "I've already told you what they did to me. God, you're obtuse."

I try to catch Ned's eye one more time, silently begging, but he keeps his gaze fixed on the floor. The betrayal cuts deeper than I expected.

Whatever hope I had left withers and dies, leaving nothing but the hollow certainty that I'm about to become the instrument of Jack's destruction. And there's not a damn thing I can do to stop it.

Something in me snaps. The fog in my brain burns away, replaced by a white-hot clarity that surges through my veins like lightning. I will not be Ruby. I will not be the thing that breaks Jack.

My body moves before my mind can catch up. I lunge, shoving Shelby with everything I have. She stumbles backward, surprise flashing across her face before hardening into something cold and terrible.

We slam into the counter, bottles crashing to the floor. "Get off me!" I scream, clawing at her arms, her face, anything I can reach.

My nails catch skin, drawing thin red lines across her forearm. The small victory fuels me, panic transforming into raw power as I fight against the fate she's designed for me. Shelby hisses, her fingers tangling in my hair, yanking my head back with enough force to make my eyes water.

"Stop fighting," she growls, breath hot against my face. "It's happening whether you want it to or not."

But I can't stop. Something primal has taken over, a desperate need to escape, that eclipses thought. My knee comes up hard, catching her in the stomach. She doubles over with a grunt, loosening her grip just enough for me to wrench away.

I stumble past her, legs shaking but carrying me toward the door. Ned stands there, eyes wide, frozen between action and inaction. For a heartbeat, I think he might step aside, might let me pass.

He doesn't.

His hand catches my arm, not roughly, but firmly enough to halt my momentum. "Eve," he says, my name a warning, and an apology wrapped into one.

Behind me, Shelby straightens, breath coming in sharp pants. "You stupid bitch," she spits. "You think you can run?"

I hear the metallic snick before I see the blade. When I spin to face her, the knife gleams in her hand, small but deadly, catching the bathroom light in a way that makes my stomach lurch.

"Put it down, Shelby," Ned says, but there's no real authority in his voice. Just resignation.

She advances on me, knife held loosely between her fingers like it's an extension of her hand. Her smile stretches too wide, eyes fever bright. "No more running. No more fighting."

I back up until I hit the wall, heart hammering against my ribs like it's trying to escape. "Shelby, please," I say, hating how my voice shakes. "This isn't you. This isn't who you are."

"You don't know who I am," she whispers, almost gently. "You never did."

The knife comes up too fast to dodge. The blade slices along my cheek—a line of fire that blooms into stinging pain. Warm wetness trickles down my skin, and I realize with a distant sort of horror that she's marked me. Cut me open like it's nothing.

I press my hand to my cheek, feeling the blood slip between my fingers. The pain is sharp but manageable. It's the violation that cuts deeper—the casual way she's marred me, like I'm a canvas she's decided to alter. Anger and hatred burns hotter than the wound itself.

"There," Shelby murmurs, satisfaction curling through her voice. "That's better. More authentic."

"Jesus, Shelby!" Ned steps forward, grabbing her wrist. "What the hell are you doing? You said no one gets hurt!"

Hope flickers in my chest, fragile as a candle flame. I will him to keep going, to be the voice of reason that pulls his sister back from this edge.

"No one important is hurt," Shelby says coldly, yanking her arm free. She turns to face him fully, knife still held loosely at her side. "Don't tell me you're getting squeamish now, Ned. Not after everything they did to us."

"This isn't about them," Ned argues, but there's hesitation in his voice. "This is about you. About what you're becoming."

Shelby laughs, the sound bitter and hollow. "I'm becoming what they made me. What Jack made me." She steps closer to her brother, voice dropping to a venomous hiss. "He took everything from me. Everything."

Each word drips with a hatred so personal, so consuming, that it seems to fill the room like smoke. I watch it wrap around Ned, seeping into him, and know with sinking certainty that he won't resist it.

"And Jack?" Shelby continues, eyes flashing. "Jack's the worst of them. He used both of us. And now he gets to play house with his pretty little wife while I have nothing?"

I flinch at the way she says "wife," like it's a curse, something foul she needs to spit out.

"The Knights destroy everything they touch," she says, turning back to me, knife catching the light. "And it's time they know how it feels."

"Shelby," Ned says quietly. "It's not too late to stop this."

She stills, something fragile passing over her face. For a moment, I think she might actually listen. Then her expression hardens again, eyes turning to flint.

"You're either with me or against me, Ned," she says, voice flat. "Choose."

The tension stretches between them, thick enough to choke on. I search Ned's face for any sign, any clue about what he's thinking. Is he genuinely conflicted? Or is this all part of their plan?

"I'm with you," he says finally, shoulders sagging with the weight of his choice. "You know I am. Always."

The betrayal crashes over me in a cold wave. Whatever small hope I had shatters, leaving nothing but the stark reality of my situation. I'm alone, bleeding, dressed in the tattered remnants of Ruby's life, with no one to help me.

Shelby nods once, satisfied. "Good. Then help me get her to the van."

As Ned moves toward me, his eyes meet mine for the briefest moment. Something flickers there—regret? Fear? Or just my mind twisting shadows into hope?

"Come on," he says gruffly, taking my arm. His grip is firm but not cruel, and I can't help wondering if there's meaning in that small mercy. Is he truly with Shelby? Or is he playing along, buying time?

Instead of being in the back, I'm shoved into the front with them. Shelby's driving, trusting her brother to keep me under control.

The uncertainty aches almost as much as the betrayal. I don't know what to believe anymore. All I know is that whatever happens next, Jack will be the one who suffers most. And that knowledge cuts deeper than any knife ever could.

As the van jolts over a pothole, it sends pain shooting through my bound wrists. I gasp as I'm lurched to the side when Shelby takes a corner way too fast.

"Oops," she sing-songs.

"Watch where you're going," Ned barks.

When Shelby's attention is back on the road, he leans closer. His mouth right against my ear. "Play along," he murmurs softly.

My mind races, thoughts colliding and splintering like glass. This can't be happening. But it is. My best friend has turned into a stranger, driven by a hatred so deep it's twisted her into someone I don't recognize. And I'm the canvas for her revenge.

But it's not myself I'm most afraid for. It's Jack.

Jack, who still wakes in the night calling his sister's name. Jack, whose grief runs so deep it's carved into the very marrow of his bones. Jack, who's finally starting to let me in, to show me the man beneath the monster he pretends to be.

What will this do to him? Seeing me like this, staged in Ruby's final moments?

I close my eyes, fighting back tears that won't help me now. Part of me wants him to stay away, to never find me. Better to disappear than to become the instrument of his destruction. But I know he'll come. He'll tear apart the city looking for me, and when he finds me—when he sees what Shelby has done—it will break something in him that might never heal.

The van slows, and through the windshield, I catch glimpses of familiar streets. My stomach drops as recognition hits me. The meat district… the warehouses… fuck.

This place was all over the news back in February. After the human auction that went wrong, the one only the elite knows about, the media spun it like a gang war. One where Ruby Knight and the esteemed Professor Valentine Grant were ruthlessly gunned down.

No one mentioned what only a few know; Jack killed Ruby and Valentine.

But since she wasn't really a public figure, no one batted an eye. Not when Nicklas Knight stood in front of the cameras and declared his sister's death a tragic accident.

Shelby parks beside a decrepit building, rust-eaten and abandoned. She cuts the engine, and the sudden silence is deafening. For a moment, none of us move.

Then, Ned reaches for the door. "Come on," he says, practically pushing me out. "Time for the grand finale."

Shelby leads the way to a side door, hinges screaming as she forces it open. Inside, darkness waits, deep and absolute.

Her brother shoves me forward, and I stumble into the void. A flashlight clicks on, casting long shadows across concrete floors and crumbling walls. The space is cavernous, once industrial, now just hollow.

At the far end, a raised platform—some kind of stage—juts from the wall. Above it, metal beams crisscross the ceiling, and from them hang hooks. Dozens of them. Rusted. Sharp. Waiting.

My legs lock, refusing to carry me forward. Ned pushes harder. "Move."

Each step feels like walking deeper into a nightmare I can't wake from. The warehouse smells of decay and abandonment, but underneath is something else—something older, darker. The ghost of violence past.

We reach the stage, and Shelby guides me to stand beneath one of the hooks. It dangles just above my head, casting a crooked shadow across the floor.

"Hands up," she orders.

I raise my arms, and she quickly loops rope around my already bound wrists, then through the hook above. With a hard yank, she pulls until I'm stretched upward, arms taut above my head, toes barely touching the ground.

The position is instantly, brutally vulnerable. My shoulders strain against their sockets, a dull burn spreading through my muscles. The torn dress rides up, exposing more of my thighs than it covers. I can't lower my arms, can't protect myself, can't hide.

I'm displayed like meat in a butcher's window, and the humiliation of it burns hotter than the physical pain.

Shelby steps back, admiring her work. "The hook wasn't used for the auction," she murmurs, circling me slowly. "But you're also missing the whiplashes on your back. Once I've given you those, I'll free your wrists. And then it'll be perfect."

The words land like a physical blow. "W-what?"

She stops in front of me, head tilted to study my face. "Ruby," she says, my blood still crusted on her knife. "This is where she died. Right here. This exact spot."

The revelation hollows me out. I knew she was recreating Ruby's death, but to bring me to the exact location, to suspend me from the same hook that held her—it's a level of cruelty so precise it steals my breath.

"How do you know?" I whisper, the question escaping before I can stop it.

Her smile is small, satisfied. "I know everything about that night. About Valentine and Ruby. About Jack finding them." She traces the knife along my collarbone, not cutting, just threatening. "I know how he screamed when he saw her. How he held her body. How he begged her to come back."

Each detail is a fresh wound. I think of Jack—my Jack—broken by grief, and it hurts more than any physical pain she could inflict.

"Don't do this to him," I plead, voice cracking. "Kill me if you have to, but don't… don't make him do it."

"That's the point," she says, eyes cold. "He has to feel what I felt when he took everything from me."

She crouches down and rummages through a bag I'm only now noticing. She lets out a delighted sound when she pulls a whip out, slowly unfurling it.

"Shelby." Ned's voice cuts through the tension. He stands at the edge of the stage, shoulders hunched, eyes darting between us. "Maybe we should wait."

She turns to him, brow furrowed. "Wait? For what?"

"For Jack," he says, stepping closer. "If you do it now, he'll just find her broken. But if we wait, he'll see her break. Won't that be much sweeter?" He doesn't finish the thought, but the implication hangs in the air between them.

Hope and horror collide in my chest. Is Ned trying to buy me time? Or is he suggesting something even more monstrous?

While Shelby considers, she taps the whip handle against her thigh. Finally, she nods. "You're right," she says. "It'll hit harder if he watches just like I did. And like me, he can be in the audience." She glances at me, something almost like regret flickering across her face. "Sorry, Eve. Looks like you get to hang around a little longer."

"Are you sure this is worth it?" Ned asks, his tone careful, almost pleading.

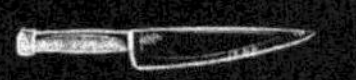

Her head snaps toward him, eyes blazing, pupils blown wide. "Worth it?" she shrieks, laughter splitting into sobs. "He was my whole life. My heart. My reason. And Jack ripped him from me!"

Her voice pitches higher, cracking into a sob.

"Don't you dare question me, Ned. Don't you dare pretend you understand!"

The knife isn't deliberate—it's desperate. She hurls herself at him, screaming and sobbing in the same breath, driving the blade into his chest with a savage thrust. He chokes, blood bubbling on his lips, but she doesn't stop. She stabs again, and again, each strike punctuated by another broken scream.

"He's gone! He's gone! And Jack still gets to breathe!"

Ned crumples under her, his hands slipping uselessly through the blood soaking his shirt. His wide eyes fix on her with shock, betrayal, and something almost like pity before they glaze over.

Shelby keeps stabbing, snarling broken words, tears and spit streaking her face until she finally shoves him away.

She staggers back from Ned's body, chest heaving, blood dripping from the knife. "I'll make him pay, John. I swear it," she mutters, wild eyes shining. Then she turns away, leaving her brother crumpled in a spreading pool.

My body aches from the unnatural position. But it's nothing compared to the ache in my heart, knowing Jack will find me like this— his sister's death reflected in my body.

And that, more than anything Shelby could do to me, is what truly hurts.

CHAPTER 34

The Trickster

My tires screech as I cut across three lanes, horn blaring, heart hammering so hard I taste copper. The phone buzzes against my thigh for the fifth time in ten minutes—Nick's name flashing, demanding answers I won't give.

I grip the wheel tighter, knuckles bleaching white. I was too late for Ruby, but not this time. Not with Eve. The thought of her name sends another surge of acid through my veins, burning away everything but the need to reach her before I lose her too.

I nearly clip a taxi as I swerve through a yellow light. The driver leans on his horn, but the sound barely registers. My mind is already ten blocks ahead, already in that warehouse, already seeing what I might find.

The phone buzzes again. I silence it without looking, knowing Nick has figured out my lie by now. He'll be mad that I tricked him into going to his own house, but I have to do this by myself. This was never his debt to pay.

A text from Ned still glows on my screen, words I've read twenty times since he sent them just after Nick left.

Ned: Shelby is taking Eve to where Ruby was killed.

Another car horn blares as I run a stop sign, the road blurring through the windshield. My breath comes in ragged gulps.

I can't stop seeing it—my sister's body slumped on the floor, the bullet wound that I put there. And now Eve... fuck, Eve in the same location, maybe in the same position.

"I'm coming," I whisper, the words scraping my throat raw. "Hold on, Little Bride. Just hold on."

My jaw aches from clenching, teeth grinding together so hard I taste enamel dust. Every red light, every slow driver, every fucking obstacle feels like a personal attack. The wheel creaks under my grip, plastic warping beneath my fingers as if absorbing the tension coiling through my body.

I slam on the gas harder, weaving between cars like they're standing still. The meat district rises ahead, abandoned factories and warehouses jutting against the sky like broken teeth. This part of town died years ago, left to rot and rust while developers argued over its bones.

My throat closes at the memory of the last time I was here. My sister's body going limp, her eyes glazing over. The thing that haunts me the most is the forgiveness I saw in her eyes as she died. Maybe even a fleeting glance of... I don't fucking know.

I screech to a stop in front of the warehouse, tires skidding on gravel. The place looks worse than when I last saw it—windows shattered, metal siding peeled back like flesh from bone, walls crumbling inward.

Weeds push through cracks in the concrete, nature reclaiming what man abandoned. But it's the same place. The place where Ruby died. Where Shelby has brought Eve to make her point.

I grab my gun from the glove compartment, check the magazine, and slam it home. The metal is cold against my palm, familiar and strange all at once. Then I'm out of the car, boots crunching on broken glass as I sprint toward the building.

A jagged hole gapes in the side wall—not a door, not a window, just a wound in the concrete where something tore through. I catch a flash of movement—a figure in the shadows, tall and angular. Shelby.

Her face is turned away, but I'd know that posture anywhere. The way she stands, shoulders hunched forward like a vulture about to feast. My blood rushes hot then cold, primal instinct recognizing predator.

I duck low, using the broken wall as cover as I edge closer. She's too focused on something ahead to notice me—something I can't yet see.

"Shelby!" I shout, unable to contain the rage boiling over. My voice echoes through the empty space, bouncing off concrete and steel.

She whips around, eyes wide with surprise that quickly shifts to something else—something like triumph. Then she's gone, melting back into the shadows of the warehouse interior.

I launch myself through the hole, concrete scraping my shoulder as I squeeze through. The darkness swallows me whole, my eyes struggling to adjust after the brightness outside. I take two steps forward, gun raised, senses straining.

That's when I hear it.

A scream tears through the darkness—high and broken and filled with so much pain. Eve's scream. The sound hits me like a physical blow, punching the air from my lungs. It reverberates inside my skull, through my bones, into the marrow itself.

Pain and fear and desperation distilled into a single, piercing note that splits me open from throat to gut.

"Eve!" Her name erupts from me as I plunge deeper into the warehouse, the sound of her agony pulling me forward like a hook buried in my flesh.

I burst through into the warehouse's hollow heart, gun extended, every nerve ending raw. The stench hits me first—copper and rust and rot. Then my eyes adjust to the half-light, and I see Ned. He's sprawled face-up on the concrete, arms flung wide like a broken puppet.

Blood pools beneath him, so much blood, black in the dim light, spreading in a perfect circle like spilled ink. His eyes stare upward, cloudier now than they were in life, seeing nothing. I don't need to check for a pulse. My friend is gone, another body left in the wake of my failure.

But I can't stop for him. Can't mourn. Can't think. Because there, in the center of the warehouse, is Eve.

 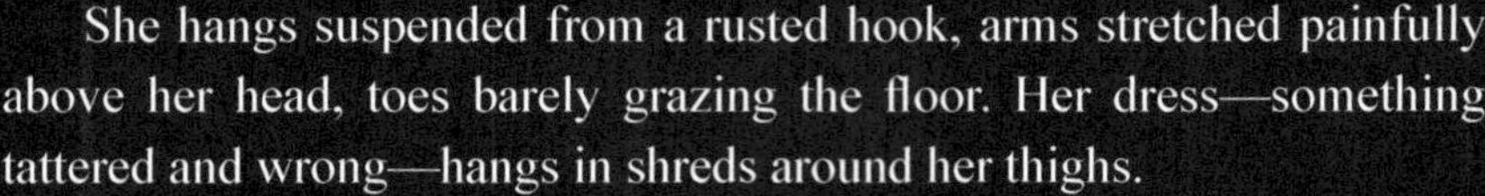

She hangs suspended from a rusted hook, arms stretched painfully above her head, toes barely grazing the floor. Her dress—something tattered and wrong—hangs in shreds around her thighs.

Her skin is split open, each lash bleeding, crimson rivers running down her body. Shelby stands behind her, arm already pulled back, whip unfurled. Her face distorts, and her features twist into something feral and hungry.

As I watch, the whip arcs through the air, its crack splitting the silence a heartbeat before Eve's body jerks with the impact.

Red floods my vision. Something primal rips through me, tearing past bone and sinew, a roar building in my chest that I swallow back.

My finger is already tight on the trigger. I've killed before. I'll kill again. For Eve, I'll burn the world down and salt the ashes.

"Shelby!" The name tears from my throat, raw and ragged.

Eve's head snaps up, eyes finding mine across the space between us. There's dried blood on her cheek, but it's the recognition in her gaze that guts me—the way relief and terror war across her features in a single, fractured moment.

"Jack! Run!" she screams, voice broken with desperation. "She'll kill you!"

Run? The word doesn't compute, doesn't register as anything but static. Run from what? From Eve? From the woman who's carved her open? Something hot and dangerous floods my veins, scorching away hesitation, burning through restraint.

"Let her go," I growl, advancing, gun trained on Shelby's head. One clean shot. That's all it would take to end this. One bullet between her eyes and Eve would be safe.

Just as I pull the trigger and release the bullet in the chamber, Shelby moves. In a blur of motion, she lunges sideways, fingers clawing into Eve's hair, yanking her close. Using my wife as a shield. Using her like a fucking prop in her sick revenge fantasy.

"No!" I roar, agony ripping through me.

Time stretches, warps, fragments like shattered glass. I see it all in excruciating detail—the flash of the muzzle, the jerk of recoil against my palm, the spray of blood. But not from Shelby. From Eve.

My wife's body jerks, a sharp, surprised gasp escaping her lips. Her gray eyes widen, meeting mine across the space between us.

"No." The word is more breath than sound. "No, no, no, no…"

My brain fractures, reality splintering around me. This isn't happening—it can't be happening. Not again. Not Eve. Not by my hand.

Fuck.

Ruby's face superimposes over Eve's in my mind. History repeats itself with cruel precision. Something breaks inside me. Something fundamental holding me together snaps like a wire pulled too tight.

The roar that tears from my throat isn't human. It's the sound of something feral and wounded, reverberating through the warehouse rafters, shaking dust from the beams above.

"Eve!" Her name is a prayer and a curse and a plea all at once. "Eve, look at me. Open your eyes. Please. Please…" She doesn't move. Doesn't lift her head. Just hangs there.

I killed Ruby. I killed Valentine. And now I've killed Eve—the only person who saw through the monster to the man underneath. The only one who made me feel something beyond the rage and grief that's consumed me for months.

"What have I done?" The words scrape raw from my throat, barely audible. "What the fuck have I done?"

Shelby's laughter cuts through my agony, high and brittle. She steps out from behind Eve's suspended form; the whip dragging behind her like a serpent's tail. Blood smears her face, her hands, her clothes—Ned's blood, Eve's blood. She wears it like war paint, like proof of victory.

"Exactly what I wanted you to do," she says, voice cold with satisfaction. "How does it feel, Jack? To destroy the thing you love most? To watch the light leave her eyes? To know it's your fault?"

My vision goes red. Then black. Then red again, pulsing with each thundering beat of my heart. I can't speak. Can't breathe. I can't think beyond the animal need to tear Shelby apart with my bare hands. To make her suffer for every mark on Eve's skin, for every drop of blood shed.

Blood runs down her arm, dripping steadily onto the concrete. *Drip.*

Drip. Drip. My world is ending one drop at a time.

"Why?" The question tears from my throat, raw and guttural. I need to know. I need to understand what twisted her into this monster standing before me.

"Why Eve? Why like this? What the fuck is this about?"

Shelby's laugh is like cracked glass, sharp enough to cut. "You still don't get it, do you?" She stalks in a half-circle, whip dragging behind her. "John!" she screams, the name echoing off the walls. "John Simmons! Does that name mean anything to you, Jack?"

The pieces click together with sickening clarity. John Simmons was my sister's husband's brother. I killed the fucker, but his death wasn't as gruesome as he deserved.

"He was everything," Shelby continues, voice pitching higher. "Everything to me. And you took him from me like he was nothing. Just collateral damage in your precious family drama."

"He got less than what he fucking deserved," I sneer.

"You Knights think you own this city, that you can take whatever you want without consequences. Well, here's your consequence, Jack." She gestures at Eve with the handle of the whip. "How does it feel to destroy what you love? To be too late to save her?"

Something breaks loose inside me—hot and toxic and hungry for blood. Before I can move, Shelby's arm snaps forward. Metal glints in the dim light—a knife, spinning end over end toward my chest.

I twist sideways, the blade slicing air where my heart beat a moment before. It clatters against the concrete behind me. I look at the gun still in my hand. Instead of using it again, I throw it to the side. I want to feel Shelby break under my hands for what she's done to Eve.

As I kick the gun away, I watch Shelby's eyes widen at the deliberate choice. "You made it personal," I growl. "Let's fucking go, bitch."

I quickly bend, scooping up the knife she threw, the handle still warm from her grip. The blade catches light as I straighten, edge gleaming with promise.

Shelby's mouth twists in a feral grin. The whip cracks through the air between us, a vicious snap that sends concrete dust swirling. Before I can dodge, it wraps around my thigh, leather biting through denim into flesh. Fire blooms across my leg, but I don't feel it.

The whip cracks again, catching my forearm this time. The pain is distant, unimportant, belonging to someone else. I advance another step, knife gripped tight.

"That all you got?" I taunt. "Are you too much of a fucking coward to come closer?"

Her face contorts with rage. The whip lashes out again, catching me across the chest. The impact drives air from my lungs, fabric shredding, skin beneath it opening in a perfect line.

Better me than Eve. The thought is crystal clear amid the red haze of pain. Every strike she aims at me is one my wife's corpse doesn't have to take.

I lunge forward, closing the distance between us. The whip is deadly at range but useless up close. Shelby backpedals, but too late—my body collides with hers, driving her back against a metal support beam. The knife in my hand presses against her throat, drawing a thin line of blood.

Her breath comes in sharp pants, eyes wide but unafraid. She knows I could kill her right now. Knows and doesn't care.

"Do it," she taunts, voice breaking. "Do it, you fucking spineless coward."

My hand tightens on her throat, squeezing until her face flushes red, until veins stand out in her forehead. The knife bites deeper, blood welling around the blade.

But Eve is still hanging there, still bleeding. Even dead, she's still my priority.

I slam Shelby's head against the beam hard enough to daze her, then spin away, knife still clutched in my fist.

Three long strides bring me to Eve. Her head hangs forward, hair matted with sweat and blood, body limp in her restraints. The knife saws through hemp, fibers parting reluctantly. In my haste, the blade skips, nicking the pale skin of her wrist.

Fresh blood wells from the cut, joining the stream already running down her arm. Horror freezes me for a heartbeat—I've hurt her again, added another wound to the collection Shelby's already given her.

Then... a gasp. Tiny, ragged, but it slams into me harder than any bullet. She's alive. My wife isn't dead. Her eyes flutter, lips parting on a shaky exhale.

Relief floods through me, so intense it makes my knees buckle. I catch her as the last rope gives way, her weight slumping against my chest. She's warm. Breathing. Heart beating against mine.

"I've got you," I murmur against her hair, throat tight with emotion I can't name. "I've got you, Eve. Fuck… I thought I'd lost you. But you're here. I love you so much. I've got you." The words of relief fall from my lips.

Behind me, Shelby's laugh rings out, high and unhinged. "How sweet," she mocks. "Too bad it won't last. You think you can just walk away from this? Take her home and play house like nothing happened?"

I lay Eve on the ground, and now that she's no longer slumped, it's all too easy to see the shoulder wound. I add pressure to stem the bleeding. Then I turn back to Shelby, something cold and calculated replacing the blind rage from before.

She's managed to retrieve the whip, holding it loosely in one hand, the other pressed against her bleeding throat. Her smile is all teeth, sharp and feral in the dim light.

"You're going to pay for every mark on her skin," I promise, advancing on her again.

She lashes out with the whip, but her aim is off, the strike going wide. I catch the leather in mid-air, yanking hard enough to pull her off balance. She staggers forward, and I'm on her in an instant, driving her to the ground.

We grapple in the dirt and blood, neither willing to yield. Her nails rake down my neck, tearing skin. My hands find her throat again, squeezing until her eyes bulge. The knife lies forgotten inches from my hand—I could reach it, could end this now.

"Jack." Eve's voice is weak but clear, cutting through the red haze of my rage. "Jack, stop. Don't kill her."

I freeze, hands still locked around Shelby's throat. "What?"

"Don't," Eve repeats, struggling to push herself upright. Blood soaks half her dress, her face pale with pain and blood loss, but her eyes are clear. Determined.

"Baby," I rasp, wanting her to understand it has to be this way. Shelby can't be allowed to live.

Eve weakly shakes her head. "I'm not your baby," she chokes out. "I'm Dr. Motherfucking Death. And Shelby isn't just yours to kill."

Fuck, if there was ever any doubt as to whether I love this woman or not, there's none now. Even while bleeding and beaten, she's all fire.

Shelby's laugh bubbles up beneath my hands, wet and rasping. "Are you really going to let your wife make the decisions?"

My grip tightens reflexively, rage surging fresh. One squeeze. That's all it would take to silence her forever, to end the threat she poses to Eve, to me, to everything I've finally allowed myself to want.

Slowly, reluctantly, I loosen my grip on Shelby's throat. She sucks in a ragged breath, coughing and sputtering beneath me.

"Jack." A note of panic creeps into Shelby's voice, and I'm pretty sure it has nothing to do with my hand around her throat. "What if I told you this is the whip John used on R-Ruby?"

Instead of feeling more heartbreak or anger, I smile. Fucking smile. It's cold and ruthless. "You saying that just shows how desperate you are to die."

Eve's hand finds my shoulder, trembling but firm. "Don't listen to her," my wife whispers. "She'll pay."

"We're taking her with us," I say, voice rough with restraint. "And once you're healed, we'll have some fun, Dr. Death."

I pull Shelby's arms behind her back, using my belt to bind her wrists.

"This isn't over," she promises, voice scraped raw.

"No," I tell her, tightening the makeshift restraints until she winces. "We're just getting started."

Without sparing her a glance, I throw Shelby to the side and turn my full attention on Eve. I've missed this woman so much I've been fucking aching. Yet nothing has been as excruciating as being this close to her without being able to touch her until now.

I drop to my knees, hauling her into me, her body folding against mine. She's trembling, bleeding, but warm. *Alive.* I bury my face in her hair, the taste of copper on my lips, proof I didn't lose her. Proof I still have something to fight for.

"Fuck, Eve," I choke, kissing her everywhere—her temple, the cut on her cheek, her mouth. "I thought I lost you. I *can't* lose you. Not *you*."

Her hands, weak but determined, fist into my shirt. She drags me closer, lips seeking mine with a hunger that steals the air from my lungs. "You won't," she whispers against my mouth, voice torn but fierce. "Because I love you."

The words break me open. The kiss that follows isn't gentle—it's raw, desperate, survival itself. Relief and hunger and love all tangled in blood and salt. I can't get enough of her. I'll never get enough.

"It's us," I murmur against her lips, words ragged and true. "You and me against the world. Always."

Her gray eyes lock on mine, steady despite the pain. "Always," she echoes, and it's the only vow I'll ever need.

CHAPTER 35

The Trickster

I carry Eve through the warehouse doors, her body a weight I refuse to surrender. Blood seeps through the tattered fabric on her body, warm against my skin, binding us together in ways I never wanted.

Her breath comes in shallow gasps against my neck, and each step I take causes her to whimper. It's a fucking dagger to my heart.

"Stay with me," I murmur against Eve's hair, not sure if I'm ordering or begging. Her eyelids flutter, gray irises fighting to focus on my face.

I'm ten steps from my car when tires screech against asphalt. Nick's car slides to a halt. Marco jumps out of the front passenger side while my brother erupts from the driver's side, face twisted with fury.

He opens his mouth but whatever he was going to say dies on his tongue when his gaze catches on Eve in my arms.

"What the fuck happened?" he asks, rushing to my side.

I shake my head. "We need a doctor for Eve."

Nick's eyes darken, hardening with purpose. He doesn't waste time asking questions I won't answer. Instead, he pulls open the rear door of his car, helping me maneuver Eve inside without jostling her injuries.

"Shelby's still inside," I tell him as I slide onto the back seat,

cradling Eve across my lap. "Marco can get her, but she needs to stay alive until Eve's ready to deal with her."

Nick nods once, already barking orders at his head of security, something about cleanup and other things that turn into white noise. My focus narrows to Eve, to the rise and fall of her chest, to the flutter of her pulse beneath my fingertips.

"Nick," I growl, not liking how long this is taking.

"Coming."

He gets into the car and, wasting no time speeding away, drives with the precise aggression that's gotten us out of trouble our entire lives. Eve screams in pain as Nick swerves to avoid the car that's stopped in front of us.

"Easy," I whisper, angling her so the pressure on her shoulder eases. "I've got you."

Her eyes open, glassy with pain but clear enough to find mine. "Jack," she rasps, "she... I..."

"Don't talk," I cut her off, pressing my lips to her forehead. The copper tang of blood clings to her skin, to mine, to everything. "Save your strength."

The city blurs past the windows, Nick weaving through traffic with single-minded determination. I keep my hand pressed against Eve's shoulder, feeling the steady pulse of blood against my palm.

My own injuries are nothing but background noise. The only pain that registers is hers, each wince and muffled groan like a knife between my ribs.

"Almost there," Nick announces, eyes meeting mine in the rearview mirror.

The gates of Nick's estate swing open before we reach them, someone having called ahead. We tear up the long driveway, gravel spitting beneath the tires. The mansion looms ahead, and when we get closer, I see Carolina standing on the front steps.

Nick barely puts the car in park before he's out, yanking open my door. "Carmichael's ready," he says, helping me slide out with Eve still in my arms. "Everything's set up."

I nod, unable to spare a breath for gratitude. Eve has gone

terrifyingly still in my arms, her head lolling against my chest. Only the faint warmth of her breath against my neck tells me she's still fighting.

Carolina gasps when she sees us, one hand flying to her mouth. "Oh my God," she whispers, but there's no hysteria in her voice—just controlled horror, the kind that comes from understanding exactly what stands before her. "This way."

She leads us through the foyer, past the grand staircase, down the west wing corridor. My boots leave bloody prints on the marble, a trail of violence through the pristine halls of my brother's home.

The hospital wing occupies the entire first floor of the west wing—a necessity in our line of work. Dr. Carmichael stands ready in the central treatment room, flanked by two nurses in crisp scrubs.

Her face remains impassive as we enter, only the slight widening of her eyes betraying her shock at Eve's condition. "On the table," she instructs, already pulling on gloves.

I hesitate, my arms tightening around Eve. The thought of letting her go, even to save her, coils like a viper in my chest.

"Jack," Nick says, voice quiet but firm. "Let them work."

Slowly, I turn Eve and lower her onto the examination table. She's on her stomach to spare the lashes on her back, but that doesn't stop her blood from immediately staining the white sheets. Her fingers clutch weakly at my shirt as I pull away.

"I'm not leaving," I tell Carmichael, a statement, not a question.

The doctor doesn't argue, just nods at one of the nurses. "Set up a second station. Mr. Knight needs treatment as well."

"Focus on her," I growl.

"We'll do both," Carmichael replies, already cutting away what remains of Eve's dress. "Sit down before you fall down."

I move to the head of Eve's table as a nurse drags a stool beside me. From here, I can watch Carmichael work while keeping my hand on Eve's uninjured shoulder, a tether between us that I refuse to break.

The nurse cleans my face with antiseptic wipes, the sting barely registering. My gaze remains fixed on Eve as Carmichael methodically catalogs her injuries. The bullet wound through her shoulder, the deep lacerations across her back from the whip, the knife cut on her cheek, and the rope burns circling her wrists.

Each wound leaves a hollow ache in my chest, as if it had been carved into my own flesh. I should have been faster. Should have known. Should have protected her.

"The bullet went clean through," Carmichael reports, voice clinically detached. "No major vessels hit. She's lost blood, but not enough to be critical."

Relief washes through me, a momentary reprieve from the guilt consuming me. Eve's eyelids flutter at the sound of my exhale, her gaze finding mine through the haze of pain.

"Still here," she whispers, the ghost of a smile curving her lips.

"I'm not going anywhere," I promise, ignoring the nurse as she cleans the whip marks across my back. The pain is distant, belonging to someone else entirely.

Carolina steps up behind me, one hand on my shoulder, careful to avoid my injuries. "She'll be okay," she murmurs, as much for herself as for me. "She's strong."

Nick paces at the periphery of the room, phone to his ear, handling the aftermath of what we've left behind. His voice is a low rumble of controlled authority—cleanup crews dispatched, Shelby secured, all traces of our presence at the warehouse erased.

The routine of it would be comforting if I could feel anything beyond the bruised tenderness of watching Eve being stitched back together. Every needle through her skin, every bandage placed, every careful cleaning of blood feels like it's happening to me.

Carmichael works with methodical precision, her hands steady as they close every wound. "You'll both need rest," she says as she finishes the last stitch on Eve's shoulder. "No exertion. No stress."

Her gaze flicks between Nick and me, clinical assessment tinged with knowing resignation, and a heavy dose of scepticism.

"They'll follow every order," Nick answers before I can. "They're staying here until they're healed."

I don't argue. Here, under Nick's roof, with guards and security systems and family watching over us, she'll be safe.

"I'm putting her on antibiotics and pain management," Carmichael continues, inserting an IV line into Eve's arm. "She'll need the stitches out in about ten days. The shoulder will take longer to heal completely."

Eve's eyes are closed now, her breathing steadier, the pain medication taking effect. Her hand rests in mine, fingers loosely curled around my palm. Even unconscious, she refuses to let go.

"Thank you," I say to Carmichael, the words inadequate for what she's done.

She nods once, understanding what I don't say. Then she turns to the nurse tending my injuries. "Finish cleaning him so we can finish up."

I submit to their ministrations without complaint, my eyes never leaving Eve's face. The worst is over now. She's alive. She's here. She's still mine. Everything else—Shelby, the warehouse, the blood—can wait.

One week passes. I measure time by the healing of her wounds—the stitches in her shoulder tightening, the cut on her cheek scabbing over, the welts on her back fading from angry red to dusky pink.

Every morning, I trace these markers with my fingertips, a ritual of possession and care. Eve watches me through half-lidded eyes, still drowsy with sleep, her lips curved in a smile that's equal parts surrender and defiance.

"You're hovering again," she murmurs as I adjust her pillow for the third time this morning. We're still in the guest suite in Nick and Carolina's home. It's become our sanctuary.

"I'm taking care of you," I correct, voice low as I smooth the sheet across her lap.

My own wounds have mostly healed, but I still stay here with her, refusing to let her out of my sight.

Eve sighs, pushing herself upright against the headboard. "I can sit up on my own, you know."

"You shouldn't strain yourself."

"It's been a week, Jack." Her fingers trace the bandage on her shoulder, testing the edges where medical tape meets skin. "I'm not made of glass."

I take her hand, moving it away from the wound. "Obey the doctor's orders," I say, pressing a kiss to her palm. "Please. For me."

She rolls her eyes but doesn't pull away. This is our rhythm now—her pushing, testing boundaries, me drawing her back, keeping her still.

I settle beside her on the bed, reaching for the book on the nightstand. It's something Carolina brought—a thriller taking place in a mental institution in the forties. Even though Eve loves to point out all the implausibilities, she lets me read it to her.

"Chapter fifteen," I begin, finding our place from yesterday.

Eve's head tilts against my shoulder as I read, her body softening into mine by increments. I feel each shift in her posture, each small twitch and sigh. When her breathing deepens, slowing toward sleep, I close the book.

"Don't stop," she murmurs, eyes still closed. "I'm listening."

"You're sleeping," I counter, setting the book aside.

Her lips quirk. "Maybe I like falling asleep to your voice."

Something warm uncoils in my chest at her admission. I lean down, brushing my lips against her forehead. "Later," I promise. "You need to eat first."

I retrieve the tray Carolina left outside our door—soup, bread, sliced fruit. Eve's appetite has been slow to return, each meal a negotiation between us. I sit on the edge of the bed, loading the spoon with broth.

Reaching for the spoon, she protests, "I can feed myself."

I hold it just out of reach. "Humor me."

"Then feed me something other than soup," she whines. "I want cake and butter and chocolate and… fries. I miss fries."

I chuckle. "Would this be a good time to point out that I *know* Carolina is sneaking you daily chocolate bars?"

My beautiful wife averts her gaze. "I don't know what you're talking about."

"How about this," I suggest. "We'll compromise. You'll eat the soup, and I'll let you have two chocolate bars today."

Her sigh is theatrical, but she opens her mouth, accepting the soup with a pointed look that says this isn't over. The spoon slides between her lips, metal against flesh, an intimacy that feels deeper than it should. I watch her throat work as she swallows, my own mouth going dry.

"Is this going to be our life now?" she asks after several more spoonfuls. "You feeding me like I'm helpless?"

"Like you're precious," I correct, tearing a piece of bread and offering it to her. "Only until I'm sure."

"Sure of what?" She takes the bread, her fingers brushing mine.

"That I won't lose you." The words come out rougher than intended, scraping past the knot in my throat.

Eve's expression softens, something tender and sharp in her gaze. "Jack," she says, my name both benediction and chastisement. "You're not going to lose me."

I don't answer. Can't answer.

The memory of her hanging from that hook, bleeding and broken, is still too fresh. The terror of holding her in the car, feeling her blood seep through my clothes, certain she was slipping away—it haunts my sleep, drives me to check her breathing in the darkest hours.

Instead of telling her that, I finish feeding her in silence, watching with fierce concentration as she takes each bite, as color returns to her cheeks by slow degrees. When she can't eat any more, I set the tray aside and retrieve the medical supplies Carmichael left for us.

"Time to change your bandages," I say, gesturing for her to turn, before I quickly snap on a pair of plastic gloves.

Eve complies and shifts onto her side, exposing her back to me, a trust that still steals my breath. I peel away the gauze covering the worst of the lash marks, relief washing through me at the clean, healing lines.

Luckily, there's no infection. Just new skin forming, scars that will fade but never disappear completely.

"How does it look?" she asks, voice muffled against the pillow.

"Better." I apply the antibiotic ointment with careful fingers, tracing each mark with a reverence that belies the rage still simmering beneath my skin. "You're healing well."

She hums, the sound vibrating under my palm. "And my shoulder?"

"That comes last." I finish with her back, securing fresh gauze over the wounds, then help her onto her other side to access the bullet wound.

"It looks good."

"It's itchy and sore," she admits, wincing as I clean around the edges. "But not as bad as yesterday."

I work in silence, methodical in my care, my touch clinical even as my gaze devours every inch of her. When I finish, I help her into a fresh t-shirt, easing it over her injuries with practiced gentleness.

"Thank you," she says, settling back against the pillows. There's something in her tone—a weight, a decision reached—that makes me pause.

"For what?"

"For finding me." Her fingers twist in the sheets, knuckles whitening. "For not letting her win."

I sit beside her, taking her hand in mine. "I will always find you," I promise, the words a vow carved in bone. "*Always.*"

She nods, swallowing hard. The room feels suddenly charged, like the air before a storm breaks. "I'm not sure I deserve it," she says, looking away.

"Why the hell not?"

"I…" Pausing, she licks her dry lips and runs a hand through her hair, twirling a strand around her finger. "I'm not completely innocent," she says, voice dropping to barely above a whisper.

Unless this is some poorly timed joke about not being a virgin, I have no fucking clue what she's getting at. "Spit it out," I order, taking her hand and squeezing it. "Whatever it is, you can tell me."

"It's about my dad."

I go still, recognizing the importance of this moment, this offering. "I'm listening."

"I killed him." The words fall like stones between us, heavy with truth long carried. "Some think it was Valentine, but it wasn't. It was me. I did it, and he helped me cover it up."

While I wait for her to continue, I trace circles on her wrist, feeling the rapid flutter of her pulse.

"Valentine was going to kill him, and he nearly did. He attacked us in an alley. But he… well, he didn't finish the job."

"But you did," I state.

She nods. "Yeah, I killed my dad. Instead of getting him help, I sliced his throat and let him bleed out in an alley. If I'd had more time or been better prepared, I would have dragged his ass into a coffin like he used to do to me."

I don't interrupt as she tells me about the years of abuse she suffered at her dad's hand. When she explains the coffin of shame, I nearly lose my fucking shit. Especially when she describes in gruesome detail how he shoved her in there and locked the fucking lid.

"When that happened, I had to convince him to let me out." She lets out a sad laugh. "Even when I was eight, he made me convince him. It was harder when I was younger and I remember this one time where it took me two days."

My vision goes red, and my nostrils flare with barely constrained all-consuming rage. "Fuck!" I roar.

She exhales shakily, and just when I think she's going to clam up, she carries on. My beautiful, strong wife straightens and tells me how he used her entire upbringing as teachable moments and published her failures as medical papers.

"That's fucked up," I growl, squeezing her hand harder. "Fuck, I wish you hadn't killed him."

"You do?" Her voice is small.

I nod. "Yeah. But only because I'd love to make him fucking cry for mercy. If I could, I'd bring him back to life just so we could lock him in his own coffin of shame."

That makes her laugh, a sound that's too rare these days. "That would be something," she giggles. She places her hand against my cheek, cupping it. "I got the last word when I told him just how much I hated him while he bleed out in a dirty alley—"

"It's not enough," I seethe. "He deserves—"

"Nothing." She raises her chin. "He deserves nothing. To men like Charles Mortis, nothing is their worst nightmare. But I canceled his book deals and Valentine helped make sure no college or uni use my dad's books. I also sold the family home. That's partly why his final resting place is on a mantle I hardly ever clean."

I whistle slowly. "Fuck, Little Bride. When you say nothing it really means…"

"Nothing," she smiles.

A pregnant silence falls over us, and I wonder what she's thinking. Judging by the way she's biting into her lush lower lip, it's not anything good.

"What's on your mind?" I ask when I can't take it anymore.

"You said I was the doctor who did nothing, and you're correct." Her voice rises. "I could probably have stopped Valentine from getting involved with Ruby. You were right to blame me. But, Jack, I need you to know something."

"What?"

"Even if I could go back and change things, I wouldn't." Finally meeting my gaze, I see the challenge in her gray depths. "Because he loved her. Like I love you. Even the damaged and broken deserve love, don't we?"

Refusing to give her the fight I feel her angling for, I bend and fuse my lips to her. "You have no idea how true that is, *wife*."

She lets out a low moan as I nibble on her bottom lip, but instead, I pull back. "I knew about your dad."

Her eyes widen. "What?"

"I didn't know all the things he did to you. But when I looked into you before my first and only therapist appointment, I already knew you'd killed him." I lift her hand to my lips, pressing a kiss to her knuckles. "So I know what you did."

"And you don't care?" Disbelief colors her voice.

"You're misunderstanding me," I chuckle. "I care very much. But only about what he did to deserve it. Now, if you're asking if I care that you took a life, the answer is no. No, I don't give two shits. Do you?"

She scrunches her nose in confusion. "What do you mean?"

"I've killed plenty of times. Do you care about that?"

Eve's never been more beautiful to me than right now, as she shakes her head and looks at me from beneath her long, black eyelashes. "I don't care who you've killed or that you've killed. All I care about is us and our future."

CHAPTER 36

The Bride

I want to cry as I look at myself in the bathroom mirror. This is the first time I see my reflection, something I've avoided until today. But it's been nine days since the attack, and, well, in my mind I thought I'd look better.

The cut makes me look absolutely hideous. I know it'll fade over time. It's already scabbed. But… oh, who am I kidding? I'm hideous.

"It's not that bad," Jack soothes, gathering my hair and dragging it off my neck so he can cup the nape.

My fingers trace the contours of my face, applying precise pressure to gauge the depth of the damage, wincing when the motion tugs at my shoulder.

"Yeah?" I sniff. "Do you want a matching cut?"

Jack's answering laugh is deliciously dark and low. "If you want to cut me, wife, all you have to do is say so."

I gape at his words. Would he really let me? When I meet his gaze in the reflection I know he's serious. The truth is right there in his green orbs. He'd let me slice him open and bathe in his blood if it would make me happy.

Rather than answering, I allow myself to admire his broad shoulders

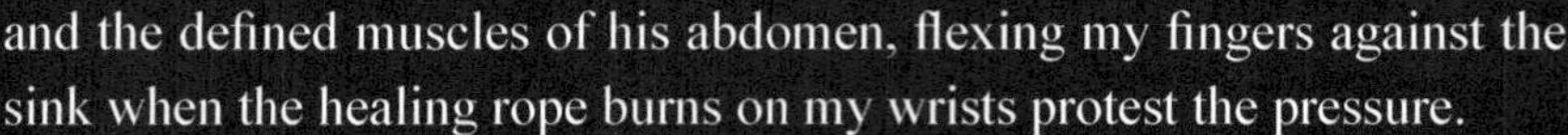

and the defined muscles of his abdomen, flexing my fingers against the sink when the healing rope burns on my wrists protest the pressure.

My eyes land on his scar, and I subconsciously lick my lips while tracing it all the way to the flesh marred by the bullet that killed him months ago—before they dragged him back. He shifts, and my gaze follows as though he's commanding my attention with movement alone.

I study the pumpkin tattoo on his deltoid. "Why did you get that tattoo?" I hear myself ask.

His eyes capture my gray ones in the mirror. "I lost a bet to Nick and Ruby," he explains.

"What was the bet?"

He inhales sharply and furrows his brows as though something's annoying him. "You know, I don't even remember anymore." There's a beat of silence before he continues. "I was only sixteen when I got it. But I'm sure it was something super serious."

My lips pull into a smile. "I'm sure it was," I agree softly.

"Eve." Goosebumps erupt all over my skin when he says my name in that breathy and husky way of his. "We should talk about—"

"Not yet," I interrupt. I know he means Shelby, but I'm not ready.

To my surprise, Jack chuckles. "You never broke once when I tormented you. But now you're crying over a cut that'll be completely gone in no time."

"I'm not crying…" I stop talking as I realize tears are soundlessly trailing down my cheeks. "Oh."

I can't help laughing because it does sound ridiculous when he puts it like that.

"You still want me like this?" I test, not because I doubt it, not really—because I *want* to hear it.

"Always," he says, no hesitation.

He reaches for my hand—the one he sliced into at our wedding. The silence stretches between us, thick with something unspeakable, as his fingertips dance across the scar.

I yank my hand back before he can brush it again. I know it's irrational, but I don't like that he hasn't kissed or touched me since we were at the warehouse. Rationally, I know it's because we've both been healing. But irrationally, it feels like an insult.

"You think this…" his finger traces the outline of the thin line on my cheek, "… makes you less fuckable?"

"I think it makes me look weak," I admit, the honesty surprising even me.

"Weak?" He makes a sound that might be a laugh. "Eve, I've seen a lot of weak people. You're not one of them."

Turning away from my reflection, I take a step to the side, surprised he lets me. "I came in here to shower." I infuse my tone with confidence I don't feel right now, even roll my shoulders back and lift my chin.

I step into the shower without looking back at him, leaving the door open. Picking up the detachable head, I adjust the temperature until it verges on scalding and angle the spray low, keeping my stitched shoulder and back dry.

Steam rises around me, creating a thin and constantly moving veil of tendrils between my naked body and Jack's watchful gaze. I can feel him still there, just beyond the glass—a presence that radiates through the barrier, that prickles against my awareness like static electricity before a storm.

Water sluices over my stomach and hips, between my thighs, washing away the lingering traces of hospital antiseptic and the phantom touch of strangers' hands. The warmth penetrates muscle and bone, thawing something frozen within me, something rigid with anger and helplessness.

I reach for the soap, lathering it between my palms until bubbles foam white and thick, gliding the suds over my stomach and legs. Just as I close my eyes, I hear it.

"Allowing yourself to be content is a weakness, Eve." My dad's words slither through my mind, just an echo from the grave I put him in. *"And when you're content, you let your guard down. Do you want to be let out of the coffin? Then make me want to set you free."*

Charles Mortis was a sadistic asshole, one I don't regret killing. But being unlikable doesn't mean he was wrong. If I hadn't said goodbye to everything he taught me and embraced a life with no rules or regulations, I never would have ended up in Shelby's clutches.

Or maybe I'd have sensed her intentions sooner and then been able to do something about it before she made me shed blood and tried to kill Jack. The bitch is tied up in Nicklas' basement. According to Carolina, Shelby's all alone in the dark—fed only while sleeping, cut off from any human contact.

While I ponder all that, my hands slide over my skin of their own accord. Thoroughly cleansing each inch of my body with slow precision. I turn slightly, offering Jack a better view through the glass. I imagine his eyes tracking my movements, cataloging each curve and angle.

The thought sends an unexpected current through my nerves, not unpleasant. It settles low in my belly, a warmth distinct from the shower's heat.

My fingers travel lower, sliding between my legs. When I find my clit, I use my middle finger to apply pressure. God, that feels good. I circle the bundle of nerves faster, harder. I hear Jack's breath catch, the sound barely audible over the shower's steady drum.

"Do you want to kiss my lips now?" I ask, never looking away from him.

As he clenches his jaw, I notice the muscle jump beneath his stubbled skin, eyes narrowed and dark with what can only be hunger.

He watches my hand work between my thighs, his own hands curled into fists at his sides, like he's physically restraining himself from storming in here.

"Yes," he growls, finally answering me.

I slide two fingers inside myself, feeling the walls of my pussy contract around the intrusion. My thumb takes over the circular motion against my clitoris, creating dual points of stimulation that make my back arch and my thighs tense.

"Mhmm," I purr. "I bet you do."

Jack's expression has transformed—the detached observer replaced by something feral and hungry. His eyes burn with an intensity that should frighten me but instead fuels something darker, something greedier within me.

"Don't test me, Eve," he growls. "My restraint only lasts so long."

Smirking, I circle my clit faster. I love knowing he wants entry to this private domain, this self-pleasure that excludes him even as it's performed for his benefit.

"Oh, God," I moan, closing my eyes for a moment as pleasure zips through me.

When I open my eyes again, Jack's in here with me, and I didn't even hear him move. Unashamedly, I look down at his crotch. He's still wearing his black boxer briefs, which immediately cling to every contour of his rigid cock.

The metal rungs of his Jacob's Ladder are visible through the soaked fabric, a ladder of pleasure I've only begun to climb.

He makes no move to remove the underwear, no attempt to join my self-exploration. He simply watches, his restraint more arousing than any touch could be.

Water streams down his chest, running in rivulets through the grooves of his muscles. He doesn't touch me. Doesn't speak. Just stands there, watching up close as my fingers continue their steady rhythm between my thighs.

"Don't stop," he says finally, his voice roughened by desire. It's not a command but something close to a request—the closest Jack Knight has ever come to asking rather than taking.

I push my fingers deeper, curl upward, finding that spot inside that makes sparks shoot behind my eyelids. My thumb circles faster, the pressure increasing as I approach the edge of release.

Jack's presence changes everything and nothing—I'm still touching myself, still pursuing my own pleasure, but now his gaze adds another layer of sensation, another dimension of intensity.

This moment belongs to me—my pleasure, my body, my choice to share the visual feast with the man who claimed to own me. Water streams between us, washing away boundaries but creating new ones, more complex, more deliberate.

His breath comes faster now, matching my own accelerating rhythm. The air between us thickens with something that feels dangerously like understanding.

Then, just as I'm close, he drops to his knees with such sudden force that water splashes outward in a corona around him. His hands grip my

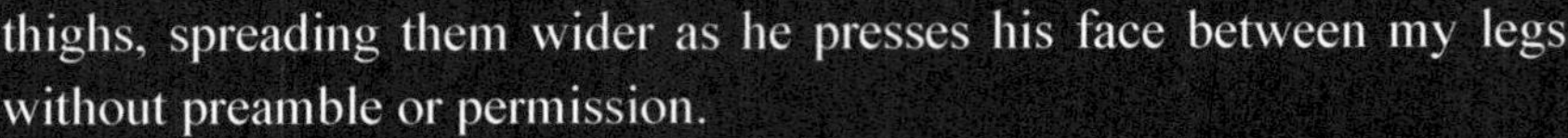

thighs, spreading them wider as he presses his face between my legs without preamble or permission.

"You asked if I wanted to kiss your lips," he rasps. "These are the lips I want to devour."

The first stroke of his tongue against my already-sensitive flesh tears a gasp from my throat.

"Jack."

I steady myself with one hand against the slick tile, my injured shoulder twinging under the pressure, while my other hand fists in his wet hair, fingers curling to control his movements with cruel precision. This isn't surrender; it's direction.

"Harder," I instruct, yanking his head closer.

He lets out a throaty chuckle. "First, I have something to ask you."

"What? Now?" My tone betrays my irritation. But seriously, this isn't exactly the time to play twenty questions.

"Yes. Now is the perfect time," he rasps.

"Fine," I huff.

His tongue flattens against me, then stiffens to a point that circles my clitoris with merciless accuracy. The pressure sends shocks of pleasure up my spine, electric and brutal in their intensity.

"Will you stay married to me?"

"W-what?" I stammer, not sure I heard him right.

"Be my wife forever, Eve Mortis."

I pull harder at his hair, directing his mouth exactly where I need it, using his face like a tool calibrated for my pleasure. Jack groans against me, the vibration adding another layer of sensation that makes my inner walls clench around nothing.

"Yes," I moan, both in answer to the way he's eating my cunt and his question. "I'll be yours forever." His stubble scrapes the sensitive skin of my inner thighs, a pleasurable burn that borders on pain.

"Then fucking use me. Take what you need to feel better, wife," he growls, breaking contact. "Your pussy tastes so fucking good when you're in control." His words buzz against my flesh, making me shudder.

The praise shouldn't affect me, but something about the raw honesty in his voice cuts through my defenses.

The man who caged me, who humiliated me on a stage, who married me without consent, and then told me he loves me—the man *I* love—is now on his knees worshiping me with genuine reverence and hunger.

His tongue dips lower, pushing inside my cunt in a crude mimicry of fucking before dragging back up to circle my clit. My hips buck against his face, chasing the sensation.

I tighten my grip on his hair, pulling hard enough to hurt, but he doesn't flinch. Just doubles his efforts, adding suction that makes spots dance behind my closed eyelids.

"Jack," I gasp, the word neither plea nor prayer but simple acknowledgment of the man bringing me to the edge of dissolution. "Don't stop."

"Wouldn't dream of it," he murmurs against my pussy. His hands slide from my thighs to grip handfuls of my ass, fingers digging into the muscle hard enough to leave bruises. "Come on my tongue, Little Bride. Drown me in your arousal."

The command triggers something primal within me. My body tenses, thighs clamping around his head as pleasure crests and breaks in a violent wave. I cry out his name, the sound echoes off tile and glass as my orgasm tears through me with a force that feels like revenge.

My fingers pull his hair tight enough to make him groan as I grind against his mouth, riding out every aftershock, taking everything his tongue offers without gratitude or shame.

Before the final pulses subside, Jack rises with predatory grace, and quickly discarding his soaked boxer briefs.

He doesn't speak—just grabs my face and kisses me, mouth slick with my release. It's carnal and wrong and hot as fuck, and I kiss him back like I'm claiming his mouth the way he just claimed my cunt.

Then he spins me around and slams me face-first against the wall. He cages me with his body, taking the impact, before his cock presses at my entrance from behind, the metal barbs of his Jacob's Ladder dragging against my sensitive flesh.

"Is this what you wanted?" he growls against my ear, one hand gripping my hip while the other tangles in my wet hair, pulling my head back at an angle that exposes my throat. "To make me so fucking

desperate for you I can't think straight?"

He doesn't wait for an answer. With a single brutal thrust, he buries himself to the hilt inside me, the intrusion so sudden and complete that it steals the breath from my lungs.

My body yields to the invasion, wet and ready from his tongue and my own earlier ministrations, but the stretch still burns in the most exquisite way.

"Jack," I choke out, palms flat against the marble, fingers scrabbling for purchase as he begins to move.

Each thrust drives me harder against the wall, my breasts dragging across the cold surface with friction that sends contradictory signals of pleasure-pain through my nerve endings.

I reach back, nails raking down his arm hard enough to draw blood. The thin red lines well up immediately, droplets mixing with shower spray in pale pink rivulets that disappear down the drain.

Jack hisses but doesn't slow his pace—if anything, the pain spurs him on, makes his grip tighter, his thrusts deeper.

He pulls all the way out, but before I can complain, he pushes back in. He feeds my pussy his length one rung at a time, and it's so fucking hot I wish I could see it.

"Yes," he pants against my neck, teeth grazing the sensitive skin beneath my ear. "Fight back, wife. Claim me like I've claimed you."

The words unleash something in me—permission I didn't know I needed, validation of the rage that's been building. I push back against him, meeting each thrust with equal force, no longer a passive recipient but an active participant.

He pulls my hips back, changing the angle. And suddenly, he's hitting that perfect spot inside me that makes my vision blur at the edges.

Pressure builds again, faster this time, coiling tight at the base of my spine.

"I'm going to come," I moan, the words torn from my throat in ragged fragments.

"Do it," he demands, reaching around to find my clit with unerring precision. His fingers circle the swollen nub, adding the final stimulation needed to send me careening over the edge. "Come on my cock like a

good fucking wife. Show me how much you fucking need this."

My second orgasm crashes through me with even greater intensity than the first, my inner walls clamping down around his length in rhythmic pulses that make him curse and stutter in his pace.

I scream wordlessly, the sound primal and raw, bouncing off the shower walls and coming back to me like an echo of my own release.

Before I've fully descended from the peak, Jack spins me around to face him, lifting me with his hands beneath my thighs.

He's careful to carry all my weight, keeping my back clear of the wall, as he slides back inside me in one smooth motion, the new angle sending aftershocks ricocheting through my oversensitized nerves.

He kisses me mid-thrust, tongue driving in like he's trying to own my breath. My legs lock around him tighter, needing the kiss almost more than his cock.

"Look at me," he commands, one hand leaving my thigh to grip my chin, forcing my gaze to his. "See who's fucking you. Who's making you feel this good."

I meet his eyes, refusing to look away even as he resumes his punishing rhythm. His thumb finds my clit again, circling with deliberate pressure that has me gasping and clawing at his shoulders.

"Such a perfect fucking cunt," he growls, the words filthy, but the tone almost reverent. "So tight. So wet. So goddamn responsive."

The combination of his cock filling me, his thumb working my clit, pushes me toward a third peak I didn't think possible. My nails dig crescents into his shoulders, drawing fresh blood that mixes with the water still streaming over us both.

"I'm close," he warns, his rhythm faltering as his own release approaches. "I want to see my cum all over your face."

"No," I gasp, locking my ankles behind his back to prevent retreat. "Inside me. I want you to come inside me."

His eyes widen fractionally, surprise flashing across his features before being consumed by raw hunger. "You sure about that, wife?"

I don't know why he's hesitating now when he's been fucking me raw all this time. But it's oddly sweet.

"Fill me up," I demand, tightening my inner muscles around him in deliberate provocation.

I don't tell him I'm on birth control. Either he knows, or he doesn't. Even so, nothing is one-hundred percent certain. But right now, I don't care about the consequences. I just want to feel his hot cum inside me.

The words trigger something primal in him—his thrusts become erratic, desperate, the metal barbs of his piercing dragging against my inner walls with delicious friction.

My third orgasm builds and breaks in tandem with his, my body milking his release as he erupts inside me with a guttural groan that sounds like my name and a curse combined.

Hot pulses of his cum fill me as my own pleasure crests, my pussy squeezing every drop from him.

Instead of pulling away, he leans in, catching my mouth in a kiss so deep it steals what little breath I have left. His tongue snakes around mine like a final claim—wet, unrelenting, and cruelly tender.

For long moments, ragged breathing and the steady drum of water against tile are the only sounds. It's… nice doesn't feel like enough of a description. It's more than that.

When he finally lowers me to my feet, my legs are unsteady, muscles trembling from exertion and aftermath. His cum trickles down my inner thigh, mixing with water before disappearing down the drain.

The cut still marks my skin, but something fundamental has shifted. I feel less damaged, more whole. Not because *he* healed me—but because *I* allowed myself to let him help me.

"I'm ready," I whisper, knowing he heard me.

"Are you sure?"

Squaring my shoulders, I lift my chin. "Yes. I'm ready to fucking break her."

363

CHAPTER 37

The Trickster

It's hard to believe it's already been ten days since I carried Eve out of the warehouse. And now, I'm watching her dress for dinner.

Her movements are careful but steady, determination threading through each one. This morning Dr. Carmichael removed her stitches, declared our recovery on track, and gave Eve the all-clear.

My wife's wounds have all closed, leaving behind pink scars that will eventually fade to silver. But some marks go deeper. I see it in the way she pauses before mirrors, in how her fingers sometimes trace the line on her cheek as if to confirm it's really healed.

A stretch of days can't erase what Shelby did to her. Maybe nothing will.

"Stop staring," Eve says without turning, her voice lighter than it's been in days. She pulls a soft sweater over her head, wincing slightly as she raises her arms. "It's creepy."

"It's appreciation," I correct, coming up behind her to help smooth the fabric over her shoulders. "You look beautiful."

She turns in my arms, gray eyes assessing my face with the clinical precision she never quite sheds. "And you look like you're plotting an escape route."

"I'm not," I grin, dropping a kiss on her forehead. "But if I'm honest, I'm ready to get the fuck away from our wardens." It's only half a joke. They've both been acting like they have a say on any movements we've made.

Eve's eyebrow arches, skepticism etched in the gesture. "Carolina went to a lot of trouble for this dinner. The least you can do is pretend to want to be there."

I sigh, conceding the point. "For you, I'll endure small talk and my brother's insufferable smugness."

"Such sacrifice," she mocks, but there's warmth in her voice, a spark of the Eve from before. It makes something loosen in my chest, a knot I didn't realize I was carrying.

We move through Nick's corridors, my hand at the small of Eve's back—support without show. Her gait is stronger, but I feel the lean into me on the stairs, the measured breath before each step.

Golden light spills from the dining room, pooling across polished floors. Inside, Carolina has clearly gone all out. Candles flickering on the long table, fine china gleaming, wine already poured into crystal glasses. In the bassinet near Carolina's chair, Willow sleeps, tiny fists curled against her cheeks.

"There you are," Carolina says, rising to greet us. She kisses Eve's cheek, then mine, her smile genuine but careful. "I was beginning to think you'd changed your minds."

"And miss your cooking?" Eve replies, squeezing Carolina's hand. "Never."

The ease between them still surprises me—this friendship forged in the aftermath of violence. Carolina has been Eve's most frequent visitor during our convalescence, bringing books, food, and the quiet solidarity of someone who understands what it means to love a Knight man.

Nick guffaws from where he's sitting. "She hasn't—"

"If you want to get laid tonight, you better leave that sentence unfinished," my sister-in-law threatens.

"Sorry, Kitten," he grins, not looking contrite at all. My brother's eyes track me as I help Eve into her chair. "You look better." I'm not sure which of us he's addressing until he adds. "Less like death warmed

over."

Taking the mature route, I flip him off while Carolina admonishes him. Eve just smiles as she settles her napkin in her lap.

"I'll take that as the Knight version of a compliment."

"It was," my brother confirms, lifting his water glass in a silent toast.

The first course arrives—a salad that looks anything but appetizing. We eat in companionable silence broken only by the clink of forks against china and Nick's occasional glances toward Willow's bassinet.

"She'll sleep through anything," Carolina says, noticing my brother's vigilance. "Just like her father."

Nick's expression softens in a way I rarely see, a tenderness reserved solely for his wife and daughter. "A useful trait in this family."

The words land heavier than he means, the reality of being a Knight thick in the air between us. I feel Eve tense beside me, her fork pausing halfway to her lips.

"Speaking of family traits," Nick continues, his gaze shifting to me, "Jack has made a decision I think you should both know about."

I roll my eyes at the way he phrases it, like he didn't run and tell his wife the second I told him. Eve's eyes find mine, questioning. I reach under the table, squeezing her knee gently.

"I've already told you. He's talking about me being out," I say simply.

"Right." She nods. "I'm still not sure what that means."

"Of the family business," Nick clarifies, as servants clear the salad and bring the main course—steaks so rare I lick my lips in anticipation, roasted vegetables, fresh bread still steaming. "Jack's retiring from Knight Enterprises."

Carolina starts serving, passing plates with practiced grace. "Which means more time for you two to figure out what comes next," she adds, her tone deliberately light.

Eve doesn't look away from my brother, her face neutral. "And you're okay with this?" she asks him.

When I told her about it while we were holed up in our recovery room, she kept nervously asking if I was sure I could leave, and if Nick would hold it against her or me. That's why I told him to bring it up

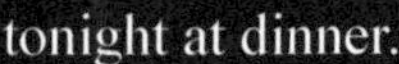

tonight at dinner.

He shrugs, slicing into his meat with precision. "It's his choice. Always has been."

"So, what now?" Eve asks, turning to me. "If you're not a Knight in practice, what are you?"

"Still figuring that out," I admit, meeting her gaze. "As long as I'm your husband, I don't really care."

Leaning closer, she lowers her voice. "Is this because of the curse?"

I'm not sure I believe in the Knight family curse, or superstition, anymore. But that doesn't mean I want to jinx it by saying that out loud.

"It's because I want to discover what life's like with you," I rasp. "Away from all of this."

A smile tugs at the corner of her mouth, something sharp and knowing in her eyes. "Well, if it was because of the curse, I was going to say you could take my last name and become Jack Mortis," she quips. "It has a certain ring to it, don't you think?"

Carolina chokes on her water, laughter sputtering past her surprise. "God, Eve," she gasps, reaching for her napkin. "Warn a girl before you say things like that."

None of us point out that a change in last name didn't save Ruby. She died a Simmons, not a Knight. But... maybe it'll be enough since I've already died once. That means, Nick is the only one of us that never did. The last Knight standing by that logic.

Nick rolls his eyes, but I catch the twitch of his lips. "I like it."

"Me too," Eve laughs, the banter coming easier now, her shoulders relaxing by degrees.

I watch her, something warm unfurling in my chest at this glimpse of the woman beneath the wounds. For this moment, in this room, with our family, she's safe. The scars are still there—visible on her cheek, hidden beneath her sweater—but they don't define her.

Not here. Not now. Not fucking ever.

"You'd take her name?" Carolina asks me, with genuine curiosity in her tone. "Like, for real?"

I consider the question, rolling the idea around like wine on my tongue. "Knight, Mortis... what matters is who I am to her," I say finally.

my eyes never leaving Eve's face. "Everything else is just paperwork."

Something shifts in Eve's expression, a softening around the edges that makes my heart stutter in my chest. She doesn't speak, but her hand finds mine under the table, fingers intertwining with silent understanding.

Talk drifts to mundane topics—Willow's sleeping habits, Carolina's plans for the east garden, Nick's latest acquisition. The details of family life don't thrill me, and when I look at my beautiful wife, I'm relieved to see I'm not the only one looking bored.

When Willow stirs, fussing in her bassinet, Carolina lifts her with practiced ease. The baby blinks up at us, dark eyes curious, tiny fingers flexing in the candlelight. Eve leans forward, her smile softening as Willow grasps her offered finger.

"Cute," Eve murmurs, though she sounds more polite than sincere.

"Want to hold her?" Carolina's already rising from her seat.

Eve hesitates, uncertainty flickering across her face. "I don't know if I should—"

"You won't break her," Carolina assures, placing Willow carefully in Eve's arms before she can protest further.

I watch my wife cradle my niece. Eve's hands, capable of both healing and harm, are now gentle against Willow's delicate form. The baby settles against her chest, trusting in a way that only the innocent can be.

"She likes you," Nick observes, the pride in his voice unmistakable.

Eve doesn't respond, her attention wholly captured by the child in her arms. But I see the way her jaw flexes, like she's waiting for the right time to give Willow back to her parents.

"So, I actually have an idea," Carolina interjects, smirking as she looks at Eve. "Because if tonight's taught me anything, it's that this kind of life would bore the both of you to death."

"Are you going to tell them now?" Nick asks, straightening in his chair.

She grins wickedly. "Not a chance," she sing-songs. "Let's wait until after the Sanctuary closes. There are only four days left until Halloween."

Later, when dinner is done and Willow's in her nursery, we linger at the table. The ease thins as the talk turns to the best way to get rid of Shelby. Though my sister-in-law makes it clear she prefers killing to be done off the premises, she graciously offers to waive the rule this once.

My cock hardens as Eve looks at me, and when she shoots me a chilling smile, I stand abruptly, quickly pulling my wife with me and positioning her in front of me to hide my growing arousal.

"Time for bed," I rasp, my lips near the shell of her ear.

CHAPTER 38

The Bride

Nicklas' basement feels like a vault beneath the earth, the kind of place where sounds go to die. Harsh fluorescents buzz overhead, casting no shadows, leaving nowhere to hide from the truth of what we're about to do.

The concrete walls trap the scents of bleach and iron, the antiseptic smell failing to mask older stains that have seeped into the foundation.

Shelby sits before us, wrists and ankles bound to a metal chair bolted to the floor, her lips twisted in a superior sneer I can't wait to wipe away. I feel Jack shift beside me, his patience stretched thin after days of waiting, or maybe he, like me, is buzzing with anticipation.

Jack's hand finds the small of my back, warm through the thin fabric of my shirt. "Are you sure you want to do this?" he asks, though we both know the answer. This isn't a question of whether, only how.

"Absolutely." I lean into his touch, drawing strength from the solid presence of him. "She took me apart. Now it's *my* turn."

"Fuck, you're so sexy right now." His mouth crashes over mine, all teeth and heat, a bruising claim that tastes of promised violence.

When he lets go of me, I'm panting and lightheaded. I take a moment to gather myself again. Damn, Jack's kisses always leave me wanting more.

I step forward, my heels clicking against concrete, the sound sharp as a metronome counting down the minutes she has left.

"Happy Halloween, Shelby," I say, savoring the way her body tenses. "Today you get both a trick and a treat."

I don't know if she even realizes what day it is after all this time in isolation. Time loses meaning in the dark. But I want her to know—want her to understand that while the world above celebrates with candy and costumes, she'll be meeting a different kind of darkness.

Jack moves to stand beside a folding table where a laptop waits, screen black but ready. His fingers hover over the keyboard, green eyes fixed on me, waiting for my signal.

"You know, I've been thinking about what drives people," I continue, circling Shelby like she's a specimen pinned for study. "What made you do what you did? All that pain, all that rage. It was for love, wasn't it? For John."

At the name, she jerks against her restraints, something frantic and desperate in her muffled cries. I smile, reaching behind her head to loosen the gag.

"I want to hear you," I explain, pulling the cloth free. "Every sound."

"You bitch," she spits, voice raw from disuse. "How dare you talk about him? He was the love of my life and you don't know the fucking meaning."

I hum softly. "Yes, so I've gathered. He was your ultimate love." I circle her once. "But one question remains." I circle her again before crouching in front of her. "Were you his one true love?"

Doubt flickers across her face, just for an instant, before hardening back to hate. "Of course I was."

"Were you?" I gesture to Jack, who brings the laptop and table closer, setting it right in front of Shelby. "Because I think it's time you saw the man you've been mourning. The man you killed your own brother for."

Her eyes dart between my face and the screen, fear wrestling with defiance. "What trick is this?"

"No trick." I lean close, my lips nearly brushing her ear. "Only a treat. After all, when we lose someone, all we want is to see them again. So we're about to make your wish come true."

I nod to Jack, who presses play. The video is grainy security footage, but clear enough. John Simmons—alive, unharmed, and exactly one day before his death—in a hotel room with a woman who isn't Shelby.

The date stamp in the corner doesn't lie. Nor do the naked, writhing bodies, or the carnal sounds they make.

"That's not…" Shelby's voice breaks. "That's not him."

"It is." Jack's voice is low, certain. "And judging by his groans, he's having a great time."

Her face contorts, grief cracking through rage like lightning through storm clouds. The scream that tears from her throat isn't human—it's primal, wounded, the sound of something fundamental breaking apart.

Her body convulses against the restraints, every muscle straining as though trying to physically reject the truth before her eyes.

"No!" she shrieks, over and over, the word shredding into meaningless syllables as the video continues. John moans on screen, his hand around the woman's throat as he thrusts deep into her pussy. "Turn it off! It's a lie!"

But she knows it isn't. I can see the knowledge bleeding into her, poisoning everything she thought she knew. Every moment of those weeks in captivity, every lash of the whip against my skin, every word spat in hatred—all of it based on an unrequited love.

I move close again, my lips at her ear while she sobs, her eyes still fixed on the screen where her world is ending frame by frame. "This is the last thing you'll ever see," I whisper, the words soft as a lover's promise. "The truth about the man you killed for."

Her breath hitches, and she tries to turn her head, to look at me instead of the screen, but Jack is there suddenly, hands steady as a surgeon's as he grasps her face.

"Eyes forward," he commands, voice colder than I've ever heard it. Not even when he caged me did he use that tone. "Watch until the end."

I step back, letting him work. The spoon in his hand gleams dully under the dim light, obscene in its simplicity. Shelby thrashes, her shrieks scraping the walls, but the restraints hold her fast. She knows what's coming.

The first puncture makes her buck against the chair, a sickening pop as pressure gives way, a suctioned rip dragging wet against the air.

Blood sluices down her face in thick sheets, crimson tears streaking over her teeth as she screams, the sound shredding into a high, animal pitch that makes the walls vibrate.

He is detached, deliberate, the spoon moving with terrible efficiency until the first orb comes free, glistening in the light. Then the second.

Her cries collapse into ragged sobs, vibrating so hard it feels like my ribs are shaking with them. Bile claws at the back of my throat, but I force myself still, my eyes locked on hers as blood leaks into the hollows where sight used to be. This isn't cruelty—it's justice. Balance.

When it's done, when her sockets gape empty and her body sags against the chair, Jack finally steps back. Blood coats his hands, but his eyes are steady as they meet mine—merciless and unwavering.

"Are you ready?" he asks, his breath ragged with exertion.

"Yes," I nod, punctuating the words while I pick up the gun from the table. "Together."

I move to stand before her, this woman who was once my friend, who became my tormentor, who is now nothing but a broken vessel for pain.

Jack steps behind me, his chest against my back, his hand covering mine on the handle. Both our index fingers curl around the trigger. His breath warms my neck as we raise the gun together.

Shelby thrashes, blind and broken, a ragged sound clawing from her throat. I lean close enough for her to hear me over her own sobs. "This is a treat you don't fucking deserve," I hiss. "But we're running out of time."

Together, we pull the trigger.

Her head snaps back, chair rattling against its bolts, and then she's still. Blood trickles from the perfect circle at her temple, spreading in quiet lines down her face. The silence afterwards is deafening.

Jack's heartbeat against my back is both steady and strong as he lowers the gun, taking it completely and engaging the safety before tossing it aside. Then he turns me in his arms. His lips find mine hard, unrelenting. The kiss is deep, claiming, sealing us in the violence we chose together.

"It's done," he says simply.

I nod, feeling lighter than I have in weeks. "It's done."

Behind us, Shelby's body cools in its metal chair, eyes gone, heart stilled. The video plays on, unnoticed now, a loop of betrayal for an audience that can no longer see. In the harsh fluorescent light, Jack and I stand entwined, monsters made from the ruins of what others tried to break.

And I've never felt more alive.

CHAPTER 39

The Bride

The Sanctuary pulses with Halloween madness, smoke curling through flame-lit walkways like beckoning fingers. Tonight marks its final hours—the last gasps of October breathing across the island before tomorrow strips it back to abandoned military structures and wind-swept paths.

But now, it thrives on the bodies twisted in grotesque performances, their skin painted in symbols I recognize from ancient grimoires. Masked revelers watch from shadows, medallions gleaming at their throats.

Jack's arm settles around my waist, his fingers splayed possessively across my hip as we move through crowds that part instinctively, sensing something deadly and satisfied about us.

No one here knows what we did hours ago. No one can see the blood we've washed from our skin, the death we've carved together. But they feel it—this power radiating between us—and they give us space to breathe it in.

"Where do you want to go first?" Jack asks, his voice low against my ear.

I scan the grounds, taking in the various spectacles. A contortionist

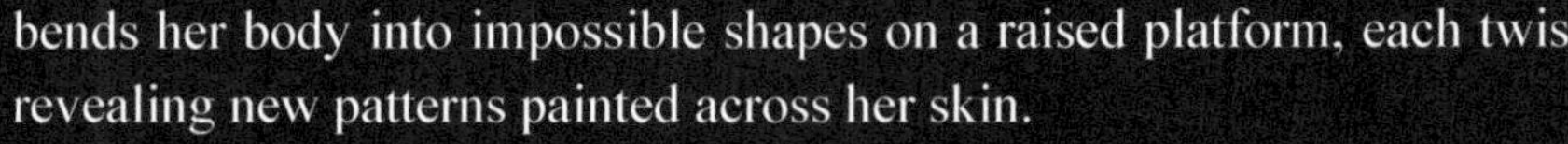

bends her body into impossible shapes on a raised platform, each twist revealing new patterns painted across her skin.

Further along, a man in a plague doctor mask performs mock surgeries on willing victims, extracting ribbons of red silk.

"There," I decide, nodding toward a performance circle where a woman with silver-painted skin is swallowing fire, her throat working visibly as flames disappear into her mouth only to reappear when she exhales through her nose.

Jack guides me through the press of bodies. Unlike the night of our wedding, we aren't part of the show—we're part of the audience. But I feel the weight of eyes following us anyway, drawn to something they sense but can't name.

The scar on my cheek no longer feels like a mark of weakness. Tonight, it's a badge of survival, proof that I've stared into darkness and emerged changed but unbroken. And most importantly, together.

We stop at the edge of the circle, close enough to feel the heat from the performer's flames. Jack stands behind me, his chest against my back, arms wrapped around my waist. His chin rests on my shoulder, stubble scraping pleasantly against my skin.

Around us, masked spectators gasp and murmur as the fire dancer takes a burning torch and presses it against her arm, leaving no mark but a shimmer of silver paint.

"That has to be an illusion," Jack whispers against my ear. "I think I read something about mirror dust in the paint reflecting the flame, making it look like she's untouched."

I lean back into him, savoring his warmth. "Why are you spoiling the magic, Mr. Mortis?"

His laugh rumbles through his chest, vibrating against my spine. "Just appreciating the craft." His teeth graze my earlobe, sending a shiver down my neck. "I prefer real scars to fake ones, Little Bride."

His fingers trace the line on my cheek, the touch reverent rather than pitying. I turn my head, catching his wrist, pressing my lips to his pulse point where blood thrums steady and strong.

The crowd surges and shifts, attention captured by the performer's finale—a burst of flame that momentarily blinds, leaving ghostly afterimages dancing across my vision.

When the spots clear, Jack is watching me with heat in his eyes. "Come on," he says, taking my hand. "Let's see what else this place has to offer on its last night."

We drift through the grounds, pausing to watch a mock execution, people being chased across the grounds, and hear the screams from somewhere farther along the path.

Jack's arm tightens around me, his other hand brushing hair from my neck to press his mouth against my throat. I feel the scrape of teeth, the warm press of his tongue, and I laugh into the night air, head falling back to grant him better access.

The freedom is intoxicating—to be touched like this in public, to feel desire without fear, to know the worst has already happened and we survived it together.

"I think," I say, my voice husky with want, "we should find that fortune teller again."

Jack raises an eyebrow, curiosity lighting his features. "Really?"

I shrug. "I want to know what she sees for us now."

We make our way toward where the fortune teller had been stationed before, but the tent is gone, replaced by a booth selling grotesque candy sculptures that bleed when bitten into.

"She moved," a passing server tells us, noticing our confusion. "Near Slaughter Stage B. The small black tent with the silver symbols."

We find it tucked between two larger attractions, almost hidden in shadow. The entrance is a slash of darkness in black fabric, guarded by nothing but a thin strand of silver bells that chime softly in the night breeze. Jack pushes the fabric aside, allowing me to enter first.

Inside, the air is thick with incense—not the cloying sweetness of cheap sticks, but something deeper, earthier, like freshly turned soil and crushed herbs. The fortune teller sits behind a small table draped in midnight-blue velvet.

Her face is different from what I remember—older, lined with deep grooves around eyes that seem too pale to be natural. But her hands are the same, fingers long and elegant as they spread cards across the velvet.

"The Bride returns," she says, voice like autumn leaves crushed

underfoot. "But not a Bride anymore. Something else now." Her gaze shifts to Jack. "Both of you have changed."

"We'd like a reading," I say, taking a seat on the cushion across from her. Jack settles beside me, his thigh pressed against mine, a warm anchor in the tent's cool darkness.

As she begins shuffling the cards she throws her head back and cackles. "Yes, yes, you were right."

"Excuse me?" Jack asks, sounding perplexed.

The woman side-eyes him. "I was answering the cards." Then she frowns and looks between both our hands. "You've killed today," she says matter-of-factly, not looking up from her task. I don't deny it. Neither does Jack. The knowledge sits between us, acknowledged and accepted.

She lays three cards on the velvet, face down. When she turns the first, it shows a tower struck by lightning, figures falling from its heights.

"Destruction," she murmurs. "But not yours. You are the storm, not the structure." She turns the second card—two figures bound by chains, standing at a crossroads. "Choice made. Paths joined. There is no untangling of what has been woven."

The third card shows a figure walking into darkness, lantern held high. "The journey continues. Not into light—into endless night. But together." She looks up, her eyes finding mine with unsettling precision. "This is no soft love, no gentle heart. This is obsession. Possession. Survival entwined with destruction."

Jack's hand finds mine beneath the table, fingers lacing together. I feel the calluses on his palm, the strength in his grip, and I squeeze back, accepting what she offers.

"Your path stretches beyond ages," she continues, voice dropping lower. "Beyond death itself. What has been forged in blood does not easily break." She gathers the cards, returning them to the deck without another glance. "You will face trials in every lifetime. Pain. Loss. But always, always, you will find each other in the dark."

"And is that a blessing or a curse?" Jack asks, his voice steady but curious.

The fortune teller's lips curve in a smile that doesn't reach her eyes.

"For creatures like you? It is simply the truth."

She offers no more, and we understand we've been dismissed. As we rise to leave, I reach for my wallet, but she shakes her head.

"I told you before that I don't want your money. I don't accept payment from those whose fates are bound to mine." Something ancient flickers in her gaze. "We will meet again, when winter turns the world to ice and you require different truths."

"You know," I gasp. It's not a question but a statement. I can see it on her face.

"Yes," she nods slowly. "The cards told me. That's why I moved my tent." She points to her bags next to the table. "I'm ready to go."

With those words, she ushers us out of the tent, unwilling or unable to answer any more questions.

"I can't decide if she's creepy or awesome," I sigh once we're outside, the night air feels electric against my skin, charged with possibility.

Jack pulls me close, his lips finding mine in a kiss that tastes of smoke and destiny. When we part, his eyes hold mine, something fierce and tender in their depths. "Definitely creepy," he decides.

"Do you believe her?" I ask as his thumb traces the line of my jaw.

I think of everything we've survived—his revenge, my captivity, Shelby's death. I think of how he looked standing in Nick's basement, offering me the knife, giving me the choice to end a life that had tried to end mine.

"I believe in us," I answer simply. "Whatever comes next."

His smile is slow, predatory, promising. His fingers tighten on my hip, drawing me deeper into shadow where revelers can't see the way his hand slips beneath my shirt, tracing bare skin with deliberate intent.

"Then let's enjoy our playground," he murmurs against my lips. "After all, we've earned it."

And as his mouth claims mine again, more demanding this time, I surrender to the knowledge that the fortune teller was right—this isn't soft romance. This is something sharper, darker, a love carved from violence and sealed in blood. And I wouldn't have it any other way.

We go from attraction to attraction, taking in as much as we can before our time here is up. We don't need a clock to tell us when we're nearing midnight. The crowd gravitates toward the central stage—the same altar where Jack once claimed me as his Bride.

Tonight, it's transformed by hundreds of black candles, their flames perfectly still in the windless air, smoke rising in straight columns toward a moonless sky. The scent of melting wax mingles with incense, with sweat and anticipation from the bodies pressing closer.

The stage looms ahead, draped in heavy velvet the color of dried blood, illuminated from beneath to create the illusion that it floats above the ground. Nicklas and Carolina are already waiting in the wings, their silhouettes sharp against the ambient glow of fire pits.

"There you are," Carolina says as we reach them, her voice pitched low beneath the growing murmur of the crowd. She looks ethereal tonight in a gown that shifts between black and midnight blue with her movements, her hair swept up to reveal the elegant line of her throat. "I was beginning to think you'd gotten lost in the festivities."

Jack's fingers tighten almost imperceptibly at my hip. "We had unfinished business with a fortune teller."

Nicklas raises an eyebrow but doesn't question further. He seems to understand that some things belong only to us, wrapped in privacy despite our public presence. Instead, he nods toward the stage where technicians are making final adjustments to microphones and lighting.

"Five minutes," he says. "Carolina will open, then call you up at midnight exactly."

I nod, oddly nervous despite everything we've already survived. This feels significant—a threshold being crossed, a door closing on one chapter and opening to another. Jack senses my tension, his thumb tracing small circles against my spine.

"Breathe," he murmurs against my ear. "This is just a formality. The real work is already done."

He's right. Shelby's body is already being disposed of, her blood washed from our hands, her memory fading with each passing hour.

Carolina checks her watch, then squares her shoulders. "It's time."

She steps out from the shadows and onto the stage, her appearance triggering a hush that spreads through the crowd like ripples in still water. The spotlight finds her, bathing her in cold light that turns her skin to alabaster.

Like a queen acknowledging her subjects, she raises her hands, and the silence deepens, expectant and hungry. "Welcome," she begins, her voice carrying without strain, "to the final hour of the Sanctuary of Shadows."

The crowd responds with a low, collective moan—part disappointment, part anticipation. Carolina waits for it to subside before continuing.

"When we created this place, we sought to build more than a spectacle. More than entertainment. We wanted to create a sanctuary in the truest sense—a place where darkness could be embraced rather than feared. Where grief and pain could be transmuted into something powerful."

Her gaze sweeps the crowd, finding faces in the sea of masks and makeup. I watch from the wings, Jack a solid presence at my side, as she speaks of transformation, of survival, of turning trauma into strength. Her words resonate with something in me—I, too, have been transformed by darkness, have learned to wield it rather than fear it.

"The Sanctuary of Shadows was born from loss," Carolina continues, her voice softening. "From the ashes of what was taken from us. My sister, Willow, never saw what we built here." She pauses, emotion briefly tightening her features before she masters it. "But her spirit infuses every shadow, every flame. Willow's Foundation rose from these grounds and has already begun to change lives, to create homes and safety for those who need it most."

The crowd is utterly silent now, captivated by her raw sincerity. Even Jack seems transfixed, his breathing synchronized with mine as we listen.

"Tonight, as we close this chapter, I want you to remember that Halloween isn't just a date on a calendar." Carolina's voice gains strength, conviction. "It's a state of mind. A willingness to look into the darkness and see not just fear, but possibility. Not just endings, but transformations."

The clock ticks closer to midnight. I feel it in my bones, in the electric anticipation that courses through the crowd.

"And transformation," Carolina says, her gaze finding me in the shadows, "is what we celebrate tonight. Not an ending, but an evolution." She extends her hand toward the wings. "As the clock strikes midnight, I invite Dr. Eve Mortis to join me in sharing what comes next."

The crowd cheers at my name, recognizing it from the launch only one month ago. Jack squeezes my hand once before releasing me, letting me step into the light alone. The stage feels different beneath my feet now—not a trap but a platform, not a prison but a pulpit.

Carolina embraces me when I reach her, the gesture genuine despite its theatrical setting. "Thank you," she whispers before pulling away, her smile private and warm before she turns back to the audience.

The first chime of midnight rings out, deep and resonant. I turn to Jack, still in the wings but visible now, and extend my hand to him so we can have this moment together. He shakes his head, smirking.

Carolina waits until all twelve chimes have sounded before speaking again. "The Sanctuary of Shadows closes tonight," she announces, "but darkness doesn't vanish with the dawn."

I step forward, feeling oddly at home beneath the spotlight. "It merely changes form," I continue, our voices weaving together as practiced. "Which is why we're pleased to announce that the Sanctuary will rise again."

"Not next October," Carolina adds, "but this December."

The crowd stirs, confusion rippling through them. This wasn't the expected announcement—they were prepared for farewell, not continuation.

"The Sanctuary of Secrets is coming," I explain, the words rolling off my tongue with delicious weight. "The first ever launch will be in another city. New grounds, new terrors—but the same soul."

Carolina's hand finds mine, our fingers interlocking as we face the audience together. "Tickets will be available next week, and you'd better hurry. Our Sanctuary of Secrets event will only be one week long."

The announcement triggers a wave of excitement—people clutching at their medals, whispering to companions, already imagining what horrors await in December's darkness.

Somewhere in the crowd, a chant begins, wordless at first, then coalescing into a rhythmic repetition of *"One list. Two options. Have you been naughty or nice?"* that swells until it seems to shake the very foundations of the island.

Behind us, fire erupts from hidden containers, columns of flame reaching toward the night sky in perfect synchronization with the chant. The heat washes over us, not burning but cleansing, marking the end of one era and the birth of another.

Feeling giddy, I turn to look for Jack, but I don't see him. When my eyes land on Nicklas, he just shakes his head and smirks. I'm beginning to think smirking is one of their damn family traits.

"Have you seen—" A scream erupts from me as I'm suddenly pulled backward.

When I turn around, I look into twin circles of black glass, his mask inches from my face, his breath rasping through the filter in steady pulls. The world narrows to the hiss of the mask, the weight of his grip, and the silent claim in the way he holds me still.

"Mine," he says. "Always."

I curl my fingers into the front of his shirt, pulling him closer, making my own claim in the press of my body against his. "Yours," I agree. "But only if you can catch me."

Around us, the crowd surges and celebrates, anticipating the horrors, and delights December will bring. But all I see is Jack sprinting after me.

As I run from him, all I feel is the promise of our future—dark and twisted and perfectly, beautifully ours. Whatever cities, whatever altars, whatever transformations await, we will face them together.

I don't make it far. His hand clamps around my waist, dragging me back mid-stride, my cry swallowed by the hiss of his mask as my spine slams into his chest. I thrash once, twice, before his arm cinches tight and I know it's useless.

"You can run," he growls through the filter, breath hot at my ear, "but I'll always catch you."

Pinned in his grip, heart hammering, I can only gasp the truth back to him. "Always."

EPILOGUE

Nicklas

5 years later.

It's Christmas Eve, and the house is quiet except for the slow hiss of logs collapsing in the fireplace. Our girls are asleep, one curled with a stuffed reindeer, the other still clutching Carolina's hair ribbon like a talisman.

Though Willow usually sleeps in her own bed, tonight she's sharing with Lily, our youngest. They're both excited for tomorrow morning and wouldn't shut up about when Santa would get here. Little do they know their dad is Santa.

I sit on the edge of our bed with my mom's diary in my hands—the last relic that ever dared mention curses and superstitions. After all these years, the binding is worn smooth at the corners.

The bedroom door opens, and Carolina enters, wrapped in a sexy as fuck negligee, legs bare beneath it. Her hair falls loose around her shoulders, and the sight of her still catches in my chest, sharp and sweet.

"Is that the last one?" she asks, nodding at the diary in my hands.

I run my thumb along the edge of the book. "Yes." The word feels heavier than it should, like a confession. "The final record of the Knight curse."

My Kitten sits beside me, close enough that our thighs press together. She takes the diary, opening it to where my mother's handwriting flows across the yellowed pages in elegant, troubled lines.

"It feels like ages ago I discovered this old thing," she grins. Her expression somber. "Nick, are you sure—"

"Yes." I think of Jack and Ruby—one died and came back, the other claimed by a family disease that ate her from the inside out. " I'm done letting ghosts dictate how we live. I refuse to let it become Willow's or Lily's burden."

The fire pulses in the hearth, shadows dancing against the wall.

Carolina watches me with those eyes that see everything—the parts I try to hide, the parts only she gets to touch.

"Then burn it," she says. "End it tonight."

I take the diary back, its weight familiar in my palm. Then I walk over to the fireplace, Carolina following. The heat pushes against my skin as I stand before the flames. For a moment, I hesitate. Not because I believe, but because this was hers—my mother's.

"It's okay," my Kitten murmurs, her hand at the small of my back. "She'd understand."

I toss the diary into the heart of the fire. The leather blackens immediately, curling at the corners like dying flowers. Pages catch and glow, illuminating my mother's handwriting one last time before ash claims it. The binding cracks, exposing more pages to the hungry flames.

"The curse died with Ruby, or with Jack's name change," I say, watching the last of the superstitions burn. "Not because it was real, but because we made it real by believing it."

My wife's arms wrap around my waist from behind, her cheek pressed between my shoulder blades. "And now?"

"Now we live," I say, turning to face her. "No more ghosts. No more curses. Just us."

The diary collapses in on itself, pages consumed, binding fractured beyond repair. The fire hisses as it devours the last record of the Knight family's darkest beliefs.

Carolina's hands slide up my chest, finding their way to the nape of my neck. Her touch grounds me, pulling me back to the present—to her, to us, to the life we built from wreckage.

"So," she says, lips curving into the smile that still haunts my dreams, "does this mean you're not dressing as Santa tonight?"

The question breaks through the heaviness, unexpected enough to pull a laugh from my throat. "Only if you've been very, *very* naughty," I growl, hands finding her waist, tugging her closer.

"I'm always naughty," she reminds me, pressing her body flush against mine. Her eyes darken with familiar heat. "That's why you married me."

I kiss her hard, one hand tangling in her hair, the other sliding beneath the hem of the negligee. She tastes of toothpaste and promises kept, like every choice that led me here.

She tugs me toward the bed, but I pause, remembering something. "Check your email first."

"Now?" Her brow furrows, confusion clear in the tilt of her head. "It's Christmas Eve, Nick."

"Trust me."

She huffs but reaches for her phone on the nightstand. I watch her unlock it, navigate to her inbox, find the message I had our lawyers send this morning.

Her eyes widen as she reads, then lift to mine. "The breeding contract is complete?" The playfulness in her voice can't quite mask the emotion beneath it.

"No more kids," I murmur against her mouth. "Three would've been too many."

Her smile turns feral as she drops the phone and pulls me down onto the bed. "Agreed," she says, already working at my belt. "Though that doesn't mean we can't keep practicing."

I lower myself over her, claiming her mouth as she claims my body, the last ash of the diary drifting up the chimney and out into the winter night, taking with it the final shadows of the Knight curse.

Carolina's scream wakes me before dawn, sharp enough to splinter the dream I'm in. Instinct takes me first—I reach under my pillow for the gun and sprint down the hall, heart hammering with every step.

"Nick! The girls are gone!" she shrieks.

The cold metal of the Glock warms to my palm as I move, barefoot and silent, listening for whatever threat has made my wife cry out.

Every door, every window, every possible entry point flashes through my mind as I calculate how quickly I can eliminate whoever dared enter our home.

The Christmas tree lights cast uneven shadows down the staircase as I descend. I pause at the bottom, eyes scanning for movement, ears straining for sounds of struggle. Nothing but Carolina's voice, pitched high with what sounds less like fear now and more like—surprise?

I burst into the living room ready for war, weapon raised, only to find chaos of a different kind. Jack and Eve, uninvited and unapologetic, sitting at our dining table feeding the girls pancakes drowning in syrup.

My daughters giggle, their mouths sticky with sugar, while Eve winks at Carolina, who's too stunned to speak. Relief floods me so fast it's almost painful. My body's still hunting for a target, adrenaline with nowhere to go.

I lower the gun, exhaling a string of curses under my breath that makes Jack smirk wider. "Merry Christmas, brother," he says, casually as if he hasn't broken into my home before dawn. "You're out of maple syrup."

Eve sits beside him, looking more relaxed than I've ever seen her. She's wearing an oversized Christmas sweater; her hair is completely green this year and hangs loose down her back.

"We brought presents," she says, nodding toward a pile of packages under the tree that weren't there when we went to bed.

Carolina recovers first, crossing the room to kiss Jack's cheek, then Eve's. "You could have called," she scolds, but there's no heat in it.

I second that sentiment with a grunt. If it wasn't because we don't get to spend a lot of time together, since my brother and sister-in-law travel with the different Sanctuaries all year long, I'd chew them out for this rude awakening.

"Where's the fun in that?" Jack asks, sliding a plate of pancakes toward an empty chair. "Besides, Willow and Lily wanted to help make breakfast for their dad. So when they called and asked us to help, we couldn't say no."

My older daughter beams at me, face smeared with syrup, utterly delighted by her uncle's presence. "We called them last week," she giggles.

"Yes, Uncle Marco helps," Lily adds.

I set the gun down on a high shelf, out of reach, then take the offered seat. "How did you get in?" I don't know why I'm asking. If Marco's in on this impromptu visit, he obviously let them in.

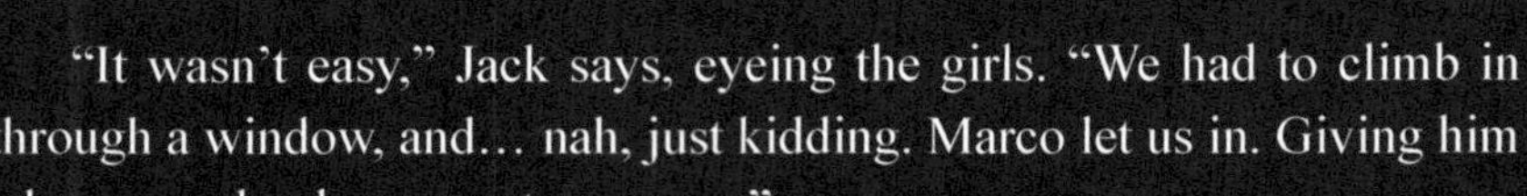

"It wasn't easy," Jack says, eyeing the girls. "We had to climb in through a window, and… nah, just kidding. Marco let us in. Giving him a key was clearly an amateur move."

Looking at my brother now, seeing the ease in his shoulders, the clarity in his eyes, I can feel a knot loosening in my chest that I didn't realize was there.

"We finished the Sanctuary of Secrets in San Francisco early," Eve explains, wiping syrup from Willow's chin. "We sold out every night."

"And made enough to award three more Willow's Foundation scholarships," Jack adds, pride evident in his voice.

Carolina squeezes my shoulder as she moves past me to the coffeepot. Her touch says more than words—she's glad they're here, glad to see this piece of our family returned, even if just for a visit.

"Uncle Jack said you used to put tinfoil on your windows," Willow announces, eyes wide as she looks at me. "To keep out the aliens."

I arch an eyebrow at my brother, who shrugs innocently. "Just sharing family stories."

"That never happened," I sigh.

"Says you," Eve adds, deadpan, and Jack laughs, the sound filling the kitchen with a warmth I didn't realize I'd missed.

We eat together, laughter and stories filling the room. Eve describes the stray cat that's adopted them, a one-eyed tabby they've named Cyclops.

"He sleeps on Jack's chest every night," she says, and the image of my brother—the man who once tortured information out of people without blinking—cuddling a cat is almost too much to process.

Willow climbs into Jack's lap, sticky hands clinging to his shirt as she demands to know if they have Christmas trees in San Francisco. Or, as she called it, *Sanny Franiso.* He assures her they do.

"And Santa always stops by," he tells her solemnly.

I watch them, this strange, cobbled-together family of ours. Carolina leans against the counter, coffee mug in hand, her smile soft as she observes Eve helping Lily with tiny bites of pancake. The tension that's lived in my shoulders since Jack left New York finally eases.

The morning light strengthens, filtering through the windows and

catching on the ornaments of our Christmas tree. Willow giggles at something Eve whispers in her ear, and Jack's smile—genuine, unguarded—makes him look younger than I've seen him in years.

It feels like family again. Not perfect, not unmarked by the scars we all carry, but real. Present. Alive.

Later, when the girls are sated and Carolina has Eve trapped in conversation about the Sanctuary's expansion plans, I drive Jack out to Ruby's grave. The cemetery is empty on Christmas Day, paths barely cleared of snow, silence deeper than any church I've ever entered.

Ruby's headstone stands apart from the family plot—Jack bought it for her. I used to feel guilty I hadn't thought of it, but it doesn't matter. Here, in death, she finally got to be only herself.

The snow is thin here, clinging to the stones, melting where the winter sun touches it. Jack carries a small bundle of red roses. He kneels to brush snow from the base of the headstone before laying them down, his movements careful, almost reverent.

I stand beside him, hands in my pockets, watching my breath cloud in the cold air. We don't speak at first. Don't need to. The quiet between us has always said more than words.

"Hey, Rubes," Jack finally says, his voice low but steady. Not like the first time we visited, when his words broke apart before they left his mouth. "Merry Christmas."

I smile at the greeting, so normal, as if she might answer back. "The girls are getting big," I add, continuing our tradition of talking to her like she's listening. "Willow's into dinosaurs now. Carries this little T-Rex everywhere. Carolina says she gets her obsessiveness from me."

Jack laughs softly. "Definitely not from me." He adjusts the roses, making sure they won't blow away.

The wind picks up, carrying the scent of pine from nearby trees. I study my brother's profile, the steadiness in him that wasn't there even a year ago. Not just the absence of rage, but the presence of something else—purpose, maybe. Peace.

"Will you ever come back?" I ask the question I've been holding since he left. "To New York, I mean. For good."

Jack stands, brushing snow from his knees. He meets my gaze

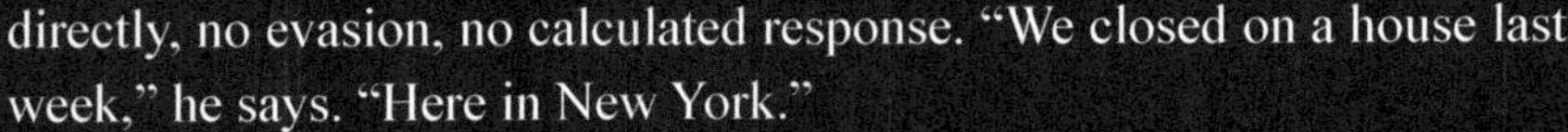

directly, no evasion, no calculated response. "We closed on a house last week," he says. "Here in New York."

"Tell me about it."

"It's an old Victorian," he continues. "Needs work, but Eve loves it. Apparently our fortune teller told her it has good bones." His mouth quirks in a half-smile. "Considering our professions, that's probably not the best way to describe it."

The joke lands between us, unexpectedly light. I find myself laughing, the sound strange in the solemn quiet of the cemetery.

"You're happy," I say. Not a question but an observation.

He considers this, his gaze drifting back to Ruby's grave. "I'm… at peace," he says finally. "With what happened. With what I did." His shoulders rise and fall with a deep breath. "Eve helps. She understands the dark parts without trying to fix them."

I think of Carolina, how she sees my shadows but never flinches from them. How she accepts the violence in my blood without letting it define me.

"I get that," I tell him.

Jack nods, knowing I do. We stand in companionable silence, two brothers bound by blood and memory, by the sister we mistakenly thought needed safety. But that's not what Ruby needed. She wanted to be free, and now she is.

"So, Mr. Mortis," I tease. "Does your house have spare rooms?"

He rolls his eyes and scoffs. "Of course it does. But they're for Willow and Lily. We don't want kids."

"Good," I reply. "That means you have time to babysit mine."

He shudders theatrically. "Eve's already planning to convert the sunroom into a playroom for them."

I burst out laughing. "Fair warning, Willow will bring her entire dinosaur collection."

"Eve will help her name them all," he grins.

I laugh again, the sound less jarring this time against the quiet of the cemetery. We turn back toward the car, but Jack pauses for one more look at Ruby's grave.

"She'd be glad," he says softly. "That we're both okay. That we found our way."

I think of our sister—her fierce independence. "Yeah," I agree. "She would."

When we reach the car, I smirk at my brother. "I wasn't joking about babysitting, by the way."

"Oh?" He narrows his eyes, probably guessing I have something planned from the tone I'm using.

"The next Sanctuary of Secrets starts December twenty-seventh, and I have plans for my Kitten."

9 781917 740111